PARADISE
PASSION
MURDER

10 Tales of Mystery from Hawai'i

PARADISE
PASSION
MURDER

10 Tales of Mystery from Hawai'i

READ ALOUD AMERICA

CONTENTS

FOREWORD

I was quite determined to be a newspaper reporter at a very young age. When I was growing up during World War II, I thought there could be no more important job than to be a reporter. I saw that the bigger the headline, the more important the story. I thought I would be the next Maggie Higgins. When I grew up, I even had a trench coat and smoked Chesterfields.

My career in writing began after my new husband and I moved to DC and started a family. I hadn't written in a while and missed writing. I had read mysteries and saw an ad in a magazine for a contest, so I wrote "Secret of the Cellars," which was a young adult novel. That one story eventually led to more than fifty other books.

Had I not been able to read, I would never have known about Maggie Higgins, would never have written "Secret of the Cellars," nor any of the subsequent books. My career and my life would have been wholly different. It would have been far less rich and I far less informed.

Because millions learn to read every year, I've enjoyed a wonderful career as a writer. I never would have been able to write so many books, however, if it weren't for those readers. Imagine growing up and never reading Dr. Seuss or Nancy Drew or Sherlock Holmes—not for lack of interest, but because you couldn't. Reading is fundamental to our lives, yet so many never learn how to do it. Adults who cannot read are plagued by the stigma of illiteracy.

In Hawai'i, a state known for its beautiful scenery and weather, the inability to read tarnishes that beauty every day. There's a saying in Hawai'i that their best and brightest leave for mainland schools and never return. Unfortunately, this talent migration only worsens the literacy problem.

The purpose of "Paradise, Passion, Murder" is to raise money to help Read Aloud America, a Hawai'i 501(C)3 organization, promote literacy. One of the things I liked most about this project was that all of the proceeds go directly to Read Aloud America. The proceeds will be used to put on programs designed to help children and adults learn to read—hopefully, together.

Most of the authors who participated in this anthology have existing mystery series. From funny amateur sleuths to police thrillers, these writers tackle their stories with a love of the islands and an ear for a good tale.

If you love fiction that shimmers with the lure and fascination of Hawai'i, grab "Paradise, Passion, Murder" for a Hawaiian revel. This great collection of stories and novels will benefit literacy in the lovely islands while bringing you hours of enjoyment. That's a winner on all counts.

Carolyn Hart
Author of Death in Paradise

Editor's Note

My husband, Larry, and I set our mystery series in Hawai'i because we love the islands. We try to get back there every year, since Larry is a surfer. When Terry discussed this project with me, the rest of the authors had already had several months to work on their stories. Rather than rush a contribution, I volunteered to put on my editor's hat. This gave me the chance to preview all the wonderful contributions. I have thoroughly enjoyed working with the authors and feel privileged to have been part of this special project to benefit literacy in Hawai'i.

Lorna Collins

About the Editor

Lorna Collins and her husband, Larry K. Collins, helped build the Universal Studios Japan theme park in Osaka. Their first book, a memoir of that experience, is *31 Months in Japan: The Building of a Theme Park*. They have co-written cozy mysteries set in Hawai'i as well as a historical novel set in San Juan Capistrano. They are working on sequels to these.

Lorna also co-authored six sweet romance anthologies set in the fictional town of Aspen Grove, CO. Her fantasy/mystery/romance, *Ghost Writer*, is set in Laguna Beach, CA. In addition, Lorna is a professional editor.

You can learn more about her on her website: www.lornalarry.com.

INTRODUCTION

Read Aloud America promotes the involvement of the whole family in making reading an integral part of a child's life. The organization designed an early evening program that operates in public schools, offering a series of high-energy, motivational sessions over the course of one school semester. Some (perhaps many) parents and grandparents who attend Read Aloud America's program do not read themselves. The program motivates families to work and learn together and lessens any feelings of anxiety that may hinder the home learning environment.

Families receive resources and tips on how to transfer this positive experience into the home. Read Aloud America's research shows the program leads to more time spent together as a family, increases interest in and time spent reading, and improves work in school.

Schools have been trying to engage parents for generations. The Read Aloud America program does that. Attendance figures gathered since 1999 show the Read Aloud America Program has served over 334,000 adults and children at 90 Hawai'i public schools. It has become the largest and most effective family literacy program in America.

Jed Gaines
Founder and President
Read Aloud America

MURDER ON THE ROAD TO HANA
Terry Ambrose

McKenna

Never could I have predicted the twists of fate that brought me to this nineteenth century Hawaiian church. I hadn't lost my way in life, though deep down I might feel the need for guidance. You see, my path had turned bittersweet. My name is McKenna and I've become quite adept at stumbling onto murders—and finding killers. And that was part of my problem.

I've long since retired from the field, but I was once a skip tracer—someone who found people not wanting to be found. That was my job. I was a people finder. My employer called me the best. The people I tracked used far different adjectives. Their suggestions of what I should do to myself were invariably rude and focused on acts that were, quite frankly, impossible to perform.

Four plain white walls surrounded me. They lent an air of simplicity and innocence to the Palapala Hoʻomau Congregational Church. Simplicity had never been an element in my life. Perhaps it never would be. But, in this moment, it felt right.

We were fifty miles and nine stops from the country club where our Road to Hana Tour had begun. Here, in this sanctuary, in this most remote spot on Maui, killers and criminals felt a lifetime away. Counting our driver, we were a baker's dozen of curious souls exploring one of the twistiest roads in the world. The architect of that road had either been a diabolical engineering genius or drunk. Perhaps both.

Forest green pews atop wooden plank flooring. A single, simple chandelier. Even the plain white balusters separating the red-carpeted pulpit from the main body of the church reminded me how simple life had once been. There was a time when I would have been content to be a crack amateur sleuth. Now, life had become more complicated. It was a good complicated, not bad. Somehow, this chapel had maintained its elegance—its simplicity—despite the complicated world around it. Could I do the same?

You see, Benni Kapono had become the complication in my life. We came to Maui to get a little time away. She's a good twenty years younger than me and don't think that hasn't gotten us our fair share of snide looks and pointing fingers. The biggest issue we face, however, is that we live on different islands. As the cliché goes, it's complicated.

I glanced up at the stained glass window depicting Jesus in feathered robes. Those robes were once worn by the ruling class of Hawai'i. I considered it a compliment that the church builders chose to use them. Of course, there were always the purists on either side of the aisle crying blasphemy and sacrilege. Let the purists make their claims elsewhere. I felt every element complemented the others.

For the moment I was alone. My tour companions were either exploring the grounds or visiting the grave of Charles Lindbergh, which is the church cemetery's claim to fame. I took a deep breath. What the heck? This wasn't my usual thing to do, but my time alone gave me an unexpected opportunity to ask for a little free advice.

I checked the inside of the church again. Still empty. Clearing my throat, I whispered, "Hey, big guy? Can you hear me? I'm, uh, thinking of asking Benni to marry me. Should I—you know—pop the question?"

I waited for a sign, any sign.

One thunderclap for yes, two for no.

A spider spinning a web to catch a fly.

The silence in the room overpowered me. I felt stupid. This wasn't a decision anyone else could make. It was mine and mine alone. The sound of rushing wind drifted in through the open front doors. Turning in my seat, I saw the source. A drone. An all-white, four-propeller, remote-controlled flying camera.

"Val," I hissed. The moment I started to stand, the drone rose into the air and disappeared.

One of our fellow travelers on this tour was Valentine Ilsley, a five-foot-four, dark-eyed beauty who had a nasty habit of asking embarrassing questions. She was the queen when it came to that particular talent. I'd taken somewhat of a dislike to Val when, during our stop at the rugged Keʻanae Peninsula, she'd shadowed me with the drone for a few seconds. In retrospect, she'd probably done it because we'd exchanged barbs after I made a crack about her profession.

—So you're a magazine technical writer, Val? How come you people can't write in plain English?

—Gobbledegeek Magazine is targeted at millennials. Why's someone your age even interested in it?

—Someone my age? I'm only sixty-five.

—Oh, then maybe you should stick to AARP's magazine. That might be more your speed.

—I'm surprised you can even spell that.

I'd turned away, not letting her get the better of me. For the most part, I'd almost enjoyed trading little semi-nasties with another smart ass. Val, however, was a true techie and a "Millennial with Money." That's what Benni had called her, anyway. I suppose it was true. Val had a real Gucci bag—Benni clued me in on that. She'd also bought the drone for this trip.

With the flying spy machine gone, I settled back into my pew, but was immediately interrupted by two voices.

—Did you see? I almost had it.

—Awesome, Lenny. You could have played pro basketball.

—C'mon, Judy, you're not still mad, are you?

Crap. These two started the day friendly enough. Lenny was one of those guys who could talk your ear off and Judy had a quick wit, which had dulled considerably as the day wore on. For the first time, I suspected I knew the reason she'd become more introspective and the reason appalled me. In her hand she held what looked like a bottle of beer, but the label read "Jim Beam Red Stag."

When I glared at them, Judy raised her eyebrows and held my gaze. "I don't think we're welcome here, Lenny."

"I'm sorry we disturbed you," Lenny said. "You're McKenna, right? How come you don't use your first name? You know, I had an uncle who was just like you. He didn't want to be called Mr. and he insisted everyone call him Jackson, which was his last name."

Lenny was still babbling about his uncle as Judy pushed him toward the door. "Stuff it, Lenny. Nobody cares. Especially him. Or me."

They passed Benni on their way out. She approached. Sat next to me. Then, took my hand. "It's beautiful," she said.

"I'm surrounded by beauty." I smiled. The troubled couple was gone. Serenity had returned. And, Benni was here. What more could I ask for?

She winked. "Not here. This is a church. Show some respect."

"I wish everyone did that."

"Let it go, McKenna. They're still young. Why'd you come here first?"

"I don't know. It just seemed like the right place for me to be. Where have you been?"

"I went to the cemetery before the others, then toured the gardens. I found a few things I want you to see."

"That sounds good." Was that a sign? The gardens? I could do the one-knee bit. Crap. I didn't have a ring.

Benni took my hand and stood, but before either of us could move, a woman's scream pierced the air.

Lenny

Benni and I rushed out the front door of the church and ran straight into a half dozen others from our tour. Around us, the crowd was in chaos. They were all glancing in different directions. Some clung to their spouses. They all jabbered at once.

—What was that?

—It came from the cemetery.

—No, no, it was back by the bus.

—It was a woman.

—Someone call the police.

The conflicted yammering went on as Benni and I pushed past the others. I didn't care who thought what. We'd definitely heard a woman's scream.

"Which way is the cemetery?" I asked Benni. As she pointed to my left, I said, "You check by the van. Yell as loud as you can if you find anything."

I hurried around the side of the church. At first I saw nothing, then about fifty feet away I spotted Judy. She stood a few feet away from a short, lava-rock wall. It was the perimeter of a gravesite. Next to Judy, Lenny knelt over the body of a man lying spread-eagled on the grass. My breath caught. It was the grave of Charles Lindbergh.

Good God. Lindbergh was an American hero. The first man to fly across the Atlantic. And now some joker on a tour bus died, not only in the same cemetery, but right next to him? I took a quick look at the positioning of the body. Head against one of the rocks. Torso and legs extended out onto the grass. The face was that of Ramon Gilligan. One of our tour members.

Lenny poked at Ramon's neck while glancing up at me. "I'm trying to find a pulse. I saw this done once, but you know how it is in the heat of the moment."

Blood had turned the grass near Ramon's head crimson.

I pushed Lenny to one side. What kind of idiot didn't know how to take a pulse? "I understand." He could have interpreted my words as an apology for shoving him out of the way, but right now I couldn't care less about Lenny's feelings. A man was dying before my eyes.

I pressed my fingers against Ramon's neck. One weak thump. Another, this one just a flutter. Then, nothing.

Ramon Gilligan was dead.

A wave of remorse surged through me—more at my willingness to get a laugh at someone else's expense than the gravity of the transgression. The whole incident had been stupid. Why had I insulted Ramon's family name? During our picnic lunch at a quaint roadside store in Hana, I made cracks about the old "Gilligan's Island" TV show. Ramon, an autoworker from Detroit, didn't appreciate my "three-hour tour" jokes. He quickly told me he'd heard them a thousand times. It seemed so petty, poking fun at a man's name—

"Is he—dead?" asked Judy.

I reined in my feelings, telling myself that they were just knee-jerk reactions. Judy stared down at Ramon, her jaw slack, the bottle of Red Stag no longer visible. When had she ditched that?

I nodded. Stood. Watched Benni rush toward us. Nausea washed over me. We'd been moved from a different tour group to this one at the last minute. Was this the reason why? Had the cosmos put me here to watch a man die? What kind of cosmic conspiracy was this? Shaking my head at how ridiculous it seemed for the cosmos to be concerned with me, I peered at Lenny, who stood a few feet away, framed by a backdrop of tropical foliage, volcanic stone walls, and palm trees.

"Did you see anything?"

Lenny was tall with a large upper torso and a small head. He reminded me of a crime-fighting action figure in some ways. Of course, given his propensity for palaver, it was entirely possible he'd simply talk any wannabe villain into submission. I fully expected to receive an overly abundant and detailed description of what he and Judy had seen. He astonished me by simply staring at the ground.

"Lenny? Did you see anything?"

He squinted at his red fingers and hands. Finally, he said, "No, no, man. We went to the gardens first. Came right here from the church. You know, we wanted to check out the grave thing. Judy saw the body on the ground before me. I tried to check for a pulse, but had no idea where to put my fingers." He swiped at his left hand with his right as though he could somehow brush away death. "I'm a stockbroker, man, not a doctor."

Oh, a stockbroker. That explained everything. He was used to having money, not common sense. He had the look of a Wall Street pro with dark hair, cut short and brushed back. He wasn't overweight, but did seem like the kind of guy you'd find in the Big & Tall store. Of course, being a stockbroker, he probably had a private tailor, which would explain the perfect fit of his aloha shirt.

Lenny was still going on about something or other. Nerves? Probably. I wondered if his tongue was this loose with his clients. Instead of letting him ramble, I held up my hands to form the letter T. Lenny seemed to get the concept right away. He'd received a Time Out. How many of those did he get as a kid?

"So, what did you actually see, Lenny?"

"Oh, uh, see? Me? Nothing important."

"Why don't you let me decide what's important?"

"I'm a stockbroker, not a detective."

What was that, his standard response for everything? To the side, Benni was gritting her teeth. Lenny must be irritating her, too.

"Cut the BS, Lenny. You said Judy saw the body first."

"Hey, there's no need to get nasty. Who put you in charge, anyway? I don't take orders from you. I'm a—I need to get this crap off my hands."

I dismissed his comment with a flip of my hand. "I know, I know. You're a stockbroker." You're also a moron, I thought. "I'm only asking a question."

Lenny sneered at me. "We didn't see anything. We just showed up and whacko there was laying on the ground. Come on, Judy. Let's go back to the bus. I've got to get cleaned up."

Judy, whose eyes had a healthy glaze now, said, "I'll be right there, Lenny. You go ahead."

Why had Lenny called Ramon a whacko? I hadn't seen any bizarre behavior. Lenny marched off in the direction of what he called "the bus." It was really a twelve-passenger van, something more intimate than a bus and capable of going where the full-sized behemoths couldn't. When Lenny was about twenty feet away, he yelled over his shoulder. "I was only trying to protect you, Judy. You do what you want."

Judy

I stared after Lenny as he disappeared from view. The guy was obviously hiding something. Had Judy witnessed the murder? Time to find out. I turned my attention to her. "What was that all about?"

She rolled her eyes and let out a huff of exasperation. Under her breath, she swore. "Damn you, Lenny."

"Well?"

Judy was about five-foot-four with fiery red hair. She had a sharp, well-defined nose, but soft cheeks and little pixie ears. She reminded me more of a Disney elf than someone whose anger could be taken seriously.

She swayed as she spoke. It made the universe feel out of kilter—pixies didn't get drunk. At least, not in public.

"I'm done with him," she snarled.

The rest of the group, a half dozen curious rubberneckers trying not to seem the part, swarmed toward us.

"Benni, can you hold them off?" I asked. "The less damage we do to this crime scene, the better."

She nodded and left me to question Judy while she kept the lookie loos at bay.

Based on Lenny's and Judy's responses, I doubted that either of them was as innocent as Lenny claimed. I'd learned long ago how to prime the pump when asking for information. That practice worked especially well with the "guilty" people, those who had secrets eating away their souls. My plan was to let Judy talk about Lenny. Once she started talking, she might open up about herself.

"Okay, then, what did Lenny do?"

She stared at me with piercing blue eyes reminiscent of glacial ice. "It's what he hasn't done. I have no patience for men who can't make up their minds. I thought Lenny was 'the one.' You know, the guy I was meant to be with. Instead he's just a loser with a capital L."

"Right," I said. Lenny the Loser. Having spent several years feeling myself a part of that category, her venom made me uncomfortable. Forget the whole pixie analogy, too. This was like talking to Judy, the Queen of Anger. What the hell did any of this have to do with my question? There was only one way to find out. "Yeah, I can see that. He doesn't have much on the ball, does he?"

"Are you kidding me? My biological clock is ticking and Lenny waits four freaking years to tell me he's not 'the dad' type. I can't believe I gave some of my prime childbearing years to a loser who doesn't want a family." She glared in the direction Lenny had gone. "All he wants is money, money, money. I should have seen it in the beginning."

So, Lenny's title was growing—Lenny the Loser, Money-grubbing Stockbroker, Not a Human Being or the Dad Type. In the midst of that thought, I remembered overhearing this same conversation with Benni. It had happened at the Ke'anae Peninsula while I'd been waiting for her outside the women's restroom after a walk along the spectacular rocky shore. There I was, the loitering pervert hanging around the entrance when Judy launched into a rant about periods and timing.

As the exiting women eyed me, I stammered, "I'm waiting for my girlfriend." My excuse probably made me seem more like a pervert than my actual presence.

Finally, Benni and Judy emerged together engaged in a deep conversation of reproductive cycles and fertility. I didn't think much of it at the time, but Benni gave Judy a big hug and encouraged her to "keep trying."

When I asked if everything was okay, Benni replied, "Just girl talk. You don't want to know."

But, now I did know. "So Lenny doesn't want a family and you do. Is that why you've been drinking today?"

"He told me this morning."

My jaw dropped. "Whoa. This morning? Right before the tour? That's when he broke up with you? That's cold."

"He doesn't want to break up. He doesn't want to commit, either. All his talk about the future was just a load of crap." Judy glared at the space where Lenny had been standing moments before. "Lenny would be perfectly happy with a hooker on retainer."

Okay, that was awkward.

It took me a couple of seconds to come up with a response. Even if Lenny did deserve the full title. Now what? "Judy, was he lying to me? What did you see when you got here?"

She buried her face in her hands. Her fingertips were stained with red.

"Let me rephrase my question. Did you touch the body?" I pointed at Ramon.

Judy's eyes teared, her lower lip trembled, and she gripped her sides. "No. He was just—there. On the ground. I knelt down, but the grass was all wet and sticky." She wrung her hands as though she could remove the stain. "There was blood everywhere. I tried to wipe it off. That just made things worse. I know, it was stupid. I didn't kill him. He was dead when we got here."

I wasn't about to quibble over technicalities, but Ramon had been alive when these two arrived. I doubted Judy or Lenny the Loser could have done anything to save the dying man, so it made little sense to burden Judy with more guilt. Her eyes drifted closed for a moment and I wondered why she hadn't cancelled the trip after Lenny's morning bombshell. "How much have you had to drink today?"

"I had a couple of bottles stashed in my bag. I wanted this to be a good day, and Lenny totally screwed it up. When we got here, I split up with him and found a quiet spot in the garden. I was just going to get drunk and say to hell with it all when he showed up. He said he'd been watching me. He decided he'd made a mistake and proposed on the spot."

The last thing I cared about was whether these two were making wedding plans, but if they hadn't been together, maybe Lenny didn't have the alibi he claimed. "Was he there the entire time? Watching you, I mean."

"I don't know." Judy seemed to be having a hard time focusing. She gave her head a slight shake. "I'm glad I told him to go to hell."

"Why? You were getting what you wanted."

"I want a marriage, not a pity party. As for Lenny, I really don't know how long he was watching me before he showed up."

Jerod

As far as I was concerned, Judy was doing a good job all on her own of turning this trip into a pity party on wheels. So she stayed with the wrong guy too long and got bad news on a day when they would be stuck together for ten hours. Was that a reason for her to drown her sorrows in cherry-flavored whiskey? Who was I to judge? I'd done worse. Or, did that give me the right to be critical?

Our driver, Jerod, pushed past Benni and the five people she had in a holding pattern. He bellowed, "What's goin' on here, brah?"

His strong island dialect had me envisioning Jerod Hayworth as the kind of guy who could laugh and joke with his friends in Pidgin while simultaneously holding a conversation in English with tourists.

I didn't answer him right away. I was trying to account for the members of our group. Benni plus her five made six. I'd already talked to Lenny and Judy. That was eight. Add in Ramon, Jerod, and myself, and that accounted for eleven. Two people were missing.

"Well?" asked Jerod.

"Oh, sorry. Judy was just telling me how she and Lenny found the body."

Judy gripped her sides. Tight corded muscles bulged against the skin of her jawline. "Can I go?" she asked. "I don't feel good."

"Maybe you wanna go rest in the van, yah?" Jerod took her arm by the elbow, looked straight into her eyes. "First aid kit's behind a panel near the fire extinguisher inside the door. Just in case."

Did he have caffeine shots in that kit? At least then she'd be a wide-awake drunk. When Judy left, I recapped what I knew. Jerod's face remained grim throughout my description. A couple of times he shook his head as he watched Judy weave away. He squatted next to Ramon. Was he taking stock of the situation? Getting ready to tell me to mind my own business?

"I gotta report this. You kinda taken charge. You ain't a cop, yah?"

"I've done some work with a PI back in Honolulu." Would I go to hell for lying in a cemetery? It wasn't a full-fledged lie. Sort of a stretch of fourteen strands of truth. For starters, I was never hired by Chance Logan. Did it matter that Chance was really just a young PI wannabe? His education consisted of courses from the Phillip Marlowe Online Detective Agency. I suspected the "agency" was a straight-out scam, but that was Chance's problem to deal with, not mine.

What the hell? Jerod nodded, apparently accepting my status as an official member of law enforcement. Worked for me. No harm, no foul. "How long will it take the police to get here?"

"Nearest station is thirty miles in Hana."

The road to Hana was about as rural as you could get. We'd travelled through rain forest, seen towering mountains on one side, and jaw-dropping coastline on the other. One-lane bridges were the norm here. Of course, the road to Hana was just the warm-up, the truly nasty part was yet to come.

Jerod gazed around nervously. He was probably more comfortable on a hairpin turn behind the wheel of his van than in front of a crowd. The one thing I knew for sure was that the collective anxiety level in our little group was rising fast.

"Everybody needs some kind of guidance," I said.

"You kinda like a cop. You handle 'em while I radio dis in."

I stared at his face for a moment. The poor guy was petrified. "Sure," I said. "Before you leave, what happened after we got here?"

"Brah, I no got time fo' stand 'round."

He started to walk away, but stopped when I rested a hand on his shoulder. "I understand you don't want to answer a lot of questions. But, this is important. And you're pretty upset. I can see it on your face."

Jerod stared at Ramon's body. "Brah, dis no boddah me. I seen dis *kine* thing all da time in Nam. Thing is, might get me canned when boss find out. No look so good if tourists get killed on tours."

Judging by how deeply Jerod had slipped into Pidgin, I suspected the stress had him on overload. I'd seen the pattern many times. "Wait. Did anyone stay behind? On the bus?"

Jerod's eyes darted from side-to-side.

Odd, I thought. It seemed like an easy question.

He jabbed me in the chest with a finger. "No touch nothing. Company ain't gonna be happy on dis." He started to walk away, then stopped. "And, no. Nobody else on da bus."

Conchita

The small cemetery consisted of a large expanse of overgrown lawn dotted with grave markers. Periodic tropical plantings consisting of ornamental figs, ti plants, and small shrubs surrounded by volcanic stone walls rounded out the landscaping. This was a place of peace and tranquility. It was where the dead should rest. Not a place where lives should be taken.

With only one tree near Lindbergh's grave, securing the area with crime-scene tape, rope, or braided ti leaves was impossible. The best thing I could do for Ramon was keep the masses away and hope his killer faced justice.

The inscription on the simple gravestone read, "Charles A. Lindbergh Born Michigan 1902 Died Maui 1974." Footprints from the day's visitors had matted the turf, reducing the possibility of retrieving even one footprint. Blood spatter stained the otherwise green carpet. Did the evidence corroborate Judy's statement about kneeling down near the body?

Based on positioning—head against the rocks, the rest of the body stretched out with arms wide on the grass—it wasn't hard to imagine scenarios in which Ramon had fallen, been pushed, or had someone smash his head against the rocks.

Grumbling from Benni's group caught my attention.

Jerod was practically begging them to remain calm. Help would be on the way soon. He didn't tell them it could take an hour for that help to arrive. A chorus of complaints arose when he said I would be investigating Ramon's death, but none was louder than the obnoxious Conchita Brunet.

I screwed up my courage and made my approach.

Conchita was a big-boned woman. Though a few inches shorter than me, she was a solid size sixteen. It was a fact I'd learned within ten minutes of this morning's introductions at the breakfast buffet when a sweet and charming Conchita commented on Benni's "cute top." Almost immediately, she launched into an annoying diatribe about prejudice in the fashion industry and how "full-bodied women" didn't have the selection available to "women like you." The whole thing sounded almost vicious and left me wondering how many personalities Conchita had.

While walking back to the van after breakfast, I asked Benni if she'd taken offense at Conchita's jab.

She smiled and said, "No. She's a Libra."

Being an expert in the art of misunderstanding women, I nodded as though I understood and returned her smile. Right now, it appeared I'd be dealing with Conchita's pushy side. Well, I could get pushy, too. I approached her and asked, "Can you help me out?"

Conchita smiled, bringing out the same bubbly personality we'd seen before the body-size discussion. "Sure. What do you need?"

I strolled away from the crowd with Conchita dutifully following until we stood side-by-side next to Ramon's body. "Here's the thing, Conchita. From what I can see, none of these people ever met prior to this tour. And yet, we have a dead guy in a cemetery right near the grave of Charles Lindbergh. Maybe there's no connection, but it might mean something. Do you have any ideas?"

"I do." She stuck her chin out, then glared directly at me. "You're dealing with this thing?"

"I've been volunteered in a way."

"Good. You can be our representative. This is absolutely unconscionable. The company should never have let this sort of thing happen on one of its tours. You need to tell them we'll go to court, if necessary. There are others who feel the same way. We need to get our money back."

I blinked, unable to believe what I'd heard. She was worried about a refund? Now? Shouldn't she be more concerned about her own safety? A killer was on the loose, after all. "That's not really what I'm concerned about right now, Conchita."

"Well, you should be."

She shifted her bulk. Perhaps a beautiful woman in her younger years, the curl of her lip now gave her an intimidating presence. It was like watching a rhinoceros shift from sedentary to first gear. No need to wonder how much damage an impact might cause, you just wanted to get the hell out of the way.

"My immediate concern is finding out who killed Ramon."

"I can help you with that, too." She smirked as she dismissed any concerns with a wave of her hand.

"Then maybe you could enlighten me." I nudged her elbow. "Help me wrap this up."

Conchita licked her lips and her smile faded. I was half expecting Crabby Conchita to return, but she was rational when she spoke.

"There were a lot of questions about Lindbergh while we were here. A couple of the really young ones had no idea who the man was. And, among the older ones, only a few knew he crossed the Atlantic, not the Pacific."

"No way," I said.

"Way." She nodded. "But Ramon, now he had the whole story. At one point, he began acting like he was our tour guide. He was very familiar with the baby kidnapping. He even knew Lindbergh had three wives with children in different countries. He said he was positive there was a fourth wife, and that's when the group broke up. A couple of them said he was just telling tales. He was convincing. Almost had me believing the story. Anyway, after that everyone moved off. A few went to the gardens. Others headed to the church."

"This is very helpful," I said. I doubted that it was, but what the heck? I had Conchita on my side, at least for the time being. "Did you hear or see anything else?"

"Yes, there was a big argument after the group split. I didn't recognize the voices, but I'm sure it was two men."

"Okay, two men. An argument." Now that was something I could work with. "What else?"

"I couldn't tell what they were saying, but it was obvious they were very angry with each other. I'm not a busybody, so I decided to stay out of it."

That was about as phony as the fake designer bag she carried around. Once again, I had Benni to thank for that bit of insider knowledge. I nearly asked her which of her personalities didn't like getting into other people's business, but decided she could easily knock me down and shove my face in the grass until I sneezed to death. "Sure, sure. Weren't you even curious, though?"

Even during the breakfast buffet, it was obvious Conchita had no qualms about telling everyone what to do. Not once, however, had she even feigned interest in what the others said. Her apparent indifference had me almost believing she really did ignore the whole argument.

Conchita's lips curled in something resembling a smile. If she were a rhino, I'm sure she'd be wagging her fifty-pound tail, encouraging me to come closer.

I kept my distance. Let her talk.

"I told you. I'm not a busybody. I don't interfere in other people's lives. You may not mind being nosey, but it's not my style. Now, if you'll excuse me, I'm sure you have more prying to do."

Olivia

Conchita stomped away, leaving me in a quandary. Apologize? Say to hell with it? I followed her, then decided an apology was unnecessary when we met up with Olivia Smith,

"Relax, Conchita." Olivia took Conchita's hand. "You're getting all worked up."

"I am not."

"Sure you are."

They reminded me of squabbling children I'd seen in grocery stores. In those cases, even the most oblivious parent eventually stopped the game. But, without adult supervision, these two could go on forever. I wondered how many times a day they did this. They were probably best friends, golf widows, most likely, who passed the time irritating each other with their own little quirks.

Jerod returned from the van, looking decidedly unhappy. "Cops gonna be at least an hour, brah. Big kine accident up the road. Some local kids joyriding in a pickup. A couple of 'em fall out. Road's blocked and Hana cops gotta deal wid dat first."

While Jerod filled me in on the traffic issues, Olivia and Conchita continued their banter.

"I can see it on your face. You're upset."

Conchita jerked her hand away. "You're wrong." Her lower lip protruded in a pout she probably learned in kindergarten.

Jerod nodded at the two women. "Nothing worse than two women married to each other. See if you can solve this thing. My job's on the line." He shook his head and left.

What? These two didn't have husbands? They were—oh, crap. Now I had another problem. Who called who what? Was one the husband? Were they both wives? I caught Benni's gaze, tried sending her a telepathic message. *Please, Benni, please help me.*

She smiled, gave me a thumbs up, and turned away. So much for lovers reading each other's thoughts.

And, forget being politically correct. What I wanted to know was why the company would hassle Jerod over a killing on his tour. Unless, of course, this was a regular thing with him and I was dealing with a three-strikes kind of guy. Maybe I could find out before the cops arrived. Right now, though, Olivia was just a few feet away.

I approached the women and asked if they'd been together the entire time at this stop. Call it my lie detector test. I already knew the answer was no.

Conchita glanced at me, then spoke to her friend in a silky smooth voice. "I've already talked to him, Liv. McKenna's trying to solve the murder. Then he's going to help us get our money back. I'm going back to the bus. What an awful day."

Olivia let out a deep sigh and fingered one of her earrings as she watched Conchita leave. "I love her so much, but she can be such a handful."

"How long have you two been together?"

"About five years. This was our honeymoon. We decided to make it official and blow our wad on the vacation of a lifetime. I'd say it was worth it. Until today."

"Were you with each other the entire time we've been at this stop?"

"Not the entire time." Olivia's smile revealed bright, white teeth straight enough to make the pickiest orthodontist proud. Even the boy-cut of her blonde hair cried sex appeal. "I was on the bus getting a snack. I'm diabetic and my blood sugar goes crazy when I don't eat on a regular schedule. Days like today are tough."

I nodded my agreement. For someone like me with celiac disease, finding a meal could become quite a challenge at times. "Did you hear the screams?"

"No, not really." She paused as though considering her options, then wet her lips before continuing. "Jerod had been asleep. He asked me not to tell, but I don't see what the big deal is. He said one of his kids was sick all night, so he was whipped."

"Oh," I said, trying to mask my surprise. So that's why Jerod's tour-guide commentary had become more lethargic as the day wore on. It had faded fast since the last stop. "If you didn't hear the screams, and Jerod was asleep, how'd you know something was wrong?"

"It was TC. He came charging up to the bus yelling about a lack of organization. I tried to wake Jerod before TC saw him. I didn't want our poor driver being hassled because he was a good dad."

Sex appeal. Compassion. But, no help as a witness. Bummer. What I needed was someone who'd seen something other than the inside of the van or the backs of their eyelids. I was striking out. "Was there anyone else on the van?"

"Valentine came on for a bit. She was flirting with me again. She seemed to think I was interested. She's been trying to impress me with her video footage all day. To tell you the truth, I think she buys toys to compensate for her unhappiness. When I told her I was married to Conchita, she sulked off to play with her drone."

Based on what I'd seen today, Olivia appeared to be the only member of the "I heart Val" club. And, let's put the emphasis where it belonged, on the heart. Now she was telling me she wasn't interested? I took what I considered the only sane route, avoidance. "When did this happen?" I asked.

"Let's see, Conchita and I came to see Lindbergh's grave first, then I made a beeline for the church. You were there— pretty deep in thought from the looks of it. Anyway, I was probably off the bus for a total of maybe five minutes. It all happened so fast."

"Conchita said she was caught up in a big discussion about Lindbergh. Ramon was leading it. I guess you missed it."

Her giggles took me by surprise. "Don't worry. When something catches Conchita's fancy, she'll keep revisiting it until she's an expert. You might have noticed she likes being in charge. Anyway, if Ramon was giving a history lesson, I know I'll be getting the graduate-course version soon."

"You two are so different," I said.

"You and Benni aren't exactly alike. Why should we be?"

"Point taken. Is there anyone else you think I should talk to? TC maybe? You said he came running up to the van."

Olivia rolled her eyes. "He's a waste. Try Valentine. She was flying that silly drone all over the place. You never know, that thing might turn out to be helpful."

Valentine

I didn't relish the idea of confronting Val again. Her Millennial with Money attitude kind of irked me. I really didn't want to get into the whole Olivia-Conchita-Val triangle either. Solve this murder, that I could do. Understand those three? No way.

What I needed to know was if she or her drone could shed any light on the murder.

I found her showing off the day's videos to Judy. Oh, happy day.

"Ladies," I nodded to both of them.

"You here to accuse me again?" Judy's glare could have melted glass.

"Or maybe you want to harass me about my drone." Val said. She took up a confrontational stance with her arms crossed over her chest.

Sheesh. Had I walked into a hornet's nest, or what? I raised my hands in surrender. "Neither. The cops are hung up and won't be here for another hour. Right now, we have a killer running around. Wouldn't you like to know who it is?"

"I already told you what I know," Judy said.

Val's lips pursed. She glanced at Judy, then reached out. When her fingers came to rest on Judy's arm, their eyes met. "Remember what we talked about. Maybe Lenny's just confused. He proposed. Okay? If nothing else, you've got a few days left to get him out of your system."

Judy nodded, gave Val a final hug, then glared at me. "I have nothing more to say to you." An awkward silence engulfed us as Judy marched away.

She waited until Judy was out of earshot. "Are you always so insensitive?"

My jaw dropped a bit, then I remembered who I was talking to—the Queen of Embarrassing Questions. "Are you always so direct?"

"Direct is good. It avoids all the little games people play. That's the nice thing about technical writing, McKenna; everything is black and white. You might have some "if this, then that" sets of conditions, but there are always a finite number of options."

"Very...um, direct."

She nodded enthusiastically. "Right. People are much more complex. Anyway, you don't want sensitivity lessons, because you want to solve a murder. Let's cut to the chase. I didn't see anything. That's it. Period."

"Direct, but lacking detail." I thought it a pretty good comeback for dealing with a technical writer. Val, on the other hand, looked unimpressed.

"That's not a bad analysis for someone who probably thinks their smartphone is a paperweight."

Crap. I just did it once. Well, maybe a couple of times. If I admitted my techno-crime to Val, I'd expose myself to more insults. Forget it. I needed to diffuse this situation fast. Time to cut my losses. I put my hand up and waved it back and forth a few times.

"What are you doing now?" she demanded.

"Can't you see it? It's a white flag. Truce?"

Val snickered and, for the first time, gave me a slight smile. "You might be past your use-by date, but you're determined enough to pull this off. What do you want to know?"

"Let's begin with where you set up shop to fly the drone."

"I was just wandering. While it videoed from above, I checked things out on the ground. If I came across something I wanted to see from a different view, I maneuvered the drone to where I wanted it."

"You've had it in the air a lot today. How far can it go?"

She beamed. "About a mile and a half. This particular model gives me a couple of hours of flying time. It's getting kind of low on power, but we're past all the really cool stuff anyway."

I felt a little surge of satisfaction. She was dropping her guard. Maybe not as fast as the drone would fall from the sky without power, but I could see progress. I pointed at what she held in her hands. It reminded me of a white, plastic gaming console. "Did you have any trouble navigating around here?"

"Not at all." She held out the device. "The controller clip holds a cell phone. The controls are super simple to master. See?" She pointed. "Just a couple of joysticks and a 'Return to Home' button. It has trouble in high wind, so Jerod told me not to fly when we stopped at the Kīpahulu Visitor Center."

"Sure. The Pools of Oheʻo. He was probably worried you'd be tempted to go after the drone if it went down."

"Too dangerous," she said. "I read the sign. Father, daughter, missing shoe. Both drowned. Believe me, I don't want to be somebody else's example of a tragedy. Anyway, it's easy here as long as you avoid the trees." She winked at me. "It's nothing like the Keʻanae Peninsula."

The skip in my heartbeat wasn't because she'd hassled me with the drone, but because I was sure Val had just decided I was a friend. I smiled at her. "Yeah, lots of open space, picnic areas, real restrooms, crashing surf on a rocky coastline, and a flying camera to catch it all. It was a great stop."

Casting her gaze downward, she bit at her lower lip. "My husband is a bit of a stick-in-the-mud. He got really ticked at me when I buzzed you. I'm sorry about that. It was kind of childish."

"Tell Lowell, no worries. I think I might have had a little payback coming." I raised both eyebrows and gazed in her eyes. "We're good?"

She gave me a little shrug, then nodded.

I wondered if maybe I'd hurt her feelings at some point. Rather than pursuing opening the wound, I said, "Terrific. So, let's focus on what happened here. Where was Lowell during this stop?"

Val rolled her eyes. An exasperated, "Ugh" escaped her lips. Val pocketed the phone she'd been using to show Judy the video and set the controller off to one side. I really wanted to see the video, but I felt like I needed to work through the facts first.

"This is his ideal stop," Val said. "He's a history buff. This was his big event. Lindbergh's been his fascination since before we met and I wasn't about to get in his way. Knowing Lowell, he was off educating everyone about Charles Lindbergh. You think I'm a nerd. Well, he's exactly the same, but he's focused on the dead past. I prefer looking at the unborn future."

I nodded as though agreeing with her, but her analysis felt slightly off. It would have been closer to the truth to say she was focused on technology. "So you didn't see him?"

She paused for a second. "Off and on. You know, we stayed in touch."

Her eyes had darted up and to the left, an indication she might have just constructed a visual memory. In other words, a lie. The only time I'd seen Val and Lowell together had been while they were on the van. At almost every stop, Val had gone one way, Lowell, the other. Even when Val had buzzed me at Ke'anae Peninsula, Lowell hadn't been around. He might have seen the incident from a distance, but he hadn't been a part of it.

So, what was Val hiding?

TC

I watched Val's face for a moment more, then broke eye contact. It bugged me to think she assumed I'd fall for such a naive lie. While I'd have loved to find out why she was lying about her and Lowell, that line of questioning had to wait. The person marching in our direction was the biggest complainer on the tour, Theodore Chaplin. In tow behind him was his wife, Magda.

Theodore insisted we call him TC. I had a nickname for him, one that would probably land me in a smackdown with him. He and his wife were total opposites. Where he was overly obnoxious, she was polite and courteous. She also seemed to be a chameleon, morphing into whatever TC wanted her to be at the moment.

I found it odd that everyone else on the tour was wearing lightweight clothing such as T-shirts and shorts, but Magda had on a long-sleeved cotton blouse and slacks. In that sense, she stuck out, but in all other respects, she melted into the background.

"I hear you're the one who's going to get us our money back," barked TC. "Why aren't you working on that? What the hell kind of way is this to run a tour? No guides at the stops, a driver who falls asleep when he should be giving us the history, murders—you'd better make a strong case or there's going to be hell to pay."

Val snorted, but kept her silence, even when TC glared at her.

I thought it best to ignore Val and maintain focus on TC. "Right now, TC, I've got other issues to deal with."

"Yeah, yeah, you're the big investigator. Well, right after you solve this case, you'd better be working to make us all whole again. Chiquita and me want this handled right."

"You mean Conchita?" I asked.

"He's not very good with names," Magda said.

"Did I ask you, Maggie? No, I didn't." He turned back to me. "Conchita, Chiquita, whatever. Nice gal, but kinda pushy. Back when I was on the tour, this kind of crap would never have happened. Somebody's got to get this mess squared away."

Calling TC out on the way he treated his wife would probably not help my case at all. We'd be at odds, and what I needed now was his cooperation, so I bit my tongue and asked, "What tour were you on?"

"PGA. Six years. Things were always well organized. Nothing like this." He flipped a hand dismissively, a scowl on his face.

"TC, you know things happen." Magda put a hand on her husband's arm, but he jerked it away, then silenced her with a cold stare.

What a jackass, I thought. I'd reserve my questions for Magda until I could get her alone. But, TC? If I were twenty years younger, weighed forty pounds more, and worked out every day—well, so much for superhero fantasies.

Fortunately, Benni had done a remarkable job with crowd control. It helped that most of the people I'd spoken to had lost their taste for the crime scene and were keeping their distance. Benni and Marquetta, another of the remaining witnesses, were engaged in a deep conversation. I hoped Benni could keep Marquetta occupied until I finished with the man I wanted desperately to call Totally Contemptuous.

Val harrumphed. "My husband said you were never good enough to make the top tier."

Having been the target of Val's acid tongue already, I knew it was an uncomfortable place to be. But, seeing Totally squirm under her level gaze made me want to kiss her.

He was still fuming when I said, "Can't say as I ever heard of you, TC. Of course, I was never much of a golf fan myself."

TC looked like he might pop his cork at any moment. Magda, on the other hand, was holding back a smile. Before her husband could recover, and before Magda got herself into trouble by saying something she'd regret after the reinforcements were gone, I put TC on the spot with a question about whether he'd heard the argument.

"There wasn't any argument," he growled. "That's the other thing about Conchita, she makes things up to get attention. Me, I don't have to do that. Right, Maggie? Right. See? There was no argument."

Magda hesitated. "I don't recall hearing one."

I saw Val stiffen. She grimaced when I glanced at her. "If you'll excuse me." She stormed away, shaking her head.

This whole thing made no sense. Why would Conchita have made up the story? And why would TC call her a liar? Unless he had something to hide. "Where were you when this supposed argument took place?"

"How the hell should I know? If it didn't take place, how could I tell you where I was?"

Magda shifted from one foot to the other, obviously uncomfortable with this entire discussion. TC's version of the events made it one in favor of an argument, one opposed. It was easy to see how someone could miss the loud voices, but to call Conchita a liar about it? Something was wrong with the whole scenario. I also had the impression that Magda was trapped in a marriage with a man who regarded her as he did everyone else—subservient. In his eyes, TC was the most important person in the room. I'd play to his need. Maybe he'd give something away.

"What you're telling me could be critical to solving this case, TC. You could be the man who has the information. What else do you know?"

"Well, that's more like it. That Ramon guy was kinda queer, don't you think?"

"Are you saying he was gay?"

"I knew a couple of their kind on the tour. He didn't strike me as the type. That's not what I meant. He was a queer duck. Stayed all to himself during the day. Antisocial, if you ask me."

At each stop, TC had latched onto a new victim to talk about sports. Football, baseball, pro, amateur, it made no difference. TC was a walking encyclopedia. Oddly enough, I hadn't heard him discuss golf once. Yes, he'd bragged about his "days on the tour," but he did it in the context of a bait-and-switch comparison to a different sport. It always went something like, "When I was on the tour, we always respected people's property. Nothing like these guys in pro football today. Did you see..." Then, he'd venture into a discussion of winners and losers, scores and strategies.

Ramon, on the other hand, had been quiet. A loner. Not antisocial in my opinion, but how would someone who craved the spotlight interpret his behavior?

"Did Ramon say anything to you, TC? I know you tried to talk to him this morning."

"Yeah, yeah, he was all excited over getting to visit Lindbergh's grave. He said it was going to be his coming out."

My pulse quickened at that line. Did it mean what I thought? Had this been a hate crime, a spur of the moment flash of anger triggered by Ramon revealing his innermost desires? But, why do that on a tour with twelve strangers? And what would that have to do with Lindbergh?

I glanced at Magda. "Did you hear him say that, too?"

She nodded. "I was there."

"C'mon, Maggie, let's let McKenna finish up his investigation. Remember what I said. We're counting on you to make this right." His voice took on a sinister tone. "Conchita and me are going to be watching."

He started to grab Magda's hand, but she pulled her arm away. "That one hurts, honey. I'm coming."

Staring after them as they walked away, I couldn't help but feel as though Totally Contemptuous might actually seek revenge if he felt disappointed.

Marquetta

Benni and Marquetta came to see me next. At first, Marquetta's attention was focused on Magda, who dutifully trailed behind her husband. Marquetta shuddered, then shook her head.

"McKenna," Benni said, "Marquetta has something you need to hear."

Marquetta was one of those women to whom age had been kind. She had a full head of curly, silver-blonde hair, which she wore cut at the shoulder. Her skin was still smooth and her smile bright. "I hope you didn't say anything to upset TC. He'll take it out on Magda."

"What do you mean?" I asked.

"Because Magda is a victim of domestic abuse. I can tell."

Just because TC was a jerk didn't make him abusive—although his verbal treatment of Magda treaded a fine line. "Did she say something?"

"Not in so many words, but back in Hana, when the guy had us all squeeze the ginger flower to release the scent, Magda winced. I asked her if she was in pain and she said it was arthritis. I thought nothing of it at the time, but when she reached out for one of the bracelets, I saw bruises on her arm. I suggested she try the bracelet on and she practically burst into tears when I took her wrist. She let me push up her sleeve. Her arm was purple and black from above the wrist to the elbow. When she saw TC coming, she pulled away. I think she wants help, but doesn't know how to ask for it."

"Pretty impressive diagnosis," I said.

In addition to perfect skin, Marquetta had the figure of a twenty-year-old, and the observational skills of a trained investigator.

"Thanks," she said as she unconsciously draped one of her earbuds around her neck while she continued to listen through the other.

"What are you, a psychologist?"

She smiled at me. "You're sweet. Hang onto him, honey. He's a keeper."

"I'm thinking about it." Benni snickered, then they burst into laughter.

As usual, the whole female communication thing baffled me. Of course, given the fact that one of my strengths is my perseverance—which more than one person had called obstinacy—I wasn't about to give up so easily. "Were you a cop?"

"No, sweetie, I was an exotic dancer. I started out on the streets when I was fifteen. I ran away in 1969 from a father who was just like TC. I come from the school of hard knocks and have seen it all. Anything you can imagine, I've been there. Hell, I've probably done it, too." She paused, hummed a few bars of a song I didn't recognize, then gazed at me. "Sorry, does that offend you?"

"The humming? Not at all, you have a great voice. Very melodic." Quite honestly, my mind was spinning as it worked to calculate Marquetta's age. "You don't look a day over fifty," I muttered.

She pulled out the remaining earbud and let it hang next to the other. Marquetta laughed, causing me to realize every time I spoke I dug my hole deeper. If I didn't get my focus, and fast, Benni would probably leave me behind when the tour left. Time for this captain to change the ship's course before everyone started calling me the bus bozo. I pointed at the earbuds. "What were you listening to?"

"I love music, harmonies. This setting." She gazed at the church, painted dark green and white. "I've seen so much beauty today I want to bring a hundred canvases here and paint for a year without taking a break."

"You're a painter, too. I'm impressed."

"It's okay, sweetie, so was TC. I made the mistake of introducing myself to him as a painter during breakfast. That seemed to get him all excited. I guess he's got some preconceived notions about artists and their lifestyles. I'm sure as hell glad I didn't tell him I started out as a call girl.

I haven't worked on my back in a very long time, but I'm sure he wouldn't know the difference."

I stammered, again noticing heat in my cheeks. "You, uh, don't look like you come from the streets."

"Thank you." Her smile was demure and pure. "I had a client who was very generous and helped me start my own club. I empathize with Magda's situation. I wish there was a way to get her away from TC."

"I may have an idea. But first, would you answer a few questions for me?"

"Let's see—where was I at the time of the murder? Since none of us knows when the murder occurred, our collective ignorance is our alibi. Did I hear the scream? Yes, I was with the rest of the group. I have been with them since we got here. That includes Magda and TC, by the way. Oh, what about, did I have a reason to want to see Ramon killed? I've never met the poor man before, so why would I want to kill him? Anything else?"

Marquetta had pretty much covered my entire Chief Inspector McKenna's repertoire in thirty seconds or less. It was unnerving how easily she could throw me completely off balance. I cleared my throat. "So, uh, you sound like you've been interrogated by authorities before." My cheeks felt hot the moment the words popped out of my mouth.

She smiled. "Don't forget those without any authority. It was an occupational hazard."

I cleared my throat again. "Right. I do have one more question. There supposedly was a discussion about Charles Lindbergh between Lowell and Ramon. What do you know about that?"

"We were all there. Ramon was spouting off all these details about Lindbergh, some of which Lowell refuted. Then, Ramon really pissed Lowell off by announcing to all of us that his mother had also been married to Lindbergh. Everybody but Lowell thought it was pretty funny, but you know what? Ramon was serious. He truly believed Charles Lindbergh was his father. Personally, I'd say he's off his rocker. Like my father in a way, but Ramon was the non-violent kind."

Benni put a hand on Marquetta's arm. "I can't imagine what you must have gone through."

"The streets were better than being beaten up whenever he got drunk."

"After you left, did your mother stick around?" Benni asked.

A tear formed at the corner of Marquetta's eye. Her jaw tightened for the briefest moment. "She stuck with him until the end, which was only a few years. Now that was a twist of fate." Marquetta's eyes crinkled with the memory. "Of all things, my father was killed by a drunk driver. Mom got a nice settlement. That's when she tracked me down and I helped her start her own bakery. She passed on a few years ago, just after her 84th birthday. She never missed a day of work in thirty-five years. She was the kind who loved each and every day. I think Magda has that same potential. Anyway, you said you had an idea about how to get her away from TC."

"It's more like I have a way to get TC away from Magda. Let's face it, you're a very attractive woman and if you were to make a move on him, he might just decide he could leave Magda alone for a little bit."

Benni's jaw dropped. She hissed, "No way. McKenna, are you crazy?"

"I love it." Marquetta flipped back a strand of hair. "He's been eyeing me all day, anyway. This will be a chance to even the score. Count me in, but I need a backup just in case he doesn't want to take no for an answer."

"I know just the person," I said.

Magda

The CIA had nothing on us. We had our own little black op going down on Maui. Good grief.

"We'll need a code name. How about Operation Breakaway?" Benni and Marquetta stared at me as if I'd lost my last marble.

Benni continued to stare at me. She was probably wondering how she'd hooked up with a lunatic. Marquetta, on the other hand, gave me a wink and a little salute.

I cleared my throat. "On second thought, forget the code name. I'll go get Jerod involved."

Our driver readily agreed to his role in our little venture. I think he might not have been so willing if our target had been anyone else, but TC had been a vocal thorn in Jerod's side all day. It helped considerably when I explained that TC had seen Jerod sleeping earlier. In the end, he was very willing to help take the man down a few notches.

Next, I went in search of Val. She was with Olivia, engaged in a heated debate about IOS vs. Android. When the women saw me, Olivia excused herself and left me alone with Val. "What's up, McKenna?"

"We need to get Magda away from TC so I can interview her."

"Good luck. That man's an insufferable—never mind. Sorry, but I don't want anything to do with him."

"Not you," I said. "The drone. Here's what I have in mind."

I described how Marquetta would attempt to lure TC away. Before TC could make a move, Jerod and I would "stumble upon" the two and break them up by telling Marquetta to get back to the van. We needed the drone to video the interaction, then swoop in if TC became difficult. I also explained that Benni had the questions for Magda and would do the interview for me. When I was done, Val regarded me with disbelief in her brown eyes.

"You do realize you're completely insane, right?"

I blinked in surprise. "I was just sure you would have loved the opportunity to use the drone as a witness."

"I do," she said. "What if the guy goes ballistic? You need a better backup. Something to stop him in his tracks. Here." She reached into her giant backpack and extracted a small device.

I pointed at what she held. "Is that what I think it is?"

"Tasers are perfectly legal."

"Maybe in your state. But not here."

She shrugged. "I didn't realize that when I packed it." A sly smile appeared at the corner of her mouth. "I guarantee it will stop even a hormone-crazed maniac."

"Keep it. I'm not spending a year in jail because you think I need a better plan."

"Your choice." She dropped the Taser into her backpack.

Operation Breakaway kicked off a few minutes later. Marquetta swayed up to TC. Her languid movements captured his attention in seconds. Magda didn't protest as her husband drifted away. I wondered if TC had cheated on her in the past or if she was just too afraid to complain. Either way, it was the opening we needed.

Benni moved in immediately, her list of questions at the ready. We figured we had no more than five minutes at the most. Jerod and I shadowed Marquetta and TC, who was practically salivating on himself. Overhead, the drone shadowed our target with its all-seeing eye.

The moment TC and Marquetta were away from the others, TC reached for her. Marquetta sidestepped and wagged a finger in his face. She kept her cool and gave him a playful laugh. "Now, now. You're not a schoolboy, and we're not going to hump in the woods like a pair of dogs."

TC's face reddened. "That sounds good to me. You said you wanted it. I've seen you watching me all day."

"A girl still likes a little warm-up." She pushed gently against his chest and TC stumbled backwards, his butt landing on a large boulder. "You sit there and let me do something you'll remember for a very long time. Why don't you unzip? It turns me on when I see a man respond."

TC's efforts to drop his shorts were the stuff of TV sit-com legend. His fingers shook so violently he could barely pull down the zipper. In his haste, the zipper caught and TC had to shimmy out amidst a great deal of cursing. By the time we hit the two-minute mark, his face was four-teen shades of red, he looked like he might have a heart attack, and his shorts were bunched down around his an-kles. When he started to kick them off, Marquetta stopped him by kneeling before him. She placed her hands on his knees.

"Not yet," she cooed. "Here comes your reward for in-dulging me."

TC looked like he might lose control of his bodily func-tions at any moment.

Marquetta stood and began a slow, rhythmic dance as we crossed the three minute mark. We needed two more.

Hips swaying, Marquetta ran her hands down her sides. It looked like she might strip right before us. I glanced at Jerod. "Holy shit."

"My wife gonna kill me," he croaked.

I checked the timer on my phone. Marquetta's dance had taken up another minute and a half. We were four and a half minutes into this little charade. The problem was, if this went any further, Marquetta could be in danger. Sud-denly, she stepped away from TC. "If you can catch me, you can have me."

TC jumped up, but fell flat on his face, his shorts around his ankles. "Son of a bitch. Son of a bitch!"

He extracted one leg, then kicked frantically with the other leg. The shorts clung to his foot, then flew away. We were just past the five-minute mark.

Jerod charged through the trees into the clearing. He bellowed, "What the hell's goin' on here?"

I marched in behind Jerod. TC scrambled across the grass for his shorts. He pulled on one leg, hopped a couple of times, then lost his balance and fell to the ground.

"This is mortifying." Marquetta covered her face with her hands and rushed away.

"You better get back to the bus," Jerod bellowed after her. "I ain't gonna allow no more funny stuff on my tour!"

Jerod turned his full wrath on TC. With the driver glaring down at him like a disgusted parent, TC couldn't seem to decide whether he should cover up or get dressed. We'd already passed the six minute mark. The question was, had we given Benni enough time to do her part?

I waited, a witness while Jerod spent the next couple of minutes chewing out TC, telling him to stay away from Marquetta, and instructing him that if there was any more trouble, all incidents would be reported to the company. TC, focused on his embarrassment, barely gave me a sideways glance.

Jerod and I left TC alone in the clearing. I doubted if he'd ever brag about this episode as he did with his "PGA tour" experience. When we found Val, she said Benni and Magda were in the church. I found them, side-by-side in the last pew. Magda's eyes were rimmed in red, but she sat up straight, as though a weight had been removed.

After we exchanged greetings, Benni turned to her. "Tell him what you told me."

Magda nodded and squeezed Benni's hands, which rested in hers. She grimaced before she spoke. "TC lied to you about the argument. We did hear it. He didn't want to be involved in the investigation because he shuns publicity. Val was right, Mr. McKenna. TC never was good enough for the pro tour. Oh, he always had an excuse. It was always something someone else had done—usually me. He always blamed me when he had a bad game. In reality, he always psyched himself out."

"What's that got to do with a murder here in Hawai'i?"

"TC is a very proud man, so when the papers started calling him a has-been, he hated it. The last few times he got any coverage at all, it was always about the shots he missed. He's come to think the press hates him and was petrified about what would happen if he was called as a witness."

"That's ridiculous," I said. "So he didn't make it to the top, big deal."

"To him that's exactly what it is, a big deal. TC is not a strong man. He's weak and makes up for it with all his bluster about his days on the tour. The reality is he spent six years chasing a dream. He's so ashamed of his career that he would do anything to avoid having people find out about his past."

"So what happened in the argument between Ramon and Lowell?"

"Ramon said his mother was a young artist in Paris—just eighteen—when she met Lindbergh. Theirs was a short liaison, but Ramon was born as a result. He claimed he had the DNA test results to prove Lindbergh was his father."

"And Lowell didn't like those claims?"

"Lowell is a Lindbergh purist. He believes, as he put it, the first man to fly nonstop from New York to Paris would not have had multiple wives, nor would he have fathered children out of wedlock. He was too honorable. Ramon said there was plenty of proof to show otherwise. They were like two bulls squaring off."

The whole argument seemed ridiculous to me. I said, "All I know about Lindbergh is related to his trans-Atlantic flight and the baby kidnapping. I remember the kidnapping was called the crime of the century and the cops used the classic follow-the-money strategy to pin the whole thing on Bruno Hauptmann. There were those who believed Hauptmann couldn't have been working alone, but he's the only one who knew for sure, and he's been dead for 75 years. Too bad DNA can't solve that case."

The light coming from the front door dimmed. I glanced over my shoulder. It was Lowell.

Lowell

"Thanks, Magda," I said. "Benni, why don't you stay with her?"

She nodded, kissed me on the cheek, and whispered, "We'll be with the others."

The two women exchanged places with Lowell, then were gone.

Lowell stood in the center aisle gazing at me with passive, dark blue eyes. "Hear you been asking questions concerning my disagreement with Ramon. I figured I might as well weigh in."

"Have a seat." I gestured around me. "We have lots available." We also had confirmation. There had been a disagreement between Lowell and the dead man.

"Thanks." Lowell picked the row ahead of me and casually draped his arm over the back of the pew.

He appeared unconcerned, as if he had nothing to fear. How odd, all the fingers pointed in his direction.

"So tell me about your disagreement."

"Not much to say. I got pretty ticked at Ramon, denigrating a national hero like that. It's bad enough that Charles and Anne had to go through the horror of having their first-born kidnapped, but then to be vilified by the media because he supposedly had all these affairs. It's more than any man should have to endure."

What planet was Lowell living on? He thought he was on a first-name basis with the Lindberghs? "Lowell, how did you and Ramon resolve your difference of opinion?"

"I challenged him to pony up the DNA results, and he admitted he hadn't yet had the testing done. He said he was going to do that 'soon,' as he put it. It was all BS. The guy was just a publicity hound, and I exposed him. When I left him, he was humiliated, but alive. I gotta say, he actually did me a favor."

"Why's that?"

"I can write an article on this." Lowell shifted in his seat so he was leaning against the back of the pew. "It'll get tons of media exposure. Ramon will get nothing by the time I'm done. Because of him, I'll be recognized as an expert on Lindbergh. I needed a break. He gave it to me."

Lowell seemed eager to tell his side. It was the first time during the day he'd been anything other than melancholy and serious. If his version of the events were true, who the hell had bashed Ramon's head against those rocks? "I hear you're a horticulturist."

"Going on ten years. Cal Poly grad. One of the best schools for horticulture and crop science."

"What's a horticulturist do? I mean, who are your clients? Customers? Whatever you call them."

"What's that got to do with any of this?"

"Just curious."

"My client list is my business. You need anything else?"

"Several people heard the argument, but nobody seems to be able to confirm the ending you describe. Was anyone around for that?"

Lowell glanced around the church; his breathing was shallow, his demeanor still calm. "Nope. They all upped and left before the big moment. Too bad, I would have loved to have had a few witnesses. Would have added credibility to the article."

"Got any idea who would have wanted to kill Ramon?"

"Can't help you there, either. Like I said, when I left, Ramon was alive." He snickered, "Maybe he whacked himself. Seen stranger things happen."

It was the first thing Lowell had said that made me question his story. Ramon had known he'd be up against intense scrutiny. He had to have been prepared for the criticism. Just because he didn't yet have DNA results, why would he kill himself? Unless he'd tripped—I turned and glanced out the church entrance.

"Your wife has gotten some very good video today," I said.

Lowell did a double take. His confident exterior returned a moment later, but in that brief second, I'd seen his smile fade and his eyes narrow. Maybe Olivia had been right.

The drone could tell us what really happened. I had to talk to Val—before Lowell got to her.

The Drone

My next, and hopefully most enlightening, witness stood about a foot tall. It had four rotors atop a narrow body, which was really nothing more than a white plastic frame on which a small video camera had been mounted. In theory, I had three possible killers: Lenny, TC, and Lowell. Lenny had been the man standing over the body and could easily have argued with Ramon, smashed his head on the rocks, then covered up the crime by pretending to have difficulty finding a pulse.

TC had the anger, but I could see no motive. I suppose it was possible he became jealous of Ramon's friendly conversations with Magda during the tour, but I was pretty sure his style would have been to take out his anger on his wife, not the man who'd been flirting with her.

Then there was Lowell. Val's husband. Amateur historian. Revered Charles Lindbergh. He claimed he'd humiliated Ramon, not killed him.

Who was telling the truth? And who was lying?

When I told Valentine I thought the drone's video could help us solve the case, she slumped back and said, "I've already been through it. The murder didn't happen while the drone was overhead."

"Can we try one more time?" I asked.

"Sure." She shrugged. "But, I don't think you'll find anything." She cued up the footage on her phone, then paused before tapping the start arrow. "McKenna, this is my husband we're talking about. I don't know if I can do this."

"Do you want to be married to a killer? And, if we can prove he didn't kill Ramon? Then you'll know for sure. Otherwise, you'll always wonder what happened."

The shaking in Val's fingers increased. She handed the phone to me. "You take it. I can't. Hit the play button."

The video began in a clearing. The drone rose into the air, the grassy area expanding until it was surrounded by forest on one end, the gardens on the other. The forest below went by quickly as the drone moved overhead. Soon, we were looking down at the old riding stables.

"Jerod told me those went out of business recently, but I wanted to get a look for myself. Call it morbid curiosity," she said.

The drone retraced its path. The gardens came into view. Three people walked about. Benni, Judy, and Lenny. Judy moved quickly with Lenny a few steps behind. They stopped on the perimeter, where Judy turned on her stockbroker boyfriend, said something, and removed the bottle from her purse. She took a swallow and stomped away. It was all very consistent with what she'd said. What I didn't know was how long Lenny had been watching her.

The drone moved on until Benni was the only one in the frame. She probably hadn't even realized she was being watched as she took pictures of flowers. The realization of how easily any of us could become the subject of stealth surveillance unnerved me.

Next, we were over the cemetery, where Ramon was holding court. Sure enough, Lowell stood nearby. The discussion going on in the group appeared to be quite animated. As if feeding on the energy of the people below, the drone picked up speed, hovered over the church, then descended until it was looking through the front door. I saw myself sitting inside. I turned, glared at the camera, and my mouth moved.

"You don't look happy," said Val. "What did you say?"

"I don't remember," I lied. Regret tinged my heart as I read the Palapala Hoʻomau church sign on the tiny screen. "We welcome visitors to this historic, missionary church in Kīpahulu. Out of respect for church members, relatives, and descendants of those buried in the graveyard, we ask that you treat this religious site with reverence & care."

"Why can't we just come to appreciate the history and beauty?" I muttered.

"I guess it's because we're so caught up in our own lives we can't leave our issues behind," Val said.

"What?" I asked. "Oh, I didn't realize I was talking out loud. Yeah, we didn't come in peace, we brought anger and violence." I felt more determined than ever to find out who had killed Ramon. It would be my small gesture to show respect for those who were buried here.

The drone rose above ground and moved back toward the graveyard. Below, the camera caught Judy and Lenny, then the main group approaching the church. I recognized Conchita, Jackie, and Marquetta. They were followed by TC and Magda. Magda turned back toward the cemetery, but TC urged her forward. Continuing on its course, the drone passed over Lindbergh's grave, Lowell, and Ramon.

The two men were obviously posturing for an argument, but without sound, it was difficult to tell how intense it might be. Their movements grew more aggressive and just before the two men passed from the field of view, Lowell shoved Ramon. Seconds later, we were watching the serenity of a rugged coastline. Crystal blue water and crashing waves filled the screen.

I heard Val sniffle and glanced at her. A tear trickled down her cheek. Her eyes were glassy and rimmed in red. She muttered, "He did it."

"It sure looks that way."

"My husband's a killer."

"You didn't see this when you were watching it with Olivia?"

She shook her head. "We were watching, but talking at the same time. It wasn't like we paid attention every second. Not like now. What are you going to do?"

I hadn't really thought about that. I'd been so focused on solving the puzzle of Ramon's death that I hadn't considered whether to confront him or wait for the police. "I wonder how long we have before the cops get here."

"Will Jerod know?" Val whispered.

"I'll ask him."

Together, Val and I returned to the van, where we found Jerod and Lowell talking. Jerod was in the driver's seat. Lowell sat in his assigned seat in the first row. I gave Val's hand a reassuring squeeze. "This could be awkward. Stay here."

She nodded and remained behind, not saying a word.

As I stepped into the van, Jerod glanced at me. "Cops gonna be here any minute." He stood, then went down the steps. From just outside the open doorway, he said, "I gotta take a leak."

"You figure anything out?" Lowell asked. He slouched back in his seat, again assuming the posture of a man without a care in the world.

I hoped by being slightly vague, I could avoid a confrontation. After all, it did look like Ramon might have died in the heat of an argument. It would be up to the police, and maybe the courts, to decide if Lowell was guilty of a crime. "We have video that looks promising. The drone was quite, um, helpful."

The color drained from Lowell's face. "Video? My wife's drone?"

I'm not sure what I expected. Would Lowell melt into a quivering mass and confess his sin? Would he deny it? Make excuses? No, he had to choose Option D—none of the above.

McKenna

Some guys just don't get it. The cops have radios. They have air support. And trying to outrun both of those in a four-ton tour bus just wasn't the smartest thing anyone would do. But, that's what happened. Lowell jumped up, shoved me to the back of the van, closed the door, and drove.

Apparently obsessed with the idea of making his escape, Lowell took the first turn fast enough to throw me against the glass window. It was also fast enough to wake Marquetta, who'd been napping in the back.

Bleary-eyed, Marquetta glanced around. "We're moving?"

I held onto my seat as we took the left onto the Hana Highway. "Lowell! You have to stop this. Marquetta's here, too. You'll get us all killed."

"Nobody's gonna die. I'll let you two off once I'm in the clear."

"What's happening?" Marquetta gaped at the mountainside rushing past.

"Lowell stole the van," I said, matter-of-factly. "He seems to think he can outrun the entire Maui Police Department." I spider-walked forward one row, hanging onto the seatback for support as we veered into a sharp right turn. "Lowell, you're on an island in the middle of the Pacific Ocean. Where the hell do you think you're going to go?"

"I'll figure something out. I can't go to jail."

"Better jail than the cemetery," I muttered.

In the back, Marquetta screamed, "Let me off. I want off this bus. Now!"

"Shut up," Lowell barked.

For once, I agreed with him. Hysterics would only make things worse. I had to reason with this maniac before he drove us into the ocean. We hit one of the few straight stretches on the road, and Lowell jammed his foot to the floor. The speedometer climbed to forty-five. Over my shoulder, I saw Marquetta drunk-walking her way up the aisle. She had one hand on the seat behind me when everything lurched forward. I grabbed at her just as we careened into a sharp right turn.

Marquetta and I clung to each other as the vehicle tilted in the other direction.

"I don't want to die. Make him stop," she wailed.

I looked out the window to my left. Holy crap. "I'm tired of being rational, you moron. I want off." Childish, true.

But, you try staring down a hundred-foot cliff and see if you don't panic, too. I needed a weapon. Something to bash Lowell over the head and take control of the vehicle— if I didn't get us killed in the process.

Hard right turn. Hard left. We were on a twisting rollercoaster with only one outcome—death. Then, I remembered the compartment Jerod had told Judy about. There was a fire extinguisher in front of it. I pushed Marquetta to one side and crawled on my hands and knees, bumping into the right wall, then the left. Another turn almost tossed me into the stairwell.

"What the hell are you doing?" Lowell glanced between me and the road.

He couldn't watch us both. I had to act fast. I unlatched the red extinguisher. "Last chance. Stop the bus."

"No." He kept his eyes forward.

I pulled the pin. And then the world flipped up and to the right. I tumbled into the stairwell. My hand closed on the handle. CO_2 spewed everywhere. It was snowing in Maui. In October. Inside a four-ton, twelve-passenger tour bus.

Lowell slumped from the driver's seat to the floor. Blood oozed from a cut on his head. Marquetta jumped on top of him and began punching. "You stupid, idiotic, retarded— man!"

The floor was tilted at an angle. Above me, out the side window, I saw sky. My back was killing me, but we were alive. "It's my turn. What happened, Marquetta?"

She stopped her tantrum long enough to say, "He drove us into a ditch. There was some old pickup blocking the road."

"Is the pickup still there?"

"He drove past when we went into the ditch."

I groaned. I'd heard stories about the locals in this area hating tour busses. I now understood how deep their anger ran.

"Now what?" she asked.

"We wait. The cops won't be long."

That turned out to be a true statement. Before Lowell regained consciousness, we were waving through the glass at two uniformed Maui cops. When Lowell recovered and realized he was trapped, he began to sob uncontrollably. Both Marquetta and I wanted to smack him. He'd nearly killed us all and was now upset he might live.

Like I said, some guys just don't get it.

Eventually, we were extracted from our little prison, Lowell was taken away in handcuffs, and we gave statements. The cops drove us back to the rest of our tour group. On the ten-minute drive back, I thought about the terrible thing that had taken place today. A man had been killed. Our tour group would forever be remembered as the one that had desecrated the Palapala Hoʻomau Congregational Church cemetery. We'd also done some serious damage to one of the tour company's vans.

On the other hand, I'd made a new friend with Val. I'd come to realize she had feelings, too. It saddened me to have taken away her husband. And, what about Magda? I hoped we'd given her the strength to escape her situation. That decision, however, would be up to her. I'd also gotten an answer to my question in the church. Yes, I should pop the question to Benni.

The even better news was, with a potential PR nightmare facing the tour company, I was pretty sure they'd agree to refunds for all.

TERRY AMBROSE

I started out skip tracing and collecting money from dead-beats and quickly learned that liars come from all walks of life. I never actually stole a car, but sometimes hired big guys with tow trucks and a penchant for working in the dark to "help" when negotiations failed.

A resident of Southern California, I love spending time in Hawai'i, especially on the Garden Island of Kaua'i, where I invent lies for others to read. My years of chasing dead-beats taught me many valuable life lessons such as—always keep your car in the garage.

Find me on the web at terryambrose.com.

LEI, LADY, LEI
JoAnn Bassett

As engagement rings go, it was no Hope Diamond, but it certainly wasn't charity either. My name's Pali Moon, and I'm a Maui wedding planner, so I've seen my fair share of bridal jewelry. I estimated the ring on bride-to-be Stacy Wilmot's fourth finger to be somewhere in the neighborhood of two-and half-carats, maybe three.

"That's a gorgeous ring," I said.

"Thanks," Stacy smiled as she looked at the rock. "It was Justin's grandmother's." She turned to her intended groom. "Was she your grandmother on your mom's side or your dad's?"

"Uh, my mom's. She gave it to me when I graduated from Stanford before I moved to the U of O. She told me to hang on to it until the right girl came along."

"And lucky for you, the right girl certainly did," I beamed at Stacy. I've gotten pretty good at flattery in the four years I've owned "Let's Get Maui'd," in Pā'ia. It hasn't been easy. In the early days it seemed I had nearly daily bouts of "foot-in-mouth" disease. Now, I'm down to just the occasional minor *faux pas*, and I'm usually quick to cover it up.

"Are we almost finished here, babe?" said Justin. "I'd like to make a few calls to the States before it gets too late back there."

I'd grown weary of explaining to prospective couples who come to Maui for a destination wedding that Hawai'i is a state. It's been one for more than fifty years. The reference to the mainland as "the States" grates on me, but I let it slide. After all, Justin and Stacy had hired me for a simple beachside wedding, not a history lesson. The services I'd render were the matrimonial equivalent of a "Happy Meal": a quick ten-minute ceremony, a couple of Costco leis, and a few photos with the witnesses. The State of Hawai'i would mail the newlyweds their official marriage certificate after they returned home to Oregon.

"You've got your marriage license, right?" I asked.

"Yep, it's right here." Justin pulled out a folded paper and slapped it down on my desk.

"How about witnesses?"

"Got those too. Stacy's sister is coming on Wednesday, and my best man, Brandon, gets in the next day."

"If you don't mind, I'd like to have their cell numbers. Sometimes I have to get in touch with the wedding party members for one reason or another."

Stacy carefully inked in the cell numbers on the lines for "maid of honor" and "best man."

"Then we're all set," I said. "I'll see you both next Saturday. I've got a permit for Baldwin Beach Park, and the officiant's all lined up. Let's meet in the parking lot at, say, five o'clock?"

"That's it?" Stacy's troubled look signaled she was disappointed there wasn't more to fuss over.

"Unless you have questions," I looked from one to the other.

"We're good," said Justin. "Babe, I really need to get to those calls."

Stacy stood, a shy smile on her face. "Oh, of course, darling. Thank you, Pali, for everything. This was sort of a quick decision on our part. Kind of like eloping. But when it's right, it's right. Don't you think?"

"I do."

The following Thursday, my cell phone went off while I was getting ready for bed. I checked the caller ID. It was Justin. I usually don't take late night calls, especially from a prospective groom a couple of nights before the wedding. While I may have trained myself to spout "make nice" noises, I still try to avoid anything to do with cold feet, bachelor parties, or prenuptial confessions.

But after three rings, I caved.

"This is Pali Moon."

"Pali, it's me, Justin."

"Yes?"

"Stacy's missing."

"What do you mean, 'missing'?"

"I went to pick up Brandon at the airport, and when I got back Stacy wasn't here."

"Could she have gone to visit someone? Maybe her sister? Is she staying nearby?"

"She's supposed to be staying just a few doors down, but we haven't seen her yet. Pali, this place looks like it's been tossed, and, oh my God, it looks like there's blood..." He didn't finish.

"Justin, you need to call the police. It's 9-1-1, just like the rest of the United States." I couldn't help myself, I had to throw in the jab.

I heard a garbled noise, but couldn't make out what he was saying.

"Call the police. Right now, Justin."

The call went dead.

I waited a couple of minutes, then called him back, hoping he'd hung up on me to summon help. He didn't answer. After leaving three voice messages, I stopped calling.

I tried to sleep, but a parade of grisly images played "peek-a-boo" with my melatonin. Since the night was shot anyway, I got up and drove down to my shop. I pulled Justin and Stacy's wedding planner file and jotted down the name of the condo where they were staying. I didn't write down the address and unit number, because I didn't think I'd need it. Lower Honoapiʻilani Road has dozens of small condos planted cheek-to-jowl along the two-lane road. All I'd have to do was look for the flashing lights on the cop cars to locate their property.

With no traffic it takes about forty minutes to drive from my house in Hāliʻimaile to the turn-off from the Honoapiʻilani Highway to the Lower Road. I marveled at how dark and quiet it was, even though it was peak tourist season. The beaches may have been rockin' at four that afternoon, but at three in the morning, the only sounds I heard were the faint hush of waves lapping the shoreline and the hum of the sodium streetlights.

I crept along the Lower Road with my windows down, actually going slower than the posted twenty-mile-an-hour speed limit. As I passed property after property, with names like "Maui Shores," "Maui Sunset," and "Sands of Maui," I wondered how tourists managed to find their assigned slot. The uniformity of the properties: low-rise buildings, each with a small roadside parking lot and an obligatory coconut palm or two, made it appear as if the same condominium plan had been replicated over and over again—like an image reflected to infinity in a fun-house mirror.

I drove all the way to Nāpili and there was no sign of police activity, so I pulled over and called Justin's number one more time. Again, no answer.

I left yet another message, trying hard to use my well-trained "suck up" voice instead of the strident "Where the hell are you?" voice I heard in my head.

As I slowly retraced my way down the Lower Road, I wondered if maybe Justin had had too much to drink and had mistakenly wandered into the wrong unit. It was possible, since most of the older condos don't have air conditioning and visitors leave doors open to allow the breeze to blow through.

Or, maybe Stacy had been mistaken when she'd mentioned they were staying near Kā'anapali Beach. Maybe the condo in question was, in fact, in Kīhei, or even out by Mā'aelea Harbor. There are hundreds of rental places there, too. But I remembered Justin saying it had taken them almost an hour to drive to their place, and Kīhei and Mā'aelea were much closer to the airport so it wouldn't have taken so long.

I got home at nearly four a.m. on Friday morning. I wasn't any closer to finding out what happened, but I felt a whole lot sleepier. I hit the pillow, fully dressed, but woke up two hours later. I tried to go back to sleep but couldn't.

I went into work and time dragged. I jumped every time my cell phone pinged, and when the mail carrier came in, she told me I looked "spooked." I glanced at the clock after what seemed like a full day's work, but it wasn't even ten o'clock. I'd texted, called, and emailed both Stacy and Justin numerous times, but still no response. I considered calling the police, but what would I say? Tourists are notorious for going dark for days on end once they kick into vacation mode.

Besides, I've had a few go-arounds with the local police and didn't need another incident. It's not like I've done any serious crimes. My run-ins with Maui's finest have mostly been minor slap-downs for sticking my nose where it didn't belong.

When I get stressed, my go-to activity is an hour of martial arts practice at a local *kung fu* studio. I like to kid myself that it's the kicking and screaming that calms me down, but in fact I know it's talking to Doug Kanekoa the *sifu*, or chief instructor, there.

I trotted down to the appropriately-named, "Palace of Pain" and it cheered me to see his ancient black Jeep Wrangler parked out back. I went in through the back door, savoring the lingering smell of sweaty feet and Pine-Sol that permeates the air like a welcome-back hug.

"*Aloha, Sifu,*" I said.

Doug leaned against the doorjamb to his office as a smattering of grade-school age *keiki* packed up from an intermediate class. From the look on Doug's face, he must've overheard some after-class trash talk and he was standing sentinel to make sure no one threw one last punch just for the heck of it.

"*Aloha,* Pali."

"Tough class?" I said as I got within earshot.

"They always are. I can't remember ever being so rowdy in front of my *sifu* when I was a kid." He slowly shook his head as he watched the last student leave.

"Are we really getting so old that we're already waxing poetic about the 'good old days'?"

He laughed. "Nah, I guess I'm just feeling my age. You know my own boy will be in middle school next year. Can't hardly believe it."

"I'll bet he doesn't give you any lip."

"Damn straight. I got the look down pat. You know what I'm sayin'?" He fixed his Army Ranger stare on me and I felt the urge to take a step back. I couldn't imagine the look was any less intimidating to the kids in his classes, but kids these days know corporal punishment is frowned on, if not outright illegal, so it's probably not as effective as it used to be when instructors taught classes with a thick bamboo pole resting on their shoulder.

"Have you got a minute?" I said.

"Sure. I don't have another class until three. I'll make us some tea."

While Doug filled the hot pot and measured out the loose tea, I told him about the strange call I'd gotten from Justin the night before.

"Huh. And you haven't been able to reach him this morning?"

"No. I've left like a dozen messages."

"You've got the address, though, right?"

"Yeah. You think I should run back over there and see what's going on?"

He shrugged and handed me a small handle-less Japanese teacup. The warmth of the cup contrasted with the chilliness of my hands.

"Why is it I always seem to get in the middle of this stuff?" I sipped the scalding tea.

"Good question. Seems the universe has a lot of faith in you."

"Well, I'd like the universe to pick on someone else for a while."

"Maybe if you mess up a time or two, it'll move on to a more competent person," he said.

He started laughing and I joined in. We both knew neither of us was willing to "mess up" on purpose no matter how annoying the circumstances. It's one of the downsides of having a competitive streak a mile wide.

"I guess I should take off." I drained my cup and thanked my *sifu* for the tea. The stuff tastes more medicinal than common green tea should, but it always relaxes me. I can't help but wonder if Doug laces the concoction with an ingredient he cultivates under grow lamps in a back room of his house, but there's no way I'd ask.

"You're not going to stay and work out?"

"Not now, *sifu*. Maybe I'll come back later."

We bowed to each other and then I loped back up to my shop. Within minutes I was driving back to the West Side with Justin and Stacy's full address on a Post-it note stuck to my dash. I figured I had a much better chance of finding the place since it was now light outside, but I was surprised when I pulled up and saw a phalanx of emergency vehicles blocking the entry to the Hale Maui Kai parking lot.

I left my car on the street under a sign that read, "No Parking—All times, All days." Since it looked like every cop on this side of the island was already busy, I figured my chances of getting a ticket were minimal.

"What's happening?" I asked an old guy in a so-new-it-was-stiff aloha shirt.

"Some guy drowned or something." He shook his head. "Real sad. My wife's inside crying. We're here celebrating our thirtieth anniversary, and she says this has wrecked the whole vacation."

I murmured my condolences for his distraught wife, and bobbed and weaved through cop cruisers, ambulances and knots of worried-looking condo guests until I found the unit number of the condo Stacy and Justin were staying in: 201. I knocked, but no one answered. That was understandable since it appeared nearly everyone was outside in the parking lot.

I leaned over the railing, searching the crowd for a familiar face, but came up empty. I walked downstairs and found a uniformed cop standing sentry on the sidewalk leading to the ocean side of the property.

"What's going on?"

"You'll have to step back." He held up a hand. "No one allowed past here."

"Is that Detective Glen Wong?" I pointed to a guy standing by the breakwater at the edge of the property. I'd had a few dealings with Wong over the past few years—some good, some not-so-good—and I wasn't sure how he'd view my arrival, but it was worth a shot.

The cop turned and looked. "Yeah, that's Wong."

"I'm here to see him."

The cop squinted at me. "Huh. Did he call you in on this?"

I nodded. I've always been a lousy liar, although I'm getting better at it all the time.

The cop stepped back and allowed me to pass. "You better not be messin' with me," he said. "I don't need no detective chewing my ass."

I put up a hand in reassurance. "Don't worry. He's expecting me."

I crossed the lawn which separated the condo building from the oceanfront. There was no beach here. The waves crashed against a riprap breakwater on the other side of a low stone wall. Paramedics had trundled a gurney down to the edge of the breakwater and as I came closer, I saw they'd loaded someone onto it. They hastily tucked a black body bag around the form on the gurney, then zipped it up tight leaving no question about the victim's condition.

Detective Glen Wong crossed his arms as he saw me approach, but his facial expression remained inscrutable.

"*Aloha*, Detective," I said in my most toadying voice. "You're just the man I was looking for."

"Let me guess," he sighed. "You're smack dab in the middle of this somehow."

"Uh, I'm not sure about that, but I'm worried about two guests who are staying at this condo. I thought I should tell you about it."

"Oh, really? What's the problem?"

"A groom I'm working with called me late last night and said his fiancée had gone missing, and their place had been torn up. I told him to call the police and, right afterward, the line went dead. I tried calling a little later and he didn't answer. This morning, I've called both him and his bride-to-be again and again and still no answer. I came over here to check if everything was okay."

"What's the groom's name?"

"Justin DeWilde."

"And the bride's name?"

"Stacy. Stacy Wilmot."

"I see. Do you know what unit they're in?"

"Two-oh-one." I pointed to the corner condo on the second floor.

"Huh. Well, as you can see, I'm kind of busy here."

"What's that mean? Don't you think it's strange that two people have gone missing from here and now you've got a drowning at the same place?"

He came over and stood close enough to speak in a low voice. "Look, Pali, we're on it. I appreciate you letting me know about the phone call, but we'll take it from here."

"Who's the vic, Detective Wong? Is it my bride?"

He shook his head. "You know I can't say anything until the next of kin has been notified."

"What's going on? Don't make me ask the reporters out in the parking lot. You really don't want me telling them about getting that call, do you?"

Wong scowled at me. Then he began walking back toward the condo building. He motioned for me to come along.

"Against my better judgment I'm going to let you in on what we know so far, if only to assure you we've got things under control. I'm afraid your male client who called you last night is our victim. And, from the looks of things, he didn't drown. It looks like suicide."

"Suicide?"

"Yeah," said Wong. "Snorkelers found him out on the rocks this morning. Looks like he killed himself with a spear gun. You know, the kind snorkelers and divers use to catch fish. The spear went right through his heart. We found the gun next to him on the rocks, and a suicide note in the condo. Seems he didn't want to leave a mess, so he came out here to do it."

My hands got the eerie tingly sensation I feel when I get a scare—like a near-miss on the Pali Highway, or a letter with "Internal Revenue Service" as the return address.

I followed Wong as he went upstairs to the second floor. He walked over to unit 201, and rapped twice on the door.

"Open up, it's me, Wong."

A uniformed cop on the other side opened the door. Behind him stood Stacy, red-eyed and teary. She looked at Wong and then hung her head as if preparing herself for a body blow.

"I'm sorry," Wong said. "They weren't able to save him."

"Stacy," I said. "I'm so sorry. Is there anyone I can call for you?"

She shook her head and continued staring at the floor. After a few seconds she turned and walked into the living room.

I followed her, noticing the condo seemed tidy and clean. Nothing out of order, no blood stains—or any other stains, for that matter—on the carpet or tile.

"Can you tell me what happened last night?" I said.

Wong shot me a warning look. "We'll be taking Ms. Wilmot's statement later on. You're just here to help if she needs anything."

"Okay, got it. Stacy, what about your sister? Do you want me to call her?"

"She wasn't able to come for the wedding, after all. She got tied up at work or something."

"Sorry to hear that. How about Brandon, Justin's best man? Do you know where he's staying?"

"No, I only met him once. I don't even really remember what he looks like." She started crying. "This is so horrible; like a bad dream. Tell me your name again. I can't seem to think straight."

"I'm Pali Moon, your wedding planner."

"Oh, of course. I'm so sorry. I just can't believe this." Stacy looked me in the eye. Her face was contorted into a mask of grief and confusion. Gone was the bubbly, blushing bride, replaced by a young woman who'd just tumbled into her worst nightmare. Her engagement ring winked in the morning light; a sad reminder of the happy event she and her now-dead fiancé had planned to take place the very next day.

Wong stepped over and removed a small note pad from his front pocket. "I'll need to get those names and contact numbers from you, Ms. Wilmot."

I spoke up. "What names are those?"

"The people who were scheduled to attend the wedding."

"Why do you want them?"

"Look, Ms. Moon, we're doing an investigation here. Unless you've managed to pass the bar exam since we last met up, you're not entitled to speak on behalf of Ms. Wilmot. In fact, if there's nothing she needs from you, I think this would be a good time for you to leave."

I looked over at Stacy. "If you think of anything I can do to help, call me. Okay?"

She looked up at me with the perplexed expression of a person who's come out of a coma and doesn't recognize her surroundings.

"Here's my card. I'm sure you've got another one around here somewhere, but I don't want you to have to look for it. Call if I can help in any way."

"Thank you." She stared at the card. "Right now all I want is to go home."

"Totally understandable." I said. "I'll make some calls and see about getting you on a flight today. I'll let you know what I find out."

I gave her a hug. She felt as though her body had already shrunk a size; as if by losing the love of her life she'd already been diminished.

I drove back to my shop in shock. I'd had weddings called off for all sorts of reasons: last minute cold feet, grooms going AWOL, a shrill mother-of-the-bride standing up at "speak now or forever hold your peace." Once, I even had a bride run off with the best man ten minutes before the ceremony was supposed to start.

But a groom reporting his bride missing and then killing himself? It had a certain "Romeo and Juliet" quality which seemed almost romantic, albeit wretched. Why would Justin do it? I castigated myself for my laziness in not writing down the full address of where they were staying at the Hale Maui Kai before I drove over last night. Maybe if I'd taken Justin's unresponsiveness more seriously...

But I couldn't go there. The die was cast, the deed done. Best I could do now was make sure Stacy got back to the mainland quickly where friends and family would be there to help her get through the ordeal. I didn't want her to travel by herself, though. The last thing the hard-working flight attendants at Hawaiian Airlines needed was a young woman snapping out of her detached state and freaking out three hours from touchdown.

I called Stacy's sister's cell phone number but it just rang and rang. I hung up as it flipped over to voicemail because I didn't want to leave a message. I didn't know if she'd received official word of Justin's death, and I didn't want to say something that might be construed as crass. Even though I'd been working on my personal communication skills, I hadn't gotten to the big stuff like death notification or humanely counseling someone about their severe halitosis.

Then I called the best man, Brandon. Supposedly, he'd arrived on-island the night before since Justin had said he'd gone to pick him up at the airport when Stacy went missing. I wished I'd had the chance to ask Stacy where she'd been when Justin got back to the condo, but with Wong there and Stacy appearing nearly catatonic, it would have to wait.

Brandon answered on the second ring. I told him who I was and asked if he'd gotten word about Justin. Unfortunately, he hadn't.

"What's going on? Is he okay?"

"Would you mind coming to my shop in Pā'ia? I'm afraid Justin has had a bit of an accident and I'd like to discuss it with you face-to-face." See what I mean about my being a lousy liar? I hung up knowing I hadn't handled the notification well at all, and thinking of ten ways I could've phrased it better.

Brandon came in the shop thirty minutes later. His face was drawn.

"I heard," he said, dropping into a chair across from my desk. "I got a call from the cops."

I chastised myself for the mental fist-pump I did in response to not having to give him the sad news.

"They asked me if I'd be willing to ID the body," he went on.

"Not Stacy?"

"They said she's mentally incapable, or something. Which is kind of funny, since that's usually her sister's MO."

I must've looked confused, because he offered an explanation. "Yeah, Stacy's sister is the nutcase. Stacy's always been the steady one."

"You've probably already heard by now the sister didn't come over. Something about getting tied up at work," I said. "That's why I wanted to see you. I was hoping you could accompany Stacy back to the mainland today."

"Sure, I'll do whatever I can to help. Did the cops tell you how Justin died? They only told me that he'd died and they didn't suspect foul play."

"Well, it's pretty sad, actually. It seems he shot himself."

He slammed his hands flat down on my desk. "What? That's insane. Where'd he get a gun?"

"It wasn't a regular gun. He used a spear gun. I guess he must've rented one for spear-fishing, but then he turned it on himself after Stacy went missing."

Brandon pulled back, squinting at me as if I'd insulted him.

"Total BS," he said in a soft voice.

We locked eyes.

"Why do you say that?"

"How well did you know Justin?" he said.

"Not well. I only met him once, when he and Stacy came in to finalize their wedding plans."

"Justin was what we Oregonians call a 'tree hugger.' Totally vegan, a sit-in-the-tree-so-loggers-can't-cut-it-down, kind of guy. No way he'd rent a spear gun. I'd be surprised if he'd even let someone show him one without him giving them a lecture about depleted fish stocks and respecting the ocean ecosystem."

"So, you don't think he rented a spear gun?"

"Nope, no way."

"They found one when they fished him out of the break-water," I said. "Apparently, he'd used it to spear himself in the heart. They also found a suicide note in his condo. I wasn't privy to what the note said, but the cops seem pretty sure it was a classic suicide."

"Well, they're wrong."

"I'd like to go with you to ID the body," I said.

"Okay, then let's do it."

The morgue at Maui Memorial Hospital is in the base-ment. Seems a logical place to put it, since it's cool and dark, giving it the spooky vibe you'd expect from a place where they store the no-longer-living.

Brandon was the "person of record," or POR, so he signed the paperwork, but I was allowed to accompany him un-der the pretext of being his "emotional support liaison," or ESL. I can't help but love how bureaucracies have an acronym for everything. I was actually the ASS, or "accom-panying sneaky snoop," but I didn't let on.

They put us in a small room with a glass partition sep-arating us from the dearly departed. When they brought Justin in, he was laid out under a clean white sheet. When they pulled it back it shocked me to see how close his skin-tone matched that of the sheet. His eyes were closed, and they'd placed a gauze pad over the entry wound, os-tensibly to spare us the gory details.

Brandon cleared his throat. "That's Justin."

A voice came over a speaker in the corner of the room, and we both jumped. "Please state the deceased's first and last name, and address, if known."

"Uh, Justin DeWilde. From Bend, Oregon."

"*Mahalo.* Please step outside to complete the paperwork."

Brandon shot me a quizzical look.

"*Mahalo* means 'thank you,'" I said.

"Oh. I guess I'm just kind of nervous."

"Totally understandable."

When we got back outside to fresh air and open sky, Brandon sucked in a deep breath. "I hope they pay those guys a lot to work in that morgue. No way I'd do a job like that."

"Yeah. Speaking of jobs, what did Justin do?"

Brandon laughed. "You didn't know?"

I shook my head.

"Total trust-fund baby. Justin's family started one of the biggest breweries in Oregon. They ship beer to just about every state and even to some foreign countries. He's been in college for at least ten years. I think he has degrees in, like, four different things. But the guy doesn't have a single cent of student debt."

I darted my eyes at Brandon, then looked away.

"I mean, he *had* degrees, and he *had* no debt. It's hard for me to think of him as dead."

"How about Stacy?"

"Her family doesn't have money. She works as a dental assistant or something. It's kind of funny how she and Justin got together. Her and her sister essentially share a job. Like one works on Mondays and Tuesdays and the other on Thursdays and Fridays, or something like that. Anyway, Justin met Tracy first, but when he had to go back to the dentist, Stacy was there. They only started going out a few weeks ago."

"Stacy and Tracy? Are they twins?"

"Yeah, kind of funny. They're nothing alike, though. I don't even think they look that much alike, but it's probably because their personalities are so different."

I dropped Brandon off at my shop so he could pick up his car, then I got to work on the phone. I'd promised Stacy I'd check on flights and it was already four in the afternoon.

I knew I should call Wong and let him know what Brandon had told me about the likelihood of Justin renting a spear gun, but there were a couple of things I wanted to check out first.

Hawaiian Airlines had a nonstop flight to Portland a little after nine that night, but there was only one seat available. I explained about the emergency situation and they offered to wait-list Brandon, but made no promises.

I called Stacy and told her she might have to wait until the next day to fly home since they only had one seat.

"It's okay, I'll go tonight. I don't want Brandon flying with me, anyway."

"Why? Don't you think you'd feel better having a friend along?"

"Not him. He never liked me. Besides, he probably blames me for what happened."

"Stacy, I really think you should wait until someone else can go with you on the plane."

"That's okay, I'm good. I just need you to email me the airline confirmation number."

I scrambled to come up with something. "Uh, I printed it out and then deleted the file. I'm kind of busy this afternoon. Would you mind coming up here to Pā'ia to pick up the hard copy?" It certainly wasn't a very plausible lie. I mentally crossed my fingers, hoping she'd buy it.

"All right, I'll come now. I want to have everything ready so I can get out of here tonight."

I made two more calls and then sat back and waited for Stacy to show up.

She arrived a half-hour later looking flushed and irritated. "Why in hell would you delete the file? That's just stupid. And it's a bitch trying to find parking around here, you know."

"How are you doing?" I said.

"I'm doing good, all things considered. I don't want to seem ungrateful, because I appreciate you getting me on the flight, but I'm kind of in a hurry. Can I have the airline ticket?"

I opened a drawer and fussed through a stack of papers as if I were looking for the print-out of the e-ticket.

Just then, Brandon walked through the shop door. He stopped and took a long look at Stacy. She froze.

"Hi Tracy," he said.

"What are you talking about? I'm Stacy. Tracy couldn't come. She had to work. You know, we can't both take off at the same time."

She turned to me. "Everybody always gets us mixed up."

"Where did you and Justin shop for your ring?" Brandon said. I'd coached him, and he performed beautifully.

"What?" She looked down at the large diamond on her left hand. "Oh, I can't remember exactly. I think it was Helzberg's Jewelers. Either that or Jared. What does it matter? I'm not getting married now, anyway."

I steepled my fingers. "Where did you hide Stacy's body, Tracy?"

"What?" This time she shrieked. "What the *hell* are you talking about?"

"It almost worked," I said. "You killed your sister and then you killed Justin and made it look like a suicide. You've been pretending to be Stacy, but the jig's up. I assume your motive was jealousy. After all, you met him first. All that money; all those family connections. It wasn't fair, was it?"

She pulled a knife from her purse with such speed it was as if she practiced every night, like a gun slinger whipping his gun in and out of the holster to get good at it.

"Give me that e-ticket right now." She flashed the knife toward Brandon and me in a menacing way. "I've got to get to the airport."

Wong stepped from behind the beaded curtain of my bridal dressing room, his badge held in one hand, his drawn weapon in the other. "Put the knife down, Ms. Wilmot. The only trip you'll be taking tonight is to the station with me."

JOANN BASSETT

JoAnn Bassett is the author of the "Islands of Aloha Mystery Series." A collection of eight cozy mysteries featuring wedding planner, Pali Moon, and set on the six major islands of Hawai'i: Maui, Lāna'i, Kaua'i, O'ahu, Moloka'i and Hawai'i, the Big Island. She's also the author of the "Escape to Maui" series: novels of mainland women who move to Maui for a fresh start.

Find me on the web at joannbassett.com.

CRIME OF DISPASSION
GAIL M. BAUGNIET

Sirens made conversation almost impossible, even in Nani's second floor studio apartment. She had lived here for the past three years, tucked in the far corner of the five-acre lot, her only window facing mauka. She set her soda glass on the end table and stood. "Come on, girl-friend, let's check out what's happening today in this poor excuse for a housing development."

Mimicking Nani, I placed my glass next to hers before standing. As a freelance reporter, I set my own hours. But with such a hectic schedule, I liked to visit with friends for lunch a few times a week to stay in touch. No complaints about having this one cut short, though. As a stringer, I always kept an eye out for a good story. Especially one that might make the front-page. Mo' betta yet if my name, Cacao Janus, appeared in the byline.

Grabbing my camera bag, more a third arm than a tool of the trade, I followed my slightly eccentric friend out her front door. The logic behind Nani living here escaped me, but she refused to move. Her goal was to see the entire complex refurbished. Though a noble ambition, renovation would be a slow process when everything was accomplished on Hawaiian time. She headed straight for the stairwell entrance, bypassing the elevator. A faded out-of-order sign gracing the wall confirmed my expectations of visiting her at A'ala Tradewinds Development for years to come.

Nani gripped the handrails, taking the stairs two at a time with me close behind. She had been helping me dig up stories ever since I switched careers. And sirens meant a story, whether the call involved Emergency Medical Services, the fire department, or the police.

Once outside, I again noted the rundown condition of the property. Sun-bleached paint peeled off the sides of buildings. Windows were cracked or broken out, and overgrown weeds filled the front yards. No wonder the development drew trouble like flies.

My police scanner had gotten crushed in a freak accident two days earlier and I hadn't replaced it yet. Even with the scanner, I'd seldom arrived on scene at the start of anything that involved this type of response. A semi-circle of police cars flanked a yellow firetruck and an EMS van.

All the action focused on an apartment facing the sidewalk. Its front door stood wide open. One police officer guarded the entrance. Paramedics frantically attended to a male stretched out on the browning front lawn. Blood splotches glistening on the man's chest suggested he hadn't suffered a heart attack.

My hands shook as I removed my camera from its case. Something bad had occurred here, possibly a domestic argument turned violent. It was the worst type of police call. At least this time, no officer had been injured. I took a couple of deep breaths and surveyed the situation.

Several officers maintained order. While they instructed residents to go back inside, I snapped photos of the apartment entrance, the man on the ground, emergency vehicles, anything that looked like part of the scene.

Whatever happened, the investigation had barely gotten started. As long as I stayed under everyone's radar, I was sure no one would accuse me of obstructing an ongoing case. Then a detective I knew walked out from the back courtyard and spotted me.

"Fancy meeting you here, Detective," I said, catching up with him before he reached the street. To ward off any chiding for stepping on his crime scene, I added, "Any particular reason you might be handling the case of a man bleeding from the chest?"

Alika Ouelette was a homicide detective with the Honolulu Police Department. He and my dad were best friends since small kid time on the Big Island. Dad married a local girl and returned to his roots in North Kohala. He'd made Detective Sergeant in the police department over there about the same time Alika got his stripes in Honolulu.

"Don't start with me, Cacao," Alika said. "I can't give you enough information to fill a shot glass, much less a story. What you see is what you get."

"What I see is a guy on the ground with blood on his chest." My hands had stopped shaking from my initial reaction to the scene and I'd gotten some decent pictures. But nerves had my stomach roiling over the possibility of a big story. "Nani's apartment isn't soundproof. We heard sirens and came down. What we didn't hear was gunshots. My guess is the guy got knifed. How am I doing so far?"

"I'll confirm that, but nothing else." Detective Ouelette walked out to his unmarked car parked at the curb. The department pays an allowance to personnel who use their own vehicles, and Alika had purchased the white sedan the day he made detective. He reached for the hand mic on his car radio and called Dispatch.

He had turned his back to me, so I couldn't catch his words. Nani was talking to a fireman standing alongside his truck. Edging my way closer to the building, I sidled up to the officer stationed at the apartment entrance. With my gaze focused on the flower bed, he wouldn't suspect me of anything. The tail-end of Alika's transmission came over the officer's radio, not loud but clear.

Now I had confirmation the man had been stabbed, once in the arm and twice in the chest. No suspect in custody, but witnesses had heard angry voices and reported they saw one of the man's relatives pull away from the curb. I glanced around the scene and noted the paramedics' life-saving activities had ceased. Without drawing conclusions, I scribbled the information in my notebook, recording everything in the muddled shorthand I'd devised during my first year of college.

Nani came running over and grabbed my arm, tugging me off to the side. "Cacao, you won't believe it. I know the guy who got stabbed."

I raised an index finger signaling for Nani to wait. "Okay," I said, once my notes were complete. "Who's the guy and how do you know he was stabbed?"

Getting the information from more than one source always added credibility. Besides, I didn't dare use Alika's name as a source after eavesdropping on his radio transmission. Legal or not, Alika would have my business license, not to mention my head.

Nani's heel thumped the ground in rhythm with her rapid speech. "Just overheard a paramedic say the knife must have nicked the heart 'cause so little blood seeped out before the man died."

That confirmed my suspicions. I jotted down the information, knowing I could attribute the quote to "an unknown source" in the field. Nani was investigating my story for me.

"Dang, Nani, you're gonna end up taking over my job. How do you know the dead guy?"

"Well, I don't really know him. I know one of his in-laws, his wife's brother."

Maybe that was the relative witnesses saw leaving the scene. "Who's the guy you know?" I asked. With Nani, questions often had to be rephrased to get answers.

Her forehead furrowed, as though she couldn't remember. When she did answer, I wasn't sure whether to cuss or cry. "Actually..." She looked back toward the dead body on the lawn. "The wife has two brothers."

I fought to tamp down my frustration. "What can you tell me about the dead guy?"

"Nothing. I only know the wife's brothers. The older one I know from work. Chen can get boisterous after a couple of drinks. Obnoxious might be a better word. The younger one hangs with him at the bar on weekends. He's the quiet one so I don't know him too well."

"Nani, do you know the dead guy's name?"

"Sure. It's Gabe something-or-other. He's part Asian. The last name's Young or Yuen. That's it. Gabe Yuen."

Knowing the name of the man who was stabbed to death wasn't enough for me to get an article in tomorrow's newspaper, though. Certainly not front page. My job would have been easier if Honolulu still had the Advertiser and the Tribune competing for stories. Since they'd merged, there was less space to fill. It meant more competition for freelancers like me. And the paper always used police blotter information over a reporter on fresh stories.

A woman in her early thirties driving an older model Kia pulled to the curb. She had barely skidded to a halt and turned off the engine before she whipped the door open. She ran toward the apartment entrance. A police officer grabbed for her arm but missed. She stared at the ground where the dead body lay, still uncovered while they waited for the coroner. Without a sound, she fell to her knees and cradled his head. I snapped a quick photo as her purple scarf fluttered in the breeze, shielding her face but not her sorrow.

The fire truck caught my attention when its engine revved. Having responded as backup only until the ambulance arrived, it edged away from the curb now. Alika gave me a hand signal over the hood of his car. He wanted me gone. I reached for Nani and led her from the scene.

"Let's go back to your apartment. The police and EMS don't need us loitering while they do their job." Besides, with all the excitement, I really needed to use her bathroom.

We walked around to Nani's building and took the stairs again. On the way down earlier, I hadn't noticed all the trash packed in the corners of the steps. The jagged glass of a broken beer bottle met us at eye level as we climbed toward the landing. Cigarette butts littered the hallway. Nani rented the space at the far end of the hall so she had to navigate past this mess every day.

Inside her studio, I used Nani's bathroom before pulling out my cell to speed-dial the news desk. I recited my facts about the stabbing death, naively hoping mine was the first call they'd received. After being told my details would get used to flesh out the police-reported incident, I walked over to the end table. I lifted my glass from where I'd set it when the sirens disrupted us. The soda had gone flat but I drank it anyway. Then I slumped into Nani's couch.

"Mine was the first reporter call with the story," I told Nani. "But they already had all the details from the police scanner and what Dispatch released. If I get something new, they'll consider a follow-up article."

"New like what?"

Nani handed me a bowl of chips, my reward for almost getting a newsworthy story.

"Mostly stuff the police will dig up on their own. Like who stabbed the man. And why." It was possible to do a background story on the family, or on the killer. If there really was a story there. But I didn't want to hand in another article on drug-related vengeance or domestic violence. "What's the name of the bar you hang out at with that Chen guy?"

"C'mon, I'll take you there." Nani grabbed her purse and headed for the door. "You drive."

My stomach growled as we cut through the courtyard. Should have grabbed a handful of chips on the way out. I walked over to the playground area where the only equipment available for the kids to play on were whitewashed truck tires. I kicked at one of the tires half-embedded in the packed dirt. It wobbled.

"When does the owner plan to renovate this area so the kids have a decent place to play?"

"Probably not till next April," Nani said, disgust distorting her face. "They finally got the hot water running in all the apartments. That'll probably cover their budget, or some misguided legal requirement, for the rest of this year."

The parking lot stalls were filled. At the far end, weeds grew out of the cracked asphalt. Two cars without tires rested on cement blocks. In the sea of gray, oversized pickups and compact sedans, my red Mini Cooper stood out.

Most times I didn't have two spare quarters to rub together, after shelling out for rent and gas. But I kept the Coop spit-shined at all times. My dad's mother, "Grams" to the world in general, had handed the keys over to me for my college graduation, no strings attached. She only expressed the hope I would always be proud of a life well lived. I thought to give her a call, then remembered why she had me housesitting in Mānoa. She wanted me to "keep an eye on things" for the duration of her Alaskan cruise.

"So you think Chen is the relative those people told the police about?" Nani asked, once we were moving with the traffic. "That probably means he's the one who stabbed Gabe. Maybe we should let the cops find him."

Now that she'd put it into words, I wondered if it was such a smart plan to go hunting for Chen. "No guts, no glory." I tried to sound confident but only managed to stutter my Gs instead.

"Turn here." Nani pointed to my left. She had directed me to a small strip mall on Dillingham Boulevard. "Pull into that empty spot in front of the karaoke bar. This is where we hang out most nights."

She hopped out of the car. When she slammed the door, I cringed and threw her an irritated scowl. But she was already entering the bar. A sign over the door read *M & Q KARAOKE*. Music drifted into the parking lot, someone's falsetto voice singing a Michael Jackson hit about Billy Jean. A wall of smoke met me as I entered.

While my eyes adjusted to the dark, I listened to a new melody blast from the speakers. Whoever chose to sing Cher's half-breed song was looking for trouble. And we would all suffer the consequences.

I tugged on Nani's jersey. "Why is this place so crowded on a Thursday afternoon?"

"It's the free snack food. Mele and Quinton serve the best *pupus* in town, and lots of it. Come on, let's grab a table against the wall."

The waitress took our orders for cola on ice, with a lime twist. She handed us each a sheet of paper. "Da specials same like always. Some sashimi left. You want one plate?"

"Eh, Cacao, we lucky," Nani piped in, quickly reverting to local pidgin. "Every time, sashimi da first t'ing to go."

The waitress made a beeline for the back room. She returned with a small platter of raw fish strips, bowls of shoyu, and a small glob of wasabi. Next to the platter, she set a plate of chicken wings dripping with barbeque sauce. I almost drooled as she laid out the chop sticks and napkins. She set down two glasses filled with ice and cola, along with a saucer of lemon and lime wedges.

Nani dug into the wings. I stirred wasabi into the shoyu with a chopstick and helped myself to a strip of deep red ahi. A few minutes later, she waved to someone, then poked me with her elbow. "Look, dat Chen coming in da door. He wen' get his little brada with him, too."

I grabbed a napkin to wipe shoyu off my fingers. As Chen and his brother walked toward our table, I studied them. I'd expected to see a couple of stocky boys. It took a minute to adjust to the reality of two muscular men, each at least five-ten, leaning toward two hundred pounds. Now I understood why Nani had questioned my plan to search for Chen.

"Maybe this wasn't such a good idea, Nani," I whispered, not taking my eyes off the guys headed toward us.

"Too late." She waved them over. "Eh, you guys pau work early today or wat?"

"Nah," the older one said. His laugh could have cut ice. "I wen' tell da boss we no like come work today."

"Still some sashimi left." Nani motioned for them to join us, then pointed to me. "Dis my friend, Cacao. Dis here's Chen and, uh, sorry, fo'get your brada's name."

Chen cuffed the back of his brother's head. The younger man rubbed his hand across the spot and looked at the floor. "His name's Mina. Sit, Mina. Eat some of dem wings." He turned and called out a drink order to the waitress and told her to bring some crab legs.

"Mina, he been one busy boy." Chen pretended to swat at his brother again. "Ain't you, Mina?"

"Knock it off, Chen." Mina grabbed a chicken wing and bit into the meat. Barbeque sauce dribbled from the corner of his mouth."

"See, jus' like at the Projects, mo' tomato sauce." Chen pointed to Mina's jersey.

Streaks of red marred the baseball logo on the shirt. Mina looked down at the marks on his chest. Then he picked up a napkin and made a couple of swipes, only smearing it more. Whatever had soaked into his shirt hadn't dried yet.

"Gotta take one leak," Chen said. He got up and headed toward the back of the bar where doors were marked "WAHINE" and "KANE".

The waitress arrived with Chen's drink order. She set one of the glasses on the table before the first shouts rang out only feet away.

"Freeze, all of you." The commands came from two uniformed police officers, both with guns drawn. "Don't move. Keep your hands where we can see them at all times."

The karaoke machine clicked off in mid-lament, leaving the room in silence.

Without thinking, I protectively reached for my camera case. A booming voice stopped me cold.

"You don't hear so good, lady? I said freeze."

Nani, Mina, and I were all shuffled off in handcuffs, transported to the main police station on Beretania. If the police found Chen in the men's room, they didn't bother to tell us. Nani and I were allowed to ride in the back of the same squad car. Mina was placed in a separate vehicle. While Mina was escorted into the station, Nani and I were ordered to "sit tight."

A uniformed officer stood guard outside the vehicle until footsteps announced someone approaching. "About time," the officer said. "You trying to put a scare into them?"

The back door snapped open and Homicide Detective Alika Ouelette stood looking down at me. "Yup, the operative word here is 'trying.' These girls just ain't got no fear in them. Get out of the car, Cacao. Bring your cute little sister-in-crime with you."

Alika unlocked our cuffs, yanking the metal from our wrists with more force than necessary. Then he told us to follow him. Inside the station he took us to an unoccupied office. "Sit." He pointed to two plastic chairs.

We did, looking at each other for answers that neither of us had.

Before I could get out a question, Alika took off on one of his rants. "Cacao, why do you always end up in the middle of my investigations? I know, you just happened to be visiting your friend." He stopped and gave Nani a look that suggested she was to blame for this latest fiasco. "Do you have any idea what you stepped into this time?"

"No," I mumbled, "but I have a feeling you're going to tell us."

"Actually, no, I'm not. You are both going to be interrogated by a detective who has no conflict of interest with you two. That's all I can tell you. I could receive a reprimand for just talking to you. So don't ask any questions. Just sit here. Quietly."

Moments later, heavy footsteps announced another arrival. This time, a plainclothes officer introduced himself to us as Detective Sergeant Dex Kadomo. "I'll be questioning each of you separately. Let's begin with you." He gestured toward Nani who stood and followed him out of the office.

Alika followed both of them out, not bothering to look at me. I wanted to ask what happened to my camera bag. But he wasn't taking questions.

The sun hit the wall behind me as it streamed through a window near the ceiling. I thought of prisoners never allowed to see outdoors because of the high placement of windows. O-triple-C, O'ahu's main prison for men, popped into my head, then the Women's Community Correctional Center. I shivered, unable to imagine what had me thinking about either facility.

It didn't take long to drum up an answer. Obviously, the red streaks on Mina's jersey were the dead brother-in-law's blood. He must have stabbed Gabe Yuen to death. Why? I had no idea. Nor did I know Chen's role in the situation. Whether the stabbing was self-defense, manslaughter, or premeditated murder was also up for grabs. The faster my mind spun, the more I suspected Alika had arranged for me to sit in this room by myself to make me suffer in silence.

"Miss Janus?" The detective had returned for me. "This way."

The sun had disappeared from the window. My watch said four-thirty. My stomach was growling again at having only a glass of flat soda and a few chunks of raw fish for lunch before being ordered to freeze. "Yes." I stood and followed him down the hall.

Detective Kadomo led me to another office, though I knew it would be used as an interrogation room today. "Have a seat, Miss Janus."

"You're welcome to call me Cacao," I told him. At my last job, the office was kept at a steady seventy degrees to prevent electronic equipment from overheating. I drank a lot of hot chocolate, usually topped with chocolate shavings

from a cacao bean farm on the North Shore. When someone saddled me with the nickname, it stuck.

"Fine, but you will call me Detective Kadomo, or Detective. This isn't a game we're playing. I'm not here to answer any of your questions, either, though I'm sure you
have a few. Sergeant Ouelette told me you're a reporter,
always looking for a story. This time, it got you in hot water. I hope that's all it is, Cacao, not a case of aiding and
abetting."

"Is that an accusation, Detective?"

"As I said, I'm not the one answering the questions here,
you are. So let's get to it. First of all, for the record, I will
be taping this conversation." He indicated a tape recorder
on the desk in front of me. After clicking a button, he said,
"In a clear voice, state your full name and date of birth."

I took a deep breath, processing what was happening.
My innocence was obvious only to me at this point. If I
could keep a clear head, this might be my best story to
date.

"My name..." I paused to remember exactly what it was.
I'd simply gone by 'Cacao' for years. Born on St. Patrick's
Day, I'd been named after a distant Irish ancestor, Clarissa
McKeough. "My full name is Catherine Clarissa Ma'omaka
Janus. My date of birth is March 17, 1982."

"Thank you. Other than your legal name, and Cacao, are
you known by any other names?"

Now I knew Alika had briefed this detective. If I didn't
answer, he could claim I was obstructing justice, though.
"My father, and only my father, calls me CC. That's it."

The detective stood at my back before pulling up a chair
alongside me. "Did you know the men sitting at your table
in Mele's place? I mean before today?"

Somehow, I got the impression the detective was leading
me with his questions. Nani must have told him she first
introduced me to Chen and Mina at the bar this afternoon.

"No, I never met either of them before today."

"But you were told who they were, right? I know you
were at the scene of the housing project stabbing. You

heard things. You're a reporter, Cacao. A floundering one, but still. It wouldn't take much to put two and two together. Unfortunately, you've been given the wrong numbers so it's understandable that you would come up with an inaccurate answer."

"What wrong numbers was I given?" I backtracked when he raised a finger. He wasn't here to answer questions. "Okay, fine. Nani said Chen and Mina are the brothers of the dead man's wife. I assumed there was some bad blood between the in-laws, and Mina decided to settle the situation with a sharp-edged weapon."

"You're very good at prevaricating, aren't you, Cacao? You made no attempt to name which in-laws might be involved in the bad blood. You also didn't incriminate Chen in any way. Did you assume Mina was involved because of the blood on his shirt?"

"Yes." To both questions, though fibbing was what I was most often accused of. I still didn't know who had done the stabbing, but now I knew Mina had been present when it occurred. *Another fact confirmed, thank you Detective.*

"What happened to Chen?" he asked.

"You mean before we were brought here?" I'd inadvertently asked another question. "Let me rephrase that. You want to know what happened to Chen at the bar. He went to the men's room before the police ordered us to freeze. I never saw him after that. Your question suggests no one else saw him after that either."

He reached over and shut off the tape recorder. "Something tells me you're almost too smart for your own good, Cacao. Wait, let me rephrase that. That's what Alika tells me. I only concur. You're free to leave. Do you want me to walk you out?"

Nani was at the front desk when the detective and I arrived. Alika towered over her as they talked. When I walked up, they both acted startled to see me.

"What, you thought they'd throw me in the slammer overnight?" I huffed past them and out the door.

"Wait," Nani called after me. "Alika said he'd give us a ride back to your car."

I turned and glared at them until they caught up with me. "Fine. Just explain to me, Alika, what that was really all about in there. How come that detective interrogated me like a suspect in a murder investigation?"

"Knock it off, Cacao," he said. "You know darn well Dex treated you with kid gloves. Tell me, did he even read you your rights?"

That stopped me cold. "What was all that with the tape recorder?"

"Never hurts to get a conversation on tape. What you told him might actually be of help to us."

"How do you know what I told him?" Again, I had to stop and think things over. Of course, Alika had been listening from the other side of the mirror. After all, anything said in a police station is fair game to use in an investigation, even if it isn't admissible in a court of law. No complaints. I was still compiling my story. "Tell me, Alika, what did happen to Chen? How did the boys in blue let him get away?"

"That," he said, fumbling with his car keys, "is not open for discussion."

"It's a good question though," Nani said. "I'm surprised no one asked me."

Alika and I stood stock-still, waiting for what she would say next. When she only looked back at us, he took a step toward her. "Do you have the answer, Nani?"

"Not exactly." She placed a hand on the hood of his car. "Just a good idea."

"Both of you, get in the back seat. Now."

He didn't bother looking before he drove out of the police garage and almost clipped a bicyclist on Beretania. He slammed his foot on the brake and took a deep breath before pulling onto the street. "Okay, Nani, what is this good idea you have about Chen?"

"Well, he went to the men's room before the police barged into the place. I figure he had to go bad. He must have heard the officer yell at Cacao, about her not being able to hear so good. Right?"

Everything she said made sense. But it didn't explain what happened to Chen.

"If he heard the cops yelling," Alika said, "you figure he managed to sneak out the back somehow?"

"No. Well, yes."

I couldn't believe Alika hadn't pulled over to the curb already to throttle Nani. Ready to strangle her myself, I said, "How can it be no and yes?"

"No, he didn't run out the back door. But, yes, he did run out a back door. See, the men's room is connected to the service corridor, and it leads to the storage area. The storage area has a back door to the alley. Chen was probably half way to Mākaha by the time we got hauled off to the police station."

Now I was really confused. "Why would he head to Mākaha?"

"Because his sister's ex-husband, Russell, lives in Kaimukī."

I threw my hands in the air. Talking to Nani was difficult enough on a normal day. Today, I gave up.

"Wait," Alika said. "You're saying Chen knows better than to get in Russell's way when something bad happens. Like when the sister's new husband gets stabbed to death."

"Right. I don't know why, though."

"It's okay, I might." Alika turned into the parking lot at the strip mall. He pulled up to the driver's side of my car and shifted into neutral. "Thanks for everything, girls. I'll take it from here. You work on staying out of trouble for the next decade. And, Cacao, here's something you might like back."

He was lucky I didn't tear his arm off when I snatched my camera case out of his hand.

Nani made herself comfortable in the passenger seat. "Where to now?"

After turning onto Dillingham, I said, "I need something to eat before I can think about anything else. How does McDonalds sound?"

"Sure, if you're buying."

We settled at a back table with our food and ate in silence. So much didn't add up about the Gabe Yuen case. Whether Nani could fill in any of the holes was questionable. "When you said Chen had to keep his distance from his sister's ex-husband, what did you mean?"

"I really don't know, Cacao. Honest. It's just something Chen always said. Whenever Russell was mad at him for anything, Chen made sure to get as far away from him as possible. He usually headed to his buddy's house in Mākaha."

The man's reasoning was sound. But one thing didn't track for me. How did Alika know what Nani meant without her explaining it? Maybe it was a guy thing.

We tossed our food wrappers, set the trays on the shelf, and headed back to the car. While I waited for traffic to clear, a thought hit me.

"That's it." I snapped my fingers. "Alika saw the logic in what you said, Nani. He went to hunt down Chen in Mākaha. Do you know where his buddy lives out there?"

"Sort of. I've been there for a luau more than once. The country club and golf course are off to the right. There's some side roads off Farrington, before the beach park, and a trail leads through the woods to a small cabin. He's probably there."

Once we were back on Dillingham, Nani started to fiddle with the radio dial. After finding a country station, she sat back and sang along to a Taylor Swift song.

"You think you can find the cabin in the dark?" I asked. The sun would set soon. I didn't like the idea of driving down some dirt trail with no idea what to expect at the end.

Nani gave a couple of quick nods. I hoped that was an affirmative answer, not just her keeping beat with the song coming over the radio.

I took Farrington Highway out past the Waiʻanae schools. She told me to keep going, that she would know the road when she saw it. At Mākaha Valley Road I started to get nervous. Dark was creeping up fast. When we passed Jade Street she told me to slow down.

On the right, I spotted Nani Court. I was sure Nani had used it as a landmark and would tell me to turn that way. Instead, she shouted, "This is it, hang a left."

I followed the shoreline. With the windows rolled down, the sound of splashing waves filled the car. If I hadn't been following a lead, I would've stopped for a quick dip. My beach bag always held towels and an assortment of suits for just such an opportunity. A red flashing light ahead erased the thought and I slammed on the brakes. Something told me Detective Ouellette had figured right. And found Chen.

I eased the Coop over to the beach side of the road. The sun had touched down before we arrived, so we'd missed our chance of seeing a green flash today. The flash was caused by something to do with gases. But magical events made a better story. An orange glow bouncing off low-slung clouds and red flashing lights coming from several police cars were the only colors visible in the darkening sky.

"Should we walk over there?" Nani asked. "We won't learn anything sitting here."

"Remember, Alika told us to stay out of trouble for the next decade. How do you think he'll react if we walk up to our second crime scene in one day?"

She made a face but didn't object. I glanced from the flashing lights to the beach and back to the car. Finally, I had an idea. "How about a leisurely walk along the beach at sundown? No one can fault us for that."

"Nope," Nani agreed. "No one. We can say we wanted to see the beach park. That will take us right past the flashing lights."

As we walked, I knew our reasoning had more holes in it than a pasta strainer. My camera battery still had plenty of juice, so I took a few shots of blushing clouds before the sun slipped away completely. Then I experimented with silhouettes, asking Nani to stand so the flashing lights formed a halo around her head. When she started prancing, I kept clicking until we both got the giggles.

"What in the name of Hades do you think you're doing here?"

I had always been able to distinguish Alika's voice, even in a crowd. With only the ocean waves for competition, there was no question he was the one demanding an answer. I reluctantly turned toward the sound.

"You're not the only one who can draw correct conclusions from Nani's cryptic comments."

"If you think that's funny somehow, Cacao, let me clue you into what's happening here. Yes, I figured out Chen was hiding out in Mākaha for good reason. Looking for him here made sense. So that's what I did, I looked for him. And I found him. But what if I hadn't figured right, and you had? What would you have done if you came traipsing out here on a mission and found what I found?"

I took a step toward him. "What did you find?"

"Another dead body. Only this one wasn't stabbed to death. This one got stuffed into the trunk of a car. Then the car was set on fire."

"Why set the car on fire?" I asked, feeling clueless.

Alika stared at me for a moment. The flashing lights distorted his face into a demonic expression. Or else he was building up steam because his next words spewed out as an unrestrained accusation. "To cover up the two bullet holes in Chen's head."

Waves continued to seep onto the shore and recede again at a steady pace. The moon sparkled off the water. I tried to focus on what Alika had told us, but taking mental pictures of the scenery helped to keep me grounded.

"Your silence suggests I finally penetrated that daredevil skull of yours, Cacao. Are you happy now?"

"I apologize for upsetting you, Alika," I said. "It wasn't my intention. I figured Chen was holed up here. I wanted to follow the story as it unfolded. Something Detective Kadomo said hinted that Mina stabbed the brother-in-law. I assumed Chen feared he would get caught up in the police dragnet, too, even if he wasn't guilty or even involved in the killing. I wanted to hear his side of the story, that's all."

"Well, that's not going to happen now, is it?" Alika dropped to one knee in the sand and sifted the fine grains between his fingers.

"It certainly makes a statement. Chen must have seen something and needed to be silenced." My article was beginning to sound more like a mob story. "If the police are holding Mina on suspicion of killing Gabe, the brother-in-law, then who killed Chen?"

"That's a good question, Cacao." Alika stood and brushed sand off his pants. "Now this is what I suggest you do about it. Go home, get a good night's sleep, and call me in the morning. I'll fill you in then, how's that?"

"Sounds like a plan." I walked over and gave him a hug. "Sorry you get to spend the night writing reports. I'll drop Nani off at her place and go home. Promise."

He hugged me back, warming me inside the same way my dad always managed to do. Alika worried about me, but he never realized I worried about him also. Something very bad had happened within this local family, something that knives and bullets were only making worse. I would go home and get a good night's sleep. But in the morning Nani and I were going to have a talk with a man who lived in Kaimukī. This story had a deep hole and I planned to get to the bottom of it.

The next morning, Nani was waiting at the curb when I pulled up. I had tossed and turned for a couple of hours last night, trying to figure out what could have ignited the family feud between Gabe Yuen and his wife's brothers. "How did you sleep?"

"Never have a problem sleeping," she said. "I was thinking about a few things before I fell asleep though."

"Like what?"

"For instance, what did Chen and Mina's sister tell the police when they interviewed her about the stabbing?"

The question had crossed my mind. I didn't think the sister was in any shape to tell the police anything useful, though. Not after she saw her husband's dead body sprawled out on the lawn. Learning her little brother might have been the one to kill him wouldn't have helped matters.

"Do you know the sister?" I asked. Just because Nani spent time in a bar with the brothers didn't make her friends with the female sibling. "Are they all about the same age?"

"No. Chen's twenty-six and Mina is only twenty-two. The sister is a couple years older than you and me, but I never met her."

"Does she have a name?" I wasn't trying to be sarcastic, but always playing twenty questions with Nani got tiring at times.

"Chen always called her Kami. She has two sons from the previous marriage. One's ten, the other is a couple years younger."

"She has kids from that marriage? Why didn't you tell me this before?"

"Why?"

"Maybe the brothers didn't like the way the stepdad treated their nephews. That could cause a rift in family relations." I hoped Russell, the sister's ex-husband, could give us some insight into how they all got along. "Are you sure you know his address?"

"Russell likes to party. We went over there about once a month. His house is off Wai'alae Avenue, on a numbered street after you pass the elementary school. The place is set back. Has a fence and lots of trees. You can't see the house from the road."

"Does he live alone?"

"No, with a dog. An old rheumy-eyed black lab. Can hardly bark anymore. At the next intersection, get in the left lane, take a left and go two houses down. There's an alleyway on the right. It'll take you to his property."

I parked on the street. Everything was quiet, no kids or animals running around. We went straight to the side door. Nani knocked. A man shuffled up to the door and pressed his face to the glass. He raised his hands, a signal I interpreted to mean "What?"

Nani bent toward the glass so her face was even with his. "Let us in, Russell."

Russell opened the door wide, then shut it as soon as we stepped inside. "Have a seat," he said. "I suppose you're here to ask me questions about my ex-wife's brothers, too. First the cops, then her, now you. Grand Central Station. Want a beer?"

We both declined, but accepted his offer of ripe apple bananas. I peeled one and bit into the soft flesh, the flavor delighting my taste buds. I walked over to the wastebasket and tossed the peel into the paper bag.

"We had lunch with Chen and Mina yesterday," I said, sitting at the table. "We got arrested along with Mina. Chen escaped out the back somehow. Did the police tell you they found him?"

Russell nodded. I hadn't seen the dog, but the rheumy look Nani had attributed to the black lab fit the description of this man's eyes. His kids had lost their stepfather to a stabbing. His ex-wife's brother was being held for the killing. Her other brother had been shot in the head, then stuffed into the trunk of a car that was then set on fire. Either he was good at hiding his feelings, or none of this had fazed the man.

"They came to tell me Chen was shot to death out in Mākaha. He always was trouble. But Mina knifing Kami's new husband, that don't make no sense. I always liked him."

"I'm not with the police, Russell," I said. "But I am trying to piece together what's going on with your family, why this is happening. Was there a problem with how Kami's new husband treated your sons?"

"Lennie and Oz? Never. Gabe loved those boys. He's been raising them for the past six years. I have kind of a drinking problem, never could handle the parenting thing too well. I agreed with Kami. The boys were better off living with her and the new husband. No problems in that department."

"What then, a problem with how Mina got along with the boys maybe?"

"Naw, Mina's nice to everybody. It's like I told the cops. Find out what Chen did to stir up trouble. Figure that out, and you'll find out what happened all the way around."

Back in the car, I pressed the cell button for Alika's private number. He took the call on the second ring.

"Enjoy a good night's sleep, Cacao?"

"Excellent sleeping weather. Nani and I had a short visit with Kami's ex-husband, Russell." I held my breath, waiting for the fireworks. Nothing. "You still there?"

"Yes. You talked to Russell. He told you Mina's a saint, and Chen has always been a problem child. He and the ex-wife and the new husband all get along like a church choir humming a new Gospel tune. Everybody loves everybody else. Makes a great story, doesn't it?"

"I detect a dash of cynicism in that comment, Alika. Since you already know everything I learned this morning, it means you've had more time to process the information. What do you make of the relationship between everyone else involved and the two young boys, Lennie and Oz?"

"According to the mother, her current husband treated the boys like his own. Never yelled at them. And the boys told a police woman they liked him as much as their first father. Did you get that?"

"If you're asking if I understand what's going on, the answer is no."

"What I'm asking is if you understood what I said so far. There's more. According to Mina, Chen said the new husband was abusing the kids."

"You mean sexually abusing them?"

"That's the way it reads in the statement Mina gave today. Chen got his younger brother so worked up about it, Mina decided to kill the man. He went over to the housing development and stabbed Gabe. Simple as that." He gave me one of his fierce stares. "None of this is available for publication yet."

"I understand." I wouldn't use any of this information until it was released. "Don't tell me that's the end of the story, though. Why was Chen shot?"

"One crime at a time, Cacao. I'll keep you posted."

I relayed the information to Nani. Then we headed over to a chop suey place in Kaimukī. I needed time to digest everything and come up with my next step. No one knew why Chen ended up with two bullets to the head. No one wanted to believe Mina killed his sister's new husband.

Now the kids, Lennie and Oz, were in the picture. That changed how I looked at things.

At the restaurant, the waitress brought us each a bowl of pork chop suey, two scoops rice on the side. She set a pot of tea in the middle of the table and glasses of ice water next to our plates. Then she slipped the bill under a saucer containing two fortune cookies before heading back to the kitchen. She had plenty of other customers waiting.

"Russell said Chen was the problem, not Mina," I said. "If Chen talked Mina into killing Gabe Yuen, the sister would naturally blame Chen for her husband's death."

"You're saying Gabe abused his stepsons and Chen got him killed out of revenge? Then Kami had Chen killed?"

"Okay, I agree it's too farfetched. What about the ex-husband, Russell? Maybe he had something to do with it. What if he was the one abusing the boys?"

"I don't think so," Nani said. "I partied with him when he was plenty drunk. He never did anything strange to suggest he was perverted that way."

"So we're stuck on the same questions. Why did Mina get riled up enough to kill Gabe? Who killed Chen, and why? One of the "why" questions is answered, we just don't know which one yet. According to rumor, someone was abusing the boys. For that reason, Gabe was killed. Whether he was the rightful target is yet to be proved."

"Was Chen killed because of something he knew," Nani said, "or something he did?"

"What are the chances Kami would agree to see me?" She was the only person involved in all this I hadn't talked to yet. If she couldn't give me something to work with, I was at a dead end. "You want to give her a call, explain you were one of her brothers' drinking pals, and try to set something up?"

Nani agreed to call. Two hours later, we walked from her apartment to the building where Kami still lived with the boys. She led us to the living room and offered us cola or coffee, her voice sounding dull from shock. We both went for the cola.

"What's your involvement in all this?" Kami asked, once we were settled.

I was prepared for the question. "Nani and I were with Mina at that karaoke place on Dillingham when the police barged in and arrested all of us. They held us for questioning, then released Nani and me. But that doesn't mean they don't still suspect us of having something to do with Gabe's death. We want to make sure everything gets cleared up. But we also want to know what happened to get us arrested in the first place. It only seems fair."

Whether Kami bought my story or not, she asked what it was we wanted to know. "I couldn't send the boys back to school yet. They're over at their grandmother's for another couple hours. I don't know if I can help you, but I'll try."

My list of questions was short, three to be exact. I only hoped the answers she supplied would be beneficial.

"I spoke with your ex-husband, Russell. He showed no animosity toward your new husband or to having Gabe help you raise his sons. In fact, he appeared grateful. Do you think he might be hiding his resentment and had something to do with the death of your husband or your brother, Chen?"

"First of all, Russell is not a resentful man." Kami's defensiveness suggested enabling tendencies. Or codependency. Maybe she was the one hiding resentment. But of what I couldn't guess. "And second, there was nothing to be resentful of. Gabe and I raised the boys because Russell wasn't capable of being a father to them. Alcohol was more important to him. He admitted it freely."

Maybe Russell wasn't sexually abusing the boys. But I had a hard time rationalizing his choice of alcohol over his children as not being child abuse. I didn't think his drinking was the problem that led to two deaths in Kami's family, though.

I had lumped all three of my questions together on purpose: Did Kami think her ex-husband hid his resentment? Did he have something to do with her current husband's death? Did he have anything to do with her brother's death? She wouldn't answer all of them immediately. But they would flutter around in her mind. When I asked them again, something from her subconscious might inadvertently spill out. I could wait.

"Kami, do you have any idea why Mina attacked your husband?" I asked, rephrasing the question as I often did for Nani when her mind drifted. It was another way of asking if Russell had something to do with the death of her current husband, without mentioning his name. Kami wasn't willing to admit it, maybe even to herself, but Russell fit into this family crisis somehow.

"Mina said Gabe was abusing the boys. But that's not true. Please excuse me." Kami stood and walked down the hall to the bathroom.

She had defended Russell's alcohol abuse; she defended Gabe against accusations of child abuse. I wanted to believe her on both counts. But I needed information that supported her defense of these two men she had married.

My cell phone rang. I dug it out of my camera bag and looked at the display screen. It was Alika. "Aloha. How may I be of service to you today?"

He laughed. "You always make my day, Cacao. I have something that might interest you. We got lab work back on fingerprints left at the car fire, mainly on the trunk. We have reason to believe Russell and Kami were both at the scene before the fire started."

"That doesn't make sense," I said, trying to wrap my mind around what he'd told me. "Why would Russell or Kami want to kill Chen?"

"Listen to me, Cacao. The only reason I'm telling you this is so you stay away from them. I know you already talked to Russell. I just don't want you getting any ideas about questioning the wife. We don't want her getting suspicious before we can make a case against them. Okay?"

"Okay."

"You don't sound too convincing. What are you doing right now?"

"Um, Nani and I are visiting one of her neighbors."

"Damn. I'm on my way."

Kami returned to the living room and sat at the far end of the couch. "Sorry, I'm taking nerve pills and have to make a lot of trips to the bathroom. Do you have any more questions before I go pick up the boys?"

"Only the last one I asked earlier. Why do you think Chen was killed?"

Her breath hitched as she started to speak. She grabbed a tissue from the box on the end table. She dabbed her eyes, possibly biding time to compose an answer. "He deserved what he got."

Nani sat up straighter, apparently alerted by the change in Kami's tone. I gave her a quick glance, hoping she would settle back and let Kami let out her feelings.

"Did he deserve to die because of something he did to Gabe?" I worked to make sense of that. Maybe she knew her new husband was abusing her sons. But after her brother killed him, she felt the need to defend her husband, regardless of his actions. Mina was being detained for Gabe's death. That left only Chen to blame for Kami's loss of another husband.

Kami stopped her show of dabbing at tears. "You could say it was because of something Chen did to Gabe. Now that I think about it, your words perfectly describe the situation."

"Chen talked Mina into killing Gabe for abusing your sons. Is that why he had to die?"

"I told you, Gabe never abused my sons." Kami pounded the couch with her fist. "He didn't deserve to die. Gabe threatened to file a report with the police because of the abuse."

Nani squeezed my fingers until the pain cleared my head. I silently thanked her. Kami had finally let slip what I'd patiently waited for, a reason.

"What are you saying, Kami? Someone killed Gabe for threatening to tell the police about the child abuse?" *Was Russell the offender? Would he and Kami have killed Chen to keep him from talking?* Trying to hold my voice steady, I asked, "Who did Gabe threaten to report?"

"I thought reporters were supposed to figure that kind of stuff out on their own." Kami reached for the tissue box again, her eyes already shiny with tears.

She had been through so much in the past two days. I was surprised she had held it together this long. I stood and walked toward her, wanting to give her a hug. Kami needed to know she wasn't alone in all this. But when she pulled a gun out of the tissue box, I froze in place.

"Something tells me..." She pointed the muzzle at Nani and me in turn. "You already know who was doing the abusing. Now you come snooping around trying to cause even more trouble for my family after everything is already settled. Why can't you just leave it alone?"

"You aren't going to shoot both of us, Kami." I stood frozen in front of her. "If you put the gun down now, you won't be arrested for anything."

"Of course I'll be arrested." Kami raised the gun and pointed it at my head before lowering it toward my waist. Then she slowly moved her hand until the muzzle touched her right temple. "Who do you think shot Chen?"

My chest started to hurt. I realized I'd stopped breathing and gasped in a lungful of air. The sudden motion distracted Kami and she lowered her right arm. I lunged at the gun in her hand, twisting her wrist until she yelped. The gun slid to the couch. Nani grabbed it before Kami could react and set it on the window sill by the door. Then we stood staring down at Kami, who glowered back at us.

A determined knock disrupted the eerie silence. Nani went to the door and escorted Alika into the living room.

"We're gathering quite a crowd." Kami sounded like a party hostess. "I suppose you all know each other?"

"Yes," I said. "Detective Ouelette is handling your case. Why don't I fill him in on our discussion? Would that be okay with you, Kami?"

Still glowering, she nodded. Alika took a seat in the lounge chair by the window. The backrest hid the window sill where Nani had set the gun.

I decided to hold back on the gun incident. "Kami gave me permission to ask a few questions, Detective. She told me her husband, Gabe, did not abuse her sons. She said he didn't deserve to die. He threatened to report the child abuse to the police. That's where we were when you arrived. I believe she was about to tell us who Gabe threatened with the police report."

"He didn't only threaten," Alika said. "We dug up the report. He filed it over six weeks ago. It didn't go anywhere because he withdrew the complaint the following day. The closing notes state Kami talked him out of moving forward with any action."

I looked over at Kami. "You have a tendency to support the underdog, don't you?"

"If I didn't," she said, "who would?"

Her question left me at a loss for words. Alika studied the floor, probably not wanting to risk his badge with a daring answer. While we sat there, mentally hemming and hawing, Nani stood and walked over to Kami.

"If you defend the wrong people long enough," she said, "there won't be anyone in your family left alive to defend."

Kami huffed at Nani's remark. "What do any of you know about family loyalty?"

A nervous cramp seized my stomach. I had actually started to root for Russell, even with all his faults. "Who did Gabe name in the complaint that you felt a need to defend in the first place?"

"I have to pick up my sons." Kami stood. "They are my entire family now."

"No." I blocked her from the door. "First, let's discuss the gun you pulled on Nani and me."

Alika was already on his feet when I pointed to the window sill. He took one look at the gun, then stared at me, waiting.

"Kami thought she could end everything by shooting herself."

He keyed his portable radio mic and requested backup for an unstable domestic situation. Considering the circumstances of this entire case, that about said it all.

A blue and white police vehicle pulled to the curb minutes later. Kami was handcuffed "for her own safety" and escorted to the vehicle. Alika bagged the gun and secured the apartment before running crime scene tape across the front door.

At the curb, I leaned against his car. "Out with it, Alika, who did Gabe name? I can't believe it was Russell."

"No, it wasn't Russell." He brushed me away from the fender. "Not that he was ever voted father-of-the-year. Mina committed murder because Chen convinced him Gabe was abusing his step-kids. But Gabe's report threatened to reveal Chen had made sexual advances toward Lennie, the older son."

I ran through the scenario. "Chen tricked Mina into murdering Gabe, to stop Gabe from revealing Chen's abuse. Then the boys' parents killed Chen for coercing Mina into stabbing Gabe. Two family members are dead, and three more will likely spend their lives in prison."

Alika shrugged. "That about covers it. Detective Kadomo is rounding up Russell as we speak. Kami will have to be evaluated, but the little display you described was hardly a suicide attempt. I'm not sure Mina will end up in prison. A good lawyer could get him declared insane at the time of the murder."

"What about the two boys, Lennie and Oz?" Nani asked.

Alika shook his head. "Probably end up living with Russell's parents. Not the worst thing. What's your final story going to say?" He and Nani turned toward me.

"I definitely won't get my own byline for the murders, Alika. You and Detective Kadomo did a great job solving this case."

"You helped keep us on track, though."

"Sure, I know that. Have to watch your backs all the time. The paper plans to quote me in their story so I get some credit. They'll also use a photograph I submitted, the purple scarf one. The news desk gave me an assignment to write the story of my investigation up to the arrests. They'll run it at a later date. Then they want me to come up with a follow-up angle and write a series of stories connected to the original case. After doing my research, I'll compile articles to shine light on the hidden perils of codependency and enabling."

To me, the two went hand-in-hand. People needed to become aware of the inherent dangers. Not only to the immediate parties but their extended families, innocent or guilty.

Nani gave me a hug and headed back to her apartment. Alika walked to his car, tossing me a wave before opening the door. As he drove away, I thought about my decision to skirt the criminal angle of this particular story for the follow-up articles, focusing instead on an ignored deadly threat.

My interest in pursuing a career as a freelance reporter hadn't wavered. One day, I would get the coveted byline. But the job offered endless possibilities. This latest project would take me on a path less traveled, expanding my horizons. And might even give me a glimpse of the green flash.

GAIL M. BAUGNIET

Gail M. Baugniet is the author of the Pepper Bibeau mystery series. After working as a police officer on the mainland and a dispatcher on Oʻahu, she now writes full time at her home in Honolulu. Gail is an active member of several writers groups and current president of Sisters in Crime/Hawaiʻi. She spends most of her time in writing related activities. With year-round warm weather, her lānai makes an excellent writing studio, where she is currently at work on her next novel.

Find me on the web at gail-baugniet.blogspot.com.

TRUST FALL
FRANKIE BOW

A hard nudge in the ribs jolted me awake.

"Molly," Emma hissed. "C'mon, stand up."

I had dozed off in one of the comfortable new chairs in Administrative Complex Conference Room 5B, my head resting on the shoulder of my best friend and fellow sufferer, Emma Leilani Kanoʻopomaikaʻi Nakamura.

"What?" I rubbed my eyes.

"Are you sleeping?"

"Well I *was*. Why do we have to stand up?"

"We're doing the trust fall thing now. Eh, don't let Jake see you making that face or he's gonna give us another lecture about our attitude."

"What? I'm not making a face. This is my face."

Jake Ahu, Director of Faculty Development, glared around the room, and tightened his grip on his clipboard.

"This is a *trust* fall, people. Come on, everyone out of your seats. We are cultivating a culture of *trust* here on our campus."

Jake's unenviable task was to wrangle us through a full workday of "team building": making orange, gold, green, and blue hats out of construction paper, building towers with marshmallows and dry spaghetti, and falling backwards off of chairs. Jake was maybe in his late thirties, but looked prematurely haggard. His black hair was shot through with gray, and his bright aloha shirt fit a little too loosely around the neck.

"Fine," he said. "If no one's going to come forward, we'll do it by department."

At least he wasn't insufferably chipper. I'll give him that.

Jake tapped his clipboard with his pen.

"Anthropology? Anthropology isn't here. Art, also not here. Biology, Emma Nakamura, there you are. You're going first. Come on. Everyone. Up to the front of the room. Molly Barda, College of Commerce, you're next after Emma. Kyle Stockhausen, Digital Humanities, you're after Molly."

I'm Molly. Molly Barda, Ph.D. I earned my doctorate at one of the top ten literature and creative writing programs in the country, and this is not where I expected to end up. By "this," I mean an eight-hour team-building retreat in the Administrative Complex at remote Mahina State University, in Mahina, Hawai'i where, according to our radio spots, "Your Future Begins Tomorrow." In the entire history of business and enterprise, has there been any practice less humane, less conducive to employee solidarity, and more likely to tip the garden-variety introvert into full-blown misanthropy, than the team-building retreat?

"I'm in the management department," I said to Jake. "That starts with an M."

"Well I'm still after you," said the chair of the philosophy department.

"You're both in front of me," said a man behind me. I turned to see Scott Nixon, Kyle Stockhausen's main competitor for the title of Hipster Humanities Heartthrob. Unlike the earnest Stockhausen, Nixon affected an air of bemused detachment (which the undergraduates in his Jane Austen elective reportedly found irresistible). Stockhausen was blond, and wore whimsical t-shirts to display his indifference to status; Nixon had dark hair, and bolstered his bad-boy persona by wearing a black leather jacket, which must have been torture in Mahina's sultry climate. Both men sported black-framed glasses and a fashionable sprinkling of stubble.

"Scott," I said, "in what alphabet does English come after management and philosophy?"

"I teach *writing*."

"Hey," someone said. "What about ag? Where's the person from ag?"

"He's coming in later," Jake said. "They have to testify at the GMO hearings."

I eyed the exit door, wondering if I could slip out unseen and get to grading the stack of papers waiting for me back in my office. Getting my students' assignments returned seemed like a better use of my time than standing on chairs.

All of the conference rooms in the new Administrative Complex had back exit doors. They allowed escape in case a mad gunman burst into the room. The classrooms didn't have this safeguard. In fact, the new administration building boasted several features our classrooms lacked, like recessed lighting, polished marble floors, and functional air conditioning.

"I'll go first."

Kyle Stockhausen, assistant professor of digital humanities, strode up to the Trust Fall Chair. The Trust Fall Chair wasn't one of the red, gold, or green conference room chairs (the new school colors, as decided by student referendum). Those chairs all had wheels, and anyway, I'm sure the administration didn't want us stepping all over the seat cushions with our dirty shoes. No, the Trust Fall Chair was plain, straight-backed, and made of wood. It had probably been ordered online and shipped from the mainland, just for this event.

"Thank you for volunteering, Professor Stockhausen," Jake nodded at him.

"Please Call me Kaila."

I heard Emma snort. Emma, who grew up just a few miles down the road from Mahina State University, had definite opinions about "white people who move here from Nebraska and give themselves Hawaiian names."

"*Mahalo nui loa*, brother," said Kyle/Kaila Stockhausen as Jake helped him up onto the wooden seat. He slowly stood, his spiky blonde hair almost brushing the ceiling.

"Come on, everyone move in closer." Jake motioned us forward. "You're all going to have to come together to catch him when he falls. Kyle, sorry, Kaila, turn around and put your arms out."

He did, displaying the black courier lettering on the back of his pale yellow t-shirt: *Everybody is a genius. But if you judge a fish by its ability to climb a tree, it will live its whole life believing that it is stupid. –Albert Einstein*

"Einstein never said that," Emma muttered.

"Now the rest of you, move in. Closer, you have to be right underneath so you can catch him."

"I have to apologize for my colleagues," Stockhausen said over his shoulder. "They don't yet realize what a privilege this is. I appreciate the value of these high-touch team-building activities. In fact, I use many of these exercises in my own classes."

This was the limit for Emma.

"Give it a rest, Stockholm-syndrome," she shouted. "You teach all your classes online."

Before anyone could react to Emma's outburst, the exit door at the far end of the room flew open. Everyone turned toward the welcome distraction. A man wearing shorts and a t-shirt stood silhouetted in the doorway.

"Am I late?" the newcomer asked.

"Here's our Ag person," Jake said. "Come in, come in. You're just in time for the—"

Jake's sentence was cut short by the scrape of wood on marble, and an ugly thud. We all pushed forward to get a look.

Kyle Stockhausen lay face up on the polished marble floor, blood spreading behind his head like a crimson halo.

Kyle "Kaila" Stockhausen's reputation improved markedly after his demise. In death, his virtues were magnified, while his lapses faded from memory. His self-righteous lecturing of fellow faculty, who didn't "get it" or were "doing it wrong," his refusal to impose even minimal standards in his classes, even the rumors of Stockhausen's fraternizing with students were viewed with revised tolerance. After all, Quentin Virtanen, chair of the philosophy department, was happily married to the pretty young Ife, and hadn't she been his student years ago? Because Stockhausen had been considerate enough to expire during the summer term, the administration thought kindly of him, too, as they had plenty of time to hire a replacement lecturer to take over his fall classes.

Stockhausen's death had appeared to be a straightforward accident, so neither an autopsy nor a police investigation was deemed necessary. This, however, didn't keep Emma from being found guilty in the court of campus opinion. Everyone knew Emma had tried to pick a fight with him during his last moments on earth. Some went so far as to claim Emma's harsh words had physically knocked Stockhausen off the chair.

A week after the incident, Emma and I were down at the Maritime Club, observing our customary Monday happy hour. Our reasoning was everyone is already in a good mood most Friday afternoons. Monday is when happy hour is really needed. The Maritime Club isn't terribly fancy, but nothing in Mahina is fancy. The weather-beaten little clubhouse is perpetually in need of a new paint job. The bill of fare probably hasn't been updated since 1952, good news for fans of split pea soup and baked Alaska. The Maritime Club's outstanding feature is its magnificent oceanfront location. At low tide, you can walk a few steps down the grassy bank to the tide pools and watch damselfish and little snowflake eel darting among the spiny urchins and lobe coral.

Emma and I chose a table on the outdoor lānai. Waves sparkled in the afternoon sun, breaking on the black lava rock and misting us with salt spray. I ordered a house cabernet, Emma got a Mehana Volcano Red Ale, and we settled in to wait for our drinks and ponder the curved blue horizon.

"This Stockhausen thing is out of control," Emma said. "I'm thinking I might have to start looking for another job."

"I thought you didn't care what people think," I said. "Is it that bad?"

"It's bad." Emma nodded. "I can deal with a few people not talking to me, not making eye contact, whatever. But this morning, I went to the financial aid office to drop off a recommendation letter, and the student worker, this little girl, just bust out crying, screaming how could I do it, didn't I know what he meant to her. Crazy."

"What did you do?" I asked.

"Nothing. Financial aid is across from the counseling office, so before I could tell her to snap out of it and get a grip, all these people came running and calmed her down. This isn't the only time, Molly, but it's just the worst one so far. This keeps up I'm never gonna get tenure."

"You think this is going to torpedo your tenure? I hadn't even thought of that. Emma, how awful."

"Yeah, I don't wanna talk about it. Speaking of hellish things, how's your summer class going? Any more trouble from your students?"

"It's okay." I shrugged. "Mostly. You know Virtanen's wife is enrolled. Ife Virtanen."

"Oh, little Ife? What's she doing taking Biz Com?"

"She's in the pre-nursing program," I said. "I just graded the latest batch of essays, and wow."

"What's wow?" Emma asked.

"Well, I asked them to do a one-pager telling me what they've learned in this class that they think they'll be able to use later. And Ife's paper—Okay, I'm sharing this with you as a fellow educator, right?"

"I see no FERPA violation here," Emma assured me.

"Good. So Ife—now bear in mind we work with her husband, right?—wrote about how important it was for her to go back to school and finish getting her degree, and what a mistake it had been to put her plans on hold to marry her philosophy professor."

"Ew, awkward." Emma wrinkled her nose.

"And it gets worse. For some reason, she feels like she has to explain why she married Virtanen in the first place."

"No way," Emma said. "And then?"

"Oh good. Our drinks."

I waited as the server, a cheerful young woman in black trousers and a white blouse, set out the cabernet, the ale, and a bowl of peanuts.

"Anyway," I said. "It was along the lines of, the professor seems so unattainable, all these hundreds of other students are hanging on his every word, but I know I'm the one he's paying attention to, and the feeling is irresistible."

"Gross." Emma picked up her beer and took a healthy gulp.

"I think it's sad. Poor little thing is so starved for validation. I thought one of the advantages of teaching business would be not getting these bleeding-all-over-the-page essays like the ones you get in comp classes. Anyway, she went on to describe how things go south once you get what you think you wanted and you've been in the relationship for a while. Apparently Quentin Virtanen, renowned professor of philosophy, is no longer unattainable, because after all, she attained him. And now, he's being a little too helpful to his young female students. She made him her whole world, and now she realizes that she's just a small part of his world."

"Yeah, that's depressing. Hey, wait a minute. Remember the rumor about Kyle Stockhausen fooling around with a professor's wife?"

"I do remember. It was before he was posthumously promoted from irritant to saint. You think he was involved with Ife Virtanen?"

"Quentin was at the team building thing with us when it happened, remember. Ife's unhappy in her marriage. She turns to Kyle Stockhausen for comfort. Her husband finds out. Maybe it was a crime of passion."

"Emma, Quentin Virtanen is a tiny little man, no offense."

"What do you mean 'no offense'?"

I kept forgetting how sensitive Emma was about her height.

"I'm just saying Stockhausen was much taller and fitter than Quentin Virtanen If anyone could push Stockhausen off a chair, it would have to be someone like—"

"Scott Nixon," Emma exclaimed. "Maybe Stockhausen was fooling around with Leather Jacket's wife. What's her name?"

"Nicole. Nicole Nixon. It's a possibility."

I took a sip of wine and tried to imagine how either Scott Nixon or Quentin Virtanen—or both—might have shoved Kyle Stockhausen off the Trust Fall Chair without being noticed.

"Actually, Molly." Emma frowned. "I don't think anyone pushed Kyle off the chair."

"Why not?"

"Cause Stockhausen woulda made some noise. Like when we're paddling and we *huli* the boat? Everyone's yelling and swearing and stuff. Stockhausen wouldn't have just gone down quietly if someone pushed him."

"You're right." I considered what she'd said. "It's as if he just lost consciousness, or—"

"Oh, I know," Emma interrupted. "Someone hit 'im with a poison dart. From a blowgun."

"What?"

"Well they never did an autopsy, yah? So it's possible."

"I guess anything's possible."

Emma set down her beer and leaned forward.

"We should call the police, Molly."

"Or maybe we should check with someone on campus first. Before we start getting law enforcement involved."

"Fine," Emma said. "What about Jake Ahu? He was at the session. I'll call him. I need another beer." She pulled out her phone as she signaled for another round.

Judging from Emma's side of the conversation, our Director of Faculty Development was not receptive to the idea of digging into the Kyle Stockhausen situation.

Emma mashed the hangup button.

"Typical administrator CYA."

"I'm surprised Jake was still at the office at this hour. I wouldn't want his job."

"I wouldn't mind his salary. Eh, forget our gutless administrators. I'm calling the actual police."

"Emma, don't call 911. They hate it when people call 911 and it's not an emergency."

"Molly, what kind of a schmendrick do you think I am? I'm just gonna call the tip line."

"Did you say schmendrick?"

"I went to grad school in New York." Emma dialed. "Maybe you forgot."

"How could I possibly forget you went to Cornell when you take every opportunity to remind—"

"Shh." Emma waved at me to be quiet. She stated her case to the tip line operator as well as anyone could have.

"We don't believe Kyle Stockhausen died in an accident. Yes, we suspect foul play might have been involved. And, yes, we think an autopsy should be performed. Can you check for any substances that might make someone lose balance or consciousness?"

Emma hung up.

"So what's going to happen?" I asked.

"She heard me out, but she didn't sound too impressed. I don't think they're gonna do anything."

"Well, now what?"

"I guess I gotta look for another job," Emma said.

"Emma, you grew up here. This is the only place you've ever wanted to work. And you're on the tenure track. Don't give up."

"I dunno, Molly." Emma grabbed a handful of peanuts from the bowl and stuffed them into her mouth. "What else can I do?"

We sat and stared at the darkening ocean. A chill breeze whipped through my blouse.

"We need someone who can help us figure this out." I hugged myself and rubbed my upper arms for warmth.

"We don't have a Department of Bizarre Death Studies," Emma said.

"We have Pat Flanagan. Let's see if he wants to get lunch tomorrow."

Patrick Flanagan was waiting for us in front of the cafeteria, his shaved head gleaming in the sunlight. He wore his usual ensemble, a flannel shirt, beat-up jeans, and big black work boots. Pat used to be a crime reporter at *The County Courier* before the layoffs. Now he teaches composition part-time, mostly for the library privileges, as part-time teaching pays nearly nothing. He also runs Mahina's most popular news outlet, *Island Confidential*.

"Fabulous shoes." He indicated my aqua Fluevog slingbacks with the five parallel buckle straps and the sassy Cuban heel.

"You didn't teach today?" Emma scowled at my shoes.

"I did," I answered a little defensively.

"The shoes are cool," Emma said. "But I dunno. Maybe you could get away with them in black."

"Why can't Molly teach in those shoes?" Pat examined my feet. "I think they look great."

"They don't look serious," Emma said.

"Emma's right." I sighed. "I'm probably undermining my authority in the classroom wearing these. It's safer to stick with dark colors when you teach. Dark colors signal dominance."

"Yeah, Pat," Emma said, "that's how come your leather guys don't wear baby blue chaps."

"What do you mean *Pat's* leather guys?" I asked. "Emma, what are you talking about?"

"Come on, let's go." Emma led the way into the cafeteria, which was up and running during the summer, but just barely. I had trouble finding anything I wanted to eat. The premade sandwiches were stuffed with something pale and gooey. It might have been either tuna salad or chicken salad. There was a coffee urn, but I didn't see any cream or milk, only flat white packets labeled, "For Your Coffee." I wondered if the unidentifiable sandwich filling had been scooped from white five-gallon pails labeled, "For Your Sandwich."

"Where'd you get the thing about wearing dark colors?" Pat asked as we made our way through the cafeteria checkout line.

"We're going to be covering it in Biz Com class," I said. "All the different factors that affect person-perception. Something else kind of interesting is height. There's a lot of research on that, actually. People don't see a short person as being in charge. It's why we've never elected a short president."

Emma turned around and glared at me.

"Now you gonna say, 'Oh, no offense Emma'?"

"Me? No, why would I say that?"

"So what? I gotta wear high heels now?"

"No, don't wear high heels," I said. "High heels can read as sexy."

"Ew." Emma wrinkled her nose.

"Hey Molly, what about platform shoes? Like what Boris Karloff wore in Frankenstein? I'm already tall, so according to your theory, if I put on platform shoes, my students would see me as some kind of demigod."

"You literally *would* look like Frankenstein," Emma said.

"Frankenstein's *monster*," I corrected her. "Frankenstein was the name of the scientist."

I grabbed a package of macadamia nuts from the impulse-buy rack next to the cashier's station. We ate quickly and then went across the main plaza to the library.

Emma stepped on the rubber mat first, triggering the glass door to wheeze open. Pat and I followed. I didn't see Emma stop in front of me, so I bumped into her, and then Pat bumped into me and we all said sorry to each other and waited for our eyes to adjust.

"Not the library, too," Emma said.

"Man, I can't see a thing," Pat said.

Our administration had been saving money by removing light tubes from the fixtures on campus. First the faculty offices, then the classrooms, and finally the library, which now looked like the set of a low-budget horror movie. The administration buildings, with their recessed lighting, were of course exempt from this effort. At least it was easy to spot the terminals.

"So what's this exciting conspiracy you two are going to uncover?" Pat asked as we picked our way around the carrels toward the row of glowing computer monitors. Two of the terminals, we discovered, were out of order. Only one connected to the library databases.

Emma told Pat the whole story.

Even in the semidarkness, I could see Pat slump with disappointment.

"You're talking about the Stockhausen thing? It's a freak accident, maybe worth a mention in wacky news or something. I mean, you were both there. Did you see anyone push him?"

"Well no," I said, "but—"

"Was he behaving strangely?"

"He was behaving like a self-righteous idiot," Emma said.

"There's no story there," Pat said. We were already set up at the terminal, though, so we had Pat pull up the pharmaceutical database. It wasn't very instructive. It turns out just about any substance, including placebos, can cause dizziness and loss of balance.

"What am I gonna do?" Emma wailed.

"It's bad, Pat," I said. "People think Emma's responsible. She had a student worker freak out and start crying."

"No one said anything when we came into the library," Pat said.

"No one else is *in* the library, genius," Emma said. "Look around. They cut the librarians' hours, remember?"

"You should tell people to stop being so superstitious," Pat said.

"Yeah, that would probably work really well. With *rational* people. Who, by definition, aren't superstitious. So you see my problem."

"Pat, he must have been impaired in some way. Emma and I were talking it over, and neither of us remembered him making any sound. He just fell, as if he had passed out."

"So, you know who you should probably talk to?" Pat stood up. "Someone in the nursing program."

"What about looking into Scott Nixon?" I asked.

"You want me to go up to Nicole Nixon and ask her whether she was having an affair with Kyle Stockhausen, and if so, does she think her husband Scott killed him? Or maybe I should just ask Scott directly, 'Oh, hey, by the way, did you kill Stockhausen?' "

"Eh," Emma said. "You're the reporter."

We left Pat in the library and started down to the lower end of campus. The nursing program is one of the most popular and prestigious offerings at Mahina State University. But thanks to some long-ago political misstep, it had been banished to a cluster of decaying portables on the swampy end of the university.

Zora Winfield, the nursing program director, was kind enough to give us a few minutes. Her desk was cluttered with framed photographs, stacks of forms, and a row of plants in tiny pots, each one fastened to a popsicle stick with a little bow of yarn. On the wall hung a framed print of "The Florence Nightingale Pledge." I read it as Zora finished and sent the email she'd been working on when we barged in to her office.

"...*devote myself to the welfare of those committed to my care.* That's nice. Kind of what we do as teachers, too. Don't you think?"

"Yeah, whatever." Emma's biology 101 is the weed-out class for pre-nursing majors and premeds, so she sees her role as pruning rather than nurturing.

Zora had heard about the Stockhausen incident, and probably that everyone was blaming Emma for it, although she was too tactful to mention it. She listened to us politely but clearly found our line of questioning farfetched.

"You didn't smell alcohol?" Zora tapped her long, French-manicured nails on her desk.

Emma and I shook our heads.

"And he wasn't acting out of character?"

"Unfortunately not," Emma said.

"I suppose there are several possibilities." She set down the pen and gazed up at the ceiling as if it held the answers. "Prescription drugs, panic attack, idiopathic vertigo. Without a medical examination, though, it's just speculation. Personally? I think it was just a terrible accident. You'd be surprised at the different ways people manage to die. Up at the hospital last week, we lost a patient en route to the ER. She'd fallen on a wineglass."

"That's how Molly's going out," Emma said.

"Thank you, Emma." I glared at her. "Just out of curiosity, Zora, not to do with this particular incident, but in general. Is there some prescription or recreational drug you know of that could make someone lose their balance suddenly?"

"Oh, any number of things. We have a very good pharmaceutical database. Faculty can access it through the main library site. It's a little hard to find. I can write it down for you."

She took a lined sticky pad and wrote out the directions for us. We didn't want to tell her we'd just checked the database and found it completely unhelpful.

"I'll be right there." Emma and I turned to see a young woman hovering in the doorway, staring open-mouthed at Emma. We took the database information, thanked Zora, and hurried out.

"Now what?" I said. We took a diagonal shortcut back up toward the College of Commerce, across the ragged lawn.

"I dunno." Emma sighed. "I guess I wait until I get run outta town."

"Hey, is this an African tulip tree? I never saw it before. I guess I don't come down to this part of campus much."

"Ucch, it *is* an African tulip. Someone needs to cut it down."

The tree loomed over the squat earth sciences building, its flame-colored petals littering the red metal roof.

"The last time I was at Safari Park in San Diego, they made a huge deal over their African tulip trees. Why would you want to cut it down? It's beautiful."

"It's a freaking weed, that's why. They need to bring out the chainsaws."

"You don't realize how lucky you are here," I said. "Back home, getting anything to grow was cause for celebration. Here, you turn your back and ravening jungle plants devour your house."

My attempt to distract Emma wasn't working.

"Look, Emma," I said. "People live things down. I mean, look at Rodge Cowper, right? He—"

"Oh, do not talk to me about Rodge Cowper, that self-centered schmuck. He's dead to me."

"Okay, I know you don't care for Rodge, but this is my point. He's still here after all these years, and he even has his own HR directive named after him."

"Oh yeah. The Rodge Cowper rule."

"Exactly. The one that says when a student's in your office you have to keep your door open."

"Well number one, Rodge totally brought it on himself. Me, I was just in the wrong place at the wrong time."

We walked in silence for a few moments.

"You said number one," I said. "What's number two?"

"Number two, how dare you compare me to Rodge Cowper? It's not the same thing at all. The Rodge Cowper rule is his own stupid fault."

"That's the same thing you said for number one."

"Shut up," Emma suggested. "Eh, you gonna be on campus tomorrow?"

"All day. Why don't you stop by before I have to go teach my class?"

The next morning Emma came to see me in my office. We usually meet in my office, not hers, since I have a chair for visitors, and Emma does not. I had scrounged my visitor chair from the last remodel of one of the auxiliary lounges of the Student Retention Office. It was old but serviceable, with orange upholstery and a squared-off wooden frame. Mahina State eliminated the furniture budget for faculty, and Emma refused to buy work furniture with her own money, so anyone who visited her office had to stand and look at that brain in a jar she kept on top of her file cabinet.

"How are things?" I asked.

Emma plopped down with an "oof" sound.

"I think I saw the janitor crossing himself when I walked by."

"Is that coffee?"

She proffered the Styrofoam cup. "Want some?"

I turned the cup around to the side that she hadn't been drinking from, and took a sip. It tasted horrible.

"What is this? It tastes like chocolate and chicken soup."

"It's from the old vending machine in the humanities building," she said. "The sign says out of order, but it still works."

My office phone rang. I picked it up.

"Ixnay on Nicole Nixon and Kyle Stockhausen."

"Pat?" I asked.

"Oh, yeah, it's me, sorry."

"Okay. Why not Nicole Nixon and Kyle Stockhausen?"

"Nicole has a Ph.D.," Pat said. "Stockhausen only had an MFA. Stockhausen wouldn't get involved with someone who has a more advanced degree than he does. He had to be in the teacher role."

"Wow," I said. "How did you manage to snoop around without attracting suspicion?"

Emma bounced in her seat, impatient for news.

"I teach a class in the English department," Pat said. "I'm supposed to be here."

I rang off and was about to tell Emma what Pat had just told me, when a knock on the door made us both turn.

Ife Virtanen stood in the doorway.

"Oh, hi," she said. "Do you have a minute?"

The wife of the chair of the philosophy department looked young for her thirty years: pale, round face, rosy cheeks, black curly hair at chin-length. She held a binder in front of her protectively, the way you might imagine a high school girl would.

"I'm gonna get going," Emma said. "Lunch?"

"Sure."

Ife came in and hovered next to the visitor chair.

"Why don't you sit down?" I said.

"Did you grade our assignments yet?" she asked.

"I did."

I pulled down the stack of papers that I was planning to hand back in class, and found hers.

"Your essay was very well-written." I added, "And candid."

She hunched her shoulders, a gesture of shame or shyness. I couldn't tell which.

"Could we close the door?" She moved to close it without waiting for my approval.

"We're not really supposed to—well, I guess it's probably okay. Just for a couple of minutes."

Ife took a seat, and I skimmed over her paper again.

He's unattainable. Infallible. Hundreds of students watch, listen, drink in his every word. They are under his spell. But he is under mine. I'm his favorite. They would do anything for him, and he can only see me.

Hundreds of students.

Ife's husband, Professor Quentin Virtanen, taught a philosophy seminar that struggled to break double digits. I could only think of one person who taught hundreds of students in his massive online course.

I glanced up at Ife. She was watching me read.

But lately, he's been so very helpful to his students. His young female students. He makes time for them. He meets them in his office. Or at the coffee shop. He makes me feel stupid and petty for asking. 'This is me', he says. 'It's who I am.'

"This isn't about Quentin," I blurted. "This is about Kyle Stockhausen."

Ife stared at me. "I heard you went to see Zora."

I was behind my desk. Ife was between me and the closed office door. My heart pounded. Ife had killed Kyle Stockhausen. I knew it. I didn't know how she had done it, but it was pretty clear why.

"Ife, you don't have to worry. I won't tell Quentin. I won't tell anyone."

Her cherubic face blazed with fury, and she lunged at me. I dove under my desk. I heard bumping overhead as she climbed over the desk, and then she was grabbing at me. I didn't know what she planned to do, but she clearly wasn't devoting herself to my welfare as Florence Nightingale advised. I braced myself and kicked outward. It seemed to be working until I felt a burning in my ankle and then everything went gray...

I woke up to a metallic tang in my sinuses and on the roof of my mouth. My heart was pounding, and I was soaked with sweat.

"Sour," I said, batting at my face.

"It's oxygen." I heard Emma's voice as if from a distance. It dawned on me, very gradually, that I was lying out in the hallway, on a blanket, staring straight up at the half-gutted fluorescent ceiling fixtures. Young men wearing dark blue shirts and latex gloves hovered around me.

"She attacked me," I said. "She—ow. My leg."

"Nah, nah, nah, don't move," said one of the young men. "Eh, lucky you. Your friend was looking out for you."

"Emma?"

"Rodge Cowper rule," Emma said. "I was walking away, and I heard your door close. I knew something was off. I came back and listened. I heard you scream, and I ran and got the secretary to open the door."

"Did you call the police?" I asked.

"Already come and gone," Emma said. "When you feel better, they said come by the station so they can take a statement. But I think they got what they needed. She was holding a syringe. Talk about getting caught red handed."

"Wow, what happened to *'I will not knowingly administer any harmful drug?'* "

"What?"

"It's in 'The Florence Nightingale Pledge.'"

"Yeah, she's not getting into the nursing program," Emma said.

Turns out, Ife hadn't meant to kill Kyle "Kaila" Stockhausen. To use an unscientific term, she'd slipped him a love potion. The side effects happened to include drowsiness and loss of balance—not particularly deadly, unless you happened to be standing on a chair.

For me, Ife had chosen something less fanciful: a common, untraceable heart stimulant. Very similar to something a notorious "angel of death" nurse had used to speed her charges off this mortal coil. If Emma hadn't called for help right away—well, I'd rather not think about what might have happened.

As soon as I was up and about, I went down to the police station, made my statement, and indicated I was willing to press charges, but as the wheels of the legal system were turning, Quentin Virtanen cashed out his retirement. He and young Ife disappeared, reportedly to a country without an extradition treaty with the United States.

Last Monday, Emma and I were at the Maritime Club. We invited Pat Flanagan along this time. Emma ordered a pale ale, I got the cabernet, and Pat opted for coffee. We waited quietly for our drinks and watched the waves break on the black lava rock next to the lānai.

Pat finally broke the silence. "So what did you learn from all this?"

Emma and I looked at each other.

"Learn?" I asked.

"You must've learned something," Pat said. "You go through a horrible experience like this, there should be a lesson."

"Keep your door open when you have a student in your office," I said.

"You mean the Rodge Cowper rule?" Pat asked.

"Don't trust anyone," Emma said.

"Really?" Pat said. "That's what you got out of this? Don't trust anyone?"

"I know," I said. "Don't stand on chairs."

"Yeah, I agree," Emma said. "Don't stand on chairs. It's dangerous, and you could fall off. Next time someone tries to get me to do one of those trust falls, I'm gonna tell 'em no way."

"Me too." I took a satisfied sip of cabernet.

"I don't think you two have to worry," Pat said. "The university lawyers are never gonna allow a workshop like that on campus again."

"Well there's a silver lining," I said.

"Shoots." Emma high-fived me. "Where's the food menu? I wanna get something to eat."

FRANKIE BOW

Frankie Bow is the author of The Molly Barda Mysteries. Like her protagonist, Molly Barda, Frankie teaches at a public university. Unlike her protagonist, she is blessed with delightful students, sane colleagues, and a perfectly nice office chair. She believes if life isn't fair, at least it can be entertaining. In addition to writing murder mysteries, she publishes in scholarly journals. Her experience with academic publishing has taught her to take nothing personally.

Find me on the web at frankiebow.com.

THOROUGHLY DEAD
A HONOLULU THRILLER SHORT STORY
Kay Hadashi

The Body

Finishing a mid-afternoon run on Waikīkī Beach, Keiko was almost back to her high-rise condo. In a full sweat, all she wanted was a cold shower, a tumbler of lemonade, and to finish her romance paperback. She had time off and planned to use it properly: by being lazy.

When she turned down the short street toward the main entrance of the condo, a crowd had formed on the sidewalk directly below the corner of the building in which she lived. It couldn't have been a car accident, as there was almost no traffic, just one sedan driving away in the opposite direction. Someone in the crowd pointed up at the building where Keiko lived. She had a bad feeling about the rest of her afternoon.

Tempted to keep running, Keiko nudged her way through the crowd to the front. She stopped when she saw what the others were gawking at. A man lay on the flagstone sidewalk, arms and legs in crooked positions, one arm twisted behind his back, a leg bent unnaturally at the hip. His head was crushed. She reached to where his twisted neck was exposed and felt for a pulse anyway.

There was something strange about how the man lay as if posed for a scene in a movie. Even though he had a deep wound exposing his brain and his skull was badly deformed, strangely there was almost no blood. Keiko knew there would've been massive amounts of blood splatter if he had been alive before an injury as devastating as his. He could've been hit by a speeding car and thrown from the street to the sidewalk, or have fallen from the roof of a building. Since there was no blood, and no damaged car with a screaming driver, he was most likely a body dump.

The man looked like a character out of an old gangster movie. His white linen suit was barely rumpled, and his black silk shirt and red necktie were too neat and tidy for having been in an accident. A straw hat lay on the sidewalk nearby. Maybe weirdest of all were the old sneakers on his feet. Dark skinned, he needed a shave. To Keiko, he looked like someone that owed fifty bucks to the Miami mafia. There was nothing ordinary about him.

Which led to the question of why would someone dump a dead body in full daylight in a place as public as a busy Waikīkī street? This wasn't how things were done in Honolulu, where life was civilized. Body dumps were done in the Ala Wai Canal, only a few blocks away, and late at night. A drive-by drop off to the sidewalk didn't make any more sense than any other explanation.

"What happened to him?" she asked anybody who might answer.

A woman dressed in an *I Love Waikīkī* T-shirt pointed toward the upper floors of a condominium. "He was pushed from up there!"

Keiko looked up at the building in which she lived. Her bad feeling about the rest of the day returned.

"He fell," a man said. On the opposite side of the crowd, he was wearing an Izod pullover, khaki shorts, and a sunburnt forehead, just back from a round of golf.

"He totally was pushed," the woman said again. "I saw it, the whole thing."

"I think he was thrown," said a new contestant in the witness game. "Look how far his body is away from the building. You can't get that kind of distance just by falling. I know, because I was a high-diver in school."

"He fell from the roof?" Keiko asked. She was already tired of the bickering strangers.

The woman who loved Waikīkī counted building floors by jabbing her finger in the air. "Nineteenth floor."

"Twentieth," the man said.

"Look," the woman said, starting over again. She counted aloud jabbing her finger in the air. "Nineteenth. He came flying off that corner balcony, the one with the potted plant. See it?"

Keiko looked up to where everybody else looked and didn't like what she saw. A bad case of indigestion was starting. The only balcony with a potted plant was her own, the one she shared with a roommate who just happened to be out of town.

She turned away from the dead man as a new argument started. The crowd was growing thicker with neighborhood residents coming out to see what the commotion was all about and Keiko had a hard time pushing her way out again. As soon as she was a few steps away, she got her cell phone and dialed a number she knew by heart.

"Davison, we have a problem," she told the man. Bill Davison was, in fact, the leaseholder of the condo unit. He was also a federal agent, the head of the Honolulu office of Homeland Security. Keiko and her roommate worked as contract assets for Davison, doing "jobs" for him that couldn't be on the books and needed a certain amount of discretion. A lot of discretion, actually. Part of their pay was free rent in the condo. It wasn't luxurious, but with two bedrooms, two baths, and a wrap-around corner lānai, it was good enough for the two of them.

"What is it?" he asked, in his usual hurried way. "A little busy right now."

"Yeah, well, it's a little busy here at the condo right now also." She cupped her hand around the phone to speak privately. "Some guy just jumped, or at least fell from our lānai."

"Who is it?"

"I have no idea. Never seen him before, at least that I can tell. Arms and legs in every direction. Head sort of flat. Not much of a shape, really. Just sort of pretzeled. The odd thing is that there's no blood."

"Thanks for the details. The police aren't there?"

"Not even sirens yet."

"And he definitely fell from your lānai?" he asked.

"Visual confirmation by witnesses. Right now they're arguing over whether or not we can have potted plants on the lānais."

"Okay, here's what I want you to do. Go back to the body and act officious. Tell everyone you're from a police stakeout, and just make up whatever story you can think of. Go through his pockets for ID, anything that he might have on him. Don't hang up though. Just keep telling me what you're doing. Most important: ignore what the others are saying to you."

Keiko kept him on the line as she pushed her way through the crowd again, the group dividing to let her through on the mention of police. She noticed a couple of them skulk off, and she tried getting pictures on her phone of them as they left.

"What's he look like?" Davison asked.

"Dark skinned, but not Hawaiian or Filipino. Maybe Mediterranean or Middle Eastern? He used a lot of that oily stuff in his hair. What's it called? Afro Sheen for white guys."

"Vitalis?"

"I guess. He's wearing a clean white linen suit, unlined, a black shirt and a red satin tie. Like he's some sort of model for that old *Miami Vice* TV show."

Someone tossed something at Keiko. "Hey lady, here's his hat. It flew off him on the way down."

"And a straw Panama hat, with a matching red satin band around it."

"No shoes?" Davison asked impatiently.

"No socks anyway. He's wearing those old-fashioned high-top sneakers you guys used to wear a long time ago, the white kind, but his are a nasty gray color and holes in the tops where his toenails stuck through."

"Take them off, see what might be inside."

"Do I have to?" Keiko asked, turning her nose up at the prospect.

"Just look. Sometimes guys keep their money or ID cards in their shoes to make it hard to steal them."

"Nice." Using only her fingertips, Keiko took off his shoes, tossing them aside. "Nothing but toenails."

"Needed a pedicure?"

"More like pruning shears."

"Anything in his pockets?" he asked.

She reached into a pocket and found something small and soft. "Cigarette butts."

"Smoked or fresh?"

"Smoked down to the filter, but they can't be his because these have traces of lipstick on them. They look like what Megumi sometimes leaves after she's done smoking."

"She wears lipstick?"

"Check your collars, Davison. But the weird thing is he has something else of Megumi's in his hand, like he stole it before he jumped, or whatever."

"What is it?" he asked.

"Nothing special. Certainly not worth any money. But it was like a good luck charm to her."

"What is it?"

"A little jade frog."

"A frog?"

"Just like the one she has tattooed on her thigh," Keiko said with a sharp tone. "Surely you've noticed it."

She heard a siren coming then, still several blocks off from the sounds of it.

"The cops are on their way." She hurried her pace. "Nothing else in his pants pockets, but he had a wallet in his jacket." She flipped it open. "No ID or credit cards. All he had was twenty-nine dollars in cash, a twenty, a five, and four ones. What do you want me to do with him?"

A second siren joined the first, closer now.

"Return the wallet and put his shoes back on. Try to get his thumbprint on something, and a picture of his face. No tattoos?"

"Not that I ever saw," Keiko said, snapping a full-face and profile of the dead man on the sidewalk. Two police cars turned the corner onto her street, turned off their sirens but left the flashing lights on. "HPD is here."

"Okay, blend in with the crowd and try to get pics of the cops and their license plates. Whatever you do, don't hang around or volunteer any information."

"But..."

"Don't get involved, Keiko. I mean it!"

Keiko backed out of the crowd, telling witnesses to remain and give statements, snapping pictures of the approaching cops with her phone camera. Once she was at the back of the crowd, she got a few pictures of the general scene and the people in the crowd. Satisfied there was nothing more she could do, she hurried away, ducking into a convenience store.

"Okay, I'm gone," she told Davison when she called him back. "Now what?"

"Where are you now?" he asked.

"In the convenience store across the street getting something to drink. Eventually I need to go home."

"Not for a while. Once the local cops find out he was in your condo unit, they'll seal the place up tight to investigate."

"Where am I staying then?" she asked. "And don't tell me at your place."

"I have space..."

"Forget it. You never call me anymore. You haven't taken me out in like three full moons!"

"There's a full moon coming up this weekend, if star-gazing is what you want," he said.

"Not what I meant, and you know it. Where am I sleeping tonight?"

"There's a budget hotel next to your building, the Sundowner Hotel, something like that. Check in for a couple of nights until I can get something sorted out for you."

"There's a police car in front of that place almost every night, Davison. I don't like the looks of the ladies that hang around in the lobby. Anyway, I'm sweaty from a long run and I'm not dressed for checking into a hotel."

"If you're sweaty, you'll fit right in at the Sundowner. Anyway, it won't be for long. Get a room that overlooks the condo building so you can keep an eye on what's going on, how many squad cars come and go, how often detectives visit. Maybe even get a few pics of them so I know who to lean on later."

"And I'm supposed to pay for it out of my pocket?" she asked, leaving the convenience store with a bottle of water. "You still haven't paid Megumi and me for the last job we did for you."

"Just pay. Keep your receipts. Get a decent room with a good lock and remember to use it at night. You're trained to deal with anything that comes your way, Keiko."

The call ended abruptly, Davison's usual way of dealing with a problem.

The Stakeout

After paying for two nights, the first thing Keiko did was strip the bed to check for bedbugs and stains. Satisfied the bed was at least sanitary, she went to the lānai. Leaning against the railing, she looked down at the scene that had developed on the sidewalk. An ambulance team was wrapping up the dead man's body in a zippered body bag. A police department crime scene technician was measuring distances from the sidewalk to the building, while another technician took photographs of the general area, even of the crowd of vacationers that was still forming. Several police officers were interviewing highly animated witnesses, pointing at the upper levels of the building, waving their arms through the air, mimicking the man's flight path. Another cop arrived, someone Keiko recognized as a Honolulu Police Department detective. Being cautious, she stepped back into a shadow where she couldn't be seen.

"Detective Dan Hata. You would have to be a part of this investigation," she muttered with a sigh. "It was only a matter of time before our paths crossed again. Ironically, it might end up being in a cheap Waikīkī hotel room."

Keiko thought of everything of hers in the condo unit, if any of it could lead the detective to her. It had been ages since they had seen each other, during which she had been given a new name and identity, courtesy of Homeland Security and a federal witness protection program. During that time, twenty-six year old Keiko had been trained to work undercover jobs as an asset for Bill Davison. In fact, it was her roommate Megumi that had trained her, ex-special operations and military intelligence. On the day she got her new identity, there had been a changeover of sorts, from a weekly tryst with Dan Hata in her tiny central Honolulu dive, to sharing a Waikīkī condo with Megumi. As far as she knew, neither of them had ever met. Thinking of the few things she'd been able to keep from her old life, none of it could point directly to her.

"Except Dad's war medals," she said to herself. "If he finds those, and my brother's picture, he might make the connection."

Her father had passed a few years before, and it had been through the help of both Dan Hata and Bill Davison that she'd been able to find a gravesite for his ashes in the national veteran's cemetery in Honolulu. That was the last time she'd seen Hata, the day of the funeral. She wasn't sure if she missed him or not.

Keiko watched as he went inside the building, likely headed up to the nineteenth floor, where she lived. Other cops would already be inside, and she thought of the condition in which she'd left it that morning, and if the dead man had ransacked the place.

She dug her hand into her pocket for the small jade frog. "Why in the world did he take this? It couldn't have cost more than a few bucks, and we both have jewelry worth more than that. It certainly isn't an antique, and all I ever saw Megumi do with it was to give it a rub."

She felt the slick surface of the frog with her fingertip.

"One thing is for sure, this didn't bring him any good luck." She put the green jade frog back in her pocket. "Which makes me wonder who the heck it was that pushed him off the lānai," she said.

The only other items in her pocket were her driver's license and debit card, and her cell phone. Carefully setting aside the license with the dead man's thumbprint she'd collected, she called Davison again.

"Want me to bring in this thumbprint and the pics I got of him?" she asked.

"Email the pics and I'll have a tech come by to get the print. I want you to stay put and watch the scene at the condo."

"You won't see much in the pictures. He must've landed directly on his head and shoulder. Pretty deformed."

"A computer program we have might be able to reconstruct his face digitally."

"Good luck with that. Most of the left side of his face was on the right side of his head." She finished her bottle of water from the minibar. "There's a problem with the police investigation though."

"Why? Did they see you?"

"No, worse than that. Dan Hata is the investigator. I just saw him go into my building. He's probably up in the unit by now."

"Anything incriminating sitting around?" he asked. For the first time his tone actually sounded concerned.

"Bras and undies drying on a line in the bathroom."

"Those aren't incriminating."

"They are if you're built like me. Otherwise, nothing personal that I can remember. Megumi runs a tight ship that way."

"But she's not there right now, just you. Is there anything in the unit with your old name on it?"

"Nothing. Not even pictures of either one of us. And if I remember correctly, there shouldn't even be anything with my new name on it. I'm sure Megumi took her wallet and IDs with her."

"Can't count on it though. The best we can hope for is that the police don't dig too deep into the lives of the people who live there. Once they find out the federal government owns the place, they'll get even more curious. That's when the FBI gets involved. Later, you'll have to get in unobserved, and if you do, check and make sure anything that could identify either one of you is removed."

"So what if the Bureau gets involved? Make a pre-emptive strike and put Cyntha Robbins on the case. She's still on loan from the FBI to your office, right?"

"Yes, but she's on assignment and unavailable."

Keiko flipped on the television, looking for the local news station to see if anything was being reported yet. "What if you dropped in on Hata, just to let him know who owns the unit and not to get too snoopy? Tell him you had an op going in that unit and you need to finish the investigation."

"I was thinking of doing exactly that. Can you tell if he's come back out?"

"Not that I've noticed, but he could've gone out another exit I can't see from here." She flipped from one channel to another, looking for news of the dead man. So far, it didn't look like any news vans had shown up yet, odd for Waikīkī. "If I can't be involved, what am I supposed to do while the investigation goes on?"

"Sit tight. One of my techs is on his way to your hotel room for that print. Once I know the guy's identity, I'll better know how to proceed. But for the time being, I'll let the police manage it as a simple break-in and death with suspicious circumstances. If they begin to figure out anything else, I'll deal with it."

An hour of watching daytime TV passed before the tech got to Keiko's hotel room. He retrieved the thumbprint from her driver's license and scanned it into the computerized system.

"How long does it take?" she asked the technician.

"Anywhere from five to twenty minutes."

While they waited, Keiko showed him the pictures of the dead man she had taken.

"No, we won't be able to do anything with those, I'm afraid," the technician said after uploading them to his digital work pad. An icon came up on his screen indicating the print search was complete. "Seven-point match."

"Is that good?" she asked.

"As good as we can get for a transfer of only one digit."

"And?"

"Martin Ash, also known as Metro Marty."

Keiko looked over his shoulder at the frontal and profile pictures of his face on the screen. All she could tell was similar to the dead man was the dark skin and black hair. "Metro Marty? Was that some sort of known criminal alias for him?"

"No, that's how he was known downtown in the office. Metro Marty."

"So, he was being investigated by Homeland?"

"No, at least not that I'm aware of. He was one of our assets, just like you. He's been working for the Honolulu office since it first opened," the tech said, shutting down his device and packing up to leave. "Too bad, too. He was a good one."

"Wait. You mean he was an asset that worked for Davison?"

"For anyone in the office who needed a job done." The tech looked nervous now, that maybe he'd let on too much information, and edged toward the door. "Hey, I got to get going."

Keiko was beside herself and paced a lap in the room. Or more like stomped. The dead man she'd seen on the sidewalk, the one she got the thumbprint from, the one who had Megumi's lucky charm, was an asset for Homeland Security, someone who worked covert odd jobs for under the table pay. Intelligence gathering, top security arrangements, jobs that were parts of larger federal operations. Just like Keiko and Megumi, Metro Marty got paid for doing work that he could never tell anyone else about. Somehow, someone had a score to settle with him, and in the process, Keiko got involved.

Punching at her phone with a fingertip, she dialed Davison's number.

"Who the heck was Metro Marty, and why was he in my home?" she demanded as soon as Davison answered.

"First of all, that unit doesn't belong to you. You and Megumi are only using it, rent-free I might add. Second, how do you know Metro Marty?"

"So, he really was one of your assets?"

"He's an office asset. What was he doing in your condo?" Davison asked.

"That's what I'd like to know! It was his thumbprint that I collected off the dead man's body."

"Says who?"

"Said that technician that was here a few minutes ago. He took it off my license and entered it into his work pad. A few minutes later, the results said it belonged to Martin Ash, AKA Metro Marty. He told me who Marty worked for and what he did."

"Impossible, for a number of reasons. Marty's prints are not in the system. He's just like you. He doesn't exist, not in any system anywhere. Everything about him was expunged from all legal and corporate records years ago. Another reason I know it wasn't Marty is that he's here in the office. I just saw him ten minutes ago. Hungover, but present in body anyway."

"But that tech's work pad came up with his ID."

"Keiko, the tech I sent has been stuck in downtown traffic. By the time he got through, he couldn't park anywhere near your hotel because of the police presence. He just called a few minutes ago, asking me to let you know he was running late. I was just about to call when you called me first."

"But who was the guy that was here?" Keiko asked.

"You tell me. Sounds like his work pad had been loaded with that information and all he had to do was hit enter and it spit it out for you to see. Sounds like you got conned."

"I don't think so."

"Did you check his picture ID? Did it look genuine? Did he leave a business card with you at the end?" Davison asked.

"He had a Homeland Security Data Technician ID badge clipped to his lapel." She shrugged as if he could see her. "He acted like he knew what he was doing. He got here a short while after you told me to expect someone. What was I supposed to think?"

"Did he scan the print, or dust and tape it?"

"Dust and tape, which he took with him. At least I still have the pics of the dead man's face and head, along with those of the crowd and the cops." There was a knock at her door. When she answered, there was a technician standing there with boxes of gear, not unlike the first one she'd met an hour before. He was sweating profusely. "Do you know a Samuel Silberstein?"

"Yes, he's the tech I sent."

"What's he look like?"

"Freckles. Not your type."

She waved the tech in and gave him her driver's license, along with a quick explanation of what had happened, asking him to do his best at getting any remnant of a print from it. "Well, who sent that other tech, and why was he so interested in telling me it was Martin Ash's thumbprint?"

"Again, you tell me. Whoever it was, shoved the dead man off your lānai, that's who."

"Okay, I'm really confused," Keiko said. "Why was someone pushed off my lānai, and who went to the trouble of trying to mislead us with an incorrect identification, trying to tell us the dead guy was another asset in the department?"

"I don't know, but I want you looking into it."

"Me?" she asked. "You've been telling me to leave it alone. Now you want me involved?"

"As much as possible. Is there still a crowd? Any cops still there?"

"Yeah, not as many. Most of them seemed to wander off once the body was taken away."

"By an actual county coroner van?" he asked.

"No, in an ambulance."

Davison let loose with a string of profanities, not so uncommon when he'd been out-smarted by someone. "Okay, that means they got the guy. He's probably been dumped in a shallow grave by now. Did you get pics of the squad cars that arrived?"

"Yes, the first three anyway, along with the cops that got out of them."

"They all looked legit?"

"The usual cars, the usual lights, the usual uniforms on them, yeah."

The technician handed the driver's license back to her, shaking his head. Once again, she copied the images of the dead man, police cars, and the crowd from her phone memory into his laptop. Once that was done, he gave her a business card with a case number written on it and left, letting Keiko go back to her call with Davison.

"And you said you saw Dan Hata there at the scene, right? Any doubt it was him?" Davison asked.

"No doubt at all. Why?"

"At least that lends some legitimacy to the investigation. There was at least some presence of authentic police activity there. Unfortunately, it had to be him."

Keiko went back to the balcony and looked down. All of the crowd had dispersed and most of the police were gone. Only one squad car remained and a dark sedan which looked suspiciously like the one Dan Hata used to drive. "It looks like Hata is still at the condo. What do you want me to do?"

"Whatever you do, do not make contact with him or any other officer. Once you think everyone is gone, I want you to go over and get inside your unit. The police will have tossed the place in their own investigation, but try and determine if anything was taken."

"You mean other than Megumi's frog?"

"Exactly. What's the story on that thing anyway?"

"She never told you? You've been in her bedroom often enough, Davison."

"Been in yours more recently. But no, she never gave me a guided tour of her knick knacks."

"Maybe if you would've asked for a tour, she'd still be inviting you back for more," Keiko snapped.

"Can you please tell me the significance of the frog?"

"The very basics are that the word for frog in Japanese— *kaeru*—is the same for the verb 'to return'."

"What's that supposed to mean?" he asked.

"You know how frogs return in the spring after sleeping in the mud and ice all winter? It's almost as if they magically return from suspended animation, right? When the frogs return, they bring with them the rains of spring, marking the end of winter. Well, with those rains come fertility of the land, and eventually, prosperity for people. Lots of frogs in the spring mean a good harvest and lots of prosperity in the fall. Plus, certain magical abilities have been attributed to the frog over the centuries, and in this day and age, the frog is thought to be a good luck charm, especially for children. Think of all the transformations that kids and teenagers go through. Just like the frog, right? So, they've come to represent transition, change, renewal, and their dreams for the future. Having a frog in your life means dreams can come true."

"Frogs are old time legends then?" he asked. "It's not just more Waikīkī kitsch?"

"Not kitschy at all. Stories and legends of frogs are something powerful enough to survive in the Twenty-First Century. Having the image of a frog like Megumi's is much like having a Saint Christopher's medal or a four-leaf clover. Try taking something like that away from someone that has had it for a long time. They've put a lot of belief in that object over the years, right? Well, for many Japanese, all Asians in fact, there are tons of things like that. The figures from the Chinese zodiac, dragons and phoenixes, certain written characters, jewelry that's been carved from jade. Surely you've noticed her phoenix tattoo?"

There was a short pause before he finally replied. "Yes, rising out of the volcano. Hard to miss."

"I should say so, considering its location. Getting back to Megumi's other charms, jade is especially important to the Chinese, with special health and healing properties. Wearing jade around the wrist or as a pendant has protective characteristics. Even the colors of jade have different meanings. Combine that with the image of the frog, and you have a powerful amulet to a Japanese. Who knows, maybe it was a gift from someone special, making it a prized possession?"

"Okay, some unknown guy who's dressed weird gets into your unit, steals Megumi's frog amulet, and jumps off the balcony. Does that mean anything to you at all?" he asked.

"Just that Waikīkī is getting nuttier and nuttier all the time."

The Disguise

It felt good for Keiko to share a laugh with Davison, something he rarely did. Sharing her bed with him would be even better, something that was happening far too infrequently of late. But a new job had fallen into her lap, something that directly involved her home, so it would be a while yet before the two of them could hook up. That was going to be one of the best parts of her roommate being away for three weeks, that she would have the unit to herself. It wasn't the privacy so much as having the opportunity for an overnight guest. Now that opportunity was fleeting.

"While I play chess with assets and agents, I want you to focus on the unit," he told her. "As soon as the local cops are gone, get in over there, get some pics, and copy everything from your computer memory into a thumb drive. The most important thing is to delete everything that might even remotely be associated with Homeland Security. They'll have already collected prints and whatever else they think is worth carrying away, but they'll be back in the morning once they come up with nothing from the fingerprints they've collected. It's critical that they don't identify the place with Homeland Security or any part of the federal government."

"Or we have to start all over with a new place to live?" she asked.

"Exactly, along with new identities. And for you and Megumi, that might mean Arizona or Minnesota, and not necessarily together."

"I see. Where does Homeland have hot agents? Ones with long lunch breaks?"

"TSA at the airport. By lunch time tomorrow, I want to know who that guy was and why he was so interested in that frog," he said. "And why he had a pocket full of cigarette butts."

"And whether he was pushed or jumped," Keiko added.

"Once we learn who he was and his interest in that frog, we'll know the rest of the story."

Looking down from the lānai again, she saw only the dark sedan parked in the loading zone at the curb. It had to be Hata's car. There was nothing she could do until he was gone, except get a change of clothes, something cleaner than her jogging outfit. That required only a quick trip to the convenience store across the street.

A T-shirt for three dollars was a steal. Along with a pair of boy's board shorts, a pair of girlish rubber slippers, and a bottle of green tea, it was going to cost almost nothing. Grabbing a straw fedora completed her disguise as a Japanese tourist.

Just as she was turning for the door, a man came in and stopped at the checkout counter. Fine time for Detective Dan Hata to show up. Keiko would have to walk right past him to leave.

It took several sly moves in hurried succession for her to hide in plain sight. Turning away, she raised her hand to scratch her nose and got the fedora on her head. Trying on a pair of sunglasses from a rack covered even more of her face. With her back turned toward him, she hoped Hata wouldn't recognize her.

It had been over a year since he'd last seen her, and for all he might've known, she no longer even lived in Hawai'i. She'd transformed her body through exercise, putting on ten pounds of muscle and taking off five pounds of fat during that time, and her hairstyle was entirely different. It would take a close look at her face for him to recognize her. That's what she told herself anyway, while she waited for him to go to the back of the store. He didn't, though.

"Howzit," the clerk said to Hata. Only a step or two away, Keiko was close enough to eavesdrop. Being that close, she was able to smell Dan's masculine scent, something she still missed late at night while unable to sleep.

"What was going on down the street earlier?" the detective asked. "Looked like a pretty big deal."

"Yeah, some dude took a flyin' leap off the roof. Totally landed on someone that was walking on the sidewalk. Royal mess. Blood everywhere."

Keiko couldn't believe what she was hearing. Dan was obviously out canvassing the neighborhood for eyewitnesses, and somehow she had got caught up in it. As far as she could remember, the clerk wasn't even at the scene. More important than that, however, was getting out of the store anonymously. Making contact with Dan so close to a crime scene would be disastrous. Two seemingly unrelated things that happen together are a random coincidence. Right now, she potentially had three: her long absence, Dan spotting her at a bizarre crime scene, and a man and his curious death. Beyond coincidence, it was conspiratorial.

To look inconspicuously busy, she tried on a different pair of sunglasses. Looking in the mirror attached to the sunglass rack, she watched the two men.

The clerk leaned forward like he was going to share a secret with Dan. "The rescue squad was there and the cops were everywhere looking for parts of the guy's brains."

"And you saw it?" Dan asked.

"Heck yeah! I mean, like, I didn't see him jump, but I saw the splat on the ground."

"You say that the victim landed on top of another man?"

"Well, I guess...maybe not. But there was enough of a mess that it seemed like there were two people."

Keiko wanted to emerge from her hiding place and tell Dan the truth about what happened, that there was only one man, and hardly any blood at all. She also wanted to tell him that the coroner hadn't been the one to collect the body, but somebody else pretending to be ambulance drivers. But getting involved right then would mean destroying her current lifestyle and having to start all over again, something she'd had far too much experience at in her lifetime.

"Hey, you gonna buy those sunglasses?" the clerk asked Keiko.

Still trying to avoid making eye contact with Dan, she looked at the clerk and nodded her head. "Shitsurei—pardon?" she said, pitching her voice to a higher tone than usual.

"Are...you...going...to...buy...those...sun...glasses?"

Keiko turned back to the display rack and shoved on a new pair, now trying to hide cheeks flushed red. In the tiny display mirror, she saw Dan looking her over. "Still looking..."

Dan cleared his voice. "Miss, did you see what happened earlier?"

She tried to ignore him, but sensed he was waiting for an answer. "Ah! Yes, sorry. Not speak English so good."

He cleared his throat again before attempting his same question in Japanese. "Nani ga okatta...mimashita ka?"

His accent was terrible and his grammar worse, even for a Hawaiian-born Japanese American, and Keiko had a hard time not laughing. "Sorry! Just visiting. I no have friends in Hawai'i."

She tilted the fedora even lower on her face, hoping he'd buy the story. After a moment, he seemed to, or at least gave up on his interrogation. Once Dan was back in the food section, she took one last peek over her shoulder.

"You want to buy those sun glasses?" the clerk asked her again.

She put them back on the rack. "No, thanks."

With her bag of purchases in one hand, she darted for the door and never looked back. In her hotel room, she dressed in the brightly colored new shirts and shorts, different colors than what she usually wore. She found the right position for the fedora on her head. With the cheerful daisy-topped rubber slippers, she was in her disguise, dressed entirely different than normal, the real value of any disguise. There was no doorman or front desk at the condo, but she'd still need to avoid being recognized as one of the women that lived on the nineteenth floor. The last thing she needed was trying to answer questions about what had happened in her unit that day.

"Okay, Keiko, think. Who wears a suit of clothes like that? Even going out in the evening, no one dresses like that in Hawai'i. In Miami or Central America maybe, but not here," she muttered as she hurried to the condo next door to the hotel. The lobby was crowded with residents chatting about what had happened. Eavesdropping for a moment, she could tell there were as many stories as people telling them. She got to the elevator, which thankfully opened right away.

"And who wears those dumb high-tops anymore?" She hit the button for the seventeenth floor, planning to walk up the last two floors, just in case anyone was paying attention. "And what was with those toe nails? Is that why he wasn't wearing socks?"

Off the elevator, she dashed up the stairs to her unit. There were multiple bands of yellow crime scene tape across the door, a warning sign taped to the middle of the door, indicating there was an active investigation, and to call HPD detectives for further information. She recognized Dan's old cell number as one of the contacts.

She knew there were closed circuit security cameras in the hallway, so she wasted no time in letting herself in, ducking through strips of tape. Once she was inside, she felt it was prudent to move quickly and silently. That was going to be difficult because of the mess.

Every pot and pan from the kitchen had been removed from their storage spots, the drawers and cabinets emptied onto the floor. The little food they kept in the refrigerator had been taken out, lids removed from jars, the bottle of milk poured down the drain, the container left in the sink. Jars of spices had been dumped onto the counter. Fresh coffee grounds had been spilt. The kitchen had been ransacked as though somebody was looking for something small.

Taking snapshots of the mess, she left it behind and went to the bedrooms. There was as much of a mess in the two bedrooms as in the kitchen. Dresser drawers had been hastily emptied, dresses tossed out of the closets, linens pulled from the beds, even the mattresses turned on end. She went to the bottom drawer of her dresser and looked for her father's framed set of military medals. It was still there, almost as if it had been untouched.

In her roommate's room, the few little knickknacks that she had on the dresser with the frog charm had been tossed about, mostly on the floor. She didn't see a frog anywhere, so the one in the dead man's hand must've been Megumi's.

'She's going to be pissed,' thought Keiko. 'She really doesn't like her stuff being touched.'

She went to the bathroom and found another mess. Cosmetics had been opened, hand soap dumped into the sink, which had been filled with water for some reason. Body wash and shampoo bottles were dumped in the shower. Even the cleaning supplies had been tossed and strewn everywhere.

The couch cushions had been thrown aside in the living room, the couches themselves moved from their proper positions. The newspaper Keiko had been reading earlier that morning was taken apart, pages separated and tossed around. It was as if whoever had searched the unit was pissed, only wanting to trash the place, rather than actually searching for something. Strangely, nothing was broken; just a mess that needed to be cleaned up. Out on the lānai, she found Megumi's ashtray up-ended like everything else, but no cigarette butts.

'So, that's where he got the ones in his pockets,' she thought.

Knowing there was nothing on the computer worth saving, she turned it on and deleted all files and folders, along with her recent browsing history. Even though it was password-protected, it would only slow down a crafty technician. It needed to be wiped clean.

Taking pictures of the mess as she went back through the unit, she slipped back out of the door and walked quickly to the stairwell, making a get-away from her own home.

The Investigation

Ignoring orders to call Davison back as soon as she was done inside her condo, Keiko caught the city bus for the nearby mall. There she'd be able to ask a few questions of store clerks. Never married, she knew little about men's grooming products, or even where men shopped for clothes. The first thing she wanted to know about was the oil she found in the man's hair. With that in mind, she went to the personal grooming section at a large drug and variety store.

Sniffing the contents of jars and bottles, she worked her way from one end of men's hair grooming supplies to the other. She found the cheapest products on the bottom shelf. Taking the cap off a bottle of clear golden oil, she gave it a sniff.

"Looking for something for your boyfriend?" a clerk asked her. Well-groomed, he stood over her, smiling.

"Not for my boyfriend," she said, recapping the bottle. She grabbed a can of pomade and wrestled the lid off. "I'm looking for something with a peculiar smell to it, and I think it's this stuff."

"Yeah, that's the generic brand."

"Who uses this kind of stuff?" she asked.

"Nobody, really. That's why it's on the bottom shelf. There's probably dust on each of those cans, they've been sitting around for so long."

"What do guys use it for?"

"Keeps hair in place, no matter what. Sort of like that gel women use. He could put that stuff in his hair and go out in a typhoon. His clothes might get ripped to shreds, but his hair would look nice."

Keeping the can in her hand, she stood, looking him over again. "You look like you know a thing or two about men's fashion. You know those old-fashioned high-top basketball shoes?"

He wrinkled his nose at the question.

"Who wears those things these days?" she asked.

"Ten or fifteen years ago, they were popular with rappers, but in odd colors. Neon, green, pink, purple. Otherwise, you can find them at the discount shoes stores for about ten bucks."

"But guys wore socks with them, right?"

"I would hope so. But nobody has worn high-tops since Wally Cleaver."

"Who?"

"You know, that old 'Leave it to Beaver' TV show?"

"Whatever." She was curiously attracted to the guy with a mainland accent. She decided to pour on the charm, just in case he was interested in helping her with more than customer relations. "Say, you look involved, as though you have a social life. Are there any role-playing groups in town? You know, the kind where people dress up in costumes?"

"Like Halloween?"

"More like characters in a mystery novel? I know this guy who wears that old kind of linen suit, and a black shirt and satin necktie. He even wears the Panama hat that would go with it."

"Oh, like Miami Vice?"

"That's right."

"Is the pomade for him?"

"Should be. Not for me anyway."

"And he wears high-tops and a Panama hat with his linen suit?"

"Maybe," she said, wondering where he was leading.

"Find a different boyfriend," he said walking off.

With her phone, she snapped a picture of the pomade before setting it back on the shelf. There were several department stores at the mall she could search for that style of suit, her next project.

"Okay, so nobody uses that brand of hair gunk, and nobody wears high-tops, not even rappers."

Keiko shopped her way through the men's departments of five different department stores at the mall. Not a single one had linen suits in the style of the dead man.

"Maybe you can find something like that at a thrift store?" the last clerk offered.

"Yeah, or maybe it's not so important now." Once again, she apprised the man of his taste and style, and figured him to be fashionable. "Let me ask you a personal question, if you don't mind?"

"Sure," he said, tidying suit jackets on hangers.

"If you'd just broken up with your girlfriend..."

"You mean my boyfriend?" he asked.

"Yeah, sorry, I guess so. But if you'd just broken up with him, would you go back and try and steal some little memento of his?"

"Like a keepsake?"

"Yeah. What would it be?"

He shifted his weight a bit, scanning the area for other customers. "Oh, maybe some little thing that reminded me of the better times, something I gave him maybe. Why? Did somebody take something from you?"

"From my roommate. Someone broke in and took a little good luck charm of hers. I was trying to figure out who might've taken it, and why he took that one little thing and not jewelry or something more valuable."

"Well, it was valuable to him. Maybe he bought it for her originally."

He pardoned himself to help another customer. Keiko felt as though she'd learned everything she could about linen suits and men's grooming products. Getting something to drink in the food court, she noticed it was now dark outside.

"Okay, nobody wears those suits, and they're almost impossible to find, even if someone wanted one. Nobody wears high-tops. Everybody around here wears fedoras, not Panama hats. And nobody lets their toe nails get like his, except for people that can't reach their toes."

She sipped at her drink for a moment, thinking about where her clues were leading her.

"That would be comatose people, paralyzed people, people that can't bend down into that position. Or people who just don't care. But they'd still have to be self-care, right? If someone else was doing their care, their toenails would get clipped along with their fingernails." She wrinkled her nose at the thought of something. "And all that stuff in his hair. Who uses that much gunk?"

Keiko knew that to answer those questions, she'd have to find the dead man. It was the only way. But his body had been removed by imposters, not by the real coroner. Even Davison had verified the fact that he'd never arrived at the county morgue. She had watched from her hotel lānai as the body was loaded into the back of an ambulance, the lights flashing as it drove off.

"Why put the lights on if he was already dead?"

She took another sip, replaying the scene in her mind.

"They turned toward the McCully Street bridge, which means they could've been going to the freeway, or to downtown to dump the body." Keiko tried thinking of the places bodies were normally found: one place was in the mountains that divided the island into two halves. Pig hunters often found skeletal remains in dark ravines. Another place was the old irrigation ditches in the pineapple fields during rainstorms, usually organized crime hits. But there was one other place that Keiko was intimately familiar with, most commonly used for body dumps: the Ala Wai Canal, only two blocks from her condo building, and a short walk from where she was right now.

The Confrontation

Her phone rang for probably the tenth time that hour. She finally gave in and answered Bill Davison's call.

"Still investigating, Davison."

"Find anything useful yet?"

"I went to the condo. Somebody had really trashed the place. Clothes and kitchen stuff everywhere. As far as I could tell, nothing was missing."

"Except Megumi's frog. What else?" he asked.

"Then I came here to the mall to check and see how easy it is to buy the clothes he was wearing."

"Good idea."

"I found the brand of that pomade stuff he had in his hair. Cheap. Also, nobody sells those suits, at least not at the standard mall department stores. And it seems the only place to find his kind of sneakers is at the discount store."

"What have you figured out about the frog?" he asked.

"I asked one guy, and he said people steal little mementoes sometimes from their lovers right after they break up. But if that were true in this case, it would be a stretch of the imagination, because there's no way I see Megumi making time with the dead man. Not with any guy that dresses like him and had toenails like his. No way that guy and Megumi were doing the dirty thing."

"What's your conclusion then?"

"I don't have one, not yet anyway. We need to find the body, or at least get an ID from the dead man to make any progress. Was that real technician able to pull a print from my driver's license?" she asked.

"Only a few swirls. Nothing helpful at all."

"Which means we need to wait until the body turns up and ID'd by the coroner."

"Which might never happen," he said.

"You know, with the way that ambulance left in a hurry from the crime scene, something seemed too suspicious about it. But I didn't get a pic of that, just the police cars that came to the scene. If I had, we could've tracked that down and talked to the guys assigned to it today."

"Too bad we can't."

"I have one other place to go this evening before I call it quits for the night," she told him.

"Where?"

"One place popular as a body dumping ground is the canal, the area over near the golf course. It's secluded, unlit, and mostly ignored. I want to see if I can find anything."

"Yes, you know that area quite well, don't you?" he said. "What do you expect to find?"

Keiko didn't like the idea of going alone, especially at night, after the experiences she'd had a couple of years before. She knew firsthand how often bodies were disposed of in that canal.

"I don't know. His bloated body floating on the surface of the water might be too much to ask for. But maybe I can find fresh tire tracks in mud, or just some article of clothing of his."

"You think you'd get that lucky?" Davison asked.

"I have to try anyway, or I won't sleep. All I know is that the groundskeepers pick up the litter and empty the trash cans at that park first thing in the morning. I need to look before then."

Most of the people were gone from the food court now, and custodians were sweeping. She noticed on her phone that the hour had come for stores to close.

"Davison, I got to go. I'll call you in a while."

She hurried away, taking the mall exit closest to the canal. On one side of the Ala Wai Canal were the high-rises and busy streets of Waikīkī; on the other side were park land, ball fields, rowing clubs, a giant golf course, and homeless encampments. She stopped at a small convenience store for one thing, a flashlight. Checking that it worked, Keiko set off for the grassy fields at the far end of the canal, a place near the golf course. In a hurry, it took only half an hour to get there.

The first place she went to was the edge of the slow-moving canal. Almost stationary where a smaller stream connected, there was a rock almost hidden by the deep, unmown grass. She thought for a second about the time two years before when she placed that rock there herself, a small memorial to a lost friend. It was the first time she'd been back since. Saying a quick and silent prayer, she moved on.

Moving through the dark of late evening, she could hear the murmurs of homeless people tucked away in shadowy corners, under simple tents of picnic tables and tarps, and in brushy nests inside brambles. It was far from intelligent to snoop in an area like that alone, especially after dark. Right then, she stood out like a beacon of stupidity wearing her brightly colored disguise in a place where tourists never went.

Getting the flashlight out, she shone the beam along the edge of the water. There was nothing. No tire marks, no footprints, no loose articles of clothing. Even the deep grass wasn't bent over as if someone had walked along there recently.

Keiko aimed the beam out into the murky canal. Once again, nothing. It would have to be a brightly colored piece of clothing, like the dead man's white linen suit, to show up in the cloudy water, even at a few inches deep. For a hundred feet in either direction, from where the brambles started to the edge of the manicured ball field lawns, there was nothing out of the ordinary in the water.

"Hey there, little lady," said a voice right behind her. She was startled that someone had been able to creep up on her without hearing him. When she turned to face the voice, she got a bigger surprise when she saw two pairs of eyes looking back at her.

She shone the light in their eyes and plastered a giant grin on her face. "Hi fellas! Is this the way to Waikīkī Hotel?"

One of them took another step closer to her. "I don't think so, Sweetness."

"Wanna party?" the other asked. She shone the light in his eyes when he took a step closer. He had a peculiar, greedy look to his face, as if he were rather single-minded about something right then. He moved quick to snatch the light from her hand and tossed it off to the side.

Keiko had no patience for what they wanted and took an athletic stance, ready to fight. "Why don't the two of you wise up and walk away?"

"Why don't you just get those clothes off?" one said back, taking another step closer.

"Yeah, that ain't gonna happen."

Before either of them could react, she gave a sharp kick to one in his crotch, spun and landed a solid punch to the neck of the other. Her hat flew off from the power of her punch. Planting both feet solid on the ground, she took another punch at the man squealing like a pig and holding his crotch. Landing her fist in his eye, he was done for. The man with the bad neck was just winding up to send a haymaker in her direction. Quick and agile, she beat him to the punch, sending him sprawling with a kick to the belly.

In the matter of only a moment, Keiko had broken into a heavy sweat, and tried wiping some of it away. She had a skinned knuckle and a stubbed toe, but was in far better condition than either of the men. She took her own advice and wasted no time in beating a hasty retreat, grabbing the flashlight but leaving the hat and shoes behind.

"Okay, that was fun," she muttered, hurrying away toward a dimly illuminated parking lot. She scanned the area for anyone else that might be following her. Seeing no one, she forced her mind back to the original reason she came here. "Maybe they took his clothes off."

Keiko went to the closest trashcan and lifted the lid off. Nothing. She hurried off to another can at the far end of the lot, keeping an eye over her shoulder for the men she'd just fought with. She went to the only other trash can in the area. Shining her light inside, she reached in and hit pay dirt.

"White jacket, white pants, black shirt, red necktie," she said, pulling each garment out one at a time. "No shoes though."

There were some voices, several men talking in an elated, or at least inebriated, way. They seemed to be getting closer. Shutting off the light, she got her cell phone out and dialed Davison's number.

"Hey, found his clothes, but no sign of him. At the canal, just like I thought."

"Just laying around?" he asked.

"In a garbage can at the parking lot. I bet if you got HPD out here to dredge the canal, they'd find his body."

"Best you get out of there. Just put the clothes back in the same trash bag you found them in and bring all of it to the office. We'll take a look at it once you get here."

Keiko was glad to be leaving. With one last glance around the area, she grabbed the bag and took it with her, rotting food stink and all. Hustling back to the busier area of Waikīkī, she was able to flag down a taxi to take her to the main offices of Homeland Security. Carrying the trash bag with her, she met Davison at the main entrance. He took a quick look inside the bag.

"Just take that whole thing and toss it in the dumpster," he told her, pointing toward the side of the building.

"But we need to search it. The dead man's clothes are inside. We might be able to ID him. Or maybe even get someone's prints off of something?"

"Don't worry about it. We already know who he was."

"But..."

"Time is money, and you're wasting both, Keiko."

"You sound just like a plastic surgeon I used to work with," she told him when she got back from the dumpster. "And nobody liked him either. But who was the dead guy?"

He led her to his desk on the third floor. She rarely ever had to go in to the office; rather he came to her when they needed to meet. That was a big plus, since she didn't like visiting the office. She had been interrogated there once for several hours on end, which eventually led to life-changing events. Taking a quick glance at the soundproof interrogation room, which happened to be in use right then by two men badgering another in shackles, she sat uneasily at his desk.

"That guy had something to do with our dead guy?" she asked, nodding her head in the direction of the interrogation room.

"Him? No," said Davison. "That idiot's North Korean and was found travelling on a South Korean passport. As soon as we picked him up, he asked for asylum."

"Will he get it?" she asked.

"If we let him stay and he turns out to be a spy, it's trouble for us. If we send him back to Pyongyang, he'll get an ice pick to the eye socket. Or worse. Not your problem, though." Davison looked her up and down for a moment, which made Keiko wonder if somehow she'd picked up the stink of the trash. "And by the way, one of them is your friend Marty."

"Who was the dead guy anyway?" she asked, taking a longer look at the men, trying to guess which was Metro Marty.

He looked her up and down again. "I like the outfit."

"Yeah, this is my attract-weird-guys-at-the-park outfit. Lost my hat and slippers, though. Who was the dead man?"

"Homeless guy that got clobbered by a truck on the H-1 Freeway this morning."

"What? He fell off the lānai. I was there, Davison. I saw his head, where he landed on the sidewalk. He was probably dead before that, but he was definitely thrown or fell off my building."

"You only saw his head and shoulder, how he supposedly landed. What you didn't see were the rest of his injuries. At the morgue, we got him all cleaned up and straightened out again, and dressed up in new clothes so we could pose him. And as you know, dead men don't bleed. That's why there was no blood at the scene."

"You posed him?" Keiko asked, confused. "I don't understand."

Somebody left the interrogation room and walked up to her. When Keiko looked up, she was even more confused.

"Megumi?"

Her roommate pulled up another chair and sat. "I know, I'm supposed to be in Coronado doing some advanced training, right?"

"What's going on?" Keiko asked once again, looking back and forth between them.

"This has been a test for you," Davison said. "I needed to see if you could think on your feet while still taking orders from the office."

"Mostly, it was to see if you could use your counter-intuitive thinking, to solve by thinking outside the box, and not go off on a tangent of your own or get lost in all the dead-end clues." Megumi smiled. "You did nearly perfectly, every step of the way."

"Except for going unarmed to that park late at night," Davison said. "You've made better decisions than that."

"Yeah, stubbed my toe. Almost broke a nail, too." Keiko looked down at her bare feet and thought of the two men she had beat up. The skinned knuckles on one hand were beginning to throb. Taking a deep breath, she looked at her boss and roommate. "Okay, but what about the dead guy? You guys took a corpse up there and tossed him off? Don't you think that's over-doing training a bit?"

"That's CIA training stuff. Those dudes are a bunch of cowboys. Homeland Security is much more sophisticated than that," Davison said.

"Yeah, sophisticated," Keiko mumbled.

Megumi laughed.

"Seriously. The CIA would probably take a live guy up there and pitch him off, just so they could see if he told any secrets on the way down. Here at Homeland, we like to think we have a little decorum. Which means we didn't toss him off. While I arranged his body on the sidewalk, Megumi was upstairs. Once I gave her the high-sign, she tossed a dummy off the balcony. All I had to do was load that into the trunk of my car and drive off, picking up

Megumi around the corner. The ambulance was waiting the next block over to come back for the corpse once a crowd formed. All a part of the show."

"What show?" Keiko asked. Once again, she was confused, just as she had been all day.

"It was a rather nicely choreographed scene, put on for your benefit. At the spur of the moment, I might add. I had to get Homeland employees from all over this building to pretend to be tourists and bystanders, just to make a small crowd around the man. I almost called the Honolulu Actors Guild for extras. We put on a pretty good show, huh?" Davison asked with a smile.

"Had me fooled."

"I even stood there and watched as you ran up to the scene," Megumi said, with a satisfied look to her face. "Look at the pictures you took with your phone."

Keiko got out her phone and studied the pictures more closely. Sure enough, Megumi was standing right in the middle of the crowd in one of them, the simple disguise of a fedora on her head, her hair in a braid, smiling.

"We need to work on you stretching your field of perception during a crisis," Davison said. "Megumi will work with you on developing techniques for that."

Keiko put away her phone. "Who tossed our apartment?"

"I did," Megumi said. "Nothing got broken though, and everything has already been put back again."

Keiko felt defeated, and also embarrassed. She took the charm from her pocket and handed it back to Megumi, who immediately began to rub it with her thumb. "Okay, why the frog?"

"As a red herring," Davison said. "Just like the clothes, the hat, and cigarette butts in his pocket. I wanted to see how much that would distract you. Just like the crowd, the ambulance, and the police."

"They were all plants put there to distract me?"

"Exactly. We'll have to work on your ability to sift through clues, to separate red herrings from real evidence," Davison told her, turning to his desk. "Starting first thing in the morning."

"What about Dan Hata? He wasn't involved, was he?" Keiko said.

"He was a problem, along with a few of the responding officers. Not all the cops that showed up had been briefed on our scheme. Once real cops started to show up, we had to pull the plug on it and get that body out of there. Bad luck of the draw that Hata was assigned to investigate. Like you said earlier, I can go lean on him a little, tell him I had an op running out of that unit, and I'm sure he'll back off. Once local cops find out Homeland Security is involved, they disappear in a hurry. Anything else?" Davison asked.

"Yeah, one last question. Who was that first evidence tech that showed up at my hotel room?" Keiko asked.

Davison and Megumi looked at each other. "That's what we've been wondering," Megumi said. "All we can figure is that we have a leak, and somebody has been monitoring our activities."

Keiko laughed. "That would be a surprise."

"It looks like that's going to be your next op, to find out who the mole is in my department," Davison said.

Keiko looked over to where the North Korean was still being interrogated in the soundproof room. "Leaks and spies and moles. Looking forward to it."

KAY HADASHI

Based in Honolulu, Kay Hadashi is a lifelong avid reader and has had an extensive career as a surgical nurse. Story plots for her novels come from events at the hospital and straight out of the news media. She knows that the best stories are the ones that come to life through the characters. Using elements from her family and herself, the characters she creates have qualities and failings that readers enjoy. Kay is proud to be a part of this anthology project that will long continue to benefit the residents of Hawai'i.

Find me on the web at kayhadashi.wordpress.com.

'ĀLEWA PARK
A LOUISE GOLDEN MYSTERY
Laurie Hanan

Day One

Charlie's deep bass voice carried across the park. "HEY hey hey hey, HEY hey hey hey, HEY hey hey hey ..." He rocked in time with his chant, sitting on a bench in the shade of a monkey pod tree, tossing a tennis ball from hand to hand, never looking at the ball, never missing.

Teenage boys taunted each other good-naturedly on the basketball court while they shot hoops and postured for the girls watching from the sidelines. The evening breeze was so thick with *pakalolo*, a person could get high just walking through the park.

Sage and I had come for exercise—hers, not mine. Dogs and their owners passed us on the concrete footpath while we made embarrassingly slow progress. Sage is blind from birth and senses the world through her nose. She stopped every few inches for a thorough investigation of the landscape, not wanting to miss a smell. I couldn't deny her that simple pleasure. I knew all the regulars by sight, and most of their dogs by name. Funny how much easier it is to ask someone their dog's name than their own.

Sage went into alert stance. Something in the bushes had caught her attention. She nearly toppled me as she lunged toward a dirt trail that led into a thick tangle of untrimmed vegetation.

True to her breed, she's an excellent ratter, but I'd had a long day and wasn't up for a rodent hunt. "No, baby girl." I gripped the leash and tugged. "Not that way."

She strained harder, nosing toward the bushes, letting out a desperate whine with each breath.

I spotted one of Sage's doggie buddies leading his owner in our direction. Maybe I could distract her. "Hey Sage, I see Pono. Let's go say hi."

Hearing her friend's name had no impact. It took all my strength to move her back onto the sidewalk.

Once she caught a whiff of Pono, she forgot everything else. The two dogs danced around each other, tails wagging ecstatically.

"Howzit?" said Pono's owner, a burly Hawaiian.

I pushed my hair off my sweaty forehead. "Long day."

"I don' know how you can walk your dog after deliverin' mail all day. I nevah walk my dog till I wen' retire."

"The vet says Sage needs more exercise. I don't mind, really. It's a lot cooler out here than in the house."

Sage and Pono circled, sniffing, until their leashes were wrapped together.

Pono's owner helped me untangle the leashes. "Eh, what kine dog Sage, anyways?"

"She's a Westie. How about Pono?"

"Half Jack Russell, half Satan," he said seriously, then let out a hearty laugh. "Eh, watch out!"

He grabbed my arm and pulled me off the sidewalk just as the guy in the power wheelchair came barreling down on us silently, oxygen tubes snaking from his nose, his brown and white spaniel in tow.

"Bastard," Pono's owner muttered as we watched the wheelchair retreat at high speed.

"I feel sorry for his dog."

"I know. He nevah let da po' t'ing stop fo' nuttin'."

We said our good-byes and headed in opposite directions.

Minutes later, a child's piercing shriek came from the direction of the overgrown brush at the edge of the park. It was impossible to tell whether it was a cry of glee, pain, or fear. There was still plenty of daylight and it wasn't unusual for kids to be in the park at this hour. I scanned the area I thought it had come from. No kids in sight.

Another scream, louder this time. No, this was definitely not the sound of a child having fun.

A young girl tore out of the same dirt trail Sage had been trying to drag me into earlier. Her eyes, wild with terror, locked on mine.

"What happened?" I called to her.

She came to a stop in front of me, sobbing, her breath ragged from running. "A dead lady ..." she managed between gasps.

What?

A chilling fear gripped me as a thousand thoughts fought for space in my head. My first instinct was to grab the girl and run, get as far away as possible.

But wait.

While a dead body was the last thing I ever wanted to see, the girl might be mistaken. When I was about her age, I was sure I saw a dead woman in an alley, partially hidden behind a dumpster. I ran home, hysterical, and told my father there'd been a murder. He insisted I show him what I'd seen. It was almost a letdown when the body turned out to be that of a decomposing long-haired dog.

I pushed down my panic. "Show me where."

Her head moved side to side as she mewled, "No no no no ..."

"Is your mom here with you?"

Her trembling fingers raked her tear-stained cheeks.

"Are you here by yourself?" I tried again.

She nodded.

"Come, let's sit down over here." I led her to a bench. More important than checking out her find, I needed to calm her so she wouldn't flee. If there really was a body in the bushes, the police would need to talk to her. "What's your name?" I asked.

"Danielle," it sounded like, through her sobs.

"I'm Louise. My dog's name is Sage. Would you like to pet her?"

She nodded.

I lifted Sage to the bench beside Danielle. "Sage is blind. You need to be gentle and not make any fast movements."

In reality, Sage adores everyone and knows no fear of people. But I hoped the effort at gentleness would serve to distract Danielle. It worked. Still crying silently, she wrapped an arm around the dog. Sage sensed Danielle's distress and settled against her.

I took my phone from my pocket and dialed 9-1-1.

"Police fire or ambulance," said a flat female voice.

"Police."

"Is this an emergency?"

"Yes."

"What is your emergency?"

"I'm at 'Ālewa Park. A girl here says there's a ... a woman ... a woman's body. In the shrubbery." I hesitated as I said it, only half believing what Danielle had seen was a dead person.

I told the dispatcher all I knew, ended the call, and speed-dialed Freddy.

"You at home?" I said when he picked up.

"Yeah. I'm finishing that story—"

"I think you're gonna want to get over to the park. Bring your camera."

"What's up?"

"Someone said there's a body down the trail—"

"I'm there." He hung up.

A patrol car pulled to a stop at the entrance and a uniformed officer got out. The dope smokers slipped out of sight while the rest of the park-goers watched the cop cross the manicured expanse of grass.

I waved him over.

"I'm Officer Tuala," he said when he reached us. His friendly smile radiated calm authority.

"Louise Golden."

"You called in a dead body?"

"Yes. I was walking my dog when I heard a scream." I indicated the girl. "Danielle came running out of the path over there. She told me she saw a 'dead lady.'"

"Did you see the body?"

"No. I thought I should stay here with Danielle."

Officer Tuala looked in the direction of the trail, then at Danielle, who seemed to be recovering well from the trauma. He crouched so he was eye-to-eye with her. "How old are you?"

"Seven." Her sweet smile revealed a dimple in one tear-stained cheek.

"What did you see?"

"A lady."

"Where?"

"In the bushes."

"What was the lady doing?"

"Nothing," Danielle said firmly. "She's dead."

"Okay." He stood and looked at me. "Let me go check it out. You two stay right here."

Alone again with Danielle, I was completely unnerved by the thought of a corpse so close by. Who was the dead woman? How did she die? Was she someone I knew?

I mentally urged Freddy to hurry and sighed with relief when I saw him park his truck. He got out and scanned the area. When he spotted me, he hurried over, a camera around his neck.

I stood to hug him. "Thank God you're here—"

"Where's the body?"

"Back there—"

He took off at a jog down the trail Tuala had entered minutes before.

It wasn't long before Freddy reappeared, accompanied by a grim-faced Tuala who spoke into his cell phone.

"Did you see it?" I asked.

Freddy nodded. "Got a few pictures before the big guy noticed me and escorted me out of his crime scene."

"Crime scene? She was ..." I glanced at Danielle and lowered my voice, "... murdered?"

He rubbed a hand slowly down his face. "It looks that way."

"The lady was wearing rollerblades," Danielle piped up.

My hand went to my mouth.

"You know who it is?" Freddy asked me.

"Blonde hair?"

"Yes." Danielle nodded, having brightened considerably.

"There's a blonde woman who rollerblades around the park most evenings. She wasn't here today. I don't remember seeing her yesterday, either."

Danielle eyed Freddy's camera. "Are you from the newspaper?"

"Yes, I am."

"I'm the one who found the body. Do you want to take my picture?" She now seemed unconcerned that a dead body lay just yards from us.

Freddy winked at me before turning to Danielle. "Sure. Why don't you stand over there."

She dried her face with her shirt before posing with the trail entrance as a backdrop. Freddy snapped a series of photos, then asked her to tell him how she'd found the body. She warmed to her story as she gave him a dramatic rendition of events leading to the gruesome discovery.

With the arrival of another half dozen police cars, Charlie's chanting increased in pitch and tempo. "HEY hey hey hey, HEY hey hey hey, HEY hey hey hey ..."

Blue strobes lent a macabre quality to the scene on the normally quiet street. Uniformed officers fanned out across the park. Tuala pointed two of them down the trail where the body lay. Another tied yellow crime scene tape across the break in vegetation, then took up a position to keep people out of the area. The rest of the cops gathered statements from anyone who'd stuck around to watch the commotion.

Danielle grinned up at the female police officer who'd come to take her home. As they left together, holding hands, the little girl chatted merrily.

"That kid's a real ham," Freddy said.

Here and there in the distance, downtown office windows glowed yellow. Harbor lights reflected off the calm water. A breeze blew across the lānai, carrying a chill.

I rubbed my arms.

"Cold?" Freddy put an arm over my shoulders.

I nodded and snuggled into him. "I can't believe they arrested him."

"The police seem to think he did it."

"But why? What did they find?"

"Tuala's a talkative guy but he was careful what he told me. Looks like she was killed about twenty-four hours ago, sometime last night, in the spot where she was found. I got the idea by the time we left they hadn't found a lot in the way of evidence."

"Then why'd they arrest him?"

"I overheard people talking to the cops. They never liked having him in the park. They're afraid of him."

"He's odd looking and his behavior is a little … bizarre. But I never thought he was dangerous."

"He got up and walked away pretty quick when the cops approached him."

"That's what he does when anyone gets too close. He seems to enjoy sitting in the park all day, but he doesn't want to interact with people."

"Do you know what's wrong with him?"

"Not really. He doesn't speak, just stays in that same spot on the bench, rocking and chanting, tossing his ball hand to hand. Someone drops him off at the park every morning. In the evenings I've seen a woman pick him up, usually after dark. She pulls up in a white van and he gets in."

"Do you know his last name?"

"No one knows. They call him Charlie, but that might not even be his real name." I shuddered. "To think how many times I've been alone there with him, even after dark, ... "

Day Two

Thanks to my being in the right place at the right time, Freddy got his photos in to the *Star-Advertiser* before any other reporters arrived on the scene. His story made the front page of the morning edition.

But honestly, it felt more like I'd been in the wrong place at the wrong time. All day at work, the image of the black body bag, the blonde rollerblader zipped inside, stayed with me. I battled between relief and guilt—relief at knowing I'd been that close to a violent killer and survived, guilt for being so glad he'd chosen someone else as his victim.

And I thought about Charlie. His actions hadn't been those of someone trying to flee the police. But as soon as he turned his back on the cops, they'd tackled him to the ground. He was bigger than both of them put together, but he hadn't resisted. I couldn't forget the confusion and desperate fear on his face, like a trapped animal, as they led him to the police car.

People at the park had always given Charlie a wide berth, but he'd never bothered anyone. Area residents had complained to the police, asking for him to be removed from the park. They were frightened by his unusual facial features, paired with his enormous size and obvious strength. His incessant chanting was unnerving. But because Charlie had never done anything wrong, not so much as dropped a piece of litter, the police said he had the right to stay. Had it been a mistake to ignore the public's concerns?

While I delivered the mail, I kept the radio in my truck tuned to KSSK. The afternoon news report revealed the identity of the dead woman. Patricia Vargas, age thirty-seven, single, from California, had been a beauty consultant at Macy's Ala Moana. I'd seen her often in the park, had admired her agility on rollerblades, but never knew her name. The newscaster called Charlie "an unidentified mentally retarded man who frequented the park." He was being held in relation to Vargas's death but no charges had been filed.

When they handcuffed Charlie, they'd made him drop his ball. Surely he could be allowed to have a tennis ball in his jail cell. I speed-dialed my only friend on the police force, Detective Sergeant Henry Nii.

The frigid air conditioning was a welcome relief from the sweltering afternoon heat. We sat in Henry's favorite booth at the back of Zippy's, where he comes most afternoons to enjoy better coffee than he can get at the police station.

I sipped my glass of ice water.

He kept his eyes on me as he emptied two packets of sugar into his coffee and stirred. "I saw in the report that you were the one who called in the dead body in 'Ālewa Park. Why doesn't that surprise me?"

I didn't reply. It sounded like an accusation, though I wasn't sure what he could be accusing me of.

"You knew the victim and the suspect," he said.

"Only by sight."

He blew on his coffee, took a tentative sip, set the cup down.

"Why was Charlie arrested?" I asked. "Did they find some evidence he did it?"

"A number of witnesses felt he'd been behaving in an odd manner."

"He's retarded. His manner's always 'odd.' That doesn't make him a killer." I dragged a French fry through the puddle of ketchup on my plate, then set it down. I had no appetite. "The news reports haven't said how Vargas was killed."

Henry seemed to weigh how much to tell me. "She was strangled."

My breath hitched. I tried to push away the mental image of Charlie's hands around the blonde rollerblader's neck. No doubt about it, Charlie was strong. He could crush a woman's throat as easily as wringing out a washcloth.

"There's more."

I waited.

"This information hasn't been released. I expect you to keep it to yourself."

"Of course."

"Your lover is a newspaper reporter." Henry had never spoken to me in this tone before. No longer a friend, now he was all cop.

My cheeks burned and he must've seen them turning red. I wasn't sure if I was more angry or embarrassed. "You've known me ten years. I've never revealed any confidential information to Freddy."

Okay. We both knew it wasn't entirely true.

"Patricia Vargas was sexually assaulted."

I gave a small nod.

"You knew?"

"Freddy saw the body."

Henry set his coffee cup down a little harder than necessary. "I don't think I'm even going to ask how that happened." He took a deep breath, let it out. "So he knows she was found with her clothes partially removed."

I felt the need to defend Freddy. "He kept it out of his initial story. Rape hadn't yet been confirmed. If you don't want it to get out, you should probably talk to Freddy."

"I will."

For a minute, neither of us spoke.

I used the break to do some relaxation breathing. This wasn't about me. There was no need to get defensive.

Finally, I shook my head. "It seems almost out of the realm of possibility, Charlie chasing down a woman on rollerblades and strangling her. And rape? I just don't see it."

"Why is it hard to believe? He's an adult male. Psychologists have classified him as profoundly retarded, but his IQ has nothing to do with his sex drive. He may have been acting purely on biological instincts he didn't understand."

"Like an oversized kid getting too rough with a toy." My throat was dry. I took a drink of ice water. "There must be DNA evidence, then."

"The assailant was careful. He used a condom. Apparently he also wore gloves when he strangled her. We didn't find any DNA or fingerprints on the body or at the scene. We don't know if Vargas was the intended victim. It may have been a random killing. But the assailant came prepared to commit a crime."

"That definitely doesn't sound like Charlie."

"Doctors are trying to determine whether he's capable of this kind of planning and premeditation."

"In the meantime, a rapist and murderer might be out there stalking his next victim. Are you even looking for other suspects?"

Henry tensed.

"Sorry," I said more gently. "I didn't mean to imply you don't know your job."

"At this point we're keeping all avenues of investigation open," he said tersely.

"How long can you hold Charlie with no evidence?"

"People in the neighborhood are outraged. They've reported his suspicious behavior in the past and nothing's been done to protect them. Now a woman's dead."

"Is he going to be charged with murder?"

Henry rested his arms on the table, folded his hands around his mug. "Between you and me, I doubt it. It's very likely he doesn't have the mental capacity to know right from wrong. For now, he's being housed in the psychiatric ward at Queen's."

"Housed. That sounds so much more comfortable than incarcerated."

"It's partly for his protection. If we released him, he'd head back to the park. You know he wouldn't be safe there now."

I nodded. Henry was right about that.

"The cops who tackled and handcuffed Charlie made him drop his ball," I said. "Do you think someone could find it and take it to him?"

Day Six

It was appalling to think someone I knew, even just by sight, had been brutally murdered so close to my home. After Charlie's arrest, the neighborhood remained peaceful. The public seemed satisfied that he had raped and strangled Patricia Vargas. In a way, I wanted to believe it too. He'd always seemed like such a gentle soul. An innocent. But as Henry had pointed out, the innocents have the same physical urges as the rest of us. The difference is, they don't always have the capacity to grasp the social complexities of man/woman relationships. They may never learn to keep their biological impulses under control.

Believing in Charlie's guilt made life easier. But in the back of my mind there was still a niggling doubt. The killer had been too organized. I couldn't see Charlie doing such meticulous planning to avoid leaving trace evidence at the scene. I couldn't see him engaging with another person in any way. Certainly not in an aggressive, much less violent, manner. One part of me was sure the police had the wrong man. If that was true, it meant a killer was walking free.

In the evenings, I stayed home. Any time Freddy was out, I kept the doors locked. Sage went into a deep funk, spending most of her hours with her nose wedged against the bottom of the screen door. I tried to interest her in indoor games, but she missed her walks.

Finally, I couldn't take it anymore. I snapped the leash to Sage's collar and we headed out.

Freddy looked up from his laptop. "You aren't going back to the park, are you?"

"I'm tired of being locked up in this house, and so is Sage. Wanna go with us?"

"I would, but I've got a deadline. You got your pepper spray?"

I held up the little canister.

"Your phone?"

"Yeah."

"Be careful."

"I'll be back before dark."

The basketball court was filled with boys, some shooting hoops, some smoking. Girls clustered on the sidelines, eyeing them. Were they even aware a woman had been murdered right here just a few days ago, or did their raging teenage hormones make them completely oblivious to the world around them?

The park was noticeably empty of children and young families. Dog walkers had either stayed home or taken a different route. The only other dog in sight was a Chihuahua named Roscoe, chasing a ball in the field.

"Want to play with Roscoe?" I asked Sage in my most enthusiastic voice.

She tilted her head and sniffed the air. When she caught Roscoe's scent, she gave a happy *woof* and wagged her tail so hard her whole body wagged with it. I unsnapped her leash and she took off after him.

I stood by Roscoe's owner, hands on my hips, watching the dogs. "It's so good to see her play like this. She doesn't usually get the chance to have an all-out romp."

"I figured with no other dogs around, it was okay to let Roscoe off the leash."

Roscoe's owner, a petite Japanese woman in her sixties, was one of my favorite people to talk to in the park. She was an elementary school teacher by day, and in the evening seemed to crave adult conversation. She chatted with everyone she came across on her walks, making her the best source for neighborhood scuttlebutt.

"You feel safe coming to the park alone?" I asked her.

She took a quick glance around, as if reassuring herself. "I guess so." She pried the ball from Roscoe's teeth and threw it. Roscoe sped after it, with Sage at his heels. "I mean, he's in custody, right?"

"Everyone seems satisfied it was Charlie who killed her."

She raised an eyebrow. "You don't think so?"

"I just don't know. I mean, he never seemed dangerous."

"Who else could have done it?"

"It could've been anyone."

"Did you know the woman who was killed?"

"I saw her rollerblading but never spoke to her. Did you?"

"Yeah. She lived on my street— Uh oh. Look who's coming."

The guy in the power wheelchair was headed in our direction, pulling his spaniel beside him.

Roscoe and Sage were chasing each other with gleeful abandon. Oblivious to everything else, they ran straight at the wheelchair guy and his dog.

The wheelchair came to a dead stop. The spaniel stared stoically in front of him, not bothering to react to the other dogs.

"Your dogs have to be on a leash," the guy bellowed with such venom I thought he might have a stroke.

For someone with breathing problems, there was surprising strength in his voice.

We immediately recalled Sage and Roscoe. They obeyed, but not fast enough. They guy had his phone out and was taking photos of our dogs before we could get their leashes snapped on.

"I'm calling the cops!" he screamed as he motored away, dragging his dog with him.

"What a grouch," I said. "I've never seen him smile. And his poor dog ..."

Roscoe's owner stared after the wheelchair till he was out of earshot. "You know who that is?"

"No. He's never spoken a word to me. Not till today, at least."

"Remember that big accident on the Pali?"

"The one where all those high school kids were killed?"

"Yes."

"Who could forget? It was horrible."

"Well ..." She leaned in closer and spoke in a conspiratorial tone. "That guy in the wheelchair? He's the one who caused the accident."

"You're kidding me."

"I'm not kidding. That's him."

"I thought he got ten years. What's he doing out of prison?"

"His lawyer fought to get him out because of his medical issues. He ended up serving just two years."

I could summon no pity for him as I watched the wheelchair turn out of the park and disappear from sight.

Day Seven

Almost without me noticing, Freddy had taken over the dining room table for his home office. Giving up my space, an inch at a time, was just one of the concessions I'd made since he moved in. All in the name of domestic bliss.

He tapped his keyboard, then turned the laptop to show me the screen. "This is him. Lester Pinpherk."

The photo was of a man in his fifties with brown hair and a thick mustache. "He looks a lot younger here," I said, "but it could be the guy in the park."

"This was taken eight years ago, at the trial." He hit a few keys and showed me another photo. "This one was taken eighteen months later, at his parole hearing."

In this photo, Pinpherk sat in a wheelchair and was hooked up to an oxygen tank. His hair and mustache had turned a yellowish white, his skin sallow.

"He sure aged a lot in that short time," I said. "This is pretty much what he looks like now. A little heavier, maybe."

"Prison wasn't kind to him. After he caused the accident that killed all those kids, including Castle High School's star quarterback, the locals hated him." Freddy pulled up photos of the horrific crash scene. Some were aerial shots, probably taken from a helicopter. The gray pickup truck lay on its side, sheet-covered bodies littered the highway. "He drifted into the oncoming lane. The pickup, with six teenagers riding in the back, swerved to avoid him. It hit a cement truck and flipped over. Pinpherk fled the scene. There was a witness, and police tracked him down the next day."

"I can't believe they let him out after only two years, even if he does have health problems."

"He always maintained he had nothing to do with the accident. Said he wasn't even in the area when it happened. I guess the testimony of one witness was enough to convince the jury."

"I remember it was such an emotional trial. The jury probably felt compelled to convict him so the case could be put to rest and people could go on with their lives."

"I hope there was more to it than that." Freddy pulled up another old news story and read it. "It says here he already had ongoing medical conditions before the accident. In prison, he spent a lot of time in the infirmary. His lawyer tried to get him released on medical parole, but the parole board denied it. Then some of the prisoners beat him severely. His paralysis is a result of that beating. Once he was permanently incapacitated, his parole was granted on humanitarian grounds.

"I remember Pinpherk was living in Wahiawā at the time of the accident. After he got out, he dropped out of sight. I figured he must've left the island."

"Well, he's still here," I said. "Living somewhere close by. You wouldn't believe what a jerk he is. He drags his dog along, never lets it stop even to pee. His electric wheelchair is absolutely silent. You can't hear it coming. He seems to get a charge out of sneaking up behind people and running them off the walkway. Today he stopped and took pictures of Sage and another dog chasing a ball. He told us he was calling the cops because they were off leash."

"You do know it's illegal to let her off the leash in the park."

"I know, but there were no other dogs around—until he showed up." A half-baked thought came to me. "Can you find the name of the witness?"

"Why?" he asked, but he was already typing.

"I don't know. Just a thought."

"Okay. Here it is." He paused. "Oh wow."

"What?" I leaned over to see the screen.

"I don't believe this."

"*What?*"

Day Eight

I did my best to be patient while Henry doctored his coffee. It was a ritual, and I knew he wouldn't talk until he'd performed it. At this hour of the afternoon we had the restaurant to ourselves.

"The woman who was murdered," I said when he set his spoon down. "Patricia Vargas."

I expected him to correct me on my use of the word 'murdered.' Murder is for the courts to decide. All he said was, "What about her?"

"Remember the guy who killed all those kids on Pali Highway?"

He tasted his coffee, set the mug down. "Lester Pinpherk."

"That's right. Well, you're not gonna believe this."

His eyes narrowed.

"The woman who testified against Pinpherk—it was Patricia Vargas."

By his expression, Henry already knew. But of course he did. He'd have all his bases covered.

"I guess you knew that."

A slight nod.

"Well, Mr. Pinpherk walks his dog every evening at 'Ālewa Park."

"And?"

"After he got out of prison, Pinpherk bought a house in the neighborhood where Vargas was living. Don't tell me that's just a coincidence. He got a dog, probably just so he could walk it in the same park where Vargas rollerbladed. Where she was killed."

"On an island this small, coincidences happen all the time."

"Okay. Let's say it was pure chance they ended up being neighbors and frequenting the same park. How is it possible they didn't recognize each other?"

"It's been years since the trial. Pinpherk's appearance has changed dramatically since he went to prison."

"So you've talked to him."

Henry held my gaze but didn't speak.

"Did you ask him if he knew Vargas was living nearby?"

"He claims he had no idea. I asked him if he'd noticed the blonde woman rollerblading around the park in the evenings. He said he couldn't help but notice her. At the speed she skated down the sidewalk she was a menace to anyone in her path. But did he know that woman was Vargas? He says he did not."

"That's a little hard to believe. He had to have hated Vargas. When she testified against him, she literally ruined his life. You're telling me she skated past him hundreds—maybe thousands—of times, and he never noticed who she was?"

"It's possible. In court, Vargas was a sharp dresser. Wore lots of makeup. Her hair was always styled. When she skated, she pulled her hair back in a ponytail and dressed in tights. I saw the body. She looked nothing like she did when she testified at the trial."

"Pinpherk had a strong motive for revenge. For most people, it would be a driving force."

"I agree. To this day, he denies having anything to do with the accident. He swears Vargas either lied, or was mistaken. Because of her testimony, Pinpherk had one hell of a rough time in prison. He came out of it paralyzed, stuck in a wheelchair for life. That's motive, if ever there was one. But there's also the question of means. Vargas wasn't a small woman. She was in good physical condition. Strong. I can't see Pinpherk overpowering her, much less ... well ... with his medical issues I'm pretty sure he didn't have the means to commit sexual assault."

"He could've hired someone else to kill her."

"There's no evidence he had anything to do with her death."

"Is Pinpherk even a suspect?"

"We haven't closed that avenue of investigation. But as things stand, Pinpherk received due process for the crime he was convicted of. Whether or not the system treated him fairly, he served the required time. Now he says all he wants is anonymity so he can live out what's left of his life in some semblance of peace." Henry gave me a hard stare. "I don't want to hear about you or your boyfriend going after him. You will not expose his whereabouts to the public. Do you understand me?"

"Of course."

"It wasn't easy finding Lester Pinpherk's address," Freddy said, leaning away from the laptop to stretch.

"You could've just followed him home from the park."

"I know. But I wanted to search online to see what all would turn up. I found no record of him since he left prison. Turns out he changed his name. Now he's Robert Brown."

"Henry didn't mention the name change."

"I guess you can't blame Pinpherk for wanting to hide. The public was really up in arms when they let him out after he'd served only two years."

"So where does he live?"

"Over on Judd Street. Not far from here. After you left for work, I went to see his house. It wasn't hard to find. It's the only one in the neighborhood with a wheelchair ramp built onto the front. I watched the house for a few hours. He had the A/C going all day. Stayed inside with the blinds closed."

"So he doesn't like the heat.

"Doesn't like light, either."

"Somehow that doesn't surprise me. What did you expect to find out by watching his house?"

"I don't know. I've got a gut feeling. There's a story here, I've just gotta figure out what it is."

"Like Henry says, no matter how strong his motive, Pinpherk isn't physically capable of taking down a woman the size and strength of Vargas. Much less raping her."

Freddy rested his elbow on the table, his mouth against the back of his hand, and stared out the window.

Which explained why he preferred working at the table rather than the desk. The spectacular view of downtown and the harbor from the dining room window no doubt inspired thought.

"It can't be a coincidence," he finally said. "There's gotta be a reason he bought a house in the same neighborhood as Vargas."

"That's what I told Henry. But he says there's no evidence against Pinpherk."

"The guy's up to something."

"Like what—besides enforcing the leash law?"

"Could be he just wanted to unnerve her by showing up in her neighborhood. But you saw them pass each other in the park and they didn't seem to take any notice of each other."

"Not that I could tell."

"Looks like he doesn't leave the house much except to walk his dog. So what does he do all day? I need to find a way to see what's going on inside his house."

"You're kidding me, right?"

"I am definitely not kidding."

"So much for the promise I made to Henry."

Day Nine

Sage danced around my feet as I came through the door. I stooped to give her a proper greeting.

"You've gotta see this," Freddy said, his eyes on the laptop screen. The dining table was set up as a workspace with two cell phones, their charger cords draped across the table and plugged into the wall socket. An almost empty water bottle stood next to him.

I pushed aside the remnants of Freddy's lunch and sat in the nearest chair. "Hi to you too."

"Hi." He leaned over and gave me a quick kiss. "How was your day?"

"This heat is unreal. I'm exhausted."

"Look at this." He turned the screen so I could see it.

A grainy black and white video showed the inside of what looked like a small living room. "What's that?"

"The camera's in his house."

"*What?* When did you do that?"

"Last night when he was out walking his dog."

"If you get caught—"

"No worries. It's hidden in the strip of insulation under the AC. If he doesn't suspect there's a camera, he'll never notice it. I'll go back and get it tomorrow. I've got what I need." He moved the curser and tapped the keyboard. "Just watch."

In the video, Pinpherk came into the house in his power wheelchair, his dog on a leash. He released the dog, shut the door behind him and double checked that it was locked. While he maneuvered the chair into a corner, the dog slinked down a hallway.

Pinpherk pushed himself out of the wheelchair and stood. He stooped to plug the charging cord into a wall socket, then walked to the kitchen without so much as a limp.

"Would you look at that," I said.

 Pinpherk returned with a Bud Light, sat on the couch, and popped open the can.

Freddy forwarded the video. "Watch this."

Now Pinpherk sat on a stationary bicycle, pumping the pedals hard and fast while he stared at the TV.

I was dumbfounded. "He's getting a real good workout for someone with breathing problems."

"I bet there's no oxygen in that tank. There's more."

Freddy moved the video forward again. Pinpherk had moved to the couch and was now lifting some serious hand weights, his eyes still on the TV.

"The guy's pretty strong," Freddy said. "Those are twenty pound weights."

"He's been faking it all along. He had everyone fooled into believing he's an invalid."

"That's gotta be how he caught Vargas off guard. Probably asked her for help with something. Who's gonna refuse to stop and help someone in a wheelchair?"

Looked like I was finally a step ahead of Henry. "Henry needs to know. But how do we tell him, after I promised we'd leave Pinpherk alone?"

"Henry seems like a reasonable sort."

"He is, usually."

"I could call him and claim a confidential source, but I have a feeling he'd receive the information better from you."

"I'm not exactly on his A-list at the moment."

"Give me time to get my camera out of there before you call him."

Day Ten

I set the phone to speaker and dialed.

"Detective Sergeant Nii."

"Henry. This is Louise."

"What is it?" he asked brusquely, as though I'd already wasted enough of his time.

"I'm calling about a mutual acquaintance. Robert Brown."

Silence.

"AKA Lester Pinpherk," I added.

Henry let out a long, audible breath that was surely meant to convey his irritation with me. "What about him?"

"He's faking his disabilities."

A pause. "And you know this, how?"

Here goes. "Freddy has a confidential source."

"Then I need to talk to Freddy."

I glanced at Freddy, who was shaking his head *no.*

"Freddy isn't here right now. Look, Henry. A woman is dead. Murdered, because she had the courage to testify about an accident she witnessed. An accident that killed a bunch of kids."

"We already talked about this. There's nothing to indicate that's why she was killed."

"You're holding an innocent man in custody. A man whose only pleasure in life is sitting at the park, whose only crime was being born retarded."

"There's no evidence Pinpherk AKA Robert Brown had anything to do with Vargas's death. End of story."

"No, Henry. That's not the end of the story. Lester Pinpherk can walk. I don't think he's really on oxygen, either. He's been exercising."

"Exercising isn't a crime."

"I'm telling you, he can walk as well as you and me. Some terrible wrongs have been committed. It's in your power to right those wrongs. I know what kind of police officer you are—what kind of person you are. You're going to do whatever it takes to see justice is served."

"I need to know where Freddy got his information."

"Instead of giving Freddy a hard time about his source, check it out for yourself."

Day Twelve

The waiter set three amber-colored bottles of Singha on the table.

Henry waited for him to leave before making a toast. "'*Ōkole maluna*."

We clinked our bottles and took a sip. The pale, ice-cold beer was delicious.

"I may never know how you got your information." Henry set his beer down, gave me a pointed look, then turned his eyes on Freddy. "I probably don't want to know. But we were able to confirm that Lester Pinpherk, AKA Robert Brown, is able to walk normally. The search warrant for his home turned up some interesting things. Looks like he was pretty obsessed with Patricia Vargas. On his computer we found a big file on her, including lots of candid photos taken at the park. He was arrested today and will be arraigned on murder charges."

"That's a relief," I said. "He's one scary guy to have running around our neighborhood. Was he faking his paralysis from the start?"

"I don't think so. I spoke again with his doctors. The beating he sustained in prison didn't sever his spinal cord, but there was enough nerve damage to put him in a wheelchair. People with this type of injury do sometimes recover over time. But considering Pinpherk's age and all his other health issues, doctors didn't think it was likely he'd ever walk again. It seems he defied the odds."

"Must've been sheer force of will that got him back on his feet," Freddy said.

Henry dipped a summer roll in peanut sauce, bit off half, and spent some time chewing. "Revenge is a powerful motive. Of course he still maintains he had nothing to do with Vargas's murder, but he's lost his credibility. Now that he's in jail, he's given up the farce of using the wheelchair and oxygen tank."

"You think you have enough to convict him?"

"A lot of what we have is circumstantial. A good lawyer could get the case thrown out. I'm still hoping for a confession."

"What's gonna happen to his dog?" I asked.

"We called the Humane Society to pick it up. It's a good looking purebred. I have a feeling it'll be adopted in no time."

One Month Later

Beach chairs and coolers were scattered across the grass. Parents, aunties, and uncles had gathered to watch the first Little League Senior Division game of the season. Younger siblings, more interested in their own games, chased each other and climbed trees.

I dodged kids who zoomed along on scooters and in brightly colored plastic cars. Sage insisted on stopping to inspect a collection of duffle bags strewn to the side of the baseball diamond. I used my hand to shade my eyes from the afternoon sun and took the opportunity to watch a bit of the game taking place on the other side of the chain link fence.

The girl on the mound pitched a fastball. The *crack* of metal bat against ball split the air. Raucous cheering broke out as the batter ran for first, kicking up clouds of red dirt.

Dust choked the dry air, settling in my nose and throat. I turned away from the wind. That's when I noticed Charlie in the dugout, sitting alone on a bench. He was quiet, watching the game with keen concentration. This was the first time I'd ever seen him focused on something other than his own inner world, the closest I'd seen him come to engaging with other people.

So, Charlie liked softball. I smiled to myself. It seemed a great step forward. Whether through therapy or new medication, it looked as though the weeks spent in the psychiatric ward at Queen's had done him some good after all.

Sage tugged at the leash, ready to explore new ground. Before moving on, I took one more look at Charlie.

His gaze was locked on the pitcher, a girl of about fourteen with a sweet face and a figure that couldn't be hidden by her jersey. The gleam in his eyes seemed much too intense for someone interested in a mere ballgame.

LAURIE HANAN

Laurie Hanan grew up in the picturesque islands of South Pacific with a father who pioneered air travel to some of the remotest parts of the world. Laurie eventually settled in Hawai'i, where she had a career with the Honolulu Post Office. After retiring, Laurie began writing her Louise Golden mysteries, about a mail carrier in Kāne'ohe on the Island of O'ahu. When she isn't writing, Laurie enjoys vegan cooking, photography, swimming, and yoga. Laurie lives on O'ahu with her husband, youngest son, an obese Westie, and a bipolar cat.

CURSE OF THE LOST TIKI
JILL MARIE LANDIS

"We're ready, Uncle Louie. Open the door, stand back, and let 'em in."

"Will do, Sophie." Louie Marshall smiled at bartender Sophie Chin, certain she had everything in hand as he headed for the front door of the Tiki Goddess Bar and Restaurant on the North Shore of Kaua'i, an establishment he'd owned and operated since the '70s.

Louie turned the lock, swung the door open, and flipped the closed sign to open, then stood aside as the line of tourists of all shapes and sizes filed in. He was still amazed folks lined up for lunch. Tuesdays were known as Tour Bus Tuesday at the Goddess. Ever since the bar was featured in the short-lived *Trouble in Paradise* reality television show, the Kaua'i TV and Movie Tour Company booked the Goddess as a weekly lunch stop.

Louie greeted every guest the way his late wife, Irene Kau'alanikaulana Hickam Marshall, had taught him by giving each and every one a genuine smile and a hearty aloha.

"Where you folks from?" he would ask. When they answered, he always had the same response. "Well then, lucky you come Kaua'i."

If someone asked Louie for his autograph, he'd grab a napkin off a nearby table and graciously oblige.

The burly guide in a TV and Movie Tour Company aloha shirt gave Louie a nod and a big aloha. Then he paused in the middle of the room, and as the tourists settled into their seats, he shouted, "Folks, this is *the* Tiki Goddess Bar made famous by the reality show featuring those madcap Hula Maidens." He gestured toward Louie. "This is owner, Uncle Louie Marshall, who ranks right up there with Trader Vic and Don the Beachcomber."

Louie took a bow, waved and smiled. He'd spent most of his life sharing his slice of paradise with people from all over the world, and he was proud of the place he and Irene had established over forty years before. Sure, the bar was located in a sagging old building that had been around since plantation times, but that was all part of the charm. Faded tapa cloth lined the ceiling, and woven *lau hala* mats covered the walls.

Even during the day, huge glass Japanese fishing floats crafted into hanging lamps cast a soft blue, semi-twilight hue over everything. Tiki masks, Polynesian war clubs and paddles, posters and photos of presidents and celebrities who had stopped by over the years vied for crowded wall space.

Louie handed out the lunch menus and then went back to the bar where Sophie finished filling plastic cups with water. She passed them around as she took the food and drink orders. Sophie was worth her weight in gold. In her early twenties, she'd been an asset to the place since the day Louie's niece, Em, had hired her. Sophie wore her hair short, spiked, and dyed the colors of a neon fruit cocktail. Small silver rings and studs pierced one eyebrow. Sophie was smart as a whip. No one ever put anything over on her.

The lunch orders were sent in to Kimo, the head cook. Louie manned the bar while Sophie delivered his legendary tropical beverages. When he had a second to pause and look around, Louie noticed a grizzled old *haole* with a short white beard standing in the doorway. He was wearing a faded billed cap and ratty T-shirt with a faded fishing logo on it. The man nodded at Louie and walked in carrying a small navy blue duffle bag. He slid onto one of the carved tiki barstools.

"Hey, Captain Jack. Long time no see." Louie grinned. "How you stay?"

Jack nodded, glanced over his shoulder at the tourists, and settled his forearms on the koa wood bar.

"Howzit with you, Louie?" Captain Jack nodded. His skin was bronzed from years at sea, his eyes bright blue above his beard.

"Always good. What'll it be? Pirate's grog?" Louie laughed at his own joke. Jack didn't crack a smile.

"Jack and soda," the captain mumbled.

"That's right. Forgot you're into Jack Daniels."

"My first name's on the bottle."

Louie laughed and made Jack a two-fisted double. "You still running your fishing charters?"

Captain Jack nodded. He'd been in the charter fishing business for as long as Louie could remember, which was farther back than most people would believe.

"Yep. Got the *Nanilani* moored in the bay right now."

The *Nanilani* was a custom, thirty-four foot, power catamaran Jack designed himself a few years back.

"Chuckie Robbins is still crewing for me." Jack nursed one drink until he ordered a second, apparently in no hurry. As soon as the lunch crowd in the bar polished off their meals and Mai Tais, they were herded back out to the air-conditioned mini-buses waiting in the parking lot.

"So, what's up?" Louie asked Captain Jack as quiet descended over the bar. He'd never seen Jack looking so down in the dumps. Then again, he hadn't really seen the man for a hefty handful of years.

"I might have found some trouble," Jack said.

"Better than trouble finding you." Louie smiled.

Captain Jack didn't smile.

"Fishing bad this year? I heard the water's too warm. Is that true?"

"Fishing's okay, but these damn hurricane scares don't help. I've spent more days with the boat tucked in the harbor waiting for storms to materialize than I'd care to count. It's not that."

"I'm a good listener," Louie said.

The captain glanced over his shoulder again. Only two tables were occupied. At one of them, four women were having lunch and chattering like mynah birds. A young couple at another table was trying to keep a toddler entertained. None of them were paying any attention to the old man seated at the bar.

"I need a favor." Jack met Louie's eyes. "You're the most honest man I know, Louie. There's nobody else I can trust."

Louie shrugged. He liked to think anyone could count on him for anything.

"I try," he said. "What do you need?"

Jack reached down and pulled up the navy duffle. "I need you to keep this for me, no questions asked. I'll pick it up in a couple days."

"Sure thing." Louie started to reach for the straps.

The captain pulled the bag back a few inches. "Promise me you won't open it. No matter what."

Louie frowned. "Okay. As long as you didn't rob a bank or something."

"Nothing like that."

"I get it. No opening the bag."

"No matter what." Jack pushed the bag toward Louie.

When Louie picked it up, he was surprised at the weight. He carried it into the office, put it in the bottom of an empty file drawer, and walked back into the bar.

Captain Jack finished his drink and shoved the glass toward Louie.

"Mahalo, Louie. It means a lot to me that I can trust you." Jack got off the bar stool and paused a second before he added, "Listen, if anything were to happen to me, bury that bag. Bury it deep, and don't look back."

Louie tried to laugh off the dire warning, then had second thoughts. Keeping a bag with an unknown item for a guy he hadn't seen in years might not be such a brilliant idea.

Louie lowered his voice and made sure Sophie was busy before he spoke. "You're not into drug running are you?"

"Nothing like that. No way. It's just better you don't know what's up. I'm not really sure yet myself." Jack tipped the bill of his cap, tossed a twenty on the bar and walked out.

Louie watched him go. Having second thoughts, he picked up the empty rocks glass and automatically wiped down the bar. He didn't know his niece had walked up beside him until he turned around and saw Em. Attractive and in her mid-thirties with blue eyes, and long blonde hair, Em had been managing the place since she'd moved to Kaua'i after a terrible divorce a couple of years back.

"Who was that?" she asked as she watched Jack walk out.

"An old friend. Captain Jack Parsons. Runs Parsons' Fishing Charters. Haven't seen him in years."

"You looked worried when I walked in. Everything okay?"

Louie hesitated, trying to figure out how to tell her something, and yet say nothing.

"You didn't loan him money, did you Uncle Louie?"

"Oh, no. Nothing like that." He nodded, hoping she believed him. Em had come down hard on him for handing out money to anyone and everyone in need of a loan. When she moved to Kaua'i and began managing the place, she balanced the books and reminded him that he was not the Bank of the Tiki Goddess. They were running a business and she was determined to make it profitable.

"I don't see the harm in helping folks out," he said. "I see it as living aloha."

"You are living aloha. Most of the people who borrow from you aren't. Hardly anyone ever pays you back."

"They do the best they can."

"Uncle Louie, bags of mangos, papayas, bananas and fish aren't currency."

He didn't bother to argue. She'd never understand.

"You sure everything is all right?" Em looked worried.

He put on his best smile. "Captain Jack was just telling me how these close-call hurricanes have cut into his business. Don't worry about me, honey. I'm seventy-three, I've got most of my hair, all my teeth, and I live on Kaua'i. How could life be anything but great?"

Ever since Em moved to Kaua'i and took over management of the Goddess, Louie started sleeping in until at least seven-thirty. On Wednesday, he awoke to an overcast sky and a lack of the usual trade winds which added to the oppressively hot, sultry air. Because of an El Nino weather pattern, the islands had dodged four major storms already this hurricane season.

After his usual breakfast of scrambled eggs and coffee laced with Kahlua, Louie mixed a tall jigger of his special version of a Bloody Mary he'd named Tiger Shark Attack to commemorate a close call while surfing Hanalei years ago. The mini portions of V8 Juice, Vodka, Worcestershire, Wasabi, and lime were for his taste-testing parrot, David Letterman. His fine feathered friend had a knack for knowing when a new cocktail recipe was spot on. Louie's concoctions were world-famous. Dave deserved to be spoiled.

Louie grabbed the television remote before he walked over to Letterman's cage. "You want *Animal Planet* or *Discovery Channel*?"

"Yo, ho, ho. Brrreakfast." The macaw squawked.

Louie tuned to *Animal Planet* and set the volume on medium. He walked back to a small rattan tiki bar in the living area and picked up the jigger. David Letterman watched attentively as Louie poured the contents into a small cup attached to the bars of the parrot's cage.

There was no sneaking out of the house without giving Letterman his morning pick-me-up.

He left the house and headed to the bar, where Em was filling the ice bin. Though they weren't officially open until ten, a group of older women was already gathered around three tables in front of the long banquette seating. What the Hula Maidens lacked in dancing talent, they definitely made up for with enthusiasm for hula. Ranging in age from ninety-two to late forties, the women were at the Goddess almost as much as they were at their homes. Louie not only gave them permission to meet and practice in the bar, but to perform there, too.

Only one of the Maidens was Hawaiian. Most of the others were long-time residents. The newest member was a transplant from Ohio. Kiki Godwin, Chef Kimo's wife, was their self-appointed leader. Kiki liked nothing better than to be up on all the island scuttlebutt.

Uncle Louie was arranging tiki mugs behind the bar and not paying much attention until he overheard Kiki say, "So did you hear they found that old guy, Captain Jack, dead on the beach this morning?"

"The fisherman," Flora said.

Louie dropped a tiki mug.

"What did you just say, Kiki?" He was barely able to get the words out.

"Some old guy washed up on the beach. Captain Frank, I think. No, wait a minute. I was right before. His name was Captain Jack something. That's suspicious. A body on the beach."

Louie bent over to pick up the pieces of the broken mug, which was easier than collecting his shattered nerves. He glanced at the clock behind the bar. It was nine-fifty-five. Sophie was due in at ten.

Kiki's cheeks were flushed and her eyes sparkled. Louie could see her mind turning.

For the past couple of years, Kiki and the Hula Maidens had inexplicably found themselves caught up in more than one high profile crime case on the island. Somehow, they'd actually managed to outwit the perpetrators and solve the crimes. They'd even received commendations from the Mayor of Kaua'i.

"We need to find out if there were any suspicious circumstances surrounding Captain Jack's drowning," Kiki said.

"Not again," Maiden Suzi Matamoto protested. "I've got too many pending escrows to get involved with another murder right now."

Hawaiian Flora Carillo, owner of a souvenir shop in Hanalei that sold Tiki Goddess trinkets, protested as well. "You know every time we get involved, nothing good happens."

"Say what you will, we always get our man, or woman, depending on who done it," Kiki reminded them.

While she tried to convince the other Hula Maidens they needed to get to the bottom of Captain Jack's death, Louie waited out the longest five minutes of his life. Thankfully, Sophie was always punctual. When she walked in at ten, Louie immediately headed for his office.

"I need to leave for a few minutes," he told Em as he hurried by. "Gotta go on an errand."

In the process of tying a hairband around her long blonde ponytail, Em merely nodded his way. "Be careful, Uncle Louie. Try to get back before the place is slammed for lunch. Looks like it's going to rain, and you know what that means."

Once rain started falling, tourists left the beaches in droves and headed into shops and restaurants to hang out until the sun reappeared. At the rate it had been raining this summer, the Goddess was packed more often than not.

Louie headed straight into the office and made sure the door was closed before he pulled open the bottom file cabinet drawer. He stared down at the navy blue duffle, took a deep breath and picked it up. He made sure there was no one in the parking lot before he hurried over to his beach house a few yards away.

Letterman started a ruckus the minute Louie appeared.

"It's too early for another drink," he told the bird. Then he grabbed the television remote and surfed the channels until he came up with an animal program to settle the parrot down again.

Once the duffle was stashed under his bed, Louie got into his pickup and headed for Black Pot Park near the Hanalei Pier. If he was going to get the real scoop on Captain Jack's death, he hoped he'd find it there.

A light drizzle fell all the way to Hanalei, but when Louie drove onto the beach beside the pier, the sun broke through the clouds, and a stunning rainbow arched over the wide mouth of the bay. Kids were already doing cannonballs into the water below.

Louie drove to the river mouth along the sand. It wasn't ten-thirty yet. This early in the day, just a handful of his old cronies were there gossiping and checking out the surfers, stand-up paddlers, and kayakers on the river. Out on the bay, crews off-loaded tourists from inflatables that carried them out to the tour boats for Na Pali sightseeing cruises.

When Louie parked under the ironwood pines, which shaded the park, he spotted his friend, Shelby Brown. Tall and lanky, Shell had been on island for decades. Too many hours in the sun and chain smoking had destroyed his skin, but the man couldn't care less. Louie crossed the park to join his friend, who was busy raking sand in the horseshoe pit the old guys used nearly every day of the year.

"Hey, Shell," Louie said.

Shelby raised his ball cap and scratched his head. "Hey, Louie. Howzit?"

"Can't complain."

"What are you doin' out here this early? You're usually working," Shell said.

"Coconut wireless verification. I just heard Captain Jack washed up on the beach this morning. You hear anything about it?"

"Hear anything?" Shell jerked his thumb toward his chest. "I found him. Damnedest thing. It doesn't pay to be one of the first guys out on the beach. That's what I get for sleeping in my car last night."

"Have too many beers?"

"Something like that."

"Good thinking."

"I got up to take a swim and clear my head and I see this guy laying on the beach half in and half out of the water. He had all his clothes on, which shoulda tipped me off."

"What'd you do?"

Shell shrugged. "I was too fuzzy headed to think much about it, so I went for a swim. He was still there when I got out. I was thinking a bit clearer, so I tried to rouse him. Rolled him over and recognized Captain Jack. He was looking back at me but wasn't seeing anything, you know?"

"Yeah. I know." Those same eyes had been alive and looking at Louie yesterday. A chill ran down Louie's spine as Captain Jack's last words came back to him.

"If anything were to happen to me, bury that bag. Bury it deep and don't look back."

He tried to shake off a feeling of foreboding.

Shell was still talking. "I called 911. KPD came out. Never knew them to work so fast. I guess they didn't want old Jack splayed out in the sand when all the tourists started pulling in. Said they'd let me know if they needed to talk to me during the investigation."

"Investigation? I thought he drowned pure and simple," Louie said.

Shelby shrugged. "Looks like he drowned, but you never know."

By the time Louie got back to the Goddess, the parking lot was full. Everyone working inside would be busy. He slipped out of the truck and headed back to the beach house, breezed past Letterman, grabbed the duffle bag, and headed to the old shed behind the house where he kept what few gardening tools he owned. As he passed a half-full bag of potting soil, he grabbed it, along with an empty plastic trash bag, and slipped the duffle inside. Then, he headed around to the shady side of the house.

He scanned the beach out front in both directions and found it empty. Mostly only residents used this narrow stretch of Hā'ena beach. Tourists preferred parks where they were near lifeguards, toilets, and showers.

Thankfully, the soil was soft and sandy. Louie quickly dug up a ti plant and set it aside, then deepened and widened the hole. Once he was satisfied with the size, he picked up the sack and slid his hand inside. His fingers found the zipper on the bag.

Promise me you won't open it. No matter what.

You're the most honest man I know.

Louie jerked his hand back as if he'd singed his fingertips.

Wrapping the plastic bag tight around the duffle, he knelt down and gently lowered it into the hole. He straightened and quickly refilled the hole with a little sand, picked up the ti plant, and centered the root ball inside.

It only took seconds to replace the sandy soil around the ti. He opened the potting soil and sprinkled some on top of the dirt around the stem of the plant. He was tamping it down with the shovel when a voice nearly startled him into a heart attack.

"Hey, Uncle Louie."

It was Jeanne Montrose. She owned the house on the north side of his own and lived in California most of the time.

"I didn't know you were back." Louie wondered how much Jeanne had seen.

"I've been here three days. Mostly I've been running errands to Costco and Home Depot to replace household stuff the vacation renters wear out. Makes you wonder how they live at home." She'd been renting her house to weekly guests for over twenty years. Most of the time, Louie was so busy he had no idea when guests came and when they left.

She tried to peer around him at the hole. "I didn't know you gardened."

"Just needed to move this ti plant over a bit." He realized that made no sense. "Rain's been dripping right onto the leaves. Em said the sound was keeping her up at night." He nudged the potting soil with his toe. "Still have to put a little more potting soil in. Might just plant a few flowers out here later."

He made show of grabbing a couple handfuls of dirt and scattering it around. "How long do you get to stay, Jeanne?"

She shook her head. "I'm taking the red-eye out tonight. This was just an in-and-out for me. Gave me a chance to check on the place. Ron and I will be back in a couple months, and this time we get to stay for about five weeks."

"Great. Tell Ron I said hello."

"For sure. Take care, Uncle Louie."

The smile he gave her before she walked away was fueled by genuine relief. With Jeanne flying off tonight, she wouldn't be around to tell anyone she saw him digging in the yard.

The day after Captain Jack's body was discovered on the beach, the temperature reached the high eighties by six in the morning. Because of an El Nino weather pattern in the Pacific, a constant parade of hurricanes passed the islands. The near misses stalled the trades and hiked up the humidity to the level of a Swedish sauna.

Louie woke up drenched in sweat, but not because of the oppressive heat. Nightmares had littered the landscape of his dreams. Somehow, he pulled himself together, filled a mug of coffee, and checked on Letterman. After fixing the parrot's wake-up beverage, Louie headed across the parking lot to the Goddess hoping to divert his thoughts from the lingering shock of Captain Jack's death.

Em looked up from the battered old desk in his office where she was paying bills. Concern showed on her features.

"You look terrible. Are you all right?" she asked.

"I didn't sleep much. It was too hot."

"Didn't you have your fan on?"

"Yeah, but it didn't help." He couldn't tell her that he'd been haunted by Jack Parsons' death and worried over the unknown contents of the bag he'd buried beneath her bedroom window.

"I'm sorry about your old friend. His death had to have been a shock after seeing him in here day before yesterday."

He shuffled out into the bar and poured himself a mug of strong black coffee. Across the room on the small stage, the Hula Maidens were practicing a new number, this time using bamboo *pu'ili*, musical implements made of two foot-long bamboo sticks carved into long strands with a handle at the bottom.

In the hands of gifted hula dancers, use of the *pu'ili* was exciting to watch. In the hands of the Hula Maidens, the bamboo implements were downright dangerous.

Pat, the troupe's sergeant-at-arms kept, stopping their recorded music whenever one of the Maidens got out of time crossing and tapping the sticks. Crossing them in and out of an X while keeping time to the music was hard enough for the old gals, but when they flung open their arms to tap the *pu'ili* of the person beside them, more often than not someone missed and smacked a hula sister on the arm, or worse yet, in the face.

Louie ignored the bickering and occasional yelps from the stage and hoped no one lost an eye. As he cut up limes and filled the garnish container, the Maidens put up a valiant effort, until their leader Kiki Godwin got knocked on the noggin and called a halt to the practice.

Louie stopped Big Estelle, one of the more stately, full-figured women of the troupe as she headed for the door. "Want some ice for that cut on your nose?"

She shook her head. "I'm okay. I've got bruises all over my shoulders. I'll ice myself down when I get home. Besides, I have to get home and make sure mother isn't accosting our new gardener. He's really good looking and, well, you know how she is."

Louie did indeed know. Big Estelle's ninety-plus-year-old mother, Little Estelle, had a passion for strapping young men.

Flora and Kiki slid onto tiki bar stools and leaned on the bar while the rest of the women exited.

"I'm so done, and it's only ten thirty," Flora said.

Louie set coasters in front of them. "What'll it be ladies? Something refreshing?"

They ordered white wine.

"You been down in the dumps all morning," Kiki said to Flora.

"I can't help it. Bad things gonna happen soon if the talk is true."

"What talk?"

"The guy who died, the one who washed up on the beach, you know, *da kine*," Flora said.

Suddenly they had Louie's full attention. He didn't waste a second filling their glasses to the rim, turning around and setting them on the bar.

"What about him?" Louie asked Flora.

She shrugged her shoulders. "I hear he found something that was better left lost. That thing killed him."

"What are you talking about?" Kiki set her wine glass down. "Did he find a bunch of drugs and overdose?"

The image of the navy blue bag flashed through Louie's mind.

Flora looked behind her. She saw no one there. Sophie was in the kitchen, so it was just the three of them in the bar. She lowered her voice.

"Worse than that. Coconut wireless says he found the lost tiki."

"What lost tiki?" Kiki rolled her eyes.

Louie could almost feel the size and weight of the bag in his suddenly damp palms. He wiped them on the bar towel.

"What lost tiki?" He repeated.

"I can only tell you what I heard from my grandparents, aunties, and uncles years ago."

Louie nodded encouragement. "Go on."

"Back in the old, old times, one of the *ali'i*, a chief from O'ahu, wanted to make a summer home in Hanalei. He tried to claim the land for himself, but it belonged to an old Kaua'i family. While his workers were digging on the land, they found a stone tiki long time buried. Strange thing because it wasn't made of wood. It was carved from stone, so they figured it was very, very old. Maybe from the first people who sailed here."

"How big was it?" Louie's heart was racing.

"How do I know?" Flora shrugged.

"Go on," Kiki polished off her wine.

"So right after they dug the tiki outta the ground, most of the workers got sick, and a lot of them died. Then the son of the chief died. So the man gave up wanting a house here and decided to sail back to O'ahu. He didn't know the tiki was to blame, so he loaded it on the ship back to Honolulu. You can guess what happened next." Flora finally drank some of her wine and smacked her lips.

"The ship went down." Louie barely got the words out.

"The chief drowned. Everybody drowned. The ship never got out of the bay." Flora added between sips. "Nobody ever saw the stone tiki again."

Kiki rolled her eyes. "Oh, come on."

"True dat," Flora said. "Folks salvaged all the stuff they could get off the chief's boat, finders keepers, but nobody found the stone tiki. Nobody remembers the old chief's name either."

"That thing is probably still at the bottom of the bay," Kiki started to rummage in her purse for her wallet. "If it ever existed."

"It should stay there, but maybe the crazy *haole* captain found it," Flora said. "Now he's dead, too."

Louie grabbed a napkin and wiped his brow.

"Captain Jack was a fisherman, not a diver," Louie said. "If it was on the bottom all this time, I doubt he or anyone else found it without dredging equipment."

"Remember when the Smithsonian came and dredged up stuff from that ship that went down in the bay in the eighteen hundreds?" Kiki asked.

Louie remembered. "I can't recall too much, just that it was a big deal," he said. "But Jack's just a fisherman. *Was* just a fisherman."

"I'm only telling you what folks are saying," Flora picked up her wine. "There's always a grain of truth under a rumor."

"Usually," Kiki said.

"I hope not," Louie mumbled.

The last thing he needed was a cursed tiki buried on his lot.

As soon as he could get away, Louie hurried back to the house. He'd forgotten to turn on the television for Letterman when he left. By the time he walked in the door, it was almost two o'clock, and the parrot was using its beak to try to disassemble the cage. The bars were reinforced, and Dave wasn't getting anywhere.

Once his feathered taste tester was appeased, Louie picked up the phone and called Detective Roland Sharpe of the Kaua'i Police Department.

The full-time detective and part-time fire knife dancer had been dating Em, so Louie hoped to pry a little inside information about Jack's death out of him.

After some preliminary chatting, Louie got to the point. "Roland, do you know anything about the cause of Jack Parsons' death? The fisherman who washed up on the beach in Hanalei yesterday?"

"Did the Hula Maidens put you up to this? Please tell me they're not snooping around again on this one."

"Not as far as I know. I'm asking for myself, Roland. I'm worried it wasn't an accident because, well, because of a couple of things I heard recently."

"The curse of the lost tiki theory?"

"You heard it too?"

"Kaua'i's a small island."

"So what do you think?"

"Are you asking if I think a cursed tiki is responsible for Jack Parsons' death? The answer is no."

"Jack was an old friend." Louie wasn't ready to break his promise to Jack and say any more. Not yet anyway.

There was a pause on the line before Roland said, "I can tell you the preliminary reports say it looks like he had a stroke. There was no sign of physical injury. His dinghy was found out of gas and floating near Waikoko. A little farther out of the bay and it would have been long gone. We figure he was headed back to his boat the night before his body was found. At some point, he had a heart attack or a stroke, fell overboard, and drowned. Somehow, the dinghy made it unmanned across the bay before it ran out of gas."

After Louie thanked Roland and hung up, he walked onto the screened front lānai filled with comfortable vintage rattan furniture and retro barkcloth drapes. Staring out at the ocean, he wished he felt more relieved.

Two days after Captain Jack's body was found, Louie got up and donned the colorful, long silk kimono he used as a bathrobe. Em was already up, sitting cross-legged on the sofa in the main room checking her emails and watching the local a.m. talk show.

"Kaua'i is under hurricane watch," she announced.

"Not again."

Em sighed. "I'm so tired of this. The talk show host just said islanders are experiencing hurricane fatigue."

"A 'watch' just means they're watching the storm. If they issue a warning, we batten down the hatches. We'll have hours of notice." He glanced over and saw he hadn't allayed her fears. He'd been through hurricanes Iwa and Iniki. Em had no idea what to expect.

"Besides," he added. "as long as we're okay and Dave's okay, we'll be fine."

"Still."

"I know." He wasn't sure that at seventy he had the energy to rebuild. Just now, he had worse things to worry about.

"Look at that." Em indicated the television screen. Hurricane Enrique covered a wide swath of ocean. One of its projected tracks showed it moving directly over Kaua'i but missing all the other islands.

"That's just weird," Em said.

Louie pictured the duffle bag as he lowered it into the ground next to the house. The idea of a cursed tiki was ridiculous. But what if Captain Jack had found the thing and pulled it out of the bay? Could it be cursed? Could it have caused Jack's death and be drawing the hurricane to the island?

The only way to find out what was in the bag was to open it, but he'd given Jack his word.

"You're the most honest man I know, Louie. There's nobody else I can trust."

He was fixing a mini-portion of Kahlua and lukewarm coffee for Dave when an idea hit him. Captain Jack's first mate, Chuckie Robbins might know something about the contents of the navy blue bag. If Jack was aboard his fishing boat when he discovered the tiki, surely Chuckie would have been there.

Louie had no idea how to reach Chuckie, but as far as he knew, Jack's fishing boat was still moored in the bay. If he went down to Black Pot, surely he could get someone to take him out to the *Nanilani*.

Within an hour and a half, thanks to Shelby Brown's Black Pot connections, Louie was on a skiff crossing Hanalei Bay headed for the *Nanilani*. John and Eddie, two fishermen from Mad Dog Fishing, were headed out to their Hatteras and happy to give him a ride.

"Want us to wait?" Eddie asked as he maneuvered the small skiff up to the stern of the catamaran.

"That'd be great, if you don't mind. Let me just make sure Chuckie's here," Louie said.

"We haven't seen him since Jack died. Probably soaking up a lot of rum someplace," John said.

Louie heard something making a clanking sound as he called out, "Whoo-ee," a couple of times and studied the navy awning shading the bridge above the captain's chair. Then he grabbed the ladder and climbed aboard the catamaran.

"Chuckie?"

Louie saw the body as soon as he stepped onto the deck. Chuckie Robbins was lying face down on the fiberglass deck, his head haloed in a pool of his own blood. There was a lump the size of a fat taro root on the back of his head. An empty rum bottle rolled back and forth and clanked against the deck. Bloody footprints were tracked all over the deck around the body. Louie staggered back and grabbed the stainless steel rail.

"You okay, Uncle?" John called up to him.

"I'm okay," Louie hollered, "but you better call 911. I'm pretty damn sure Chuckie's dead."

Authorities on shore notified the Coast Guard, which had jurisdiction over commercial vessel injuries and death. Chuckie Robbins was indeed dead and had been for quite a while. Not only were there footprints near the body, but the *Nanilani* appeared to have been ransacked. Louie and the two fishermen were taken aboard the Coast Guard cutter and interviewed.

Louie was in shock, but still able to think on his feet when asked what business he had aboard the *Nanilani.*

"Captain Jack, the boat's owner, was a friend of mine. He died a couple days ago, so I got a lift and came out to check on his hand, Chuckie. They'd worked together for years. I was sure Chuckie had to be pretty torn up about Jack's death. I wanted to give my condolences."

He got the feeling the Coast Guard officials dismissed him as a suspect on the spot but they asked him, John, and Eddie to stay on island in case they had more questions. The men all agreed, and then the fishermen ferried Louie back to the beach.

He wasn't two steps away from the boat when he saw Roland Sharpe step out of an unmarked KPD vehicle parked on the hard sand near the river mouth. The detective headed his way.

"Uncle Louie." Roland nodded. He held a small spiral notebook in his hand.

"Hey, Roland." Obviously, the fire-dancing detective had been waiting for him.

Roland said, "I headed up here as soon as the 911 call came in. Found out you were on the boat when I got to the beach. You okay to drive back to the Goddess?"

"Sure. Why?"

Roland shrugged.

"You asking because I'm old?" Louie lifted his hat and ran his hand through his hair. "I'll admit it was a shock seeing Chuckie like that, but I'm okay." He could still hear the sound of the rolling rum bottle in his head.

"Most people would be a little shook up," Roland said. "Em called and asked me to check on you if I was on the scene."

"Well, after I drive off you can call and tell her I'm just fine and on my way back." Louie fished around in his pocket for the keys to his truck.

"Before you go, you mind if I ask a couple of questions?"

"Course not."

"Why did you go out to Jack Parsons' boat this morning?"

He told Roland what he'd told the Coast Guard officials. "To see how Chuckie was doing. He worked for Jack for years, and I figured he had to be messed up about the captain's death."

Roland's notebook was little bigger than his palm. Louie noticed the detective was jotting down notes.

"Did you call to let him know you were coming?"

Louie shrugged. "Heck, I don't even have a number for him. Couldn't have called if I wanted to. Just thought I'd show up."

"Em said Captain Parsons was in the Goddess the day before he washed up on the beach. Is that true?"

"It's true. Why would Em make that up?"

Roland jotted and then stared at him.

"Sorry," Louie said. "This has all been a little much."

"You called me asking for information about cause of death for Parsons. Since you were one of the last people to talk to him, did he give you any cause to think he might have met with foul play?"

"You mean that cursed tiki story?"

"No, but did he tell you he was in danger?"

Two men were dead. Chuckie might very well have seen and even laid hands on the tiki, *if* Jack had found it. Louie knew if he told Roland Jack had sworn him to secrecy about the bag he'd buried in the garden, the detective would demand they dig it up and open it.

Until he knew exactly what he was dealing with there was no way on earth Louie wanted anyone else involved. Until he knew what was going on, he had to keep Roland and everyone else safe without lying.

Louie chose his words carefully. "Jack never said he was in danger. Do *you* think he might have been?"

If Roland doubted his word, he didn't say so.

He did say, "I think if Parsons told anyone about finding a lost artifact, that there are enough people around here who might just want to get their hands on it. If it's from the eighteen hundreds, it could be worth a fortune to the right buyer."

"So are you thinking that's what happened on the boat? Someone who heard the tiki rumors, went aboard and killed Chuckie, then ransacked the boat looking for whatever Jack may have found?"

"I'm thinking that's a strong possibility," Roland said. "I don't believe in curses, but I do believe greed drives some people to do terrible things."

"I hate to think somebody killed Jack over a ridiculous story like that." Louie hoped he sounded sincere because at this point he had no idea what to believe. "I'd better get back to the bar," he added. "If that's all you need..."

"For now," Roland said.

"If you hear anything from the Coast Guard, will you let me know?"

The detective nodded. "Seeing as how Parsons drowned and now this, we'll be taking a closer look at the captain's death. It might not be so open and shut. If I get any new information that won't jeopardize the case to tell you about, I'll let you know. But you'll have to do something for me, Louie."

"Sure. What?"

"Keep the damn Hula Maidens from going into sleuth mode."

By the time Louie returned to the bar, the place was suffering from late afternoon slows. The stifling weather accounted for the lack of patrons. It was almost too hot to move. Most of the locals were no doubt at home in front of fans praying the trades would return while the tourists were sequestered in their air-conditioned hotel rooms.

He was still in shock, his mind reeling. Someone, not something, had killed Chuckie. The bloody footprints on the deck were real, not something a cursed tiki would leave behind. Unable to focus, Louie headed into his office and pulled out his Booze Bible. The three ring binder was filled with his original tropical beverage recipes, the legend he'd written for each one, and doodles and sketches in the margins. He paged through the binder lethargically but couldn't blame his malaise on the heat.

A quick knock on the door gave him a start.

"Come on in," he called out.

Em stepped inside and left the door open behind her. "How are you doing?"

"As well as can be expected after Jack and now this," he said.

"Roland assured me that he'd let you know whatever he can."

Sophie walked in behind Em. "Sorry to interrupt, but there's a local guy here who wants to see Louie. Says he needs to ask a favor."

"Thanks," Louie said. "Tell him I'll be right out."

Louie stood up. Em was still standing by the door. He could tell she had something to say.

"What?" He asked.

"No more loans, Uncle Louie. You promised."

He knew she was only trying to keep the business in the black, but he missed being able to ease folks' minds by loaning them whatever they needed. Whether or not they could pay him back never entered his mind.

Em was waiting for his promise.

"Okay. No loans," he agreed, but only half-heartedly.

He walked into the bar and recognized the man waiting for him at a table near the front door. Louie knew his first name was Dane and that he was a North Shore activist for all things Hawaiian.

"Aloha, Uncle Louie," the man said without smiling.

"Dane, is it?"

"Dane Naupaka."

Louie offered his hand. "Long time since you've been in."

They shook hands. Dane said, "I come to ask a favor."

"Sure. I'll do what I can."

"You say that and I haven't even asked."

"You're a neighbor. I'll help if I can."

"I'd like to hold a community meeting here at the Goddess."

"When are you thinking?"

"Sooner the better. You know about the two dead *haole*. You heard the rumor about a lost tiki being found?"

"I've heard, but I'm having a hard time believing in a cursed tiki."

"We want to get the word out to the community, let them know that whoever has the tiki needs to put it in the rightful hands."

"And whose hands would that be?"

"Hawaiian hands. My family's. The Naupakas will see to it. The old timers say our land out in Hā'ena is where the ancestors buried the thing in the first place. This has to be handled in the proper way. Protocol, you know. This has to be *pono*. The right thing has to be done so the curse will end."

"What's the right thing?"

"The tiki must be put back into the land in a secret spot far from everything and everyone."

"What makes you think you and your family will be safe? If the legend is true, you may be putting your whole family at risk. Supposedly plenty of Hawaiians died last time the tiki surfaced."

"We'll honor it, bury it with ceremony and keep it out of the wrong hands."

"If the story is true, and I'm not saying I believe it, then what makes you think anyone is safe while it's on the island?"

Dane frowned. "It's our *kuleana*, our responsibility, no matter what happens. We believe the tiki was created by our ancestors. It should be in Hawaiian hands." Dane was getting steamed up.

Louie debated how to answer. What if Dane was wrong, and his family wasn't safe? The last thing he wanted was for anyone else to die. If the thing buried in his garden was responsible, he didn't want it to strike again.

"Can we hold the meeting here or not?" Dane demanded.

As much as he wanted to say no to protect Dane and his family, Louie nodded in agreement.

"Of course. Let's go tell Em to put it on the calendar."

The night of the North Shore community meeting at the Goddess, Hurricane Enrique was two days closer to Kaua'i. Meteorologists were predicting a direct hit in the next thirty-six hours unless the storm took a miraculous turn and changed course. Record high temperatures and humidity had everyone crankier than usual. Every seat in the room was taken. Folks were standing around the edges of the room two and three deep. The front lānai was filling up as well.

On stage, the Hula Maidens were decked out in bright green-and-white mu'umu'us and jaunty straw hats. They'd pinned huge anthurium blossoms on the sides of their heads beneath their tilted hat brims. According to Kiki, one can never wear too many adornments.

All went well with the Maidens' performance until they tried to execute a simple line switch maneuver. Two of the front row dancers, Precious Cottrell, a Little Person, and Lillian Smith, a nervous Midwestern transplant, danced backward when they should have stayed in place, which threw everyone else out of step. Chaos ensued. Big Estelle stormed off the stage along with two other back row dancers. Lillian burst into tears. One by one, the Maidens fled.

The band forged on until Kiki was the only one left on stage. She made a dramatic, sweeping bow at the end of her number and toddled over to the bar.

Louie had volunteered to act as emcee for the evening, so as soon as Kiki left the stage he thanked the band and welcomed everyone.

"We're here at the request of Dane Naupaka and his 'ohana. It's great to see such a wonderful turnout. Before I hand the mic over to Dane, I have a couple of requests. First, as you probably know by now, tonight we're only serving water, sodas, and juices until the meeting ends. Second, please remember to keep your cool and speak with aloha and respect. You've all got opinions and tonight we're going to hear all sides."

He and Em agreed they didn't want anyone to get drunk and overheated causing fights to break out on the premises. In the two days since Louie agreed to hold the meeting in the bar, Hurricane Enrique wasn't the only thing to heat up. There were now three solid factions in contention for possession of the lost tiki—a tiki no one could actually prove existed.

Not only did the Naupaka family want it, but so did the Smithsonian Institute, and also representatives for Fredrico Quintana, a billionaire developer and owner of the Quintana Corporation who planned to develop a five-star hotel up the hill past Princeville.

Louie scanned the crowd until he spotted Roland standing beside Em near the far end of the bar.

"Now Detective Roland Sharpe wants to say a few words." Louie waved Roland forward.

Roland walked up, and Louie handed him the mic.

"Aloha. We're not expecting any trouble, but I'm here tonight with two of my fellow KPD officers to make sure all voices are heard. I'm also here to let you know the Coast Guard investigation found that Chuckie Robbins was not murdered. Blood and hair samples found on board show he died at some point during the night. Chuckie was so drunk, he either slipped or passed out and hit his head on a railing aboard the *Nanilani*. Whoever went aboard, presumably looking for the legendary lost tiki, walked through Chuckie's blood and tracked it around while ransacking the boat after his death."

Roland paused and studied the crowd. "So as far as Chuckie being murdered, or Captain Parsons for that matter, we have no evidence to support either theory. They died of natural and accidental causes. There is no proof Parsons ever found a lost tiki, and no proof anyone stole it off the *Nanilani*." He reminded everyone to stay cool, handed the mic back to Louie, and left the stage.

"You all know Dane Naupaka, who called this meeting," Louie said. He handed the mic over.

Dane had walked on stage surrounded by a contingent of angry-looking Hawaiian men in matching black T-shirts. Barbed wire designs were printed around the neckline and down the sleeves.

"By now everybody knows what I'm going to say, so I'll make it short. Two men are dead. No matter how they died, they're dead. We believe the captain found the tiki and the curse is still very powerful. The tiki belongs on Naupaka 'āina. My family has owned the land for centuries, so we are the rightful owners. If some no-name chief hadn't tried to take our land in the eighteen hundreds, if his workers hadn't dug it up in the first place, a lot of lives would have been spared back then and now." He looked around slowly, eying them all.

"Whoever has the idol is not gonna last long. If you have it, bring it to me. If you don't, but you know who has it, let me know, and we'll get it back. Me and my *'ohana* will take care of it in the most *pono* way."

Someone yelled from the back, "How you know you not going to die, too? How you know we not all going to die if that thing stays on Kaua'i? It's gotta be put back in the ocean, back in the water where it can't hurt anybody else."

"He *don't* know," another man called out.

Dane's burly entourage glared around the room, effectively silencing the crowd.

Louie took the mic. "Mahalo, Dane. Mahalo for being concise. I'm sure we all heard Dane's message loud and clear. Now I'd like to introduce a representative from the Smithsonian Institute in Washington, D.C."

The men in black accompanied Dane off the stage as a clean-cut, middle-aged *haole* wearing a powder blue Polo shirt, gray slacks and carrying a brief case took Dane's place. His assistant, in a nearly identical outfit, passed out flyers as he moved through the crowd.

"This is Dr. Timothy Bleumenthal from the Smithsonian." Louie handed him the mic.

"Aloooooooha!" The museum official shouted as enthusiastically as an emcee at a hotel luau.

The audience stared back in silence. The man cleared his throat, and then introduced himself and listed his many credentials.

"As you probably all know, the Smithsonian was founded in 1846. It's the world's largest museum and research complex and consists of nineteen museums and galleries, the National Zoological Park, and nine research facilities. There are one hundred thirty eight million artifacts, works of art, and specimens in our collection. The information sheet my assistant is passing out now gives an overview of how we professionally and carefully store these national and world treasures and also how we use radiocarbon and thermoluminescense dating techniques to determine exactly how old an archeological treasure might be. In the case of the idol, which was supposedly unearthed in the early eighteen hundreds, we intend to date, catalogue, and protect it while in our possession, and then eventually return it to the Kauaʻi Museum.

"As you may know, we recently gave the Kauaʻi Museum items recovered from the shipwrecked Royal Hawaiian Yacht Haʻaheo o Hawaii, also known as Cleopatra's Barge, in the 1995-2006 dredging of Hanalei Bay."

"So you wanna take the curse to the mainland?" Dane shouted.

"Let him," a woman in the crowd suggested.

"Surely in this day and age you don't honestly believe in curses," Bleumenthal said.

The crowd remained silent. No one nodded in agreement.

A young man in his late teens raised his hand. When Bleumenthal acknowledged him, the young man stood.

He waved the information sheet. "It says here you got almost one hundred and forty million artifacts. Why you need ours?"

Applause broke out around the room.

When it was finally quiet again, Bleumenthal said, "Thank you all for listening. We're sure that you'll do what's best for the future generations of Kauaʻi."

Louie was in the middle of fantasizing about digging up the captain's duffle when he realized the Smithsonian representative wanted to turn over the mic. Two minutes ago he had almost made up his mind to give the tiki to the Naupakas, *if* there was a tiki in the bag. But, what if the curse was legitimate? He was an author of legends himself. He had embellished his own life experiences for years while working on his Booze Bible recipes. There was always a grain of truth behind each of his tales. What if there was some truth to the legend of the lost tiki?

Representatives from the Quintana Corporation were signaling from the back of the room. They had finished setting up a PowerPoint presentation.

Louie announced, "Our next speaker is a representative from the Quintana Corporation, which just purchased property near Princeville for a new hotel development."

A round of boos went up.

"Remember folks, aloha," Louie said.

He handed the mic to an Asian American dressed in a Reyn Spooner shirt, khaki pants and Topsider shoes. Suddenly, a watercolor rendering of an upscale resort filled a screen set up on the wall behind the stage. A collective gasp filled the room. Expressions of shock and anger were on most of the faces of those in the audience.

The speaker went on as if he hadn't heard or noticed.

"This is an artist's rendering of Indah, the planned hotel and resort just north of Princeville. The name Indah means beautiful in Indonesian. As you can see, the main building is done in Balinese style. The hotel cottages are the pod structures on paths that trail out and away from the main building like raindrops on a spider's web."

The picture changed to another showing an open-air wooden structure with a vaulted ceiling.

"This is the main building, the lobby where guests will register. As you can see, there is a reflecting pool in the center of the lobby. There is a pedestal in the center of the pool which is where we plan to display the Legendary Lost Tiki of Kaua'i for all the world to see and admire."

An old man in the back stood and called out, "You mean you'll put it on display for all the hotel guests who can afford to stay at your hotel to see."

A man beside him appeared to be related. He stood up. "What about the maids and the gardeners and the other workers? They gonna be allowed in the lobby? They gonna get to see it?"

Hoots of encouragement filled the bar and started a free-for-all.

"You got the land," a woman yelled. "Now you want our ancestors' gods too?"

"Go back to the mainland."

"I was born in Honolulu," the Quintana rep replied.

One of Dane's cohorts hollered, "Go back and tell 'em enough hotels up here already. No more."

Louie saw the Smithsonian representatives scurry out the door. The Quintana rep was visibly shaken. He handed the mic back to Louie.

Louie had no fear of the community members in the bar. He commanded the stage with ease. He'd been around long enough to know that given enough time, island upheavals worked themselves out more often than not.

Dane Naupaka signaled that he had one more thing to say. Before Louie handed over the mic, he whispered to Dane, "Folks are hot and tired. Not too long, eh?"

Dane nodded. "Okay, so you guys heard everybody now. You know what's *pono*. You know where I live. If you don't, ask somebody. We'll take the tiki no questions asked, and put it back into the land, into its rightful place on our *'āina*."

Louie thanked everyone for coming, including Roland and the men from KPD. The room soon cleared of old folks and youngsters. The regulars hung out and ordered drinks when the bar opened. Within a quarter hour, it was business as usual.

Just before closing, Em asked Louie if it was all right for her to drive Kiki home.

"Kimo's still got things to do in the kitchen, and Kiki didn't drive her own car," Em said.

"Sure. Sophie and I can handle things and close up." Kiki and Kimo lived just up the road. He figured Em would be there and back in twenty minutes or less.

Two hours later, he was worried sick, wondering where Em was. He'd tried calling but she didn't answer her cell phone. He knew there were dead spots on the highway where cell service was spotty at best, but Kiki wasn't answering her home phone. He waited another ten minutes and then called Roland.

"Em's missing." Louie tried to keep the panic out of his voice and failed miserably.

"What do you mean missing?"

"She left over two hours ago to take Kiki home, and she's not back yet. I can't reach her by cell, and Kiki's not answering her phone either. Kimo left and same thing. No communication."

"I just heard cell phone calls aren't going through to the North Shore. I'm outside of Anahola. I'll head back. You sit tight in case she gets back. You can let me know."

Louie agreed. He paced the bar, sick with worry. Sophie refused to leave. The television in the corner was tuned to a local news channel now broadcasting twenty-four-hour storm information. Enrique was bearing down on Kaua'i with a slim to none chance it would pass them by.

Running his hands through his hair, Louie thought about the hurricane, Em's disappearance, the upheaval in the community, Captain Jack and Chuckie's deaths.

"Here." Sophie put a gin and tonic on the bar in front of him. "She'll be okay, Uncle."

"You sure?"

"I have to be. You do, too."

"Right." He swallowed the shot.

"Another?"

"No thanks. This is no time to get plastered."

They waited for what seemed like eons for the phone to ring. It was pouring rain when a car pulled into the deserted driveway, and both of them ran out onto the lānai.

Louie recognized Roland's undercover KPD cruiser. When he spotted Em in the passenger's seat, his legs nearly gave way with relief. He leaned against the railing for support.

The detective and Em got out of the car. Roland hurried her up the steps with his hand riding at her waist. Em hugged Louie and then Sophie.

"I'm so sorry you had to worry," she said.

Louie noticed her upper lip was swollen. "What happened?"

Sophie pulled out a chair for her. "Want to sit?"

Em shook her head. "I was driving home and thought I saw a dog right in the middle of the road. It walked straight toward me, so I swerved to miss it. I ended up in a deep ditch. It nearly swallowed up my car. The airbag went off, and I guess I passed out. When I woke up, I tried to call 911, but my cell wouldn't work. I tried to call you, too."

"It's nuts, but cell and phone lines both seem to be out up here," Roland added. "I tried to call you when I found her car. The car lights were off, and I nearly drove right past her in the dark."

"Good thing you didn't drive off the makai side and end up in the ocean," Sophie hugged Em again.

Em shivered. "I hope my car is all right overnight."

"I'll have a tow truck bring it to you tomorrow so it's here before the storm hits."

"Sheesh. I forgot about the hurricane." Em glanced at the television screen mounted in the corner. "Is it still headed this way?"

"We have time to pack things up and get ready," Sophie said.

Louie couldn't stop staring at Em. If anything had happened to her because of the promise he'd made Captain Jack, he would never forgive himself.

He was the one who'd accepted the bag, the one who buried it in the yard. He was the one who was going to have to do the right thing to save Kaua'i and everyone on the island.

Louie made sure Em was comfortable and tucked in before he went back into the main room. He planned to stay dressed and sit up all night if he had to in order to carry out his plan in the wee hours of the morning.

He woke up with a kink in his neck from sleeping on the sofa. The clock on the microwave in the kitchen read five a.m. Walking past Letterman's cage on the way to the front door, he touched the Hawaiian print cover over the cage and whispered, "Don't drink yourself to death, little buddy."

The first thing he did when he left the house was pull an old, one-man outrigger canoe from beneath the house. It was still rigged, and the paddle lay in the bottom of the canoe he hadn't used for years. For all he knew the canoe might be full of holes, but right now his only concern was making it to Hanalei Bay.

He wasn't going to worry about getting back. If he was meant to survive, he would.

A full moon cast milky moonlight upon the sand. The crests of the small waves along the shore were a frothy blue-white as he pulled the boat across the beach toward the high tide line. It was a small craft, old style made of wood, but still not too heavy for him to move alone.

Once the boat was at the waterline he went back to the shed behind the house, got out his shovel and then dug up Captain Jack's duffle. He pulled it out of the plastic trash bag and stored the bag and shovel in the shed.

Without looking inside, he hung the straps of the bag over his shoulder and headed back to the canoe. Once there, he gently laid the bag inside, lifted the canoe over the worn coral shelf at the edge of the water, and set it in the water. Louie stepped into the canoe, lowered himself onto the single seat, and got his balance. Then, he picked up the paddle and headed away from shore.

He paddled carefully, using muscles he hadn't used in years as he traveled along the coast south toward Hanalei, guided by the lights of the St. Lexus Hotel at Princeville. He was outside the huge crescent bay when dawn lit the sky. Odd streaks of high cirrus clouds seemed to quickly turn from gray to pink to red.

Red sky at morning, sailors take warning.

Louie put some more muscle into his paddling and was moving along at a smooth pace when he felt something bump the bottom of the canoe. He automatically leaned toward the *ama* for balance and looked down into the water.

He thought he'd hit something, but something had hit the canoe. In the dim light, he could just make out a six-foot tiger shark slowly circling the boat. It nudged him again and again.

Slowly, carefully, Louie set the paddle down in the bottom of the boat and picked up the duffle. His hand shook as he unzipped it. The bag opened to reveal an old beach towel, faded and ragged. It had been wrapped around a two-foot long object.

From the shape and feel of it, Louie knew what he'd find beneath the towel.

Sure enough, it was a stone idol. The image of the tiki had been carved so long ago, its features were nearly worn smooth. As he stared down at the ancient god, he wished it could tell him where it had come from and why it was so angry.

Reverently Louie lifted it out of the bag and cradled it on his knees. The shark still slowly circled the boat.

"So, old man. Here we are. I don't know if this is where you want to be, but it's where I intend to be at the end of my own life. It's peaceful down there on the bottom. Maybe that's where you were when Jack found you. Legend has it this was your last resting place, somewhere here in the bay, so I'm putting you back. I hope that will make you happy. If not, I guess I'll know soon enough."

Louie gently lifted the idol with both hands and held it over the side of the canoe. The shark had moved a few feet away but was still circling, watching, and waiting.

Louie closed his eyes. Before he let the tiki go, he whispered, "Aloha. *A hui hou.*"

The idol sank out of sight in less than a heartbeat.

When Louie finally picked up his paddle, the sun appeared over the mountains that hugged the Hanalei Valley. The shark swam beneath and beside him all the way back up the coast until Louie turned toward shore and slipped through an opening in the reef. That's when his deadly escort finally disappeared.

Dead tired emotionally and physically, Louie pulled the old canoe up onto the beach. He didn't breathe a sigh of relief until both feet were firmly on the sand. He left the canoe on the shore and carried the paddle up to the house.

He opened the front door, intending to creep in and not wake Em until he heard the television in the main room.

Em was lying on the sofa with a cup of coffee in her hand. Letterman's cage was uncovered. The parrot started squawking as soon as Louie walked in.

"Yo, ho, ho. Brrreakfast."

Em waved Louie over to the sitting area. "I woke up worried about the storm and came out to hear the latest update. You won't believe it. About forty minutes ago, the hurricane suddenly veered away from the island."

Forty minutes ago he'd let the tiki slip back into the waters of Hanalei Bay.

"Whew! It looks like we're safe." Em's smile was radiant with relief.

Louie nodded and smiled back. "It sure looks that way. I guess time will tell."

JILL MARIE LANDIS

Jill Marie Landis lives on the North Shore of Kaua'i where she has just completed book #5 of her hilarious Tiki Goddess Mystery Series. *Mai Tai One On*, *Two to Mango*, *Three to Get Lei'd* and *Too Hot Four Hula* are published by Bell Bridge Books and available in book and all ebook formats.

Her thirty novels have earned distinguished awards and slots on such national bestseller lists as the USA TODAY Top 50 and the New York Times Best Sellers Plus. She is a seven-time finalist for Romance Writers of America's RITA Award for Historical and Contemporary Romance as well as a RITA Award winner.

You can learn more about her on her website: www.jill-marielandis.com.

KE AHI PIOʻOLE
THE FIRE THAT NEVER BURNS OUT
A. J. Llewellyn

Though the weather outside my storefront Waikīkī office was frightful that hot, humid August Wednesday, the fire inside wasn't damned delightful.

Some hotel guest at the Holiday Inn next door had been smoking in the laundry room, which was forbidden, and I seemed to be the first one to detect it.

Rushing through the maze of glitzy stores and restaurants that fronted what used to be the old Waikīkī Beachcomber Hotel, I followed the stench of acrid fumes, then discovered the fire in a trash bin. He'd made a futile effort to stamp it out with a towel, only to make the flames spread. I doused them with my own mini extinguisher, but scorched my shoes, and even managed to singe my socks in the process.

The guy who started the fire wasn't happy either. I recognized him as a homeless man who hung out around the beach. So he wasn't a guest, but everybody has to do their laundry someplace.

"Don't call the cops, man," he begged. "I have a job interview and I didn't hurt anybody."

I realized my shoes didn't count. Neither did my socks. Somehow, he'd managed to get hold of tokens for the washer, but they were stuck in the slots. Most of his clothing, which had been sitting on top of the washer, had caught fire except what he was wearing: saggy Y-fronts and a woman's pink bikini halter top.

I felt bad for him, slipped him ten bucks, and told him to try the thrift shop around the corner. Two fire trucks took up a lot of space out front as I stomped back to my office and tried to ignore the sky full of moisture-laden ominous, grey clouds. *Something feels off.* I'm a former cop and sometimes I get a little paranoid thinking everything's suspicious, but was surprised to see a woman standing on my side of the desk. I didn't panic, but I didn't get excited either. I hadn't landed a single case since I'd moved back to Waikīkī four weeks ago.

So far, every single person who's come in here is either trying to book a scuba trip, or a luau because they think my office still sells discounted tickets. I hadn't counted on the free holiday magazine ads still floating around out there. Often people stopped and wanted to know where the club Don Ho used to perform in before his passing was located. More strangely, I've had people ask me where they can find Don Ho's Zom Zom Boutique.

They've also asked me, "By the way, what is a zom zom?"

I had no idea but have since discovered zom zoms are fictitious foods. And as far as I know, the online listing for this restaurant is a complete hoax.

"Mr. Morales?" the reed-slim Asian beauty asked me.

I stuffed the extinguisher in its box and made a mental note to order a new one as fire-retardant foam kept oozing out of the nozzle. The woman watching me was stunning. Her shoulder-length black hair, sweet face with just a touch of makeup, and what looked like a vintage white and lemon sleeveless pantsuit gave her the appearance of a China doll from another era. Without even looking, I knew she'd be wearing dainty, feminine shoes. Not sneakers or running shoes.

"Yes," I said. "I'm him. He is me. I mean, I am he." *Could I possibly sound a little more stupid?* She moved to the "client" side of the desk.

I glanced down. As I suspected, she wore pretty, slingback sandals.

"Mr. Danny Morales?"

I was tempted to respond, "No, I'm his cousin Fred," but said yes, hoping she wasn't trying to sell me a timeshare. Or zom zoms.

"I'd like to discuss a delicate matter with you." She wrinkled her nose. "What is that awful smell?"

"It was a fire. It's out now, though."

She cast a doubtful glance at the extinguisher, and I didn't blame her. The odor suddenly seemed worse.

"You wanted to see me about something?" I kept wondering where I could take her for a private talk. Not for the first time I cursed my idiotic decision to convert this space into an office.

Her eyes flickered in what I interpreted as anguish, and behind her, I noticed the beach police hauling off the homeless man who'd started the fire. He kicked and spat at them, but they kept a firm grip on him. Man, Waikīkī is getting crazier every day.

"Please, take a seat. Tell me what's going on."

I was almost surprised when she sat, especially when the homeless man suddenly shrieked obscenities at the top of his voice.

She pulled a face. "He sounds like my husband." I had an idea she wasn't joking.

"Would you like some tea?"

She looked surprised.

Maybe I should have been offended, but I know I'm a long, tall blend of Japanese and many Polynesian strains merged into a Neanderthal height of well over six feet, four inches. With my jeans, aloha shirt and big, cheesy grin, maybe she thought I looked more like the beer and burger type than the tea and talk type. Her glance seemed to rest on my short, dark hair, which never stays neat, probably because I am always sticking my fingers into it and grabbing chunks in frustration. And lately, I've been getting frustrated a lot.

"I have two kinds of tea," I said. "Japanese cherry and green coconut."

"Cherry sounds great."

I had stainless steel thermoses filled with each and poured her a cup then one for myself.

She held her pale blue porcelain cup with delicate fingers, staring at me over the rim.

I wondered who'd referred her to me. I wasn't sure why this spectacular creature wanted my services, but if she'd mistaken me for a gigolo I would have said yes, even though I'm gay. She was that gorgeous.

I waited for her to sort her thoughts. Besides, I had nothing better to do. I moved here from Kaua'i to try out a new career as a private eye. At the age of forty, I needed a break from the sometimes harrowing work I did in the cold case unit. Charlie, an old Punahou school buddy of mine back here who used to sell vacation and time share packages and discounted island activities out of the tiny storefront space, quit to relocate to a more peaceful life in Kaua'i. It's hard to hawk the excitement of a shark swim when one has just taken off your left arm and part of your right foot.

So, Charlie and I did a straight swap. He took over my Hanalei Bay condo. I took over his storefront space. We haven't talked much, probably because we're both severely depressed and it wouldn't take much for either one of us to convince the other to swap back again.

I sipped my tea, grateful that the smell of burning clothes seemed to have receded. "Take your time," I said. "Tell me what's going on."

She took her first sip, closed her eyes briefly and with a twist of grief in her expression, glanced down into the cup. "If I tell you something, is it confidential?"

"Well, that depends. As my client, anything you tell me remains between us unless you confess you're about to murder your husband, or you're going to put a bomb in 'Iolani Palace."

She seemed to consider this, then tilted her lovely head to one side. "Do you have a problem with infidelity?"

Boy, what a loaded question. I did in my own life, but as a public servant, I'd learned to withhold judgment on other people's lives.

"Not unless it's related to me."

"So if I tell you of a…marital indiscretion, you wouldn't feel the need to report it to uh, to my husband?"

"No."

She nodded. Her eyes were filled with pain when she looked at me. "The murder has already happened."

I gaped at her. "Who was killed?"

"My next door neighbor." She swallowed the tea in one gulp and slid the cup toward me. She knocked her forefingers together on the desktop. I wondered if she knew I have a Japanese mom or if this was just an old habit, but Mom does the same thing. She once told me it came from the old country and was a polite way of saying, "More please." I gave her a refill, thinking she needed a stiff belt of cognac instead. She took another sip. "Ah, that's good." She tilted her head at me. "My name is Sachi Hammond, and I'm married."

"Yes, you mentioned that." I was still trying to follow everything, but so far this trail of breadcrumbs wasn't falling into a straight line.

"For the past year, I've been having an affair with my neighbor, Takeo Watanabe, and well, he disappeared about five weeks ago. He came back last Monday, but he's not the same man."

Oh, poor lady's been rejected and can't handle it. I tried a tactful approach. "What do you mean? He's acting strange? Is he—"

"No, I mean he's a completely different person." She shifted in her seat. "I'm in a very bad marriage. I won't deny it. My husband and I have lived separate lives almost since the day we got married two years ago." She held up a hand. "It sounds like a line, I know, but it's true. I live in the downstairs portion of my house, and Bobby, my husband, lives upstairs. We rarely speak, but I am respectful, and I keep my private life private."

"Where do you live?"

"Mānoa."

"Go on."

"Takeo moved next door a few months after Bobby and I got married. I used to see him often and we'd talk. We began a...er, relationship about a year later. He's the best thing that ever happened to me, but for obvious reasons, I have kept it a secret. Even my closest friends don't know."

I looked at her. "May I ask you a personal question?"

"You're going to ask why I stay with my husband." Her cheeks flamed and she squirmed again. "I married him to help him with his green card. Believe me, if I didn't need to keep up the façade, I would have left long ago." She arched a brow at me. "He's a horrible man, but he paid me a lot of money. I needed it to save my home and pay off the debts my father left me when he passed. I grew up in that house. My father grew up in it, too. He had three mortgages, including one he took out in my name. I had no idea. He'd also opened credit cards in my name...oh, it's been a mess."

Her story sadly, wasn't unusual. As a cop, I'd had teenagers report their parents fraudulently using their credit. Identity theft had become an international pastime.

"I have to stay married for eleven more months to fulfill my end of the bargain and to receive the other half of the money Bobby owes me."

"How much is that?"

"A hundred thousand dollars."

I stopped myself from letting out a whistle. That was a lot of clams. "I assume he's paid you that much already." When she nodded, the obvious question became why he'd shelled out so much when obtaining immigration status would have been much cheaper.

Before I could even ask, she said, "Bobby is from Yemen. He grew up in England but he was born in Yemen. It's not exactly a popular country to be from when you want U.S. residency." She sipped her tea again, and her expression grew dark.

"We met at a book signing one night at The Pacific Club. In fact, it was his book signing. He's a retired boxer, and he'd written his autobiography. Have you ever been to The Pacific Club?"

I shook my head. "I know it costs a gazillion dollars to be a member." I paused. "And you need something like seven other members to sponsor you just to join."

"Exactly. So I went. I'm an aspiring writer, and he zeroed in on me. I was impressed. I'll admit it. He swept me off my feet. Literally." Once again she looked embarrassed. "I was taken in by his charm, good looks, his elegant clothing. I'd never been to a book signing like his. I mean, they served the most delicious food and drink, and the club makes you feel like you've gone back to the old Territory days. It's elegant and gracious. He's a member, so..."

"How did he swing that?"

She shrugged. "He has a lot of friends in high places."

"When did he bring up the issue of his immigration problems?"

"A few weeks after I met him. He really played me. I've lived here all my life and I fell for a classic con artist."

"A rich one, apparently."

She nodded. "He knew I wanted to be a writer and said when I finished my novel he'd help me get it published and he'd guarantee me that I'd have a book signing at The Pacific Club. He had no idea I was drowning in debt until he was with me one day and the bank served me with a foreclosure notice." Tears glistened in her eyes. "It was devastating, but he was so understanding, and so kind. He mentioned his attorney told him he should get married. According to this attorney, Bobby had no special skills that would make it easier for him to become a legal resident."

"And you believed him?"

"Yes. I met the attorney and he showed me all the paperwork he'd filed for Bobby."

"What's the attorney's name?"

"James Ivy."

I knew the guy. He wasn't an ambulance chaser. But he was dangerously close. "Go on," I said.

"Well, I learned a lot in the hour we were with him. Apparently before 9/11, Bobby's boxing career could have been enough to get him a green card, especially if he was actively fighting. Since he planned to coach football at the University of Hawai'i at Mānoa, that held extra appeal, but without the green card they wouldn't take him."

"And his friends in high places couldn't help him?"

"Not when it really mattered, no."

"So, getting married was mutually beneficial."

"Absolutely." Her eyes still shone with unshed tears. "We had a beautiful wedding with a big luau at The Pacific Club. That was the happiest day of my life. At first, Bobby was sweet, but it didn't last. He's moody and gets angry easily. He hit me once, and I called the police. There's a report on file with Honolulu Police Department. It's the Beretania Street division. After that, Bobby apologized and promised it would never happen again, but I took my little dog, Susie, and moved downstairs. It's a much smaller space, but I've made it very comfortable. He has the better part of the house, but Susie is safe with me, and I never leave her alone."

My God. The things people got themselves into for the almighty dollar.

"I have a contract with him for everything I told you. I can email it to you. In a little under twelve months when we complete the final immigration interview and his green card comes through, he'll move out, and my life will be mine again. We'll get divorced, and I don't care what happens to him after that."

As I tried to absorb all of this she added, "Right now, he's petrified I'll divorce him. We both stand to lose a lot if our true arrangement is ever revealed. I could go to jail. Did you know I could face a five-year prison sentence and a $250,000 fine for marriage fraud? And after what I went through with my dad? That's more than Bobby even has to pay me, but it would be worse for him. He'd be forced to return to Yemen, and he'd never be allowed back into this country again. Something happened there. And in England. The idea of going back frightens him."

"Have you Googled him?"

"Yes. There's nothing there but he doesn't talk to his family or anyone involved in his past. It's strange, don't you think?"

"Sounds like it." Still curious, I asked, "What's he doing for work now?"

"He trains boxers. That's partly how I've managed to keep my relationship with Takeo a secret. We meet when Bobby's out of town with his fighters, or when he takes them to camp on one of the other islands. He's fond of high-altitude training, and he'll go to one of the cabins at Haleakalā or Kīlauea with his clients."

Suddenly the trail of breadcrumbs of this woman's story seemed to lead straight to Bobby.

"Is there any chance Bobby found out about you and Takeo?"

She shook her head. "No. Absolutely not. I've been very careful. Bobby thinks I've become a frigid bitch, and I prefer it that way."

"When was the last time you saw Takeo?"

"Friday, July fifth. I saw him at our favorite coffee shop. We usually get together Friday nights because Bobby has dinner and watches the ESPN fights with some of the guys from the gym over in Pearl City. Takeo and I have a ritual. He comes to my entrance downstairs through the hibiscus forest at the back of my property. There are no lights, and it's hard to see. We keep an ear out for Bobby. It isn't hard to tell when he's home. First of all, Susie goes berserk and secondly, he's usually drunk and he hits the fence as he's coming down the driveway."

Wow, he sounds like a gem. "So that night, Takeo didn't come?"

"No. He didn't. His car was there when I looked over the fence. I called him. I even sneaked next door and knocked, but he never answered. The house was dark. The next day, the car was gone and I didn't hear a word from him."

"You tried to contact him again?"

Her dark hair bounced around her shoulders as she nodded. "Yes. Several times. I stopped leaving messages and then his voice mail got full."

"And nobody saw any sign of him during this time?"

"No."

"And nobody thought to call the police when he disappeared?"

She winced. "Believe me, I thought of it, but he's an unusual man, Takeo. He's a hermit who ventures out sporadically. He doesn't even go to the market. He shops by phone, and they deliver. It isn't unusual for him to skip a cooking class. That's his passion, vegan cooking. We also do, er did, volunteer work together, and it's not unusual for him to skip that, except he skipped delivering two Meals on Wheels. His day is Friday. That's when Amy got concerned, too."

"And Amy is?"

"Our district coordinator."

"So she got concerned and did...what?"

"When she couldn't reach him by phone, she went to see him. By that stage, I'd encountered the man next door and knew he was masquerading as Takeo. She met the guy and realized it too."

I looked at her. "So please explain why you think Takeo isn't um, Takeo."

"Because he isn't." She leaned on the desk, her eyes lit from within. I could tell she loved talking about him. "When he came back, I saw him on the lānai. I was so pleased to see him. I waved, but he didn't wave back. I thought it was odd. I thought he looked different." She blew out a sigh. "I was really concerned about him. From afar, he looked thinner than he had before, but it was Friday night, and he didn't come to my house, so I went to him."

"The man who opened the door was a stranger, even though he'd cut his hair to look like Takeo. There was no recognition in his eyes when I greeted him. He was rude, actually. I tell you, it was weird because unless you knew him, he could pass for Takeo, but I promise you, he is not."

She rifled through her cell phone and showed me a photo. "This is Takeo."

I studied the image of a young, very handsome Asian man with a boyish haircut, the front flopping into his eyes.

"I have a few of photos of the two of us together." She showed me three, and in each of them, it struck me how in love they seemed. They complemented each other perfectly. They appeared to be on a beautiful Asian sandalwood bed. Right beside them was a small black dog.

"Is that Susie?"

Her smile told me it was. Then she showed me a photo she'd taken of "Takeo" since he'd returned.

"There are three." She handed me her phone.

"How did you get this?"

"I followed him when I spotted him in the Ala Moana center a couple of days ago. I couldn't believe it worked. I had just bought these eye glasses that have a camera hidden in them. I noticed him, followed him into to Barnes and Noble and pretended to bump into him. I said hello but he wasn't happy to see me, that's for sure. I couldn't wait to get home and download the images. As you can see, there's a very strong resemblance but it is not the same man."

"Have you ever confronted him?"

"Yes. The first time I went to his door. I asked for Takeo, and he said, 'I'm Takeo.' I said, 'No, you're not.' I thought it was a joke at first, then I realized there was something about him. His manner was chilling. I knew he wasn't Takeo, but I wasn't going to stand there and argue. Quite frankly, he scares me."

She let me download the images to my laptop. Until I compared the photos side-by-side, the differences weren't obvious. Looking at them together, it was clear that Takeo and this new guy looked nothing alike. The big giveaway was their teeth and the shape of their faces. Takeo's front teeth had a gap. The new guy's didn't. The new guy's face was longer and lacked Takeo's unusual, downturned eyes. He could have had dental work and a facelift, but it didn't explain why he had no idea who Sachi Hammond was.

"Wow. And you haven't taken your suspicions to the police because of your involvement with him, and of course, Bobby?"

"Exactly." She nodded emphatically.

I stared at the photos. "Why would somebody impersonate Takeo?"

She spread her hands. "I have no idea. But it's obvious he kept our relationship a secret too, because this new guy had no idea who I was. None at all."

"And you think he killed Takeo?"

"I know he did. Little things have been happening. Takeo was an amazing person and this man knows nothing about the life he actually led. Takeo stopped volunteering at the local animal shelter. People think it's odd, and when Amy Jaeger went to visit him, the man didn't know who she was, either. Amy freaked out and called me. Takeo, I mean the real Takeo, would have known who she was because she's not only our Meals on Wheels coordinator, but Takeo's ex-fiancée."

This case was getting interesting. "You've discussed this with her?"

"Yes." Sachi Hammond seemed relieved. "We've talked a couple of times. She's the only other person who thinks this man is an imposter. Takeo is—was—a very private person. Up until he vanished, he was a relentless Facebook user but he never posted much about his day-to-day activities. He posted slogans, you know, the feel-good stuff a lot of people post. He was proud of his cooking classes. It was a big deal for him to try new things. I encouraged him. The new guy just took a class yesterday judging by the new posts, which have begun cropping up again. But that's all. I'm telling you, this man is a phony, and I think, a killer."

I nodded. "And you want me to prove it."

"Yes."

"Okay, I'm intrigued. I'll bite. May I ask, who sent you to me?"

She smiled for the first time. "A mutual friend. Noni Kolima."

I returned her smile, but it was fake. I reeled through the Rolodex in my mind. The name was familiar but I couldn't recall how I knew it.

"Could we get started right away?"

"Of course." I opened my top drawer and extracted a contract.

She read through it. "You require a three-thousand dollar cash retainer." She reached into her purse. "Here's five." She pushed a slim envelope toward me then scrawled her signature on the agreement. The envelope didn't look bulky enough to contain five grand. "All present and correct, I assure you." Once again, she seemed to be reading my mind. It was spooky.

As if on cue, a small puppy face peeped out of the purse opening.

"Well, well, well," I said. "Miss Susie, I presume?"

Sachi laughed. "Yes, this is Susie."

Her cell phone rang, and she dipped into her purse once more, checking the readout. "It's Bobby. He needs me to pick him up from the airport. He just got in from L.A." She pulled a face. "His boxer just lost the middleweight world championship two nights ago. He's going to be in a foul mood."

As she stood, she handed me a folded piece of paper. "Here are my details. My address, Takeo's address, my cell phone number, and his. By the way, somebody cleared his inbox and the phone rings, but I haven't left a message." She frowned. "We contacted each other with a series of codes. I made a note of them on the page in case you need them. I also gave you both of our social media links."

"I'll call you at six o'clock to give you an update." I said.

"Please don't leave messages on my cell phone. If you don't reach me in person, there's a number at the bottom of the page. It's a burner cell phone for you and me to stay in touch." She handed me one more item. A champagne glass in a baggie.

"This is a sample of Takeo's fingerprints. Oh, I've also given you Amy Jaeger's number. She knows I'm worried about Takeo, but only as a friend and fellow volunteer." Her cell phone chirped. "Gotta run."

I stared after her. Several things bothered me about the case. First, if she and Bobby rarely spoke, why was she picking him up at the airport? I opened the envelope and saw five crisp, thousand dollar bills. I'd never seen anything like them before except on drug busts. But what really got to me more than anything was I remembered who Noni Kolima was. And if she was the same person Sachi Hammond was talking about, then we had a problem because the Noni Kolima I knew was dead.

And had been for twenty-eight years.

I had a lot to do on this investigation and I was more excited than I'd been in weeks. Before anything else though, I needed to make sure the money she gave me was real. I checked in my top drawer for the counterfeit detector pen I was certain I'd put in there. Then remembered I didn't have one. Not that I thought the cash was fake but better safe than sorry. Before I left for the bank, I went online and Googled "Takeo Watanabe." I found his Facebook page, which was set to semi-private. I was able to see some things, such as the fact that he belonged to a vegan cooking club on the site and that he had joined two years ago.

His photo was not of himself but of a bowl of noodles. *Interesting.* Next, I looked up Bobby Hammond. Man, he was handsome, and just the kind of guy I'd go for, which meant he was a total doucheweed. He had a sullen look to his olive complexion and dark eyes. His hair had been shorn to the scalp and he had a huge grin. A cocky mofo to be sure. His Facebook avatar was a photo of him and Sachi. She looked ecstatic in the image, so I assumed it had been taken in happier times. His profile had been set to public, so I was able to discover the photo had been taken at their wedding, along with many others in his album.

Bobby's timeline was filled with boxing photos. The only reference I could find to Sachi was a birthday greeting the previous month. "Happy birthday to my gorgeous bride." There was a photo of the two of them at one of the outdoor tables at House Without a Key. Outwardly at least, he was keeping up the pretense of a happily married man. I made a mental note to come back and take a closer look at his posts.

I shut down the computer, stuck it in my laptop bag, slid the contract and the notes Sachi gave me into a pocket of the bag then locked the office. I wasn't worried about somebody coming and not finding me. It was too much to hope that I'd land two clients in one day.

Any passerby would have to ask somebody else about zom zoms.

Outside, I felt like a kid being let out of school. Born and raised on the island of Oʻahu, I'd known Waikīkī well in my school days, college, and later as a beat cop, but transferred to Kauaʻi. I hardly recognized Kalakaua Avenue now. Upstairs in the old Beachcomber tower, I had a small one-bedroom apartment I'd rented from a friend of Charlie's. It wasn't bad, but weekend nights, the noise level from the tourists was deafening. Located right opposite the Cheesecake Factory—my new, lethal obsession—and my least favorite place, Jimmy Buffet's aggressively loud Margaritaville, I got out of the office and away from the noise as soon as the sun started to set.

It still took some getting used to seeing all the big, fancy stores that had nothing to do with Hawai'i. I moved down the street to hit the bank and remembered it wasn't there anymore. There used to be one at International Marketplace but it was a construction site now, empty except for the massive banyan tree and another small one behind it. Not much seemed to be happening, except a lot of noise. The project was taking for damned ever to complete. I sped over to the First Hawaiian Bank on Luxury Row and raced inside.

One of the tellers took my notes, held them for a moment, an odd look on his face. He ran them through a counting machine, swept a counterfeit pen across them and stared at me. "They're real. I gave her this money myself."

I gaped at him. "She came in here? That's a huge coincidence."

He shrugged. "Small island, I guess. She ordered them about a month ago." He stared at the notes so long, I felt compelled to tug them from his grip. "I remember this transaction because we don't usually give out thousand dollar notes."

"I know. That's why I wanted to come in and check."

He smiled. "Beautiful, isn't she?" He sighed and fiddled with his wedding ring in a distracted way. "I keep hoping she'll come back."

I returned to the hotel where I kept my car in the maze called the parking lot, and drove off to the police station on Beretania. The constant and massive construction along Kalakaua and Ala Moana Boulevards was irritating and slowed the already impossible traffic congestion. I still couldn't get used to Foodland being gone from Ala Moana center. I needed a gift for my cousin, Kathy, since I was about to call in a huge favor. Several, actually. I drove up to King Street and headed to the Foodland there. I found parking instantly and began to think it was my lucky day. Inside the store, I wondered what I should give her as a baby gift. I saw a display for diapers. Yeah. That was the ticket. Babies went through a lot of those. I bought a big bag of them and zipped on through the checkout.

A few minutes later, I was on my way to the Beretania Street police department. I went over my to-do list in my mind and parked in one of the massive structures lined with meters designed to swallow up every last dime you've earned. Sauntering over to the station, I admired the emerald green lawn around the station and the other important buildings, such as the court house.

At the entrance, I went through the security check and didn't mind the gentle ribbing from some of the guys. They liked to make fun of me. I was surprised any of them remembered me, and it made me feel good when they said, "Welcome home, big guy."

Inside, I took the elevator down to the basement where my cousin, Kathy, worked in the crime lab. She was in her cubicle and looked up at me. Her happy expression faltered after she saw the diapers.

"Put them with the others," she instructed, a sour look on her face.

I was shocked to see a stash of them under her L-shaped desk. She was fuming, and I wondered if she'd get angry if I asked for the favor I needed.

"How's the baby?" I glanced around the walls of her cubicle. I remembered he was a boy but couldn't recall his name.

"Thanks for asking. He's great. May I ask why you brought diapers? Why does everyone give me diapers? You think I got a poopy baby or something?"

"No," I said, embarrassed by her tirade. "I'm just a bad shopper. Sorry, cuz."

She simmered down a little. "You can take me to lunch."

"What, now?"

"No. Right after I do whatever favor it is that you want."

"Okay. Any place you want." I can see my five grand disappearing faster than you can say zom zoms.

"Auntie Pasto's."

I stifled a groan. I liked the food, and it was close to the station, but the restaurant had a chronic problem with getting orders out quickly.

"Okay." I adopted a game face.

"What do you need?" She turned to her computer.

"I'm looking for a missing man. I need to pull up any background info we have on him and ah, can we request his cell phone records?"

"We, huh? Well, *we* can do both. I assume this on the QT and you're not going through official channels for his phone records."

"Not at this time. If I suspect foul play, I will report his disappearance, I promise." I noticed a photograph of a Desert Eagle, the weapon, not the bird, tacked on the wall of her cubicle. Right next to photos of her and her hubby and the baby. *What the heck is his name? William? Warren?*

"Nice gun," I said.

Kathy's face turned dreamy. "We never get weapons like this. We had a shooting death at Tally's restaurant."

"Hey, if I was forced to eat there I'd go postal, too."

She shook her head. "Oh, you. I was so excited when I found the weapon."

"Where was it?"

"In the men's toilet, shoved into the garbage bin."

"Good work. And you're right. We never get weapons like this. If you watched the TV series *Hawai'i Five-O* however, you'd be forgiven for thinking everyone carries Uzis on the streets of Waikīkī." As far as I could recall, I'd only ever come across one Desert Eagle in the course of police work. Those fifty-caliber guns mean business.

"Gimme your deets."

"The subject's name is Takeo Watanabe."

"That's a nice French name."

I grinned, glad to know that motherhood hadn't robbed Kathy of her sense of humor.

"Address?"

I gave it to her. She turned to me. "The cell phone records will be here in seventy-two hours. I'll let you know
as soon as I have them." She fixed me with a penetrating
stare. "You know this is going to take more than diapers
and a plate of pasta, right?"

"What else do you want?"

"Baby sitting. Friday night and then again two weeks
later."

"Sheesh. You drive a hard bargain."

She smiled. She'd always been a tough girl, even when
we were kids. She stood and waved me into her seat. "Have
at it. I'll give you fifteen minutes to noodle around. I'll go
make myself a cup of coffee. You need to print anything
out, the printer's over there." She pointed to a corner of
the office and left the cubicle.

I dive-bombed her computer and began my background
check on Takeo Watanabe. He had no arrests I could find,
no criminal activity sprang out at me, but he'd moved
around a lot. I went back over the last ten years, and he
appeared to move every two years. He'd traveled from California to Nevada, then to Arizona before settling in Hawai'i.
He'd lived in the islands for four years, and his previous
address had been in Kīhei, Maui. I printed off everything,
then ran a criminal record. Nothing.

Doing a credit check was illegal but I did it anyway. He
had several revolving credit card balances. One of them
was taking a real hammering, and he'd been late on the
last payment, which had dinged his credit enormously. It
didn't take much these days. I thought this was a huge red
flag since the installment had been due during the time
he'd disappeared but had been paid two weeks ago. It was
still too late to keep his credit score high.

Again, I took a copy of the report and I swung over to the
Honolulu land titles section. He'd bought the Mānoa Valley house two years ago. It appeared he'd been renting in
Maui since that residence was owned by a couple with the
last name of Alvarenga. Probably Portuguese.

Out of curiosity, I checked on Sachi Hammond's house. It was listed in both her name and Bobby's. Ouch. I had a sneaky suspicion he'd make her sell it if they got divorced. *Why, oh why did she put him on the title?* Then again, maybe she'd been forced to do it in order to save her family home. I hoped he wasn't going to make her sell the place once they got divorced.

I pulled up the police report on the domestic dispute between the Hammonds over a year ago. It was pretty much as she had told me, though there were photos on file of her with finger marks around her neck. I printed the report then Googled Takeo and was surprised to find virtually nothing on him apart from what I'd already found. I wanted to noodle around his Facebook profile and look at his posts. I'd ask Sachi if she'd give me her login information so I could do it. There were no LinkedIn listings for him. Again, nothing. *How did this guy make ends meet? What did he do all day in that big expensive house?*

I made a list of people to speak to including the Alvarengas in Maui, and Amy Jaeger.

"You done?" Kathy asked at my elbow.

"Yep. I need to get hold of case photos."

She made a note of the case number, went off, and returned with a sealed bag of police Polaroids.

"You'd better give me something within twenty-four hours to substantiate my doing this for you."

"Will do." *I hope.* I studied the seven photos, shocked to find they were worse than the police report implied. Bobby Hammond had given his wife a severe beating. Her facial contusions were frightening, and it looked like he'd tried to strangle her. I took photocopies of everything.

"Spouse declines pressing charges," the notes said. *Yeah. She didn't want that slime bag to end up with a blemished reputation.*

"Cool. I called ahead to Auntie Pasto's. They've got orders of meatballs and spaghetti and garlic bread coming up."

"Awesome." I was starving. We made our way to my car and since Beretania was a one-way street, I had to make a complicated series of turns to reach the restaurant, also on Beretania, but about a mile away from the station. I found parking right out front and fed yet another damned meter.

Inside the restaurant, we grabbed a table, and I almost swooned at the delicious scent of garlic wafting over us. It sure beat the smell of fried underpants and scorched shoes. I turned my foot over under the table. Just as I suspected, there was a big hole in the sole. Our food arrived quickly, and we split a bottle of mineral water.

Kathy filled me in on the horrors of childbirth. "It's like pulling your top lip up and over your head." Then she described the latest cases she had. Honolulu Police Department's crime lab had limited scope with its investigations but the small crew of fifteen men and women worked hard each and every day. She was feeling tremendous guilt over returning to work, but she and her husband, a detective out in Pearl City, weren't rich and needed the double income. As she talked, I ran over the case in my mind. I didn't think Bobby Hammond was necessarily involved in Takeo's disappearance, but I'd ask Kathy's husband, Mike, if he knew the guy and the gym where he trained.

Something else niggled at me, and it was Sachi's mention of Noni Kolima. If it was the Noni I knew and she was dead, how had they communicated? I knew there were some very spiritual people in these islands, but could Sachi really be one of them? I almost slapped myself thinking these things. There was no way Sachi could have known Noni. Unless there was another one. But still the question lingered in my mind as our lunch progressed. When the check came, I didn't realize Kathy had been talking nonstop. I also had no clue she'd ordered a couple of meals to go. That was okay, she'd done me a huge favor today.

"It's so great of you to come over Friday and babysit. Why don't you come a little earlier than we agreed, say five o'clock? That way I can go over the diaper changing ritual with you. You're going to love looking after Joshua. He's the happiest kid you'll ever meet. Such a good-natured baby. He reminds me of you at his age."

I had no idea what she was talking about. She was a year older than me and since I'd been a baby, how would she remember? I still needed her, though, and simply smiled as I paid for our food. I dropped her back at the station and watched her walk up the stairs before driving off. I had dead people to visit and lei stands to negotiate first.

Waikīkī's street traffic is a nightmare in the afternoons with cars detoured all over the place and certain streets blocked from making left turns. I finally made it downtown to the King Street lei shops and bought a rose lei, then headed upcountry to the Mānoa Valley. I followed the twists and turns up to East Mānoa Road, then Old East Mānoa Road until I reached the old Chinese cemetery. I could still recall the awful day we'd all congregated for Noni's funeral. She was the first person I knew who'd had cancer and died. Her entire class of twelve-year-olds shaved their heads in solidarity the morning we said goodbye. My parents came with me and we'd marched along the unpaved road to the children's section.

At the entrance, I stopped and placed the only candy I had, the last two pieces of butterscotch Lifesavers from a tube, just inside the marble archway. We believe in bringing candy to the children. I still remembered exactly where her grave was and found it just as some fat raindrops fell from the sky.

I moaned. "I know, Noni. Been too long." Emotion choked my throat. All these years later, and her death still hurt me. Somebody had been to visit her recently. Her grave contained pieces of *li hing* mango and some crack seed. Only a local would do that. Was it Sachi? Probably. The question remained, had she known Noni?

Rain fell hard, the way it does in Mānoa, and I walked back to my car after taking a snapshot of the offerings on her grave. It was well looked after like so many of our loved ones' final resting places. As I walked back to my car, I noticed the US and Hawai'i state flags decorating some of the newer graves. Hawai'i has had more losses in the war against terror than any other state. I'm proud that we look after our dead, because my ancestors always believed if we take care of them, they take care of us.

I got back into my car and waited out the ferocious storm. It battered my sweet old Mustang as I thought about my next move. The rain might be the camouflage I needed to take a drive by Takeo Watanabe's house. After checking my cell phone, I saw that its location on Paty Drive was right off East Mānoa. I made my way down the mountain, ecstatic when a rainbow appeared high in the sky. I saw it as a good omen.

It still rained as I reached the address. I couldn't see the house from the tiny road but I almost hit a tree in shock when a man came out of the house with a garbage bag in hand. I pretended to keep going and went up the hill past the house. I quickly turned around and parked behind another car and cut the engine. The man dropped the garbage bag into the wheelie bin then pushed it out onto the road. He glanced up and down the street then turned back to the stairs leading down to the house.

From the side, it looked like it might be the "new" Takeo Watanabe, but I couldn't be sure. I sat and waited. My cell phone rang. It was Sachi Hammond.

"Hey Sachi."

"Do you have any news?" *Oh, no.* She was going to be one of those clients.

"Not yet. Listen, I have a question. Are you Facebook friends with Takeo?"

A pause. "Not under my own name, no."

"Ah. You created a fake account."

"Yes, but the new guy blocked it."

"So you can't see it anymore."

"No. I heard he dropped a lot of people and made it impossible to see anything. I hear he's signed up at Whole Foods for their vegan cooking class."

"How'd you find out?"

Her voice dropped to a whisper. "Somebody, one of our Meals on Wheels volunteers, saw him and said he thought maybe Takeo had plastic surgery." She paused. "She also accused him of having a charisma bypass. This new guy is not very nice. I gotta go. Susie needs to pee."

"Wait."

"What?" She sounded pissed now.

"What does Takeo do for a living?"

"Oh. He's a painter. He had an exhibit down in Lāhainā in Maui before he moved here, but he had a bad falling out with the owners of the gallery. All his paintings vanished from their stockroom."

"Which gallery?"

"It's called the Rainbow Goddess."

"Thanks," I said, and she ended the call. I predicted a daytrip to Maui in my immediate future.

So, the guy was an artist. It must have been devastating to lose all his work. Maybe that was the reason he'd become a shut-in. I was about to start the car again when a black BMW snaked up the driveway of Takeo's house, made a left, and drove slowly down the mountain road toward Waikīkī. I waited a few minutes, moved forward and paused outside the house. The rain pelted hard and fast. Outside the Watanabe house, I braked, threw open the door, and raced toward the garbage bin. Reaching in, I grabbed the refuse, tossed it on the back floor of my car and drove away again. I'd have to come back when it was dark. The garbage smelled already. I could tell it was rotten fruit. It was time to do some snooping, and I knew just the place to do it.

My mom's house was right off Woodlawn Drive, less than a mile from The Watanabe residence. The house hasn't changed since I was a kid. She keeps it neat, the plants well-tended, and it always smells of food cooking. My mom was surprised but pleased to see me. As usual, I almost forgot to remove my shoes at the door, and she wasn't thrilled when she saw me hauling a garbage bag.

She's tiny and feisty. She acts like she gave birth to me at my current height and often makes reference to this.

"Still causing me mischief, Daniel? Most people throw their rubbish away. They don't bring it into the house." She watched me, arms folded across her chest in the doorway of her kitchen. I donned her washing up gloves.

"I'll buy you a new pair," I promised.

"Yeah you will." She pursed her lips in the way I'd learned to dread as a kid. I opened the bag on the kitchen bench top. It surprised me to find the discarded packaging of a new iPhone. *What had happened to the previous phone?* Sachi had mentioned that the voicemail had been full but had recently been cleared.

Had the new Takeo taken over the phone number and got himself a new phone? I went through the refuse.

My mom suddenly piped up. "Somebody's a neatnik."

It took me a few seconds to realize she was talking about the bizarre newspaper-wrapped items scattered in the trash. I opened one and found hair. Lots and lots of black hair. Huh. I had no idea whose it was, but it was good evidence. I put it in a baggie. I processed the entire bag and found only one more item of interest, a chilling one at that.

The page had been ripped into quarters but I put it together and took in the details of the online receipt from an auction for a military-style pen that doubled as a knife. It had been purchased four weeks ago. I put it in a large plastic Ziploc bag and rebagged everything else, including my mom's washing up gloves.

"What the heck is that?" She peered over my shoulder. I cleaned the countertop and washed my hands. Only then did I take a good look at this macabre auction item.

"Oh, my God," Mom said. "Will you look at this? From some website called Patriot Surplus. This is a restricted item in many countries. It says so here. Why not the U.S.? Have you read this description? Designed with active-shooter callouts in mind, the Double Duty's wedge features counter-angled friction ridges to help prevent tool slippage, grip breaching surfaces securely, and increase bite when breaching even the most robust doors like those found in government and school facilities... Oh, Daniel.

Who would buy this?" She looked up at me, her lovely brown eyes filled with fear. "Whoever purchased this tool meant business. No other reason to buy something like this."

She was right. And suddenly the one thing that had seeped into my brain from my conversation with Kathy over lunch came to mind. She'd said the same thing about the Desert Eagle she'd tested and processed. "Only reason to buy a gun like this is because this person means business."

I was pretty certain Takeo Watanabe was dead. But I had a long way to go before proving it.

I called Sachi at six o'clock, but got her voicemail and per her instructions, didn't leave a message. I called her burner phone, but she hadn't yet activated the voicemail system. How frustrating. I hung up, hoping she'd call me and pondered my next move. My mom is a big fan of the vegan cooking classes held at Whole Foods in Kailua. She's been to a few, and when she told me there was one at seven o'clock, I asked if she'd like me to take her. I hoped to find the new Takeo there.

"Why are you being so nice to me?" she asked when we got into my car. "Don't think this means you don't owe me new washing up gloves."

I shook my head and laughed. The drive to Kailua was a nightmare. Honestly the traffic was horrendous and getting worse by the day, but when we got there I was pleased to see Takeo in the crowd milling about by the demonstration counter. We were too late to sign up for classes but Takeo had a seat and stared intently at the teacher, who, it turned out was a friend of my mom's and waved us over toward her.

"Stand over here." She proceeded to do things to tofu I never dreamed possible. The smell of the orange sauce she prepared with the fried strips was mouth-watering.

Takeo followed her instructions well but my mom suddenly whispered to me, "That guy has no clue what he's doing. Look, he keeps chopping toward himself."

The real Takeo was apparently an ardent lover of food and cooking, so this was worth noting. He glanced up at us a couple of times but my mom manfully resisted going over and showing him how to handle a knife. His instructor didn't have any such qualms.

"No, Takeo, like this. A gentle touch."

I thought it ironic that a man who may have murdered another with a military pen knife had trouble chopping vegetables. We hung out long enough to try free samples of the cooking. Wouldn't you know it, we got tastings of Takeo's efforts, and they weren't bad.

"Very good," Mom told him, which earned her a small smile. He had a weird grin, and suddenly I realized he was trying to hide his teeth.

The class broke up and I wished I could have followed him, but I owed Mom some gloves. I also bought her a couple of candles for her troubles.

"Sometimes you're such a doll," she said. "Except when I'm giving birth to you."

I laughed. "You only did it once."

"Once was enough." Mischief danced in her eyes.

We drove back to Mānoa, and I took her home. Dinner for my scrawny mom was probably the tiny cup of orange tofu we'd had at the cooking class. Me, I was starving, but after seeing her safely inside, I tore off for Paty Drive. I wanted to get a look at the two homes, the Hammond residence, and Takeo's.

The street was pitch-black, all the better for me. I had infrared goggles. After parking up the hill away from the house, I stood at the top of the incline looking down at the Hammond place. It was a typical sprawling ranch-style house, which sold for a couple of million in this valley. It was beautiful, but also featured huge windows that looked out onto the darkened garden. The house was lit up like a Christmas tree, but I didn't see anyone moving around in it.

I switched over to the Watanabe house. It was a completely different style. A kind of two-story Cape Cod with a wraparound lānai. I suspected it was a newer construction than Sachi's pre-war home. I saw no lights or movement. After a long, careful look, I realized one small light was on upstairs. The black BMW I saw shoot out of the driveway earlier in the day wasn't around. I picked my way down the steep lava stone driveway to the left of the Watanabe property and to the right of the Hammond home.

A white SUV stood at the far end of the Hammonds' driveway, and a small dog began to bark from the confines of what looked like a room at the base of the house. It shocked me to hear it because Sachi had told me she never left Susie alone. Also, the room was dark. The yelping sounded pitiful.

I crept over to the door. "Susie," I whispered, making a light kissing noise. "Susie?"

The dog stopped. Something was wrong. I just knew it. She panted heavily and the distressing sound freaked me out. *What the heck happened to Sachi?* I didn't want to leave the dog there but could I break into the room? Boy did I wish I had the Double Duty pen knife in my possession.

I had a small burglary kit. Not exactly legal, but effective. I took it out of my back pocket and checked around me. Nothing but the dog's whimpering and my heavy breathing. I wanted to use my flashlight to illuminate the lock, but couldn't risk it. I jiggled the mechanism, and it was harder work than I'd imagined. Headlights loomed from the top of the street. *Oh, no.*

The vehicle was coming down the driveway. I popped the lock and the frantic dog leapt into my arms. I grabbed and held her as she licked my face. Something smelled bad in the tiny room. It was probably dog poop. I closed the door and scooted out of the small area. I paused near the white SUV just as whoever was driving the vehicle at the top of the drive, hit a tree, then the fence.

"Shit." A man's voice.

Sachi had told me her drunken husband did this. Susie froze in terror in my arms and I took the moment to duck behind the white SUV and into unknown territory behind it. Susie clung to me. She gave me a small chin lick as we made our way into the back garden. The property was huge. Giant koa and cypress trees provided the perfect camouflage. Susie growled as I ran behind a large clump of bamboo.

"Shh." Her body stiffened. She didn't let out a yip because I kissed her, but she started to tremble violently. I was pretty certain I was standing on freshly turned earth. Then I saw the hibiscus trees Susie had mentioned. This had to be the pathway between the two houses Takeo had used to visit her.

"Susie?" A male voice called in the distance. "Where the fuck are you?"

The dog's breath caught in her throat and her mouth hung open. I darted through the cover of hibiscus trees and through several people's properties. I hid in a garden far from the Hammond and Watanabe homes and did what any self-respecting man would do. I called for back-up. Wielding my cell phone as the dog continued to shake in my arms, I was so relieved when my favorite person in the whole wide world answered.

"Mom?"

"What's wrong?"

"I need your help."

She came up the hill in her trusty VW bug several minutes later and I hid behind the garbage bin next to TheBus stop across the road. Several cars passed, but when I was sure it was Mom, I darted over. She looked at me, wound down the window.

I thrust the dog in her direction. "Please take her home. I'll be in touch."

For once she didn't say anything, except, "Oh, poor baby." She cuddled little Susie. I hid behind the bin again as they drove away until I was sure nobody had followed them. I had no gun on me. I didn't usually carry one, but as I walked back up the hill, I was shocked to see a man walking toward me, a leash in his hand.

Bobby Hammond.

"Hey," he said.

"Hey." I stopped, hoping he couldn't hear my thundering heart.

"You haven't seen a small dog, have you?"

I shook my head. "No. Sorry."

"Little runt. She got away from me. I could strangle her sometimes." The way he wielded that little pink leash between his big hands frightened me. He didn't want to walk that dog. He wanted to kill her.

"What kind is she?"

"Little black dog. Kind of a mix." He shrugged.

His British accent was detectable.

"Sorry. I'll keep my eyes open."

"Yeah. Do that." He looked so pissed I was definitely worried about Sachi now. "My wife and I live in the old ranch house. The one with all the guava trees."

"Okay." Phew. The alcohol on his breath and seeping from his pores almost knocked me over.

I was surprised when somebody came up to us. *Shoot.* It was the fake Takeo. I kept moving. I was sure he would have recognized me, but I kept my head down and walked to the other side of the road facing oncoming traffic. As I passed them, I heard him say, "Did you find it?"

It? What the hell? Susie wasn't an it.

I kept walking up the hill past the Hammond house. Behind me, a blonde came out of the house and up the stairs to the street. *Who the hell is she?*

She looked straight down the hill, and I turned to see her making her way toward the two men, who were still deep in conversation.

I reached my car, but by the time I got inside, only Hammond and the blonde remained. Who was she? And did he always bring home strange women?

My worries for Sachi's safety ratcheted up a few degrees. Disguising my number by pressing *67, I called her again. This time her phone rang. I was stunned to see Bobby Hammond pull a cell phone out of his pocket.

"Hello?" he said.

I hung up on him. *Oh, my God.* Something had happened to Sachi. I really hoped she wasn't lying at the back of her own home buried beneath her own private tunnel of love.

I drove to Mom's and both she and Susie were overjoyed to see me.

"Somebody hit this dog in the head," she said by way of a greeting. "I'm worried about her."

"What makes you think so?"

"She keeps tilting her head and kinda walking in circles."

"Let's watch her overnight and see how she does."

Mom looked relieved. "You're staying?"

"Yeah." I had no need to return to the miniscule hot box I currently called home. Besides, the two ladies would be great company. My old room was turned into a sewing room some time ago, but a day bed remained in the corner. Susie seemed fine to me.

I had a long day ahead of me the following day, so I turned in. Keeping the door open, I was aware of the small dog joining me a couple of times, but she was a restless sleeper. The next morning when I awoke, I found her in the kitchen eating fresh-cooked chicken out of a bowl on the floor as Mom made scrambled eggs and rice.

I took a quick shower and threw on the only clean garment I had left in the house, a slightly tight Reyn Spooner shirt. I found some old socks and replaced my singed ones.

When I got back to the kitchen, Mom didn't hesitate. "You'd better tell me what's going on."

I gave her an abbreviated version of the events. "I know Sachi Takamoto," she said.

"Well, Mānoa's a small town, so that makes sense."

She shook her head. "No, son. You all went to school to-gether. Her sister, Maya was in your year. Sachi was two years behind you."

Ah. That made sense now. Maya and Noni had been best friends. The thing about Noni talking to Sachi however was still freaky to me.

"Any idea what happened to Maya?" I asked.

"Lives in Oregon with her husband and kids. Don't know if the sisters are close. Maya hates Bobby Hammond." She pulled a face. "I can't call Sachi by the last name of Hammond. Her husband's a weirdo." She kept watching the dog and apparently decided Susie was okay. "I'll confine our walks to the garden." She swiveled a glance in my direction. "I'll protect her, son. You go help poor Sachi. She never would have married that man if her dad didn't have such a bad gambling problem."

"He did?"

"Oh, yeah. He used to play cards in Chinatown. Got beat up real bad a couple of times. Arrested, and everything."

"What was his name?"

"Hideo Takamoto. Nice man, just weak as hell." Mom dropped to the floor to play with the dog. "Funny thing, you know. I just realized I haven't seen Sachi in weeks. You tell that girl if she needs a respite, if she needs a safe house, this is her home."

"Thanks, Mom." I loved her even more than I already did. I made a couple of calls, the first to Amy Jaeger, the Meals on Wheels coordinator. She seemed surprised to hear from me.

"You want to talk to me about Takeo?"

"Yes. Sachi Hammond gave me your number."

Silence.

"She did? When?"

"Could we meet and talk?"

"Okay. Sure." She sounded nervous now. "I have a busy day but I could meet you for coffee if you can do it now. Where are you located?"

"Mānoa."

"Oh, me too. Do you know Morning Glass?"

I sure did. We made arrangements to meet in fifteen minutes.

When I arrived at the tiny coffee house, I was shocked to see Amy Jaeger was the blonde I'd seen the night before at the Hammond house.

"Hi," I said.

She looked at me and frowned. "Haven't we met before?"

"I don't think so. I just moved back here from Kauaʻi. Can I get you a coffee?"

"I have one, thanks. Are you single?"

Why did I hear the theme from Jaws as a strange gleam leapt into her eyes? I sat with her, not wanting to break the connection.

"It's complicated." I didn't want to divulge anything personal to her.

"Isn't it always?" She sighed.

"Boyfriend troubles?"

She shrugged.

"Go on," I said. "I'm a good listener."

She shook her head. "I should have known better. I shouldn't have believed him when he said they lived separate lives and he was counting the days until they got divorced."

"So he's married?" *Leaving him?* I knew there was no way in hell Sachi would leave Bobby Hammond until he had his green card.

"Yeah."

"How long have you been seeing him?"

"Are you judging me?"

"Not at all. Like I said, I'm a good listener."

She looked distressed. "Six months. And it's been hard. He comes to my place every Friday night. She thinks he's watching the fights with his buddies. I don't know. The whole thing is weird. What's really strange is that she's the woman you said gave you my number. When did you talk to her?"

I feigned surprise. "Sachi Hammond?"

She nodded. "We're pretty good friends. We volunteer together." She spooned sugar into her cup but didn't stir. She stared into the milky surface of the coffee for a moment, reminding me of Sachi staring into her tea the day before. "I guess she told you Takeo is looking and acting weird."

"Yeah. She did."

"But why? I mean, he's nice and all, but such a whiny wackadoo."

She thinks he's a wackadoo? "He is? How?"

"He's an artist. I have no artistic skills so maybe I can't relate, but he keeps banging on about this gallery that lost all his paintings. Or stole them. Or something."

"Wow. That's terrible. I could understand that. Paintings are things you can't replace. I don't know of a true artist who could reproduce the same piece exactly."

"I get that. But he's let it affect his whole life. Won't paint. Won't go out. Won't do things. Gets super depressed. I understand he was a rising talent in the business but get over it already."

Wow. She's harsh. A harsh home wrecker. She spooned more sugar into her cup. I wondered how many times she'd done it already.

"When did Sachi hire you?"

"I don't really want to say since you're ah, sleeping with her husband."

Her cheeks flamed. "I know, right? Awkward." She spooned more sugar into her cup. "It's just that I've been worried about her, too. I mean, more than I worry about Takeo."

"Why's that?" *Because you're cheating on your friend?*

"Bobby said she had a boyfriend."

My blood ran cold. "Oh?"

"Yeah. Now he claims she left him."

I couldn't hide my shock.

"She didn't tell you?"

"No. She didn't."

"And you say she hired you to investigate Takeo?"

"Yes."

"Not her husband?"

That took me by surprise. "No. Not at all."

She seemed relieved. "You're not going to tell her about me and Bobby are you? Because I like her and I don't want to hurt Sachi. Bobby told me he was waiting for his green card. Now he's saying there's a hitch."

"The hitch being that she left him?"

"Yeah. But the weird thing is he says it just happened, but I haven't seen her for weeks. Nobody has. He hates that dog of hers. I'm no fan either, to be honest, but I find it hard to believe Sachi left the dog behind." For the first time she looked concerned. She hunched forward. "The dog has been acting real weird. He'd let her out to pee at night and she'd start digging up the garden. She cries and whines all the time.

"It's freaky. I mean truly disturbing." She reached for her coffee, sipped, shuddered then tried to swallow. "Ugh. That tastes bad." She frowned. "I didn't know what a problem it was until a few of nights ago. He said it's been getting worse and he couldn't handle it. I suggested she needed more exercise. She's used to being out all the time with Sachi. But that night, we took her into the garden and she bit him when he tried to bring her inside. I've never seen him so angry. He put her in the basement. I insisted he leave her with some food and water, but it was not a good solution. The howling from that little creature was unnerving. He was going to take her to the shelter and have her humanely euthanized, but she disappeared last night. So he says. Now I wonder if he didn't do something himself."

She seemed nervous now as she toyed with the edge of her collar. "He gets so angry. And you never know what's going to set him off. He's so sweet afterward. Sweet and gentle, and apologetic. Right now though, he's acting super strange. Says he's being watched."

I opened and closed my mouth.

When we parted a few minutes later, my head was spinning. I'd rescued poor Susie just in time, but I was very worried about Sachi. Where in heck was she? And why hadn't she set up the burner phone's voicemail? I tried her regular phone once more, but she didn't answer.

I got into the car and pointed it in the direction of Waikīkī. I wanted to take the Double Duty pen knife to the Beretania division of HPD. I felt dirty after my conversation with Amy Jaeger and wanted a shower.

At the station house, I went to my cousin, who smiled. "What have you got for me?"

I laid out my case and she, too, became concerned. "We need probable cause to check out the back of her property. You have that invoice you mentioned?"

When I handed it to her, she didn't look surprised. "We'll get it checked right away."

I followed her to the forensics section of the crime lab and watched her sweet talk the woman who was checking slides. Within seconds, the woman dusted the sections of the page for prints and found a few good ones. We waited while she processed them. She handed Kathy a CD and said, "Good luck."

We returned to Kathy's desk where she entered the CD into the AFIS system, and the computer match began.

I was stunned to see an immediate match.

"Our man has a criminal history." I held my breath until she checked his stats. She swung around to me, genuine fear in her eyes. "I think our girl's in big trouble."

I gulped, trying to read over her shoulder. The photo I saw was the new Takeo Watanabe.

"His name is Cheng-Gong Dan. A well-known art forger, but he's supposed to be in prison back in New York serving a ten-year sentence for a huge art theft. Looks like it involved six other people and over fifty million dollars in faked masterpieces."

I thought a moment. "Maybe this file hasn't been updated. What if there's a big conspiracy behind Takeo Watanabe's disappearance? Maybe he wouldn't paint, and they got in this forger. He sort of passes for him, and coming from New York, Cheng-Gong Dan wouldn't need a passport. He'd just need a valid driver's license."

"Could be a stretch, but it makes sense." Kathy looked at me. "I'll look into this and see if he's back east still, but if he's not, it explains his fingerprints. You need to get over to Maui and visit the gallery. Pronto, Tonto."

She was right. I made a beeline for the airport and called my mom.

"You got my message," she said, sounding breathless.

"No, what message?"

"I took Susie to the vet."

"Why'd you do that?"

"I was worried about her. They told me Sachi was there a few weeks ago and paid to have her micro chipping information changed. You are her alternate guardian in case Susie goes missing."

What? Sachi had known weeks ago she was going to hire me? How come she'd taken so long to follow through? I thought for a moment. According to the bank teller, she'd ordered the thousand dollar bills around the same time. Why had she waited? Was she so afraid of her husband? I had to know. I wondered what had gone on before Sachi came to me. As a cop I'd dealt with a lot of domestic violence cases and most women I talked to had a defining moment that made them leave.

"Okay. Mom, I want you to go to my place for a couple of days."

"Why? You hate that place, and so do I."

"I know, but I have a bad feeling that the vet might call Bobby Hammond and tell him you were there. He was going to have the dog euthanized this morning."

"Over my dead body." Mom got hysterical instantly.

I blew out a frustrated breath. "I wish I were closer. I'd come get you."

"We're leaving right now."

"You have my spare key, right?"

"Yes." She didn't sound like herself at all. "Bobby Hammond's calling on the other line. Oh my God."

"Get out of there. Now."

"We're going. Why would the vet do that?"

"Bobby probably told them the dog was missing. No time for questions. Get going."

"I'll call you when we're at your place."

She ended the call, and I drove into the airport parking lot hoping my feisty mom could handle herself. Stress caused me to hyperventilate as I parked in the short-term lot. I crossed over to the go! Airlines terminal and booked the first flight Maui-bound I could get. Noon. That gave me an hour to sit and fret.

My phone rang. It was Kathy, who gave me an update. "Cheng-Gong Dan was released eleven days ago from Sing Sing."

"According to Sachi Hammond, the new Takeo Watanabe showed up about a week ago."

"Right. And there's no earthly reason for Cheng-Gong Dan to be in Hawai'i. As a matter of fact, he was supposed to check in with his probation officer two days ago and never did. He was supposed to serve time in a halfway house with a work furlough program the day before, but never returned. I guess because he was considered low risk, it didn't make the papers."

"So he didn't necessarily kill the real Takeo Watanabe."

"Who do you like for it?" she asked.

"I still like the husband for it, but I'm not sure. I'll call you from Maui."

"Danny, I did find out that Watanabe had a career in Japan but was a slow producer. I found what you told me about his paintings being stolen fascinating because there's nothing online about it."

"Can you get a search warrant for his property?"

"I hope so."

I spent some time on my laptop trying to find out anything I could about the gallery where Takeo Watanabe had held his show. It turned out that the Rainbow Goddess was Japanese-owned, with a chain of galleries in Japan and one in Maui. The featured artists included Watanabe, but he was the only one whose personal link to a photo and bio didn't work.

The first call for my flight sent my blood pressure up a few points.

I was relieved when my mom called. "Susie and I like it here. I had no idea you had such a great view of Diamond Head. I think we'll take a nap on the sofa."

"Do that. I'll be in touch." I boarded my flight with the last batch of travelers and clutched the armrest for the entire thirty-five minute trip, not because I had a fear of flying but because I felt time was getting away from us, and I was worried the bad guys would disappear before we could do anything to stop them.

I rented a car at Kahului Airport and drove straight to Lāhainā. Traffic was as bad here as it was in O'ahu, but I made it to Front Street thirty minutes later. Finding a parking space took longer. I found one eventually and made my way to the gallery. I was stunned to see a huge sign in the window advertising a new exhibit by Japanese artist, Takeo Watanabe.

"Meet the artist!" the signs said. "He will be painting in our studio tomorrow!"

I studied the photo of a grinning Cheng-Gong Dan and noticed he'd kept his mouth closed. Those teeth would have been a giveaway for anyone who knew the real Takeo Watanabe.

A blond man from inside the gallery approached me. "Are you a fan?"

"You had an exhibit of his work a while ago, and I loved everything he had."

The man smiled. "Come on in and take a look at his new piece. You may or may not know he takes a long time to complete a single painting."

"I had no idea." I followed him inside. Lined against one wall were some paintings wrapped and stacked. A few hung on the walls. I studied them. They were impressionistic in style with the composition made up of tiny dots. I had to stand back to get the full effect. I realized I was looking at a Maui sunset.

"Breathtaking," I said.

"We have seventeen pieces from his previous collection, which have never been seen before. Six new ones, too. But this one's my favorite." He led me to a corner of the gallery where a framed painting hung under a pendant lamp. My heart almost broke as I studied it. The painting was called "Fire Princess." It showed a man and woman entwined. Flames surrounded them, but only their passion seemed to be on their minds.

I looked at the woman. I can't explain it, but I knew, just knew that Sachi Hammond was dead. She was the woman in the picture. I would have staked my life on it. And the passion depicted in that searing image was probably what immortalized her, but extinguished her mortal life.

I went outside and called Kathy. She told me a team of detectives had gone to Takeo Watanabe's home, but neither he nor Cheng-Gong Dan were home.

"We have a unit watching the house. We've been authorized by the New York State Corrections Authority to apprehend him. I've put a call through to the U.S. Marshals. We just haven't located him yet."

"I don't know where he is right now, but he's supposed to be painting here tomorrow," I told her. Careful not to blow my cover, I took photos of the signs in the window and sent them to her.

"Can you send me photos of anything inside?"

I went back in. Whenever the gallery manager's back was turned, I snapped shots of the stacked paintings I was beginning to suspect were the "stolen" items, and, miraculously, grabbed one of the Fire Princess. I had to do it while the blond guy was on the phone. He came over at one point and smiled.

"You love her, don't you?"

"I sure do." He'd already told me the painting was selling for quarter of a million dollars.

"She looks so real, doesn't she?" His stare made me uncomfortable.

"Yes."

"You have to meet the artist." He smiled.

"I'll come back for sure."

"There are other pieces. You should come to the stockroom and look. There are a few cheaper pieces you might like."

I shook my head. "Thanks, but I'll come by tomorrow." Something about him unnerved me. Then I realized he was coming on to me. It had been so long, I didn't recognize a pickup line anymore.

Giving him a friendly wave, I went back outside and sent all the images to Kathy. I got a phone call a few seconds later from her saying that I'd be hearing from a Maui Police Department detective.

"We're grateful you're there. You need backup. We've just sent a K9 cadaver unit to the Watanabe property and they went straight for that part of the garden you mentioned."

"Oh, man." I didn't want to be right. I didn't want Takeo Watanabe or Sachi Hammond to be dead and buried.

"Are you okay?" Kathy asked.

"Yeah."

"I know you've had a rough time, cuz. You're doing great."

I blinked back tears. It sure didn't feel like it.

"Stand in the light," she said. "I'll be in touch."

I walked outside and waited. I didn't know what to do with myself. And then I saw him. That bastard Cheng-Gong Dan. He stood across the road eating an ice cream. Our gazes locked, and he stared at me. He must have recognized me from Whole Foods and took off running, dropping his cone on the ground. I bolted after him, narrowly missing getting hit by cars coming in both directions.

Front Street on its slowest day is wall-to-wall foot traffic, but I kept up with his dark head bobbing and weaving through the pack. Thank God he was moving away from the most popular area where the people were fewer, until he reached a school.

Something made him turn right. He almost hit a low branch of a banyan tree in the schoolyard. Kids started screaming as he stomped their bento boxes and stuck his foot in a basket of cut oranges. He tried to remove it, but kept moving, orange segments flying. I realized the kids were making adzes out of balsa wood. I'd done the same thing in my day.

"Kids, I'm a cop. Move."

The kids looked at me.

I tried to jump over a couple of them but their heads went back and forth.

"Is he a bad man?" One of them asked as I ran.

"Yes," I called out.

They picked up their half-finished weapons and with a united cry, converged on him. One of them bonked him in the head, and he went down. They kept yelling and pummeling him until I shouted, "Enough." I straddled his body and put his arm behind his back. I didn't even have cuffs.

"You need zip ties?" asked the coolest woman I'd ever met.

I nodded. "Yes, please." I got three of the plastic ties onto Cheng-Gong Dan and kept him sitting on the ground. I called 911, requesting backup.

The kids kept him surrounded with their wooden adzes. It made sense to me, considering our islands were once ruled under the Law of the Splintered Paddle. Their teacher looked so proud.

Then my cousin called. "Bad news, cuz. They found them both. They're saying the decomp is so bad they've probably been there about a month. They also arrested Bobby Hammond. Apparently his mistress walked in upstairs twenty minutes ago and confessed that she knew about the killings. She said Hammond killed Sachi because he was afraid she'd leave him before his green card came through. Sounds like he knew about her love affair with Watanabe."

"Amy Jaeger told them this?"

"She said she couldn't live with her conscience after she talked to you this morning. Apparently Bobby Hammond's brother was involved in the art swindle case back east."

I wanted to hear more, but I had to keep a grip on Cheng-Gong Dan.

"If only he'd painted more, none of this would have happened. What a loser."

"Oh, he's a loser." I let out a snort.

I was grateful to hand the jerk over to Maui PD when they arrived, but of course, questions remained. I told all the kids I would personally make sure they all received commendations. I posed for photos with them and their teacher.

"How exciting." The teacher clapped her hands. "See, I told you making adzes would change your lives, didn't I?"

I left her to it, then drove off to Maui PD's station on Honoapi'ilani Highway and worked my way through the crush of media and the usual "concerned citizens."

Inside the station, I answered the detectives' questions and contacted my cousin at HPD. I should have known. Kathy and the rest of the lab staff were at the crime scene.

Only when I flew back to O'ahu and went to the scene myself did I learned why Bobby Hammond had been involved with the art crew. He and his cousin had been using the paintings Cheng-Gong Dan had created to ship drugs across the country.

Somehow Bobby had remained unnamed in the ensuing trial and moved to Hawai'i, intending to start the art forging and smuggling business all over again. A chance meeting with Watanabe intrigued him. Watanabe apparently told him of the gallery in Lāhainā and how they stole his paintings.

According to what Amy told the police, Watanabe kept telling Bobby he couldn't paint, then suddenly did. Bobby happened to see a painting he thought looked like his wife, and he suspected an affair. The idea drove him nuts, not because he loved Sachi, but because he still needed her.

One thing led to another, and he connected with the owners of the gallery, who lamented their failed attempt to build some mystery and drama around the paintings. Watanabe not only threatened to call the police, but refused to paint anymore.

Having discovered Sachi was cheating on him, Hammond came up with a cunning plan. Kill them both and replace the reluctant artist with a world-class forger who could easily copy Takeo Watanabe's style.

It would have worked except somehow Sachi found me.

Nobody could understand how she contacted me a month after she died. Though I swear I spoke to her, the incoming call from her the previous night never showed up on my cell phone or the records, but the bank teller who gave her the thousand dollar notes backed up my story of going in there.

How Sachi found me is a profound mystery already gaining popular myth in the islands, but my mom and I know what happened. I worked for ten years on cold cases in Kaua'i. Our unit was called Ke Ahi Pio'ole: The Fire That Never Burns Out.

I might have left the job, but the job has not left me. I've had ghosts come to me before, telling me their secrets. It's been a burden, and I realized, thanks to the beautiful Sachi, it is also my treasured gift.

The dead seek me out. Just like our motto says, "Finding their killers, finding them justice is my life."

I have no idea what Bobby thought he would do when his wife failed to show up for his immigration hearing. Perhaps he planned to find a replacement. Who knows? And he refuses to say. He'd started telling people Sachi had left him only after people noticed she was missing. She was a well-loved girl, so he couldn't have kept up the façade much longer.

I used the money Sachi gave me to pay for her funeral expenses. My mom and I have worked hard to raise money to keep her home as a refuge for battered women, children, and their beloved companion animals.

I feel guilty I thought I could ever walk away from those long-forgotten cases, but I have to thank the spirit of my friend Noni Kolima, who knew I would help.

For me, it is the only way.

I am sure at night I sometimes see Sachi and Takeo walking in the garden. I see them, and Susie does, too. And if I ever think I will forget my truth, I remind myself I am one who walks with those who have crossed the rainbow.

I am one who knows how to help them.

I am the one who believes in them.

I am the one who makes sure the fire never burns out...

A.J. LLEWELLYN

A.J. Llewellyn lives in California, but dreams of living in Hawai'i. Frequent trips to the islands, bags of Kona coffee in the fridge and a healthy collection of Hawaiian records keep her refueled.

A.J.'s passion for the islands led to writing a play about the last ruling monarch, Queen Lili'uokalani, written from her maid's point of view.

A.J. never lacks inspiration for writing romances. With over 200 published books, this is indeed rare. When it does happen, she surfs and hangs out with friends and animal companions.

A.J. Llewellyn believes that love is a song best sung out loud.

Find me on the web at www.ajllewellyn.com.

CLIPPED WINGS
A LEI CRIME SHORT STORY

TOBY NEAL

Morning glowed through the steel wire embedded in the glass of the youth correctional facility's high window. Consuelo Aguilar lay on her back gazing up at a Jack Canfield quote she'd written out and taped to the bottom of the bunk above her. "Everything you want is on the other side of fear."

Only today, everything she wanted was on the other side of barbed wire.

There was no point in getting up. Lying here was probably the most comfortable she'd be all day, and if she got up, she might wake Fai. She could hear Fai's deep, rhythmic snores. The Tongan girl was never in a good mood when she woke up.

Consuelo could just see the waving top of an ironwood tree through the tiny window, its long, feathery needles backlit and black against the dawn sky.

"That's how I feel. Backlit and black," she whispered. Consuelo rolled over and reached under the bunk for her notebook and pen. She jotted the phrase into the notebook.

Doing so felt as vain as writing the words in sand on the beach, as if they'd blow away the minute she lifted the pen from the paper—but writing was part of her therapy. Part of her future.

She set the notebook back down and looked up at the picture of Angel, her teacup Chihuahua, right beneath the Canfield quote. She was going to see Angel soon, when Lei Texeira, her mentor, brought the little dog to visit. It was important to remember all the things she had to live for, even if some of the most important were already gone.

"It's the depression talking," Consuelo muttered. Dr. Wilson, her therapist, was always reminding her that the depression had its own voice, and fighting it began with identifying its insidious lies.

Fai snorted and turned over, making the bed's old metal springs squeak. "What'chu talking down deah?" she growled.

"No`ting," Consuelo said. Their voices held the lilt of pidgin, dialect of Hawai'i. Fai wasn't a friend, but at least she hadn't been an enemy. The Tongan girl, her homemade tattoos writhing up arms and thighs, could deadlift two hundred pounds. Sometimes she liked to show off by cracking kukui nuts in the exercise yard with her bare feet.

No one messed with Fai. Having her as a roommate had kept Consuelo out of many of the girl fights that happened on the ward.

So what was on the other side of fear?

Flying. Being free.

Folding her hands under her head, Consuelo let her mind drift back to when she'd been flying, and free. For a while, she'd gone anywhere she'd wanted to. Taken anything she wanted. She hadn't used what she'd taken for herself. She'd stolen from the rich and given it to those who needed it. She'd made a difference. For a little while, she'd been a hero.

It sucked to lie here and remember how that had felt.

Depression talking again. She was going to have a life, when she got out of here. Her mentors, Lei Texeira, the FBI agent who'd captured her, and Wendy Watanabe, the reporter who'd covered her case, had made sure of it. In fact, she owed them both, big-time. Wendy had raised money to hire a top-notch defense lawyer, and Lei had helped her get mental health help. Between the two of them, Consuelo was only in the correctional facility for two years.

"You like get out of here?" Fai's husky voice shattered her thoughts.

"What you mean?"

"What'chu think I mean?"

"I don't know." Consuelo cautiously threw back the thin blue synthetic blanket and sheet, all that was necessary for warmth in this climate. She swung her legs out of the low bunk and peered up.

Fai's round brown face, her thick black hair a tangled halo, looked down at her. "We going get out of here. Early." Fai's dark brown eyes were hard as pebbles. "You can come."

Consuelo's heart pounded heavy thuds, which filled her ears. "I'm just doing my time. I only have two years."

"I've already been here two years, and I sick of the bull-shit." Fai scowled. "I want to leave before they send me to the federal facility on the Mainland. My uncle, he goin' set us up with IDs. My cousin, he get one boat. Taking me and Jadene to one nother island."

"Why're you telling me this?" Consuelo stood up, took a few steps away from the bunk to get a better look at her roommate.

"Because. If you come, and we get caught, we all get off easy. I not stupid." Fai sat up, her legs dangling off the bunk. She pulled the correctional-issue plain black tee down over her loose breasts and combed back thick, bushy hair with a tattooed hand. "You get the good law-yer. I getting some insurance for Jadene and me." Jadene, a white-trash haole girl from Kaneohe, was Fai's current girlfriend.

"It doesn't work that way." Consuelo felt her mouth go dry. "Ask my boyfriend. He got twice my time." Her boy-friend been captured at the same time as Consuelo and was serving a much longer sentence at a facility in Utah.

"He was over eighteen, dat's why. You do this, you going give all those rich assholes the finger. Just like you was doing before you got caught. You get one whole movement going on the outside, I been hearing." Fai's eyes gleamed with excitement.

It had been two months since Consuelo had been released from Tripler Hospital's mental health ward and begun her sentence at Hawai'i Youth Correctional Facility, and this was the first time Fai had indicated she knew or cared about Consuelo's past.

"I need to think about it. What's the plan?" Consuelo pulled the plain black sleep tee off over her head, clipped on her bra, and zipped up her orange coverall.

Fai jumped down from the top bunk, landing with a thump beside her. "Not telling you unless you're in."

"I can't agree until I hear the plan." Consuelo had her back to the other girl as she stowed her sleep tee in the cheap cardboard bureau where their clothes were stored.

Fai threw a meaty arm around Consuelo's neck, hauling her up against her heavy, muscular body in a chokehold, with Consuelo's head caught in the crook of Fai's elbow. She pushed Consuelo's head forward with her other hand as she lifted the much smaller Filipina girl off her feet, cutting off her air supply.

Consuelo heaved and thrashed, clawing at Fai's arm. She kicked back at Fai's legs with her unshod feet, but the bigger girl merely grunted, twisting so Consuelo dangled off her hip. Consuelo's flailing had no effect at all.

"You think you're all that," the older girl hissed in her ear. "You nothing but a flea. I could kill you right now. And I will, if you say one word about this. You're coming with us."

She flung Consuelo like a rag doll. The petite girl flew forward and hit the wall, sliding down to the floor in a gasping heap.

Black spots gradually receded from Consuelo's vision as she caught her breath. She pulled herself together and sat up, drawing her knees close against her chest, touching her bruised throat.

There was nothing to be done at the moment but play along. Fai was right. She'd be dead any time the girl wanted to kill her.

Fai turned away as if nothing had happened. She dressed in her prison orange, humming a little as she dragged a comb through her thick hair.

Consuelo's voice was hoarse as she said, "I guess I'm coming."

Consuelo kept her hands in the loose pockets of the orange coverall as she walked into the visiting area. She kept her face still so as not to reveal the dread and excitement that filled her at the call from the office that her mentor, Special Agent Lei Texeira, was here to visit, bringing her dog, Angel.

They came every week, but due to Lei's busy FBI work schedule, it was never a predictable day or time. Consuelo hated to admit how much she looked forward to the sight of the curly-haired agent with the warm, tilted brown eyes and smatter of freckles on her nose—but she didn't have to hide how happy she was to see Angel.

The little Chihuahua, wearing a tiny therapy dog vest, bounced toward Consuelo, yipping with excitement. Consuelo scooped her up, ducking her head to hide the tears prickling her eyes.

"Hey, baby," she whispered into the dog's sleek neck. The little animal wagged her curly tail, her whole body vibrating. She licked Consuelo's neck, and Consuelo tossed her head back and laughed.

"Consuelo." Lei's voice was a little rough. "Come here."

They weren't alone in the room. Knots of girls visited with their families around the bolted-down tables. In a far corner, Fai and Jadene were twined together on one of the couches. Consuelo felt the older girl's eyes burning a hole in her coverall as she advanced to sit on one of the metal stools beside Lei.

Usually the agent let Consuelo play with Angel alone for a few minutes, or let the other girls who still hadn't really warmed up to Consuelo pet the little dog. Today the agent's gaze was intent and probing.

"Yes?" Consuelo looked up at Lei, her heart pounding. She hadn't decided if she was going to go along with the breakout, or if she was going to try to tell someone and get it stopped. Either choice was fraught with risk. She felt herself teetering on the brink of the hard choice as she looked into Lei's concerned brown eyes.

"There's a bruise on your neck." Lei pushed a hank of Consuelo's glossy black hair away. "On both sides of your neck."

"Hey. Who's your friend?"

Fai's voice came from over Consuelo's shoulder, and she felt the Tongan's bulk behind her. She kept her face neutral and voice flat. "This is Special Agent Lei Texeira. With the FBI."

"You get visits from cops?" Fai's meaty hand rested on Consuelo's shoulder.

"Back up off of her." Lei's voice cracked with authority, and she looked coiled as a spring, though the agent hadn't moved on the stool.

"Introduce me." Fai's tone was silky as her hand loosened and slid away.

"Lei, this is Fai Afa. My roommate." And this time, when Consuelo raised her eyes to the agent, she knew her expression was pleading. Much as she was tempted by the opportunity to escape, she wanted more than anything to have this awful dilemma taken from her.

"Is this girl threatening you?" Lei's gaze seemed to bore into Consuelo's, then she switched her gaze to Fai. Consuelo riffled through her choices mentally as her hand automatically stroked the Chihuahua snuggled up to her shoulder.

"No. We're friends," Consuelo said. "Fai's helped me a lot in here. Kept the bullies away." This was perfectly true, and Fai patted Consuelo's back in an approximation of friendly approval.

"That's right. No one messes with my friends."

Jadene approached. "I've noticed you every week when you come," the skinny blonde said to Lei. Consuelo's stomach turned at the girl's shy act, so sincere and so false. "It's great how someone important like you is taking care of Consuelo's dog."

The two girls hovered nearby for the duration of Lei's visit, taking turns petting Angel and making it impossible to get a moment alone. Lei seemed to be buying the other girls' friendly act, and Consuelo's stomach tightened at the thought of how her mentor would feel when she heard of the trio's escape.

Betrayed.

Consuelo knew how betrayal felt. Her situation squeezed her like the tightening coils of a boa constrictor.

Lei smiled at the other girls. "Can I get a moment alone with Consuelo? News of her family."

Consuelo had no family but her stressed-out aunt, who'd only visited once, but Fai and Jadene didn't know that. Fai gave Consuelo a last glance over her shoulder, and they moved off.

Lei leaned forward, petting Angel, who'd gone limp and fallen asleep under all the attention, and now snoozed in the crook of Consuelo's arm.

"Is there something you need to tell me?" Lei's voice was soft and a fall of her curly dark-brown hair hid her lips from the prying eyes that Consuelo could feel on her back.

"I'd like a different roommate," Consuelo whispered. "As soon as possible."

"I'll see what I can do," Lei whispered back. Consuelo felt a weight lift. She wasn't going to have to deal with this situation if she could just get Fai out of her room.

It was an emotional wrench, as usual, when she said goodbye to Lei and Angel, but there was a little more spring in her walk as she left the visiting area. Maybe Lei could get Fai away from her.

Fai caught her in the hall on their way to their room, hooking an arm around Consuelo's bruised neck in a parody of friendship that the nearby correctional officer, a big mixed Hawaiian woman they called Aunty Marcy, didn't react to.

"How's your family?" Fai asked, giving Consuelo a little push into their room.

"Fine." Consuelo tried to get some distance. The door was kept open except at night, and even then, the COs checked on the girls periodically through the wire-covered viewing window. Fai followed Consuelo in, crowding her.

Consuelo had had enough. She whirled toward the bigger girl. "Leave me alone," she hissed. "I said I'd go. I didn't say anything to Lei, even though she asked me if I was okay. I kept your secret, and I'm going along with your plan. So leave me the hell alone. You keep hassling me, someone's going to realize something's up."

"What's the problem here?" Aunty Marcy boomed from the doorway. Consuelo, hands on her hips, glared up at the big Tongan and didn't look away.

"Everything's fine, Aunty Marcy," she said.

Fai took a step back, turned to face Aunty Marcy with a smile that showed all her straight, white teeth. "This girl. She keeps trying to borrow my panties."

Aunty Marcy gave a snort of laughter at the unlikely scenario. She watched a minute longer, but Consuelo just climbed into her bunk and reached for her notebook as Fai sat down at the little desk with one of her community college textbooks.

Turned toward the wall, Consuelo opened her notebook and uncapped her pen. She had an idea of what she could do.

Lei held up her cred wallet at the exit sally port so that the guard could see it. "I need to speak to the warden," she said.

The man nodded and picked up the phone. A few minutes later, a correctional officer opened the door. "Right this way, ma'am."

Lei wondered at what point she'd crossed that invisible age line into 'ma'am.' She followed the stocky CO down the hall. Efforts had been made, in this area at least, to soften the look of the youth facility. Artwork by the kids decorated the walls. An incomplete hand-painted mural gave a sense of something abandoned, as many of the kids were.

Lei had taken a moment to put Angel back in the car with the windows down before returning to speak to the warden. She thought over her visit with Consuelo. There was no doubt something was wrong, and Lei hadn't needed Consuelo's whispered request for a new roommate to tell her it had something to do with the big Tongan girl and her haole sidekick.

The warden was an older Caucasian man wearing Hawai'i business-casual: a muted aloha shirt and chinos. A ring of keys and an ID badge bounced above his belt buckle.

"I'm Grover Smith. How can I help the FBI today?" The man's weathered skin crinkled around blue eyes faded by years of squinting. *Sailor or golfer,* Lei guessed as she shook his hand.

"I'm here on behalf of Consuelo Aguilar," Lei said.

"Ah, our famous inmate," Smith said. "What's she done now?"

Lei laughed politely. "As you may know from the media, I was the one to capture and bring her in. I've been—mentoring her, shall we say, and it appears that there's a problem with her roommate."

"So you're not here in an official capacity." The smiley crinkles disappeared from Smith's face. "The internal affairs of the youth facility are none of the FBI's business."

"I realize that, of course." Lei's heart rate spiked with anger, but she made an open gesture with her hands, still smiling. Hard lessons in the past had taught her not to show emotions to these bureaucrat types. "I believe Consuelo's being intimidated by her roommate. There could be trouble. I just thought I'd give you a heads-up that Wendy Watanabe, of KHIN-2, also has an interest in Consuelo and could pop by at any time. She's told me she's thinking of doing an in-depth piece on the facility."

Smith glared, hands on his hips. "You can't blackmail me with media pressure. She gets no preferential treatment. It sets a bad precedent."

"There has never been, nor likely ever will be, another case like hers," Lei said tightly. "She's not one to complain, but she asked me to help her get another roommate. I wouldn't be here if I didn't think it meant something serious was going on."

"I'll take it under advisement. Now, if there's nothing else…"

Lei could tell he wasn't going to budge.

"No." She spun on her heel and headed outside. There was no point in any further social niceties.

At her truck, Lei petted Angel as she thumbed through the contacts on her phone to find Wendy Watanabe's personal cell. She didn't think she and the petite anchorwoman would ever be friends, but they'd come to a mutual respect for each other over several cases—and a shared interest in the brave teen who'd captured both of their hearts.

"Texeira. To what do I owe the pleasure?" Watanabe's voice was crisp.

"I'm at Koʻolau Youth Correctional. Consuelo's got a problem with her roommate. Big Tongan girl named Afa. I'm going to look into Afa's criminal background, but I thought you might be interested in the fact that Warden

Smith blew off my warning of a problem and Consuelo's request for another roommate."

"Jerk." Lei could almost see the narrowing of Watanabe's almond-shaped, sharp brown eyes. "I wasn't kidding. I want to do a story on that place."

"This might not be a bad time to poke around. I have a feeling our girl's in trouble. She wouldn't tell me more, but for her to ask for help...."

"Yeah. I'm on it." Watanabe hung up with a brisk click.

Satisfied for the moment, Lei started her vehicle. "Gotta get back to the Bureau and run background on Afa and her friend," she told Angel. "But it's late. I'm sure tomorrow will be soon enough."

Consuelo started awake, her heart pounding. Fai was shaking her shoulder roughly.

"It's time." The older girl thrust a handful of clothing at her.

Despair nipped at Consuelo even as adrenaline hit her system. If Lei had tried to get her transferred, it hadn't happened quickly enough. She climbed out of the bunk and changed into the nylon basketball shorts and tank top Fai handed her. The older girl had received a package yesterday, and gym clothing was allowed for when the girls had exercise time, so apparently Fai had obtained an extra set for Consuelo. The box had been opened by the COs, but they had missed the little extras Fai's uncle had included.

Both girls put the few things they wanted to keep into pillowcases; Consuelo packed the photo of Angel and the Canfield quote, a few old photos of her family, and her notebook.

"Yeah, don't you try to leave that notebook behind," Fai hissed. "I don't want you giving away any clues."

"I wouldn't," Consuelo said stiffly.

The room was dim, the only illumination thin, milky moonlight coming in through the high window and an embedded night light the C.O.'s used for checking on the inmates. Fai opened the box of her package and tore open a large loaf of cellophane-wrapped banana bread. Boxes were X-rayed for metal or weapons, but only visually inspected after that.

Packages were also sniffed by scent dogs; the strong smell of banana bread must have thrown the dogs off too, because inside the loaf were two plastic vials, which wouldn't have set off any detection equipment.

"Now comes the tricky part," Fai whispered. Consuelo could tell the other girl was nervous by the tremble in her voice. The Tongan girl unscrewed the pointed caps of the vials and squeezed the contents into the crack adjacent to the door lock.

A combustible combination of acids, the chemicals began working as soon as they connected with each other. A thin wisp of toxic-smelling smoke wafted from the doorjamb.

Consuelo hid her face, breathing through the edge of her blanket and shutting her eyes against the fumes. Her mind ticked over the steps she'd taken, and what she could do next. There hadn't been much. A few minutes later, Fai grabbed her shoulder.

"I think it's ready." With no interior handle, there was no way to open the door but to push. Fai pushed. The door gave a bit, but held.

"I don't think the acid ate all the way through the wood," Fai whispered harshly. "Come help me."

The two girls ended up running and throwing their weight against the door. The remaining wood finally gave with a crack and squeal that sounded like a scream.

Once out in the hall, Fai in the lead, they hurried to the room where Jadene was locked in with her roommate. Both of those girls were awake. Fai had a plastic key to their door, and unlocked it. At the last minute, Jadene and Fai turned on Jadene's roommate, a sturdy local girl named Nani, and shoved her back in, locking her inside the room.

"Bitches!" Nani yelled. She pounded and screamed, but the walls and doors were fairly soundproof.

"We have to hurry now," Fai said. They ran down the hall. As had been arranged with one of the C.O.'s who owed Fai's uncle a favor, the door into the rec room was left unlocked. From there it was a simple matter to open the exterior door out into the yard.

There were surveillance cameras in the hall, the rec room, and on the yard, but Fai's uncle had also paid for the system to be down for maintenance. The girls trotted unchallenged across the yard, keeping to the shadows, to a chosen exit point in the shadow of one of the buildings.

Fai squatted down and dug in the soil just beneath the chain-link fence topped in coils of razor wire. She produced a pair of heavy wire cutters. Consuelo felt her heart sink. She looked back around, her gaze desperately sweeping the dim yard.

She'd never expected them to get this far.

Fai began cutting the wire in a seam, Jadene prying the wire open further as she made each cut.

Suddenly the lights went on inside the main cinderblock building, and a pulsing electronic alarm split the air.

"That stupid Nani," Jadene hissed. "I bet she got someone to come with all her carrying on."

Fai hunched her shoulders, throwing muscle into the cutting. "Almost there."

Consuelo looked back again, still hoping someone would stop them. One of the doors to the main hall flew open.

"Halt!" an amplified voice yelled, but Fai had made the opening big enough. She wriggled through, tearing the fabric of her shorts on the sharp wire. Jadene whirled and grabbed a handful of Consuelo's long hair, pushing her in front. "Get through there, bitch."

"No," Consuelo cried. "Help! Help me!"

Fai reached back through the hole and grabbed Consuelo, but she struggled harder, desperation giving her strength as she writhed and twisted in the other girls' grip.

"No! I don't want to do this!" she yelled. Jadene finally let go and dove through the hole into Fai's arms. The two older girls hit the ground, scrambled up, and ran for a black pickup truck Consuelo could just make out idling at the edge of the cleared area that marked the compound's boundary.

Consuelo fell to her knees and clasped her hands behind her head, watching the girls reach the truck, jump in, and speed off. The CO pursuing reached her and knocked her flat to the ground, cuffing her, then yanking her up roughly.

"Where did they go?" The head night watchman, Keone, was a heavyset man. He'd always been someone she avoided. All the unplanned running had made his breath short, and he puffed cigarette breath into her face as he panted. Consuelo felt his rage at being made to look incompetent. She cried out as he shook her. "Tell me now!"

"I didn't want to break out! I tried to stay here. Please call my friend, Agent Texeira!" Consuelo cried.

"I'll call someone for you," Keone said, and backhanded her so hard everything went black.

Consuelo awoke on a gurney trundling somewhere. She tried to sit up. Panic surged through her as she discovered she was restrained at feet and hands. Every part of her was strapped down.

"Help! Help me!" she screamed, thrashing. "Help!"

"You just hush that noise." The voice speaking to her was familiar—Aunty Marcy, who'd often been kind. "Calm down. You're going to the infirmary."

Consuelo forced her muscles to relax as ceiling lights moved by overhead. Her cheek throbbed where Keone had hit her. Her scalp hurt from the other girls pulling her hair.

"Call my friend Lei Texeira," she whispered to the C.O. "Please. I left a note for her in my room. I was forced. I didn't want to go with them."

They'd wheeled into the infirmary. "Just relax," Aunty Marcy said. Consuelo yelped as the medic stabbed her in the arm with a needle. A few minutes later she slid into darkness again.

Consuelo woke up to a dry mouth and pounding in her head. She sat up slowly, relieved not to be restrained, and looked around.

As she'd expected, she was in the isolation unit. This wasn't the first time she'd seen the inside of this little shoe-box from hell. She'd got in a scuffle early on, and spent a few days in here. The worst thing about "the shoe" was not having her notebook.

Consuelo hoped someone had found the note she'd left, tucked into her bedding, detailing the plan to get out, what she knew about Fai's plans and family, and that she was being coerced.

But Keone hadn't seemed like he was listening, and she couldn't tell if Aunty Marcie was either.

She looked around. The cot was a single metal shelf covered in rubber that folded up to the wall. There was a toilet, and a sink beside it in one corner. A paper cup rested on the rim of the sink. The walls were padded with berber-style carpet, to keep inmates from injuring themselves and to deaden sound, Consuelo guessed. The only illumination to the roughly six by ten foot space was a wire-covered window near the ceiling, and a couple of embedded glow lights.

Lying on the cot, Consuelo mentally reviewed the situation. If Aunty Marcie didn't contact anyone for her, she could be stuck in here for weeks.

She had to pinch herself on the arm to keep from giving in to the wave of hopelessness that swept over her at the thought. She'd made it through that dark time in the psych hospital by focusing on the things she had to live for, and that would stand her in good stead now, too.

She might be all alone with hardly any family, but she had friends. Powerful friends. And she had information, too. She'd gleaned all she could about Fai and her gangster uncles. They were connected with the notorious Boyz organized crime operation that controlled the construction trade in Honolulu.

If she could get someone to listen to her, she might be able to help get them stopped.

Lying there, she thought of the book proposal her lawyer, Bennie Fernandez, had told her about a few weeks ago.

"HarperCollins wants to publish your memoir," the cherubic little lawyer had said, polishing his round glasses. "The conditions of you getting a reduced sentence include that you have to pay back all the property damage you caused. If you write the memoir, you might be able to achieve that, and still have a little something left over for when you get out of here."

"How much are they offering?" Consuelo felt a little queasy at the thought of having to put into words the complex reasons that had driven her to steal an airplane and begin a Robin Hood-style crime spree. Even though she hadn't been involved with the destruction that had followed, she still felt responsible for that, and for the lives her actions had ended up costing. She'd been dealing with the whole situation by focusing on right now, surviving her life in prison. Some days it was all she could do to keep finding reasons to keep waking up in the morning.

"It's an advance of a hundred thousand, which is only a drop in the bucket to all the property damage caused by the anarchy movement you launched," Fernandez said.

"I'm arguing that you can only be held responsible for the houses you burgled."

"Thanks for that," Consuelo said. "I want a chance to set the record straight. I might have been the one who started something, but I never meant it to end the way it did. I just wanted to draw attention to the gap between the rich and the poor in Hawai'i."

"Well, you certainly did that." Fernandez set his glasses on his little pink bulb of a nose. "But I'd hate for that message to get lost in all that came after. So I think you should do it."

Lying on the bunk, without so much as a blanket let alone pen and paper, Consuelo felt depression and despair sweep over her. She shut her eyes.

She was never getting out of here.

She'd never be able to tell her story, or do anything to fight guys like Jose Taika, Fai's gangster uncle. She had a record, now. She was a criminal, just like they were. Just a number in a system that had no reason to do anything but shut her up.

Consuelo closed her eyes and rolled on her side facing the wall. She willed herself to sleep, but that welcome darkness wouldn't come.

Hours seemed to have passed in the dim half-light that was the perpetual state of things in the shoe, but it might have only been minutes when she heard the metallic grind of the door unlocking and it opened.

Consuelo sat up and looked into the stern face of Raynaldo, one of the CO's. "You have a visitor."

"I thought I couldn't have visitors." Consuelo's voice came out a thin rasp.

"Your lawyer isn't considered a visitor."

"Thank God." Consuelo stood, her legs a little wobbly, and preceded the C.O. down the hall. Raynaldo put her in a bare conference room with a battered table, rather than the usual group visiting area. Consuelo sat on one of the molded plastic chairs.

Bennie Fernandez, his white hair standing up in a halo, wasn't the only visitor. Lei Texeira, her brown eyes worried, followed him in, and right behind them, bright as a parakeet in a teal-green suit, was Wendy Watanabe. Bringing up the rear was a haole man that Consuelo recognized as the warden.

"I'm so glad to see you," Consuelo told Lei. She had to blink to keep tears from overflowing. Lei sat next to her and touched her arm lightly. Consuelo knew she wasn't much for hugging.

Not so Wendy.

"Oh, my God, girl. What did they do to you?" the petite reporter exclaimed, swooping in to hug Consuelo in a waft of pīkake perfume.

"She was captured breaching the wall off the property," the warden harrumphed. "She's in the isolation unit, standard intervention after an escape attempt."

"No, sir, I didn't want to escape." Consuelo extricated herself from Wendy's arms. "I was fighting to get away from the other girls. I left a note under my mattress asking for help."

"That's why Warden Smith allowed this meeting." Fernandez straightened his bright aloha shirt. "One of the CO's, Marcie Porter, found it in your cell."

"I was hoping someone would find it and know that I didn't participate willingly," Consuelo said. Warden Smith's face looked thunderously angry. She could tell he'd happily keep her in the isolation unit indefinitely. She had to hurry and say what she needed to in front of witnesses before he found a way to do that. "I have information. About Fai's uncle. He has contacts here in the prison, and he helped her escape."

"Jose Taika," Lei said. "I ran background on your room-mate Fai already. She's well connected."

Smith's eyebrows drew together. "Well. We didn't have that information. If we had, I might have taken your concerns more seriously."

Lei cocked a brow skeptically at him. "I've already called a contact at HPD that I'd like to have help with your girl hunt. I just came to verify that Consuelo was unhurt and see if she had any more information for us?" she turned to Consuelo.

"Yes, I do have information," Consuelo said. She swallowed. "But I'm afraid. Of what could happen. From Fai and her relatives."

"I am requesting a change of location for you from a judge because of this incident," Bennie Fernandez said. "And I'm sure Warden Smith plans different accommodations for you in light of all of this?"

Wendy whipped a small recorder out of her pocket and turned it on, extending it toward Smith. "This is Wendy Watanabe with KHIN-2 news. I'm here with Warden Smith of Koʻolau Youth Correctional Facility, doing a follow up story about Consuelo Aguilar. This notorious folk heroine was recently involved with a breakout and is now cooperating with authorities in the capture of the escapees. Warden Smith, what can you tell us about how the facility plans to assist in the capture of the runaways?"

"Ah. Well." Smith smoothed his shirt and sucked in his paunch. "Every resource will be deployed to assist in the capture of the criminals at large."

"And what is being done to protect Aguilar, a witness in this case?" Watanabe was relentless as she held the microphone of the recorder close to Smith's sweating face.

"We'll—move her to a protected site," Smith said, getting redder. "We appreciate law enforcement's prompt, coordinated effort in recovering the escapees."

"You heard it here, first, folks." Watanabe clicked Off on the recorder and smiled, a twitch of shapely scarlet lips. "Thrilled to hear it."

Lei made a shooing motion with her hand. "Fernandez and I need to speak to Consuelo alone regarding the case. The rest of you can wait outside."

Consuelo's heart rate was still galloping as Wendy and Smith filed out. "Please. Get me a notebook," she whispered. "I want to write while I'm in isolation."

"Done." Lei said. She drew the girl's notebook out of her backpack, along with a plain Bic ballpoint. "The pen sucks, but it passed regulations."

Consuelo clasped the notebook to her chest. "Thanks so much."

"You're welcome. Now tell me everything."

Consuelo did. She felt much lighter as she was led back to the isolation unit half an hour later, the notebook concealed under her shirt.

Lei strode out of the youth facility, Bennie Fernandez trotting in her wake. "Like I said, I'm filing for a change of venue to move Consuelo to a locked therapeutic group home," Bennie said. "It's a lot homier than Ko'olau."

"Great, Bennie. You've done good by her. But don't let me find you defending any of these scumbags," Lei admonished, shaking a finger at him. "I'll cite conflict of interest on you in a heartbeat."

"All's fair," the little defense lawyer puffed as they reached the parking lot. "In love, and in defense law. But don't worry. I checked with my office. No Taikas or Afas on the client list."

"Keep it that way." Lei beeped open her truck and jumped in, peeling out of the lot.

She put her light on and picked up her radio, checking in with Marcus Kamuela, detective in charge of the breakout's manhunt.

"Got some new information from a witness," she told the big Hawaiian detective. "Rendezvous in five minutes."

She met Kamuela and the other HPD operatives at the Kaneohe police station. There, she shared the intel Consuelo had gathered.

"We need the Coast Guard in on this," Kamuela said. "And SWAT. Making the calls."

It wasn't long before the multi-agency group approached a rusty steel warehouse down at the harbor area, an industrial zone of grubby older buildings draped in power lines, contrasting with the sparkling turquoise ocean in the distance.

Lei stayed well back, aware of her 'consultant' role, as SWAT burst in the warehouse entrance with a handheld metal door cannon. There was a mad scramble inside the warehouse, the rattle of gunfire, and a burst of yelling. The roar of engines added further chaos, and a twin-engine speedboat zoomed out of the side of the warehouse butted up against the water.

Lei hadn't entered with the team, and she ran along the outside of the building, her weapon in low-ready position to track the fleeing boat.

Looking back at the shore, faces pale with fright, were a heavyset girl with black hair and a slim blond. Driving the boat was a suspect in a black ball cap. In the stern, taking a shot at Lei with a shotgun, was another male suspect.

Lei ducked out of the way as a hole blew open in the corrugated metal wall near her. She swung back around and shot, aiming for the big twin diesel engines. She hit one, she could tell, as Fai Afa gave a cry and jumped back, grabbing the blond Jadene in her arms. Lei fired again, and hit the other engine, but the boat kept going, hitting surf and bouncing high, a tough target on a wide-open sea.

Lei didn't want to hit one of the girls, and she was already out of range for anything but a wild card shot. She kept an eye on the boat as Marcus arrived beside her, panting with exertion. "Interior secure. Looks like the girls got away."

"How far out is that Coast Guard cutter?" Lei asked. "I did get off a couple of shots. Tried to hit the motor. Seemed like I did, but it's still moving."

As if in answer to her question, they saw the smaller of the Coast Guard's intercept boats moving in on the speedboat, which had slowed significantly.

"Maybe I winged it," Lei muttered, sheltering her eyes with a hand against the glitter of sunshine on the ocean.

"Looks like you did." Marcus lifted his rifle in burly arms and looked through the scope at the distant, bobbing boats. "They're taking it in tow."

They turned away. The big Hawaiian's stern face split in a grin as he high-fived Lei. "Tell that girl of yours nice work. We scooped up some major Boyz today."

Consuelo sat on the floor of the isolation cell and used the bed as a desk.

"It all began with a drunk driver," she wrote. "Just a guy who'd been laid off, had a few, and didn't even know what he was doing when he jumped a curb in his old Pontiac."

As Consuelo wrote, she felt the pressure of locked-up pain begin to drain away.

Nothing could bring her mother, mowed down beside Consuelo on the sidewalk, back to life. Nothing could change the fact that her father had been drawn down into the hell of cancer, never to return. Nothing could save the people murdered by others in her name.

But Consuelo could tell her story, and she knew that, with the friends she had, it would be heard. It would help make things right.

There were other kinds of freedom than taking to the air in flight.

TOBY NEAL

Toby Neal grew up on the island of Kaua'i in Hawai'i. After a few "stretches of exile" to pursue education, the islands have been home for the last sixteen years. Toby is a mental health therapist, a career that has informed the depth and complexity of the characters in her books. Outside of work and writing, Toby volunteers in a nonprofit for children and enjoys life in Hawai'i through beach walking, body boarding, scuba diving, photography and hiking.

Sign up for news of upcoming books at http://www.tobyneal.net/ and receive a free, full-length, award-winning novel!

DANNY'S TALE
THE UNTOLD STORY FROM THE OHANA
C.W. Schutter

Honolulu – 1978

Governor Dan Myers knew it was time to tell the truth. His son, Gerry, sat in the soft butter leather barrel chair in the sitting room adjoining his office with his head in his hands sobbing.

Being labeled a liar could end any chance of my being re-elected, he thought.

Gerry raised his head. "Dad, she's my baby. We have to find a match for a bone marrow transplant before the cancer progresses too far, even if it means tracing our ancestry back to Portugal, Germany, the Philippines, and China. And we've got to find all the Hawaiians related to us here.

"I remember very little of my mother. You rarely talk about her. Kathy and I figured her memory must have been painful because you always change the subject when we ask. All I remember of my mom is a soft-spoken lady, who told us Bible stories and smiled a lot. I don't ever recall a time when she yelled at us or hit us. I only know what she looks like because of the old picture album."

The Governor got up from his chair and went to the Koa wood console table where pictures of his family were scattered on the smooth, golden brown top. He was proud of the way his family turned out. He picked up the 11 x12 frame with his wedding picture and marveled once again at how he, a poor boy from Kalihi and Pālolo, somehow married the richest, most beautiful woman in Hawai'i who was a *kama'āina haole*, to boot. Of course, he had no idea who she was when he fell in love with her. That was the beauty of it.

Sighing he put the picture back down.

Truth had consequences. But he didn't have a choice now.

He turned and faced his son.

Honolulu - 1930-1942

Danny Myers was born in Kalihi, one of the roughest neighborhoods in Honolulu. In 1930, at the age of fourteen, his family moved to a better neighborhood across town in Pālolo. The quiet, shy boy stayed out of trouble by keeping his nose in books, shutting his mouth, and never looking at people too long. Giving stink eye meant getting beat up in the rough streets he grew up in. And stink eye was defined by the accusers and in most cases, a complete mystery to the victims who were charged with the dubious offense.

Danny had no feelings whatsoever for the people in his neighborhood. By the time he was ten, he felt like an alien dropped into an environment with people he had nothing in common with. He even refused to speak pidgin English.

"Hey Danny, who you think you are talking like one *haole?*" the kids at school, his cousins, and even his brother, Tommy sometimes teased.

Maybe God had played a joke on him. But being different had its advantages. Knowing he wasn't like the others kept alive his hope of a bright future. On the other hand, violence in his family kept him motivated.

Instead of feeling defeated and bitter like so many of the housing kids, who found their identity in violent gangs, he chose to focus on dreams of a better future no matter how impossible they seemed. However, he was one of them—

like it or not. Success would be sweeter knowing where he came from.

"You think you betta than the rest of us cuz you make good grades?" His German-Hawaiian-Chinese father sneered. A massive brute with a crew cut, narrow hazel eyes, and a cruel mouth set in a lantern jaw, Danny's father had an iron fist he used liberally on his children. "You one loser. You nevah goin' be anything in dis life. You nuthin' but one loser. You gotta be like your brudda Tommy. You gotta be tough to make it in dis world."

"Danny, you gotta lift weights, get tough. Play football or something," Tommy advised. "Dad picks on you 'cause you let him. He's a bully. He like pick on the little guy, and you his scapegoat. So you gotta get big. Spend mo' time lifting weights with me then reading books all the time."

"Making good grades is how I'm going to get out of the housing," Danny told him. "I'm not going to live like this the rest of my life. I'm going to be somebody. A lawyer, a doctor, something where I can have a nice house and quiet family life."

Tommy laughed and patted his younger brother on his shoulder. "Okay, brah. Big dreams sometimes make big people. Me, I'm going to join the army and get outta here because I'm not a brain like you. Make it for all of us, okay? And remember your bruddah when you do."

Danny admired his big brother, who was his polar opposite. Tommy was everything he was not—athletic, strong, and protective of his brother and sister.

"I love you, bruddah," Danny said.

Tommy looked embarrassed for a moment. "Feel the same. You my only bruddah."

"What about Jolene?" Thirteen-year-old Jolene squeaked as she walked into their bedroom. Frail like their mother with curly light brown hair, golden skin, thick, long-lashed brown eyes, she had a promise of beauty far surpassing anyone in the family.

Tommy went up to her and patted her on the head. "Hey shrimp, we going keep all the boys away from you. Make sure you end up an old maid."

Jolene frowned and began hitting Tommy who pretended to be scared of her. He yelled while laughing at the same time. "Owee. Owee. You're hurting me."

Their dad strutted around his turf in a perennial bad mood because he drank. Danny suspected it was to stop feeling like a man beaten down by circumstances and poverty. Their apartment was his kingdom where he let out the aggression ground out of him day after day doing menial labor. When he was sober and feeling melancholy, he would tell his boys, "Don't be like me. My life is no good."

The three siblings were close because they shared a common bond. They didn't like their abusive father, who lashed out at his family when he was in a bad mood. Unfortunately for the family, he was in a bad mood most of the time. The target of his rage was often their frail Portuguese mother. Her mere existence seemed to bring out the worst in him.

The only time his mother fought back was when he was about eight-years-old. She had walked in the front door carrying bags of groceries in the middle of an especially bad whipping. Dropping the bags when she saw blood on their legs and arms, she cried out, "Stop. Stop. What are you doing?"

Tommy turned. "Why are you hitting us? We didn't do nuthin'." His father punched him in the face.

Their sister ran out of her bedroom when she heard her mother's voice. Running to her, Jo clutched her waist and shook with fear.

"You hit him in the face," his mom screamed. "How many times did I tell you not to hit them on their faces? And they're bleeding. For God's sake, stop before you kill them."

His dad spun around, his face black with rage. "Keep out of it. These damn no-good, spoiled rotten kids drive me crazy."

"No, you stop." She shielded her sons with her body.

"Get away." His dad stepped toward her.

His mom stretched her arms across her sons, who cowered behind her. "What's wrong with you, Bobby? How can you do this to your own kids?"

"You always put them first. Not me." He raised his belt and whipped her across the legs.

Danny sobbed, "Mom, Mom go away. Please. Don't help us."

Tommy darted out from behind her and grabbed the phone. "I'm going call the cops." He picked up the phone book to look up the number and started dialing.

Their dad dropped his belt. He marched up to Tommy and snatched the phone book as well as the phone from his hands. Throwing the book against the wall, he bashed the phone into its cradle. Without another word, he left the apartment, slamming the door so hard a figurine on a nearby table crashed to the ground.

In time, his meek mother avoided his father's tyranny by disappearing into herself. By the time Danny entered ninth grade, her paranoia had turned into full-blown psychosis.

"Your mom is a nutcase," their dad scoffed between chugs of beer. "Look at her, talking to herself and wearing the same thing every day. Hey dummy, that housedress and robe *pilau* by now. And look at your hair. Why I wen marry a *pupule*, ugly cow like you?"

Danny's mother acted as if she were deaf and dumb, ignoring her husband as she shuffled around the house in her furry house slippers and pink bathrobe, which covered the faded blue flowered housedress she always wore. Her only reaction was to clutch the top of her robe together.

"Why you no get one job? Five jobs in one year prove you *pupule*." His dad pushed back his chair and went up to his wife. He raised his fist. She cowered, but remained silent. He dropped his fist and exhaled in disgust. "No sense." He returned to his chair muttering. "I tell you, she good fo' nothing. A chain around my neck."

Danny's mother scurried back to the kitchen to prepare dinner. Somehow, despite disappearing into her own private world, she managed to cook, clean the house, and go to the market. She ceased talking to anyone but herself. Beating her became a non-event to Danny's father. Instead, he unleashed his anger on Danny and Jolene, but he left Tommy alone.

Tommy was as big as their father at fifteen—stronger and tougher too. Considered the bull of the school even as a sophomore, no one dared mess with Tommy. Having Tommy as a brother during intermediate school protected Danny from getting into trouble. Wannabe bulls prowled the schoolyard looking for guys smaller and weaker just to beat them up so they could get a rep as a tough guy. But because of Tommy, they left Danny alone.

"No worry. High school different," Tommy told him. "The guys who always like fight play football instead. Defense." Tommy winked. "They mo' interested in hitting than getting hit."

The only time Danny felt at peace was when he was either in St. Patrick's church or at St. Louis, the Catholic boys' school he attended. He was grateful to the Catholic Church as they saved him from growing up bitter and angry. The Roman Catholic order of the Marianists plucked both his brother and him from public school and took them into their fold. Tommy got a football scholarship in his sophomore year. At the same time, Danny received an academic scholarship and started St. Louis in his freshman year.

The first day of school, as Tommy and Danny walked to the bus stop together wearing their school uniforms, starched white button down shirts over navy blue pants, one of Tommy's Pop Warner football teammates, Lewis, jaywalked across the street to say hi.

"Howzit Tommy?" Lewis greeted, looking the brothers up and down. "Heard you was going to St. Louis. You sure look different in uniform. But no get me wrong. You looking good in it."

Danny knew Lewis said it to be polite. All the boys in Pālolo knew how tough Tommy was and didn't want to get on his wrong side.

Tommy ran his fingers through his short hair self-consciously. "Yeah, well. Wish St. Louis had girls, but it's always one of the top five football teams in the state so, what you going do?"

"What about your bruddah, Danny?" Lewis asked.

Tommy smiled and shrugged. "Don't you know? He's so smart he going be the governor one day. So watch what you say to him."

Danny found his calling at St. Louis. His family rarely attended church, but Danny felt pulled to the priesthood. The stained glass windows, the altar, statues of Madonna and Child, the crucifix, and the priestly vestments created an atmosphere of holiness he yearned to be a part of.

"What's with going to church all the time?" Tommy asked him. "It's boring. I can't even understand what they're saying. All that Latin stuff. So why go?"

"I like it," Danny replied. "Mass seems more holy in Latin."

"You *pupule*." Tommy chuckled.

"You should go to church. Bet you can't remember the last time you went to confession."

"You right 'bout that. Last time I went to confession, I was a little kid. Tell you what." Tommy smiled. "You go pray for me. That way I no need pray."

"You still need to go to confession."

"Nah. Father Thomas don't have hours to listen to all the things I wen do since I was a kid." Tommy laughed. "You and the Father good friends. Maybe he forgive me if you ask him to."

Danny admired Father Thomas, a kindly, soft-spoken man, so different from his father and the men he grew up around. More than anything, he wanted to emulate Father Thomas, who always had time to talk to him, especially about his interest in the priesthood.

"It's a serious, life-changing decision." Father Thomas leaned across the desk in his study. "Pray about it and think hard on it. The priesthood is a life of sacrifice and service. Personally, I can't imagine a life other than being a priest. It fulfills me to help people. But that's just me."

Danny needed very little convincing. He knew the priesthood was his calling. From then on, he worked towards entering seminary after high school. Knowing where he was headed brought him peace.

1932

Danny, Jolene, and Tommy enjoyed listening to radio shows in their free time and prior to their dad coming home. Most of the money they made collecting soda pop bottles and selling newspapers was spent on comic books. *Buck Rogers* was their favorite. After Tommy got busy with football and baseball, he stopped chipping in to buy comics and became more interested in looking good for girls. Now that *Buck Rogers* was a radio show, the Myers kids were glued to the radio every Monday through Thursday. Tommy and Danny were big fans.

Buck Rogers was a World War I vet who became trapped in one of the lower levels of an abandoned coal mine near Wyoming Valley in Pennsylvania after it caved in while he was investigating strange activity inside the mines. Exposure to radioactive gas put him into a state of suspended animation until the year 2419 when he finally woke up and joined a group called Air Lords in the strange, new world he found himself in. The Air Lords and a gang called the Bad Bloods were enemies. Buck's life was constantly in danger as the Air Lords and Bad Bloods were always fighting to gain control of the world. It was the most exciting and thrilling show on radio.

Just as the Bad Bloods were in the middle of destroying the Air Lords' airships and killing as many of the Air Lords as they could, their dad walked into the living room and slammed the door. Danny and his siblings were so engrossed, they didn't move at first. They were used to their dad slamming doors. Whenever he did, they lay low and tried to ignore him, hoping he'd leave them alone if they remained quiet.

"Children should be seen and not heard," was one of his favorite sayings.

Danny was lying on the floor with his eyes closed trying to picture the chaos and fiery explosions eradicating the airships as well as the Air Lords' camp. The descriptions were so vivid, and the narrator's voice so ominous, he hung on every word. His sister sat on the floor next to him with her back against the couch. When the door slammed, she reached out and grabbed his hand. Tommy was sprawled on the couch above them. He had kicked Danny and Jo off the sofa earlier because he wanted to lie down after football practice. Since Tommy was the closest to the door, their dad went to him first and knocked him on his head.

Tommy shot up from the couch, "What're you doing? I nevah do nothing."

Their father slugged him. "Damn kid got no respect, talking to your father like that."

Tommy jumped over the couch, grabbed the front of his dad's aloha shirt in one hand, and raised his fist over his head. "You like beef?" he yelled. "You think you so tough, old man?"

Tommy towered over his dad. Because of his height and weight advantage, their dad hadn't attacked Tommy in at least two years. Danny looked down at his dad's red eyes and bloated face. Although it was still only five thirty in the afternoon, he could see their dad was already wasted.

Their dad blinked his blood-shot eyes and shrank back. In the background sirens blared, machine guns blasted, and people screamed. Jolene, now fourteen, wrapped her arms around her knees and buried her face between them.

Fear showed in the older man's eyes, and he stepped back. Tommy dropped his hands.

Their mother entered the room and tottered over to her husband and son. Stopping next to Tommy, she patted his arm. Tommy raised his eyebrows. Before he could react, she put her hands on his cheeks and pulled his face down close to hers. Her eyes blazed for the first time in years as she whispered in the gentle, clear voice her family hadn't heard in a long time, "Good boy." She kissed his forehead.

It happened so fast, Danny might have thought he imagined it because just as quickly, the light disappeared from her eyes, and she began muttering to herself again as she shuffled past Tommy into the kitchen.

Tommy blinked back tears. He grabbed the front of his dad's shirt again, and glowered. "Don't ever let me catch you touching my mother again or I swear to God, I'll kill you."

Danny attended mass alone at St. Patrick's Church on Wai'alae Avenue every Sunday. The Romanesque cruciform structure of white stucco with a red-tiled roof built on a rocky, volcanic slope in Kaimukī, was the closest Catholic Church to Danny's apartment. Completed and dedicated in 1929, the parish belonged to the Fathers and Brothers of the Sacred Heart. It had been given to them by papal decree in recognition of their missionary efforts in establishing the Catholic Church in the Islands.

Danny sometimes went there during the week just to sit and meditate or pray before going home. It was dark and quiet inside the sanctuary, so different from the hot, noisy world outside. Embracing the peace his private retreat brought him, he sometimes simply sat in a pew, looking all around and enjoying the quiet beauty of the church. Light filtered in through the beautiful stained glass windows and became colored prisms, creating a magical atmosphere. When the bells rang, he closed his eyes. He imagined himself in Brussels, the exotic European City where stained glass windows and bells were made. *What a wonderful place Brussels must be with its historic buildings and staunch Catholic population.*

When he knelt and prayed, the presence of God, Jesus, the angels, and Blessed Mother Mary seemed to converge inside the lovely interior; further sanctifying what was already holy ground. When the world outside got too much for him, he escaped to St. Patrick's and spent hours sitting in the pews in silence, dreading his return to the chaos at home.

"Everyone has a cross to bear," Father Thomas told him.

His dad was definitely the cross his entire family had to bear.

Moved by the comforting calm of the church and grateful to the Catholics who ripped him from the public schools where he was bullied, Danny remained determined to become a priest like Father Thomas.

Danny first saw Sister Maria inside St. Patrick's Church. He was sixteen years old. In 1909, the Sisters of the Sacred Heart had built a convent and school, the Academy of the Sacred Hearts of Jesus and Mary, on the adjoining lot long before the church was built.

If there was such a thing as love at first sight, Danny fell victim.

The first time he found himself alone with her inside the sanctuary was in the early afternoon. He was surprised. He rarely saw anyone there on weekdays. After that, they seemed to be there at the same time quite a lot. Most of the time, she was already ahead of him, kneeling down in the first row saying her prayers, her rosary entwined in her small hands. Kneeling in the first row across from her, he couldn't help but stare. She looked very young and tiny. As if sensing his eyes on her, she turned. Her hair was hidden under a black veil, and the standard white coif and wimple covered her cheeks and neck. Even so, it didn't diminish the beauty of her small, heart-shaped face, big, melting almost-black eyes, and cocoa skin.

Danny's heart stopped. He couldn't stop staring at the most beautiful girl he'd ever laid eyes on. He tried to look away and concentrate on his prayers, but his flesh disobeyed. With his heart pounding inside his chest, he turned to gaze at her again. The nun with the face of an angel made him tremble.

What was happening to him? He had already decided to enter the priesthood. How could he be attracted to a nun, of all people? Nuns were married to God.

As if she felt him staring, she turned her big, dark eyes towards him. Her thick lashes fluttered down in shy alarm as she twisted a rosary in her praying hands.

After that, Danny came to the church every weekday at the same time. At first, she showed up only occasionally. But after two weeks of furtive glances at each other, she began coming regularly. They were both too shy to speak to each other.

Weeks went by. Then, one day, as if God personally helped them, he blessed them with a sudden tropical storm a minute or two after they left the sanctuary. Not only were they hit with pouring rain. Lightning split the gray sky, and a loud clap of thunder shattered the air above them. They fled back into the church, soaking wet from the sudden cloudburst. They stared at each other open-mouthed, rainwater dripping from their faces and clothes. Unexpectedly, she put her hand to her mouth and giggled.

Danny looked down at himself. They both looked like drowned cats. He started laughing, too. Wanting the moment to last, he had an idea. A strange idea, since he was the serious type who never clowned around. But she provoked unfamiliar feelings in him, and he did something he'd never done before. He acted goofy, bending his elbows and flapping his arms like wings while running back and forth in front of the altar clucking and squawking like a wet chicken.

If Father Thomas had seen him, he'd have been shocked, disapproving of the sacrilege. Danny was appalled, too. However, he quashed his guilty feelings and gave in to impulse in order to make her laugh.

She laughed so hard she had to sit down. He sat next to her, and they stared at each other.

"My name is Danny." He held his hand out to her.

She looked down at his hand but didn't take it.

"Sister Maria," she replied in a soft, shy voice with a Filipino accent. She paused as if uncertain as to what to say next. Tiny in stature, the young nun's eyes were downcast and her hands folded in her lap. She shivered, whether from the wet rain or embarrassment, he didn't know.

Mesmerized by her beauty, and proximity, Danny couldn't speak for a moment. Her face was damp, like she had just emerged from the shower. He longed to take her hand in his. Instead, he shook his head to clear his unholy, sinful thoughts.

"Maria." Her name came out like a sigh.

"Sister Maria," she gently corrected. She raised eyes glittering with curiosity and looked directly into his.

"Sister Maria." Danny sat, throwing his head back, and staring at the ceiling. He wanted to look at her, too but was timid and shy. As inexperienced as he was, he knew their attraction was mutual.

She's a nun, he warned himself.

Although they remained quiet for a while, he was intensely aware of his raging emotions. Her discomfort betrayed her interest in him. He saw curiosity in the eyes, which refused to look at him as her nervous hands played with the rosary in her lap.

"Sister I'm a senior at St. Louis." He immediately felt like an idiot. Everyone from Kaimukī to Kapahulu knew all the young men and boys who wore a starched white button-down shirt and dark navy trousers were from St. Louis. The Academy of the Sacred Hearts of Jesus and Mary were mainly elementary school students who wore white shirts and khaki pants.

"Yes, I know."

They stared at each other for a second. Embarrassed, they both looked away.

"Father Thomas told me you're planning on entering the priesthood," she said.

He was taken aback for a moment. They discussed him?

"Yes," he leaned back against the back of the pew, sighed, and began twirling his thumbs. "Why were you and Father Thomas talking about me?"

"He saw us sitting in church one day," Sister Maria explained. "After you left, he asked me if I visited the sanctuary often. I guess he knew you came here a lot. I said yes, and he asked me if we ever talked. I said no. He told me you were going into the priesthood after high school."

"I see."

"What made you decide to become a priest?"

"I found peace here with the church for the first time in my life. I knew I was called to do this." He turned to her. "And you? How did you find your calling?"

"The most wonderful person I ever met was a nun at the convent school in Manila. Sister Agnes was a saint. All the other girls thought so, too, because we all wanted to be like her." Sister Maria shrugged. "It wasn't hard deciding to be a nun. Everyone in my convent school was very poor with little chance of bettering ourselves. The Philippines is not like Hawai'i. That's why so many Filipinos come here to live. Hawai'i is paradise compared to my home country. And being a nun or a nurse, or both, is a high calling for Filipino girls."

Danny laughed. "Here in paradise, I grew up poor."

"But now, we are both lucky and rich in the Lord." Sister Maria tilted her head.

For the first time in his life, Danny felt lucky. He had just met the most beautiful, amazing girl in the world.

Whenever they saw each other at church in the presence of others, mainly on Sundays, only their eyes betrayed their growing friendship. Once, Danny brushed by her and the tips of his fingers touched her habit. It sent an unexpected thrill through his body knowing her garment touched her skin. To his dismay, images of what she looked like under her habit stirred his desire.

This isn't happening—my calling is to the priesthood.

They started meeting secretly in the church on weekdays, or sometimes under the shade of a tree in a quiet corner behind a building no one ever walked by. In the beginning, Danny told himself it was only to discuss ministry. They both knew they were caught up in a lie. What madness seduced them? Nuns married to God and priests or future priests were not supposed to fall in love. But he couldn't stop dreaming of the beautiful nun who set him on fire.

One day, he yielded to desire. Unable to stop himself, he reached out and touched the smooth satin of her dark skin. His fingers tingled, and his burning heart raced, aching with desire. It made him feel more alive and passionate than he ever felt before.

This isn't supposed to happen. But even as he thought it, he cupped her chin in his fingers and gently, hesitantly, kissed her soft lips. As his tongue probed into the soft, wetness of her mouth, she returned his passion. He was aware of tears falling on her soft, wet cheeks. But there was no turning back. They were in love.

For the first time, Danny doubted his calling.

That night, he turned his head to the wall and wept in silence so as not to disturb Tommy.

"Forgive me, Father, for I have sinned." Danny slumped in the confessional booth pouring out his story to Father Thomas, who sat behind the screen. He could just imagine the shock on the kindly priest's face. Of course, Father Thomas recognized his voice, just as he recognized his dear mentor's voice. *How shocked he must be.* As he related his story, he felt like the biggest sinner.

"My son." Father Thomas's kind voice made him feel worse. "Perhaps it isn't your calling to be a priest."

Danny dropped his head into his hands. "I planned my life around the priesthood. And Father, she's a nun, not just a novitiate."

Silence. Danny heard him sigh.

"These things happen more than the church likes to admit. At least you haven't entered seminary or taken final vows."

"But she has." Father Thomas' understanding relieved Danny yet made him feel worse at the same time. He had expected to be scolded and given a heavy penance.

"Have you sinned beyond falling in love?"

"No, just kissing, nothing more. I came here before things went too far."

"A wise decision. Does she wish to leave the convent?"

"No, she says she loves me, but must honor her commitment." Danny began to cry. "I love her more than anyone in the world. I...I don't know if I can live without her."

"But it sounds like she's made her choice." The priest paused. "The only thing you can do is to forget her. She's already married to God. You must stay away. You know that. It wouldn't be fair to her or to you to put temptation in both your paths. There are other churches you can attend."

"I know." Danny sobbed. "But I can't help it. Loving her doesn't feel like a sin."

"I'm sorry for you, my son. Choosing the priesthood or to marry God is always a sacrifice."

Danny saw her one last time. They met in a small, sterile room under the watchful eyes of the Mother Superior. Because the nun was partially deaf and sat all the way across the big classroom in a corner, they were able to speak to each other frankly. Danny was grateful for the little privilege.

Sister Maria bowed her head. "I confessed everything to Mother Superior. She's been very kind allowing me this one last meeting. My penance is to clean bathrooms for a month and spend my free time fasting and praying for forgiveness. I'm being sent to the order of the Carmelites."

"The Carmelites?" Danny sat back. "Don't they take vows of silence?"

She nodded. "I won't be allowed to speak for a while. Eventually I will be able to talk, but only when necessary. The Carmelite charism demands contemplation, prayer, and service. As a result, they are under the special protection of the Blessed Virgin Mary. It's only through silence, prayer, and contemplation that the Carmelite nuns are able to receive the visions they are known for. Mother Superior only wishes to protect me from the temptations of the world."

Stunned, Danny leaned forward. "It sounds like prison."

"Don't think like that, Danny," she replied with earnest eyes. "I think of it as a place where I can work on becoming more holy and pleasing to God."

"I wish I could kiss you or touch your hands just one last time." Danny's heart sank as he held back his tears.

"You're my life. How can loving you be a sin? Why do you have to do penance and be forced to separate from the world just because we did something so beautiful and natural as falling in love?"

Sister Maria dabbed her eyes with tissue.

"Maria." He leaned forward. "Don't do this to yourself. Don't hide from the world. Marry me."

Surprised, Maria looked up, her face wet with tears.

"Marry me. I'll quit school and we'll make a life together. Have children."

"We're both too young to marry without permission." She looked down at her fingers twisting the tissue to shreds.

"I'll be seventeen in a few months..."

"I've just turned sixteen." She sighed and bit her lip. "Perhaps I should explain why I feel so committed to the church. My mother died eight years ago after a long illness. My dad remarried, and my new stepmother treated me like a servant. After she got pregnant, she kicked me out of the house. That's why I left the Philippines."

It was the most she had ever shared with him about her past.

"I'm sorry your life was so hard. But, what does it have to do with our getting married? People get married young, even younger than seventeen."

She shook her head. "I owe the church everything. I would still be living in the streets if not for them. The nuns saved me. I owe them my life."

"No, you owe them gratitude, but not your life."

"Danny...I can't. I dedicated my life to God and the church. How can I turn my back on them? You don't know how it was for me. I was hungry all the time. The only food I got was what I could beg or steal. My clothes turned to rags, and I had to beg in the streets. I dug in the garbage for scraps of food. Finally, scary-looking men came and tried to take me away. When I tried to run, they grabbed me, and began beating me. Three nuns saw them. One of them went to get the police. The other two tried to help me. As the men dragged me away, the nuns held on and refused to let go. Thank goodness the other nun returned just in time with the police. They told us the men were known to prowl the streets looking for homeless young orphan girls to sell to prostitute houses." She looked up with wide eyes. "The nuns saved me. I owe them a debt I can never repay. They took me to live in the convent with other girls they'd saved in the streets. They gave me clothes to wear, a bed to sleep in, and food to eat. I went to school at the convent and learned English. The day I became a novitiate was one of the happiest days of my life."

"What were the other happiest days?"

"When I took my final vows and..." Her voice drifted off before she hesitated and looked into his eyes, "And all the days I spent with you from the moment we met."

Danny wanted to hold her in his arms, but as he reached for her, she shrank against the back of the chair. They heard Mother Superior clear her throat and push back her chair as she stood up. They both turned and saw her staring at them. A frown darkened her stern face. She shook her head.

"I have to go." Maria stood to leave with tears on her cheeks.

Danny held up his hand. "Wait. At least tell me your real name."

She paused, before answering, "Evangelista DeDios."

"Evangelista DeDios," he echoed. "Write to me Evangelista, if you change your mind, we're in the phone book under Robert Myers in Pālolo."

Maria nodded. "I won't change my mind, but I'll remember Robert Myers in Pālolo." Then she turned her back on him as she walked over to join Mother Superior.

Danny cried out, "I'll love you forever."

She turned one last time.

He memorized every inch of her face. Although her voice caught, she was still able to whisper loud enough for him to hear but not loud enough for Mother Superior's ears, "And I will love you until the day I die."

Danny dropped his head into his hands and cried as she followed Mother Superior out the door.

1933

Tommy joined the Marines in the fall after graduation.

"You gotta look out for them now," Tommy told Danny. He put his big hand on Danny's shoulder. "You're the big bruddah now. Keep the old man in line."

"I'm not you," Danny replied. "Why do you have to go?"

"I told you I was going into the military if I didn't get a football scholarship. I want to see the world. Only way fo' a poor bugga like me is to sign up."

"Tommy..."

Tommy peered into his eyes. "Don't disappoint me, bruddah. Take care of our sista. You hear?" Tommy swung the army duffle bag, which held all his possessions, over his shoulder. "I'm depending on you."

Danny watched Tommy swagger out the door. A sick feeling twisted his insides. How was he supposed to look out for Jo and his mom? He wasn't Tommy. He was no match for his dad.

The relationship between their dad and Jo deteriorated after Tommy left. His big brother had always protected his sister and mother. Bobby Myers watched his step when Tommy was around.

A couple of weeks after Tommy shipped out, their dad came home drunk and began picking on Jo. Nothing unusual. But this time, his father had been on a monster bender and had just got into a fight at the bar with someone who gave him a black eye. He was roaring mad and primed to take it out on someone who couldn't fight back.

"Where you going gallivanting looking like a painted whore?" Their dad grabbed Jo's arm before she could dash out the door. "What ch'ou doing with that no good boyfriend of yours? You wanna get a bad rep? You want the kids at school calling you easy meat?"

"I'm not doing anything bad." Jo yanked her arm away from him.

He hit her so hard she fell to the ground. Then he started kicking her. For the first time in his life, Danny put his hands on his father and tried to shove him against the wall. But Danny wasn't big enough or strong enough to tackle his father. He punched Danny so hard he flew against the wall and hit his head. Then he dragged Jo by her hair into her bedroom before Danny could react.

He was still stunned when he heard the click of a lock followed by the sound of a leather belt lashing skin.

Jo screamed, "Please daddy, don't. I'm sorry. Don't hit me."

Danny pounded the door with his fists. "Dad. Dad. Don't hit her, Dad."

But the sound continued. Jo kept screaming.

Danny leaned against the door and cried.

Jo went to live with their maternal grandmother in Kapahulu. Tutu needed help now that their maiden aunt had gotten married and moved to the mainland.

"Do you have to go?" Danny asked when he came home from school the next day and saw Jo packing her bags. "It won't be easy living with Tutu. She's old and frail. You'll practically be a caregiver."

"I know." Jolene bit her lip and shook her head. "But Tutu needs help, and it's my excuse to get out of here before something really bad happens. I'll have a place to live. If I wait too long, Tutu will find one of our cousins to help her.

"I can't take it anymore. You know how Dad is. He's never going to change. He always picks on me. He used to be scared of Tommy, but now Tommy's gone. He doesn't pick on Mom because he says it's no fun. He calls me a whore. I can't let him beat me up anymore.," Jo hesitated and looked up at her brother with wide, teary eyes. "Danny, I'm pregnant."

Danny put his arms around her.

"Are you angry at me?"

"No. Just sad because you're so young—too young to have a baby, if you ask me. But you're not. What will you do?"

"Billy says he'll marry me. He's the same age as you. And Tutu knows. She says we can live with her, Billy, the baby, and all."

"What about school?"

"Maybe for a little while. It depends on how much help Tutu needs. Maybe I'll go until the baby comes. I'm already three months pregnant." Jolene dabbed her eyes with a tissue.

Danny looked at her and realized he'd been so wrapped up in his own sorrow he'd paid very little attention to her. He suddenly realized she'd been wearing loose muumuus recently. "Did you tell Tommy?"

"Yes. That's why he kept Dad away and asked you to take care of me. He told me to tell you, but I was afraid you'd be disappointed in me. Tommy isn't holy like you, so I knew he would understand." She paused. "You're the smart one in the family. Tommy's the jock. You're the brains. Me, I'm nothing."

Danny put his hands on her shoulders. "You're not nothing. Not only are you going to be a mother, you're beautiful, and you make people smile. Just because you never liked books or studying or school doesn't mean you're not smart."

Danny wrapped his arms around his sobbing sister once more, and they cried together. Later that evening, while their dad was at the bar, Danny walked his sister to her boyfriend's jalopy. As she waved goodbye from the car window, he had a feeling Jo was doomed to a life as desperate as their mother's.

What a mess his family was. He longed for the calm peace of St. Patrick's Church and couldn't stop thinking of Maria, who he missed every minute of every day. But although he wrote to her, she never wrote back.

"Don't make it harder for her than it already is," Father Thomas advised. He went back to St. Patrick's a few months after Maria, or Evangelista left to join the Carmelites. "I understand she's done her penance and voluntarily took vows of silence. There's no way to get a postcard to her. You must accept it. The Carmelites are very strict and watchful. Consider her dead. Because, as a Carmelite, she is no longer of this world."

It was the last thing he wanted to hear. The thought of never seeing or even writing letters again left a hole in his heart he didn't know how to plug.

Now there was only Danny and the zombie, as his father took to calling his mother. Danny stayed away, studied constantly in the library, and eventually graduated at the top of his class. By graduation, his father's drinking had gotten worse. But at least he spent more time at the bar than he did at home, so Danny really didn't give a damn.

June 1934

Only his sister appeared on his graduation night looking like she would give birth any day. She had a carnation lei slung over her arm. Putting it over his head, she kissed his cheek. She looked drawn and tired. It made him sad to see her like that.

"Congratulations, Danny. You made a terrific speech. Everyone was impressed. You heard how loud they clapped. Sorry Billy couldn't come. He had to work the night shift. And Tutu doesn't move much from her couch these days. That's why I can't stay long. Poor Tutu isn't doing well."

The siblings looked at each other awkwardly, feeling strange in the midst of a sea of people snapping pictures and piling lei after lei on their graduate's neck. Most of the boys' faces were almost hidden under all the leis.

"Thanks, Jo. It's the best lei I've ever had," he said sincerely.

Jo burst into tears. "It's not fair, Danny. Dad didn't even bother to show up. You're the valedictorian. You should have tons of leis."

"It's okay, Jo. I don't mind," Danny lied.

That night, Danny went home, drank a cold beer, and ate some lukewarm pizza.

Boy, this is some graduation party. Maybe he shouldn't have been such a recluse in school. He went into the bathroom and stared at himself in the mirror. He wasn't handsome, but he wasn't bad looking either. He was five foot ten and a little on the skinny side. His curly medium brown hair was cut short, and he had naturally tan skin. His eyes were his best feature—big, melting brown eyes with thick, heavy black lashes above a straight, *haole* nose. Although it was harder for him to meet girls because he went to an all-boys school, it wasn't impossible. He wasn't blind to the girls who flirted with him at Tommy's football games and at the bus stop. But Maria/Evangelista still occupied his thoughts, and he was determined to succeed. He wanted to make it to a mainland college, and he did. The letter in his pocket confirmed he had won a full scholarship to Marquette University. He had a lot to be grateful for.

"So where did you get them high falutin' ideas about going to college?" his father asked when Danny finally told him about Marquette.

"I always wanted to go," Danny answered simply.

"Well, you can't. Colleges cost too much and are a waste of time." His dad guzzled his beer and ate *pupus*.

"Dad, I got a scholarship. It means we don't have to pay for anything."

Bobby stopped drinking his Primo for a second. "So, that mean you're smart or something?" He took a long swallow from the half-empty can. Wiping his mouth noisily, he burped. "Well, I don't care about scholarships. You still can't go."

Danny couldn't believe his ears. "Why, Pop?"

His father looked at him sideways. "You're a dreamer, like your ma. Always dreaming of living in Kāhala with the rich folk. Always reaching for something you can't have. And you know why? Because you were born in Kalihi, you grew up in Pālolo, and that's where you going to stay for the rest of your life. No sense going nuts like your zombie ma, always wanting impossible stuff."

"It doesn't have to be that way," Danny replied.

"Don't argue with me, boy. I'm older and got experience. You don't know nothing. Your nose is always in books. Boy, life kicks you in the balls until you're down on the ground saying uncle. I'm saving you from getting that kick in the balls. Might as well accept this is all you're ever going to be."

"You're wrong. I'm going to be somebody someday."

"You sure are. Mitch Sanchez down the road says he can get you a job at Hawaiian Telephone. Seeing as you're so smart, maybe you can start as a lineman."

"I don't want to be a lineman."

"That's how stupid you are," Bob roared. "You know how much linemen makes? Plus you get benefits and retirement."

"I don't care. I want to be a lawyer."

"A lawyer? Well, ain't that something. What makes you think you're smart enough to be a crooked lawyer?"

Danny ignored the criticism. "I just know. And they're not all crooked."

"Politicians, lawyers, and cops. They're all crooks. So you might as well put that stupid college idea out of your head." His dad slapped him on the side of his head. "Monday, you go see Sanchez for a job."

"No."

"Listen here, boy. You go see Sanchez or no come home. I ain't supporting you and your fool *pupule* dreams anymore."

Danny was silent. He'd go see Joe all right. He needed the best paying summer job he could get because he was going to Wisconsin in the fall—no matter what.

Jo came to see him the day before he left for Wisconsin. He tucked her chin in his hand and leaned over to kiss her and his nephew.

"He's beautiful, Jo."

"I think he looks like you." Jo looked tired and older than her seventeen years—like she had been robbed of her joy.

"Hey sis, looks like you're not getting enough sleep."

"Babies tend to do that to you." She lifted her baby's face to hers and rubbed her cheek against his. "But they're worth it. Wait until you get one of your own. You'll see what I mean."

"That'll be a long time from now, if ever."

Jo widened her eyes. "You don't want kids?"

"I didn't mean it. I was just saying..."

"You'll change your mind when you fall in love and get married." She nodded.

Danny put his hands on her shoulders. "You have to take care of yourself. You look so tired. What will Tutu and your son do if something happens to you?"

"I know." She looked into his eyes. "Do I look that bad?"

"Well you don't look your best." Danny dropped his hands. "Is Billy helping?"

She looked away. "He's always busy working. Marriage isn't what I thought it would be."

"Nothing ever is." He sighed.

She looked up, and her eyes flashed like the old Jo for a minute. "Tommy and me, we're not perfect like you. We make mistakes. Maybe because we're not smart like you."

"You're both smart. The only difference between you, me, and Tommy is I liked school, and I was motivated to go to college..." He paused. "I'm far from perfect."

"What do you mean? Did something happen?" Jo pulled back in surprise.

He sighed. "I fell in love with a nun last year."

"What?" Jo stared. "Goody, goody, holy Danny fell in love with a nun?"

"I'm human, too."

Jo put her hand on his arm. "I'm sorry, Danny. I shouldn't talk. I was just surprised about the nun part. Was she pretty? Did she love you?"

"She was beautiful, like you." Danny smiled. "And yes, she loved me. But God and the church came first."

1934-1940

Danny felt rejuvenated in Milwaukee. No longer was he the boy from Pālolo with a drunk for a father and a nut for a mother. He was a college student, like the rest of them. He could pretend his life in Hawai'i was as American as apple pie. Whatever that meant.

Since the scholarship didn't provide for all his needs, he got a job in a brewery working the graveyard shift. Several nights a week, he watched hundreds of bottles go by on the conveyer belt. His job was to pull out the irregulars. There were times when he thought if he never saw a beer bottle again, it would be too soon.

The guys he worked with urged him to drink after work with them. "Hey Danny, why don't you ever join us after work? Might as well drink the beer instead of throwing it away just because the bottles are screwed up."

"Unlike most of you guys, I go to school every weekday. I don't know about you but I'm too tired to do anything but sleep. And I gotta do good in school because I'm on scholarship, and the only way for me to get to law school is for me to get another scholarship," Danny replied.

"Give us free legal advice when you become a big time lawyer." One of the workers laughed.

Danny saluted them. "Will do."

Working at the beer factory was like working at the pineapple cannery. Both he and Tommy had hated working there every summer. He was lucky he was the younger brother because Tommy told him he shouldn't even try to get a job in the pineapple or sugar cane fields.

"I no can stand working summers at the cannery and in the fields," Tommy said. "But money is money, and in this family, we need money. Just don't go in the fields. It's worse than the cannery. When they burn the fields, it's like being in hell."

Danny wondered how people could endure working in those places all their lives. For him, it was a temporary situation towards his goal. For many, it was a life sentence.

Jo had a baby girl just before he graduated from college. She sent him pictures of her children along with a letter.

"My son looks like you," Jolene wrote. "Well, kind of like both you and me. I'm happy. I promise to God, I'm not going to raise my kids the way we were raised. I'm never divorcing Billy, no matter what. Even though we got married by a judge, we decided to have a Catholic wedding and make a commitment to raise our kids Catholic. Father Thomas was kind enough to marry us, probably as a favor to you. So I'm sticking to the vows I made. Both my kids got baptized. I take them to church every Sunday and hope to send them to Catholic schools if I have the money. My son seems real smart, like you. Maybe he can get a scholarship to St. Louis like you did.

"Dad got Billy a job at the Telephone Company, so he's making good money now. I miss Tutu, but I admit, its easier living on our own. I hope I don't live so long I become a burden to my kids."

1941

Danny got his BA in three years by going to summer school. Three years later, he graduated Editor of the Law Review and number one in his class. He received job offers all over the United States and decided to clerk for Frank Murphy, the only Roman Catholic in the Supreme Court. Father Thomas recommended him. It was an exceptional honor and would be an impressive addition to his resume. He couldn't turn it down even though his heart was still in Hawai'i. He promised himself he would eventually move back there and reconnect with his 'ohana again. For now, he couldn't turn down anything this important.

December 7, 1941

Danny was having a late lunch with one of his fellow clerks in a coffee shop when a police officer dashed inside.

White-faced, the policeman yelled, "The Japs bombed Pearl Harbor."

The clerk turned to Danny. "Isn't Pearl Harbor in Hawai'i where you're from?"

Danny nodded, momentarily speechless.

As soon as the war began, Tommy signed up again as a sergeant. The Army sent him to Italy. Danny was exempted from the draft because he was born with a hole in his heart. He felt guilty about not being able to do his duty to his country. Danny vowed, when he became a lawyer, he would take care of his family.

1943

Tommy returned from Italy after only a year. The war was over for him. Although the local newspapers called Tommy a war hero. The shot to his knee won him a medal and left him with a limp for the rest of his life. He showed his family the Silver Star he got for crawling on his belly under heavy gunfire to save two of his men. Although the state of Hawai'i celebrated him as a war hero, he told Danny he didn't consider himself one when he called from the VA hospital just before he was discharged.

"Congratulations, big brother. I hear you're famous in Hawai'i. You could run for office."

"Not me. I'll leave that stuff for you. Tell you the truth, I wasn't trying to be a hero or get a medal. I just wanted to save my guys. It just happened."

"Now you sound like a *haole*" Danny laughed.

"Don't you know? I'm bilingual. I speak pidgin and American English." Tommy chuckled. "I've been in the army too long. Those guys didn't understand pidgin. I got tired of them saying, 'What did you say?' Speaking like a *haole* got to be a habit."

"So tell me how you got the Silver Star."

"By going against orders." Tommy laughed again. "The captain in charge told us to withdraw. But two of my guys were down. I saw them move, and I knew they were still breathing. I argued with the captain. He told me it was too dangerous, I would get killed. But Danny, they were my guys. I know I was rough on them, but it was my job. One of the guys reminded me of you. He was a smart. I nevah understand what he was talking about half the time. Just like with you."

"There you go, some pidgin slipped in." Danny smiled to himself.

"That's what my guys used to say, 'You're doing that funny talk again.' Anyway, the guys and I went through hell together. I had to try to save him. I got him, but he died. His last words were, 'Thank you.' Made me cry. My boys thought I was crying because I was shot in three places, but I was crying because the college boy was dead."

When Tommy returned home to a hero's welcome, their dad got Tommy a job as an installer with Hawaiian Tel. He could have gotten the job himself, but Tommy, being Tommy, knew it made his dad feel good to do something for him.

It was Danny's first week back in Hawai'i as a working lawyer. Things were pretty chaotic in Honolulu. The city was packed with servicemen passing through on their way to fight in the Pacific/Asian theatre.

Danny sat amidst file boxes stacked one atop the other in his new office. He looked around him with pride at the smooth, dark oak desk, matching built-in credenzas, forest green carpets, and peaceful mountain views. On the heavy door was a shiny brass plate with his name with the hard-earned title of Attorney-at-Law engraved below it. Outside, his secretary sat in her cubby in the long hallway lined with all the other secretarial stations and law offices, which made up the silk-stocking Honolulu law firm of Smith, Winston, Kingsley, & Bradford. He couldn't help but feel awed and excited the first few times he walked through the doors. The road from Pālolo had been a long, rocky one. But he'd finally made it.

The phone rang. At first he stared at it awhile before pressing the speaker button. "Yes?"

"Mr. Myers?" Laura, his secretary said uncertainly. "Your father is here to see you."

Danny stared at the speakerphone.

"Mr. Myers? Are you still there?"

"Yes." Danny tried not to let his voice shake. Clearing his throat, he continued slowly. "You can send him in, Laura."

"Okay." She hung up.

Danny leaned back in his chair and felt a slow, sinking feeling in his stomach.

Why now?

Although he'd visited his sister and brother and even stayed with Tommy and his new wife from Italy while he looked for a job and apartment, he didn't visit his dad in Pālolo. His mother was dead, and he had no interest in seeing his father ever again. While living on the mainland, he had half forgotten his father and his old life.

When his dad walked in hesitantly, he looked much smaller than Danny remembered. He had more lines around his face, and his hair had gone completely gray. Otherwise, he looked the same. The big difference lay in not only their perception of each other after so many years, but the changed circumstances surrounding their lives.

Bob Myers glanced around the office and shuffled his feet nervously.

Danny caught the disbelief he tried to hide from his son. Danny smiled. His father was dressed in his best clothes. It gave Danny some degree of satisfaction seeing his father uncomfortable, and even a little awed.

"Sit down, Dad." Danny indicated a chair.

His father was still checking out the office, but when Danny invited him to sit, he turned his eyes on his son and stared at him as if he were a stranger, an intimidating one at that.

Danny straightened up, acutely aware of what he wore. The white dress shirt over khaki trousers and tie were perfect. His dad's eyes lingered on the navy sport coat hanging on the coat rack before clearing his throat. "Nice office. Fancy. You just moving in?"

He eyed the boxes.

"Yes. You must want something or you wouldn't be here." Danny narrowed his eyes. "Just get on with it. I'm busy. I don't have time to waste talking about my office."

"Yeah, I get it, Mr. Big Time Lawyer." His father frowned and became his old, cocky self again. "You think you're a hot shot now, but me, I don't think so. Anybody who forgets his family and where he comes from, well, that person is a shit as far as I'm concerned."

Danny was taken aback. His father still managed to intimidate him. The thought roused him to anger. "I don't care what you think."

"I'm your father. Maybe you forgot. You owe me." Bob pounded his chest with a fist.

"I owe you nothing." Danny trembled. "What did you ever give me but humiliation, abuse, and sorrow? All you ever wanted was for Tommy, me, and Jo to do exactly as you said. You wanted to run our lives. You never respected our dreams or ambitions. You never thought I was good enough or smart enough, despite my accomplishments. I earned everything I have with no thanks to you."

"I did what I thought was best," Bob spat out. "So you wanted to be a hot shot crook, big deal. Don't go insulting us guys who sweat on the streets so guys like you can push paper. I tried to make sure you boys grew up decent. And what did I get for it?"

Suddenly aware the people outside his office might hear their angry exchange, even through the closed door, Danny lowered his voice. "Keep your voice down."

"Why? You ashamed of me and where you came from?" His dad sneered. "I don't argue with fancy lawyers. I only came to tell you about your sister."

"What about Jolene?"

"Oh, so the big time lawyer remembers his sister's name."

Danny sat back in his leather chair and snorted. "Stop wasting my time and just tell me what you came here for."

"She's in the hospital."

Danny's eyes widened and he sat up straight. "She's in the hospital? Is she sick?"

"Billy shot her."

Danny stood up. "What?"

"They called me cuz Tommy's out in the field. And maybe you forgot, but I'm still you guys' father. Don't exactly know what happened, but Billy was drunk or something and they got in a fight. The two of them always fighting. This time he beat her bad before getting his gun and shooting her..." Bob bit his bottom lip, looked down for a minute, and rubbed his eyes.

Danny was speechless.

"The cops said it was the third time this month they wen go to her house to break up a fight. The neighbors called when they heard the shots."

"He shot her more than once?" Danny ran his fingers through his hair. He couldn't wrap his head around what his father was telling him. Billy always seemed like a good-natured, if somewhat quiet, hard-to-get-to-know kind of guy.

"Yeah, then he shot himself in the head. Billy's dead."

Danny stepped back. "Dead? What about the kids?"

"The cops said they was screaming, so I got them and took them to my sister's so I could go to the hospital."

Danny felt like he was in the middle of a nightmare. "Is she at Queen's?"

He nodded. "She's having surgery. But before they wen wheel her in, she asked me to call you, hot shot. I nevah even know you was in town. Nobody told me. Anyway, she like see you."

Danny pressed the Intercom button on his phone. "Laura, get Hawaiian Tel on the phone. Tell them to locate one of their linemen, Thomas Myers, immediately. Tell them it's an emergency and he needs to get to Queen's hospital to see his sister. And cancel all my appointments for to-day."

He shot out of his chair and grabbed his sport coat.

He turned to his father. "That's how you find Tommy. You don't ask, you tell. Let's go."

Danny had to listen to his father complain about him all the way to the hospital.

"I'm cursed, I tell you, cursed. Because when I married your motha, her *pupule* sista cursed me."

"My mother had a sister?"

The older man folded his arms and nodded. "She's in Kaneohe Mental Institution. Been there since before you was born. Your motha nevah like tell you kids 'bout her crazy sista. The two of us hated each other the first time we met. Crazy people run in your motha's side of the family. So don't think you too good for us. You might go crazy one day like your motha and her sista. They was normal, and all of a sudden...cuckoo. Now your sista in the hospital. Maybe *make*. Who going take care of her kids?"

"Shut up. Just shut up." Danny pounded the wheel of his new car with the palm of his hand.

To his surprise, his father shut up.

Jo was in ICU when they arrived. Tommy was already there, pacing the floor. He ran up to them and hugged Danny then his dad when he spotted them.

"I was just coming back from a job when Hawaiian Tel paged me. They told me Billy's dead. It seems he was drunk." Tommy shook his head. "I told him to slow down on the drinking. Damn stupid Portugee."

"Where's Jo?" Danny asked.

Tommy blinked back his tears. "Inside ICU. The surgery's *pau*, but she's still passed out. The nurse told me the doctor's going talk to us soon as you two get here."

Danny sat in a chair and put his head in his hands. The three men remained in silence when the doctor came out.

"I'm sorry, we did everything we could, but I don't think she's going to make it." The doctor looked stern. "It would be a miracle if she did."

"What? She's just one kid. And she got two little ones at home. She no can *makei*. Who going to take care of the kids?" Bob jumped out of his chair.

The doctor shook his head, "Before she went into surgery, she asked for a priest to conduct final rites just in case. A priest from The Cathedral of Our Lady of Peace was here seeing patients, and he was able to see her before she went into the operating room. He's with her now. He stayed in the hospital and asked to be called when she came out of surgery. You may want to go in and say goodbye. There's a possibility she might not even wake up."

Bob flopped into the chair behind him. He dropped his head into his hands and sobbed.

Tommy sat next to his dad and put his arm around his dad's bowed shoulders.

Tommy looked up at Danny. "Go in by yourself first. I'll stay here with Pop. Better for us to go in one by one anyway." Tommy wiped tears from his eyes with the back of his hand. "I'm glad Mom's not here."

Danny walked into ICU alone. His sister lay in bed hooked up to machines and bags. A nurse injected something into the tube that ran into her veins. The priest sat in the chair next to her bed, holding her hand. The nurse turned when she heard Danny approach and nodded.

Jo's eyes were closed, her head bandaged. She had cuts and bruises all over her face. Her nose was broken, and one of her eyes was swollen shut.

The priest got up and motioned to the chair.

Danny sat down and took his sister's hand in his. He cried until he felt her hand move. He looked up and saw her eyes focused on him.

"Danny," she whispered.

Danny brushed her cheek with the back of his hand. "I'm here, sis. I love you."

"Billy's dead. He tried to kill me."

He nodded, and she began to cry. He took a handkerchief from his pocket and dabbed her cheeks gently.

"This is Father Paul." She nodded her head to indicate the priest. "This is my brother Danny. Isn't he handsome? He's a lawyer." Her voice conveyed her pride before she started coughing.

"Shh, Jo. Save your strength." He continued to hold her hand in both of his.

The priest got up. "I'll leave the two of you alone. If you need me, I'll be right outside in the hallway."

After he left, Jo turned to him with a wan smile. "I'm dying."

"Don't say that. You must fight to stay alive. You need to take care of your kids."

"Take care of them for me," she whispered.

Danny nodded. He was crying too much to talk.

"Promise?" Her hand tightened in his.

"I promise." He nodded again.

She sighed and managed to smile. "I love Tommy, but I want them to be like you. Make believe you're their real daddy. Tell them Billy and I were just watching them for you and their real mom."

"What?" Her request was insane. He was shocked. *Maybe she's confused and delusional coming out of the anesthesia.*

She tried to raise herself.

Danny shook his head. "Don't try to get up."

"Swear to God and the Virgin Mary that you'll raise them and make them believe they're your kids."

"They won't believe me. Maybe Kathy's too young, but Gerry's old enough to know it's a lie."

Jo fell back on her bed. She struggled to speak. Her voice was hoarse, and the words rolled out with effort. "Kids understand secrets. You're a lawyer. Convince them."

Danny slumped in his seat and shook his head. "They won't believe me."

Jo clutched her blanket. "I can't have the kids growing up burdened by the sins of their father. Swear, so I can die in peace."

No matter how crazy her idea, he couldn't deny his sister her last request. Danny raised his hand and said, "I swear to God and the Virgin Mary I'll raise them as my children and try to make them believe I'm really their father."

He turned back to Jo. Her lips looked bluish.

"Thank you." She closed her eyes. In a few minutes, she flat-lined.

Jo's funeral had an unexpected visitor. Tommy and Danny stood at the graveside listening to Father Thomas with their nephew between them. Billy's father showed up with Billy's stepmother. His mother was absent. She ran off with another man when Billy was only six and was never heard from again. Bob Myers stood behind his sons, grandchildren, and his mother, who flew in from the Big Island to attend her granddaughter's funeral.

As Father Thomas quoted from the Bible, Danny saw a woman walk toward the graveyard from afar. She wore a black dress with a gathered skirt down to the middle of her calf. A pillbox hat perched at an angle atop her long hair that fell in a pageboy down to her shoulders. Dark netting covered her face.

Despite the distance of time and space, he recognized her. She was the air he breathed, the subject of his dreams and imagination. There would never be anyone else for him. She was the only woman who set his senses on fire— Evangelista.

She waited until she was the last person to offer her condolences. His hand trembled when they touched.

"Evangelista." His voice caught in his throat.

"I'm so sorry," she whispered, and began to withdraw her hand from his.

He trapped her hand in both hands of his. "Let's talk." He turned to his brother and whispered in his ear. "She's the nun I told you about. Give me a moment."

Raising his eyebrows, Tommy looked at Danny, then at the petite, beautiful woman standing next to him. He shrugged and turned to the children.

Holding on to Evangelista's hand, Danny walked her to a quiet spot under the shade of a tree. He put one hand on her shoulder and lifted her chin with the other.

"Have you left the order?"

She nodded, and he embraced her. It was all he needed to know.

Evangelista was dying.

"I left the convent because I'm of no use to them anymore. I have a rare blood disease I inherited called thalassemia." She choked on her tears and stumbled on the word. "It's a form of anemia, which will eventually kill me."

Danny took her in his arms as she wept.

After a few minutes, she pulled back and dabbed her cheeks with a handkerchief. "That's one of the reasons I'm so small and have very little appetite." She shuddered. "The doctor said it's a miracle I'm still alive. Most people die as children."

"Marry me. I'll take care of you."

Evangelista sobbed. "Oh, Danny, I didn't come here for you to save me. I came to say goodbye."

Danny held her shoulders with his hands. "I don't care if you're sick. I'll take care of you. I'm a lawyer and make good money. If we live simply, we can and will survive this illness."

She looked away. "I can't. It's not fair to you."

"Let me be the one who decides what's fair. I've never stopped loving you, although God knows I've tried."

"Danny, I have a few years at most."

"I don't care. Maybe science will come up with a cure. In the meantime, you'll be a great help. I promised my sister I'd take care of her children. I need you. More than that, we'll be together. I don't care about anything else except being with you. Together we might be able to beat this disease."

They both wept when they said their vows before a judge. Tommy stood by his side and his wife on hers. The only other person was their father.

His dad seemed different now. Since Jo's death, he'd quit drinking, attended AA meetings, and went to church most Sundays. Becoming sober had changed him.

"Wish he'd quit when we were kids," Tommy whispered.

"Wish he never started," Danny replied.

Tommy and his wife volunteered to watch Jo's children so they could go on a honeymoon, but the bride needed a blood transfusion.

The transfusion helped her feel better for almost a year. Jo's children took to her just as Danny knew they would.

Our children, he reminded himself. He had to stop thinking of himself as their uncle, but as their father instead. Unexpectedly, as if God ordained it so, he was able to grant Jo's last request.

The shock of the murder and suicide completely wiped out his son's memory of his entire childhood up to that day. As for Kathy, he didn't know what she remembered or believed until the night he heard her weeping in bed.

Danny tapped on her door. When he heard her sniffling, he called out, "Kathy? Are you all right, sweetheart?" There was no response except for more sniffling. He opened the door. She lay on her side, sucking her thumb and clinging to her doll. He sat on the side of her bed and gently turned her onto her back. Her parents' wedding picture was tucked between her chest and the doll.

"Do you know who these people are?" He pointed to the picture.

Kathy nodded. "Mommy and Daddy. They went to heaven."

"That's right." Danny stroked her hair.

His daughter sat up, her eyes wide. "But Gerry said they're not. I showed him the picture, and he said I was stupid because we live with our mommy and daddy."

Danny hugged her. "Well, he's right, too, because I'm your daddy now and my wife is your mommy."

"Can I keep the picture?"

"Of course you can keep it," Danny replied. "But better not mention it to Gerry until he's ready to talk about it."

"I know. He gets mad." Kathy nodded, then brightened. "Can it be our secret?"

"Sure it can."

She smiled and kissed him on his cheek before melting his heart by saying, "Good night Daddy. I love you."

She never brought up Jo and Billy again. Sometimes he wondered what became of the picture.

Danny gradually grew optimistic because some of the bloom Eva had when he first met her returned to her cheeks. It was the happiest time of his life.

"I never knew such happiness existed." Eva snuggled in bed with him. "Do you think there's any other married couple in the world who loves each other as much as we do?"

"Impossible. No one could love as much as we do." Danny laughed then traced her face with his finger. "You're so beautiful—the most beautiful girl in the world. And I'm the luckiest man in the world."

"Not so lucky," she said softly.

He cupped her chin in his hand. "Not lucky. Blessed." He kissed her gently on her nose.

1948

The day he dreaded finally came. The whites of her eyes yellowed and her energy level plummeted alarmingly. Eva, as he called her, picked at her food. He made an appointment to see the doctor.

Dr. Arakawa took off his glasses and laid them on his desk with a sigh as he faced Danny and Eva. "I'm afraid I have bad news. Your spleen is enlarged. We have to remove it."

"Can she live without a spleen?" Danny asked.

"Yes," the doctor nodded. "That's the good news. The bad news is, without it, she'll be prone to infections."

"What about another blood transfusion?" Danny did all the talking. Eva remained quiet. He felt somewhat irritated by her listless acceptance.

"The blood transfusion is partially at fault for her spleen's condition. You remember me telling you it might cause an iron build-up, which might damage her organs? At the time, it was the best and only option to keep her alive."

"There's got to be something else. What if we go to the mainland? Maybe there are new discoveries that haven't reached the islands yet." Danny ran his fingers through his hair.

Dr. Arakawa shook his head. "I keep up with the latest developments. I haven't heard of anything."

"But it's possible," Danny insisted.

"Anything is possible." The doctor nodded. "However, at this point, we shouldn't wait too long to perform the operation."

Danny turned to Eva. "You have to do the surgery."

"Whatever you say." Eva nodded as she fiddled her fingers. Danny was perturbed by the resignation in her voice.

"Will she be okay?" he asked. "She's so frail."

Dr. Arakawa sighed. "For now, it's the only thing we can do to try to prolong her life."

The removal of her spleen was a success, but as Doctor Arakawa warned, her immune system became compromised. When the flu season came around almost a year after her surgery, Eva got so sick she had to be hospitalized.

Every evening, before Danny visited her, he went to the chapel in Queen's Hospital to light a candle and pray. But Eva failed to get better.

"I can't live without her," he sobbed to Father Thomas.

"You went into this marriage with your eyes wide open. To her credit, she told you the truth. All you can do is make her last days happy."

"That's not what I want to hear."

"What do you want to hear, my son?"

"God can do miracles. He will do miracles. Or there is someone somewhere who does healing miracles."

Father Thomas put his hand on Danny's shoulder. "God does do miracles sometimes. But it's up to Him whether or not He does. We have to accept His decision."

Danny looked up, his anger barely contained. "She's the best person I ever met. She deserves to live. She doesn't deserve to die so young and in this way."

"Death comes to us all. How and when we die is in God's hands. How can we presume to know better than the Almighty?"

Danny stood up and glared down at the priest. "Maybe you can accept his will, but I can't. I won't. He has to heal her."

Father Thomas shook his head. "He doesn't have to do anything."

"Then forget God. What good is He if he refuses to heal someone as deserving as Eva? I refuse to accept a God who would kill my wife. I'll go to a Kahuna, to anybody, who might help."

"Danny," Father Thomas put a hand on his arm.

Danny shook him off. "Let me go." He stalked out of the chapel.

"I want to be with my children," Eva begged from her hospital bed later the same evening. "Please take me home. I want to be with them for at least a little while."

"But you need full-time medical care." Danny kissed her hands.

Eva looked at him with her big, dark eyes. She was so thin now they were sunken into hollows in her small, heart-shaped face. They looked huge and out of proportion because of the dark circles. She reminded Danny of one of the waifs in a Margaret Keane painting.

"Danny," she whispered. "I'm going to die. You must accept it. I have."

"No. I won't accept it. I'll find someone who has a cure."

"Please Danny," she begged. "Let me be with my children before I die."

Danny cried, but eventually agreed to do as she wished.

They had a week of barbeques, picnics, and watching the sunset. They celebrated her birthday with their family. Even Father Thomas and Mother Superior came. When Mother Superior hugged Eva's frail body, she wept.

"I'm sorry, Maria, I mean Evangelista. This should be a happy time, and here I am ruining it for you."

Eva smiled. "Do you know that's the longest sentence you've ever spoken to me?" Eva put her hand out and patted the Mother's gnarled, arthritic fingers. "Don't worry about me. I've lived a lot longer than the doctors predicted. And I've been so happy. God blessed me with a family."

Mother Superior brushed the bangs from Eva's forehead. "I never realized you were so beautiful, my dear." She sniffled again. "Oh my, here I go again."

Everyone brought gifts. Eva acted as if each one was a treasure. After opening the presents, she blew out the candles on her cake. Everyone clapped.

"I'm tired," she whispered to Danny. "Can I go back to bed now?"

Danny nodded and picked her up. She was shockingly light.

The next day, Eva wanted to go to the beach.

"Not a busy beach. A quiet, country beach like Waimānalo. I want to see Rabbit Island and go fishing." Her eyes brightened. "Please, Danny."

"You want to go fishing?" he asked with surprise.

"My father was a fisherman." She smiled. "He used to take me with him because my mother was sick a lot and couldn't take care of me. Maybe she had what I have."

"Shall we take the children?"

"Another time. I just want to be alone with you this time."

Danny gazed down at the frail woman he loved with all his heart. She had lost so much weight and was so weak he had to carry her everywhere. He bowed. "Your wish is my command, your highness."

"You've made me the happiest princess in the world..." She began coughing.

Then, to his relief, she giggled. For a moment, she looked like the old Eva.

When they got to the beach, he took off his shoes and carried her barefoot to the sand. They were alone and had a perfect view of Rabbit Island. She took a deep breath and smiled. Her eyes sparkled.

"Can you carry me and run at the same time?" she asked. Her eyes twinkled with mischief.

"I can do anything," he bragged. "As long as you're with me."

She laughed. Optimism surged in Danny. He ran. She kept laughing.

"Faster," she ordered. "Faster, Danny, faster."

He ran as fast as he could. Suddenly, he realized she had been silent for a few minutes and felt limp in his arms.

He stopped. Her eyes were closed. She wasn't breathing.

Danny fell to his knees in the sand. Holding her to him, he buried his face in her neck and cried.

For a time after Eva died, Danny tortured himself with the thought her death was his fault. If only he hadn't compromised her calling, perhaps the Lord would've taken mercy on her and let her live. The guilt plagued him in dreams, and he had many sleepless nights. Because the Catholic Church reminded him of all his failures, he stopped going.

It was an easy transition as his children attended Episcopalian schools. Both of them were very smart. Kathy went to St. Andrew's Priory, an all-girls school and Gerry attended 'Iolani, an Episcopalian boys' school in Kapahulu with an education second to none. Both schools were originally founded as Anglican schools by Queen Emma, who had been raised Anglican.

Now that both his children were steeped in the Protestant world, Danny wanted them to grow up in a church. He chose Central Union Church. It was perhaps the grandest and most magnificent church in Honolulu. Surely the imposing gray stone structure had the most extensive and expensive piece of real estate of any church in the Islands. The Congregational church was often called the Church in the Gardens. One couldn't help but admire the statuesque beauty of the iconic structure with its towering steeple set back on acres of prime real estate. No small country churches for Danny. He felt comforted inside a structure as grand as any Catholic church he'd ever gone to.

1960

Danny watched the slender, blonde woman sitting in the back of Central Union church. He'd noticed her only recently, probably because he no longer had to attend services at the same time as the youth groups and started going to a later service instead. It was there he first saw her. Her shy nervousness and uncertainty mixed with a patrician air attracted him. For the first time in twelve years, he felt drawn by the intangible winds of fate. Something told him they were alike—two lost, lonely souls born into a bewildering world in which they didn't belong.

Danny wondered briefly where the last twelve years since Eva died had gone. He'd dated occasional women, some for as long as a year. But his grief and guilt over his loss had been so great, he couldn't open himself to any of them. Besides, his commitment to his family and job effectively stopped him from marrying again, despite his children's urging. He was so busy with his kids and the law firm, time had flown by. Kathy was now a married schoolteacher with children of her own. Gerry had just graduated from college and was entering law school in the fall.

Somehow, I did a good job with them, Jo. You would be proud of them.

A sudden need welled up in him, and he approached the woman before she could slip out the back door.

"Hello. I'm Danny Myers. I've seen you here before." He smiled.

The woman looked up at him timidly. She was a bit older than he'd initially thought. Older than he was, anyway. Still, she had the same fragile quality as Eva, the one which had made his heart stop.

"I'm Meg, um, Duncan." She smiled.

Her radiant glow blinded Danny momentarily, catching him off-guard.

My God, she's beautiful.

"Meg Duncan," Danny offered her his hand. "Would you allow me to take you to brunch?"

1978 – Governor's Office

"So now you know the truth, son." Danny sat back in his chair.

"I'm not part Filipino?" Gerry smiled. "I think I've always known the truth. Kathy and I used to talk about it because we vaguely remembered our real mom and dad. But it was all in the shadows because of the trauma. Thank you for being honest with us. And thank you for honoring our mother's final request."

Danny sighed with relief. "Your mother loved you so much she sacrificed her identity and memories of herself as your mother to give you better lives."

"I understand." Gerry nodded. "But we've always been one big 'ohana. Uncle Tommy and his family, Mama Meg, and even Grandpop. As for Eva, she really was a mother to us after our mom died."

The two men stood up and hugged. Danny grabbed his son's arms and stood back. He had to look up at Gerry.

"We are a strong 'ohana, and we're going to get through this. My granddaughter will find a donor. Nothing is going to shake our 'ohana."

THE END

This story is based on the untold story of a character from the novel, *The Ohana* by C.W. Schutter.

C.W. SCHUTTER

C.W. Schutter grew up in Honolulu dreaming of becoming a novelist.

After graduating with a BA in Psychology from the University of Hawai'i, she worked in Hotel Management, later became an Editorial Assistant, and Realtor. She sat on the board of a commercial real estate company, and chaired benefits for non-profits in Aspen, Colorado.

Her first screenplay, *September Dawn*, became a movie starring Jon Voight, followed by a novel. *The Ohana*, an award-winning novel about Hawai'i took 1st place in the Golden Scrolls Awards. Danny's Story, is an untold story from *The Ohana*. She enjoys writing in different genres.

Find me on the web at www.cwschutter.com.

Acknowledgments

As the architect of this project, I wanted to say a quick thank you to those who made this project a reality. First, of course, there are the writers. This anthology wouldn't have been possible without the generous support of ten other writers, who all had one goal in mind, to help improve literacy in Hawai'i. So, thank you to JoAnn Bassett, Gail Baugniet, Frankie Bow, Kay Hadashi, Laurie Hanan, Jill Marie Landis, AJ Llewellyn, Toby Neal, and CW Schutter for joining me in this effort to do some good with our imaginations and words.

I mentioned ten writers. The tenth is Lorna Collins, who is also an editor and agreed to edit each of the stories. Thank you, Lorna, for finding our mistakes, redundancies, and moments of pontification.

Laurie Hanan did double duty on this project by volunteering to read and edit each story for the Hawaiian words. Our attempt was to be true to the language and we all hope each and every 'okina and kahakō are used correctly.

Kathy Ambrose at Pen 2 Ink Designs deserves all our gratitude for the book layout and cover design.

We all want to thank Jed Gaines and the staff at Read Aloud America for their tireless efforts to help improve literacy in Hawai'i. You truly are the ones who help make this world a better place.

Thank you to Caroline Hart for your inspiration to all mystery writers and, of course, for the foreword.

And last, but not least, thank you to everyone who purchased a copy of this book. We hope you enjoy our stories and thank you for your support.

Terry Ambrose
Project Manager

Made in the USA
San Bernardino, CA
26 August 2017